T0103901

J.A.P.

(Just Another Pilot)

EDWARD LANDERS

Order this book online at www.trafford.com
or email orders@trafford.com

Most Trafford titles are also available at major online book retailers.

© Copyright 2013 Edward Landers.
All rights reserved. No part of this publication may be reproduced, stored in a retrieval
system, or transmitted, in any form or by any means, electronic, mechanical, photocopying,
recording, or otherwise, without the written prior permission of the author.

Printed in the United States of America.

ISBN: 978-1-4907-2063-0 (sc)
ISBN: 978-1-4907-2064-7 (e)

Because of the dynamic nature of the Internet, any web addresses or links contained in
this book may have changed since publication and may no longer be valid. The views
expressed in this work are solely those of the author and do not necessarily reflect the
views of the publisher, and the publisher hereby disclaims any responsibility for them.

Any people depicted in stock imagery provided by Thinkstock are models,
and such images are being used for illustrative purposes only.
Certain stock imagery © Thinkstock.

Trafford rev. 12/03/2013

 www.trafford.com

North America & international
toll-free: 1 888 232 4444 (USA & Canada)
fax: 812 355 4082

The front cover portrays two different sets of wings. The first set is standard Navy wings worn by Naval and Marine aviators. The second set is the wings worn by aviators of Northwest Airlines. It signifies the fact that Northwest Airlines was the first airline to carry United States airmail, a historic event.

Front cover design by R. G. Bensen, Capt. Northwest Airlines; LCDR United States Naval Reserve

For Barbara

For a princess from a man who believes that he can slay dragons for the fair maiden. You are the fair maiden. The world is the dragon.

This is the third book in a series beginning with <u>EDDIE</u> and followed by <u>SMOOTH</u>. <u>EDDIE</u> is an autobiography while <u>SMOOTH</u> and <u>JAP</u> are listed as fiction. There are several reasons why the latter two books are "fiction" and I won't go into those here but nevertheless both of those two books are true to life. The things that happened in them actually happened and some, probably most, of the conversations are true also. Names have been altered to protect persons still alive. This book has two faces; one that of flying with the Navy, the other of flying with what used to be Northwest Orient Airlines, after that Northwest Airlines and now defunct, having been bought by Delta Airlines.

The author is a retired Commander, United States Naval Reserve, with 23 and ½ years of service. As to Northwest Airlines the best that can be said of it is that it was a nice job but not a nice company to work for. In 1968 Donald Nyrop was the head of Northwest Orient. He was a draconian CEO and all expenditures had to be routed through him. Northwest Orient was known for its harsh treatment of its employees and its habit of paying its bills late. This was a "mixed blessing" in that the company was an uncomfortable one to work for but all of its assets were owned, outright, by the company so it was a solid company and not one that was doomed for failure due to economics. Nyrop was a tyrant but he tried to do his best for the company. Future CEOs did not have that goal in mind and selfishly stripped the company of assets, selling them in order to enhance their pockets and those of their friends, leading to the demise of Northwest Orient aka Northwest Airlines.

Under the Railway Employee Act a contract written between management and employees (mostly the unions) could not expire in the interests of passenger travel and convenience. Those contracts could only become "amendable". That meant, to Northwest Orient, that you could talk, harangue, argue and draw out labor talks for years without paying the employees any extra in terms of money or perks. It was a modus opperandi with Northwest Orient for any employee group to have to resort to a strike in order to solve any contractual dispute. That usually came after years of negotiating and it accomplished what Northwest wished to do, that is, save money.

Northwest Orient belonged to a group of airline companies that helped each other in the event of a strike on any of its members. The group was called the Mutual Aid Pact and it aided the "bottom line" of any struck airline. Its effect was to make strikes very long in time while each side tried to outlast the other. The airline employees who were affected by the strike, both strikers and the others who were laid off (or, as the British say, "made redundant") tried to supplement their meager strike benefits paid by the unions or their unemployment benefits by finding work anywhere and wherever they could. With most airlines this was a once in an era event. With Northwest it was a chronic one. Employee groups, Pilots, Flight Attendants, Customer Service Agents and other unions on the property would withdraw their services (strike) about every two years. Northwest Orient became a laughing stock in the trade as other airlines called it "Cobra Airlines" because it would "strike at any time". The longsuffering public became used to this and were usually on the side of the employees.

Nevertheless, it was a super job, whenever one could work at it. The people who actually worked for the airline were wonderful, the pay scales were good and the time off was very good. If you could ignore the management and the bean counters it was an unbeatable job.

Some of the pilots, like Kruger, kept their perspective by flying for the various military reserve establishments. The military flying was fun and challenging and acted as an ace in the hole for those times when the airline flying stopped, as in strikes.

Military pilots are a tight knit group that operate like a close fraternity. Without any announcements or braggadocio any military pilot can readily identify a brother military pilot within minutes. It is one of the tightest brotherhoods you can find and it operates with a unique secrecy that rivals that of the Masonic order. No handshakes, winks or other paraphernalia is needed. The only thing needed in order to identify a member of the brotherhood was a few words and a meeting of the eyes. Most of the pilots at Northwest Orient were military and the non-military pilots felt on the outside and were jealous of the obvious tight-knit group. The military pilots casually disdained the civilian pilots and called them "flaps" for "fucking light air plane pilots". It was perhaps unfair as any pilot has to undergo much training and learning before even getting into a plane. After all of that one has to learn how to fly and has to accrue hundreds of hours in the air in order to be truly vetted as a pilot.

As much as the military cadre disdained civilian pilots that disdain was doubled when it came to female pilots. Female pilots had a real uphill battle in their attempts to gain the cockpit. They got little or no aid from the established pilots. In the authors experience female pilots had to work twice as hard as any male pilot in order to gain any recognition for their efforts.

The author loved flying and his first love was the US Navy. Airline flying was tame in comparison. Working for the airline entailed years of "flying" as a Second Officer or a copilot before attaining the "left seat" as a Captain. Flying as a copilot was still flying but flying as a Second Officer was demeaning. Flying is a perishable skill and sitting sideways, monitoring a panel of switches was tantamount to losing that fragile skill. Some pilots simply gave up and resigned themselves to that type of job as it still paid well and the time off was comfortable. Those "pilots" were dead pilots flying. It was unfortunate but that was flying for the airlines.

JAP is an attempt to show what airline flying really is like and, as an aside, to show what real flying is like as in flying for a military group. As always the author tries to show the humorous side of flying whether military or civilian. Most pilots tend to be flamboyant, in-your-face, irreverent, independent and risk takers. People who do not posess those attributes tend to be accountants, economists and census takers. Northwest Orient never acknowledged those attributes of their pilots and, as a result, all of the bargaining between the two groups was adversarial. Northwest pilots all had a good sense of humor while Northwest management had none. The result was that in any of the adversarial bouts between the two groups the pilots usually won. The pilot's goals were primarily honor and pride while the company's goal was merely money. In every strike or a "withdrawal of services" by the Airline Pilots Association the pilots used their military skills in engaging in guerrilla warfare. They also utilized a lot of humor in their battles, something that the management of Northwest Airlines was very short on. The results almost always figured on the side of the pilots notwithstanding that it took a long time to accomplish.

Civilian neighbors of Northwest Orient pilots could never understand exactly why the pilots always seemed to be on strike. Trying to make someone understand the adversarial syndrome that operated at a modern airline, especially Northwest Orient, was counterproductive. After all, the pilot's lifestyle seemed ideal to the average civilian. Pilots made lots of money, had exciting jobs, got to travel to exotic countries and had a lot of time off to enjoy whatever they wished. Who could ask for anything more?

One pilot explained this dilemma to his neighbor in the following way. The neighbor had asked just what the pilot group was asking for during the current strike. After all, pilots had an outstanding job and made lots of money. What else could they possibly want?

The pilot answered, "We are asking for the most time off all of my neighbors think I have, the most money my in-laws think I make and the most extra-marital sex my wife thinks I get, and we want it all retroactive to last year".

Flying for Northwest Orient Airlines was like living the old Chinese curse; "May you live in interesting times".

Edward Landers

CAVEAT

This volume is presented as a fiction novel. Regardless of that label the things that are presented herein are true to life and actually happened at one time or another. The reason for the label as fiction is to preserve the thought thread from the second novel "Smooth" where the main character's name was Ed Kruger. As in the second novel everything in this novel actually happened. Only some of the names have been changed in order to protect the people who star in this book.

Part I

The Evolution

CHAPTER I

"Bail out! Bail out! Goddamn! Bail out!"

Kruger was talking to himself. He was driving along US-1 just south of Folkston, Georgia skirting the Okefenokee Swamp on his way to Minneapolis, Minnesota to join Northwest Orient Airlines in order to fly for that company as a commercial pilot. He was driving an old Volkswagen that his daughter considered a family disgrace. The VW had been purchased from a local gas station in Jacksonville, Florida and proudly bore a "Jack's Esso Service" sign on both sides in bold letters, much to the chagrin of Lorrie, his six year old.

Ed Kruger, a thirty-two year old pilot, had just resigned a regular commission in the US Navy fifteen days prior to this. He had immediately accepted a reserve commission in the same service, as he didn't really want to quit flying for the Navy. His decision to resign from the Navy on active duty had been prompted by the inept and, (in his opinion), useless officers senior to him who insisted on fucking up by the numbers and, in that manner, bringing disgrace down on the Navy that Kruger held in high regard. He had finally decided that he couldn't stomach the idiocy any longer and had decided to throw in his lot with the commercial airlines as a second choice for a career.

Kruger had resigned his regular commission, a highly sought for title among Navy Officers, in spite of regular entreaties from officers senior to him to stay in the Navy. He thought, "If the stupid shits only knew . . . .". He intended to stay in the Navy he loved only he would do so as a Reserve Officer instead of a Regular Officer.

As soon as the ink was dry on his resignation he hot-footed it over to the Wing hangar at NAS Jacksonville where an old Commanding Officer of his was on staff. Kruger asked Commander Falkenstein if he would administer the oath of office for his Reserve Commission, which he readily agreed to do.

In short order Kruger was back in the Navy once again after a hiatis of about twenty minutes.

Kruger didn't hold airline pilots in very high regard. He firmly believed them to be a lesser form of aviator who had to kiss-ass on a daily basis in order to draw down the high pay and low duty times the airline types were known for. Still, all in all, it probably would be a nice life and he would still be flying, something that had become paramount in his life.

His Volkswagen was packed with ammunition that he had accumulated throughout his eight years on active duty. Each Naval Officer had an allotment of ammunition that he could draw and shoot annually in order to maintain some semblance of proficiency with firearms. Most Officers didn't know about the allotment or didn't care and didn't draw their whole allotment. Kruger was not counted in that group. The government contract movers wouldn't handle ammunition or explosives so it had become necessary for Kruger to move all of the precious munitions himself as the cost of replacing them on the civilian market was prohibitive. Kruger loved to shoot almost as much as he loved to fly. He was aware that if he ever had a collision anywhere during the trip there was an outside chance that the Volkswagen and its inhabitant would be instantly transformed into a lot of smoke and a large hole in the pavement accompanied by a considerable amount of noise. Such is life.

He had adapted, as all pilots do, to habitually scanning everything around him along with all of the instruments available to him, which, in the case of the Volkswagen, were markedly lacking. The lack of instrumentation just made it possible for him to scan his surroundings better. Glancing in his rear-view mirror he discovered that the pickup truck following him had begun to smoke. The smoke seemed to be coming from a large cargo of old tires the truck was transporting.

There were two men in the truck. They were engaged in what seemed to be a lively conversation and were generally ignoring anything outside of a six-inch radius around their respective heads. Terms like target fixation, situational awareness and space myopia ran through Kruger's head as he watched the smoke rapidly grow to gigantic proportions and finally blossom into a roaring fire fed by the 60 mile-an-hour speed both vehicles were maintaining. Kruger knew that the fire would soon reach the gas tank with possible disastrous results for the two men.

He began to honk the puny Volkswagen horn as he waved his arm out the window and tried to brake while maintaining a position ahead of the truck in order to become noticed.

"Goddamn it, bail out! Get the fuck out of the truck!" he shouted as he gestured and honked.

Finally the driver of the truck noticed Kruger's distress and glanced into his rear view mirror to see what the problem was. The sight of a wall of fire greeted him. He began to brake as his passenger started to open his door and exit the truck, which was still traveling at 30 to 40 miles an hour. All Kruger could do at this point was to stop the Volkswagen and stand by to assist once the truck had come to a halt.

The pickup drove erratically into the right ditch, both doors flew open and the men inside jumped out running at top speed as they did. Kruger got out of his small car positioning himself so that the VW was between the fire and himself. Suddenly the gas tank in the pickup ignited and the load of tires flew a hundred feet into the air with a resounding roar. Both men who were in the truck either dove to the ground or were knocked there by the blast. The truck continued to burn as Kruger ran over to see if they were OK.

"Jesus, how the hell did that happen?" one of them commented. The other trucker thanked Kruger saying, "Damn, Mister, I'm sure as hell glad you saw that fire. We could have been blown up if we'd stayed in the truck any longer."

The truckers continued to babble as Kruger made sure that they weren't harmed. He gave them his address and promised to write a summary of what had transpired for their insurance company. He also told them that he would stop at the first place that promised to have a telephone and call the local sheriff along with the fire department. No one had cell phones at that time, in fact, they were generally unknown. He apologized for not offering them a ride but he explained that he had so much ammo in the car that there was not really room for anybody. The truckers hurriedly assured him that, under the circumstances, they really didn't relish riding on top of thousands of rounds of explosive items.

The excitement being over, Kruger's hegira continued. He spent the night in northern Georgia and was on his way early in the morning. Pressing on he made Minnesota that evening and called his old friend from VP-11, Ted Sorenson, as he got close to Minneapolis. Ted had left active duty a few months prior and was now on the seniority list for Northwest Orient Airlines. He was delighted to hear from Kruger and told him to "pick up a pack of Grain Belt and come on up here."

"Two questions," was Kruger's response. "What the hell is Grain Belt and just where in the hell are you?"

Ted laughed at his buddy's ignorance and explained that Grain Belt was the name of a local brand of beer. It was well known in the Twin Cities.

"Twin Cities?"

"Yeah, you might as well get used to the term. Minneapolis and St. Paul are side-by-side up here. They are really jealous of each other and insist on getting equal billing. Northwest insists that we refer to each of them anytime we mention either of them"

"Jesus, a bunch of prima donnas!"

"Well, you might as well just bite the bullet and get used to doing things that way up here. That's the way things are."

Kruger followed Ted's directions and soon knocked on the door to an apartment in a large complex of apartments. The door opened and he was treated to a raucous scene consisting of a number of young men and women. Ted explained that they were all pilots and stewardesses, the latter called cabin attendants by Northwest Orient. Kruger was divested of his load of Grain Belt by a stranger who obviously had consumed more than a few cans of the local drink. Introductions were attempted.

Kruger observed that none of the furniture possessed any legs. He wondered if this was a local idiosyncrasy and Ted informed him that the lack of legs was simply due to the boisterous activity of the pilots who belonged to this apartment. All activity in the apartment seemed to be oriented around drinking and attempting to get into the undergarments of the cabin attendants who were present.

Kruger decided that the party was too much for him and begged off in order to get a motel room so that he could relax and get some rest. As he left the apartment he shook his head. He expected that life as a civilian would be markedly different from what he had come to expect as a Naval Officer but this was, he thought, outside the envelope. He chalked it all up to his friend being a bachelor. "Things have to be more civilized in other quarters," he thought.

On a whim he drove by the Naval Air Station located on an obscure corner of the airport known as the "Twin Cities International Airport" or "Wold-Chamberlain Field", probably named after some equally obscure pilot. The sentry box seemed friendlier than anything he had seen for the last few hours so he drove into the Naval Base, produced his ID card, received a salute and had the distinct feeling that he was home once again. As he hunted for the Bachelor Officers Quarters, known to Navy people as the BOQ, he had the fleeting feeling that maybe; just maybe; he wasn't cut out for civilian life anymore.

Ed Kruger had originally wanted to live his whole life as a Naval Officer and a Naval Aviator. He had worked harder than most in order to make the cut as a Navy pilot and, once in that elite club, had never wished for anything more. Early on he had requested to be allowed to augment into the Regular Navy from the Reserve Officer Corps that he had signed on for. He was given an audience with a board of senior Regular Officers who scrutinized his record diligently and asked a number of piercing questions as to why he wanted to become a Regular Officer. "Regular" Officers were usually drawn from the Navy's Academy at Annapolis, Maryland and were part of a "good old boys" network. They tended to look out for each other. When promotions were in question it was well known that the Regular Officers would be selected over the Reserves unless the Reserve Officer had distinguished himself beyond all of his peers.

"Why do you wish to become a Regular Officer, Ensign?" The question was not unexpected. Becoming a "Regular" was tantamount to joining a very exclusive club. Not everyone was invited nor wanted. The question was asked after most of the other expected ones had been tendered.

"What is your vision for the Navy in the future?"

"Do you believe in God? Do you attend church regularly?"

"Are you married? Are you a family man? Do you have any children?"

"What did you do prior to enlisting in the Navy?"

"What were your grades in collage? What did you study? How can your studies benefit the Navy?

As to the question of why he wished to become a regular officer Ens. Kruger replied, "Sir, I wish to become part of the team, part of the club. I wish nothing more than to serve my country and I think that the best way to do that is to become more of a Naval Officer than I am at the present. It is my intention to make the Navy my career and I will do so whether or not I am selected as a Regular Naval Officer. Becoming a "Regular" is my idea of becoming closer to the service I have come to love."

Apparently the screening team was impressed by Ens. Kruger's answer as they gave him an "up" and shortly thereafter he was requested to resign his Reserve commission in order to be inducted into the US

Navy as a Regular Officer, to serve at the pleasure of the President of the United States. The Commanding Officer of his squadron, AEWBARRONPAC, swore him in. It was a very happy moment in Ensign Kruger's life.

Eight years later Lieutenant Kruger, USN, reversed the process and resigned his Regular commission to pick up a Reserve Commission in the United States Naval Reserve once again. He did so with much trepidation. He had always loved and revered the Navy but he had become disillusioned by senior officers who only paid attention to their own career patterns and who disregarded the welfare of their squadrons, the people in those squadrons and the US Navy. A common cry from officers like those that Kruger disdained was, "I don't want to jeopardize my career" as they sought to refrain from doing anything that was required under the circumstances and the time. As Lt. Kruger often remarked, "Those dummies don't even know that they don't have a career. They destroyed it long ago and are too ignorant to know it."

Lieutenant Kruger was a far cry from the thin Ensign who had originally embarked on a very new journey with the Navy. He still had black hair, although not as much as he once had. His teeth were still crooked as was his smile. At five feet eight and a half inches he was still not as tall as Northwest Orient wished him to be but they had hired him nevertheless. Perhaps they were scraping the bottom of the barrel. Who knew? At any rate Kruger was "aboard", but with misgivings.

Checking into the BOQ was like coming home from a long deployment. BOQs were not five star hotels. They existed solely to allow an officer to rest for a short period of time prior to going on duty once again. They were Spartan in their makeup. Their saving grace was that they were populated only by Navy personnel; officers and stewards. The stewards were enlisted men recruited from the Philippines under an agreement made between the two countries in the early 1900s. No one in a BOQ would think of breaking off the legs of a couch, trying to smuggle a number of stewardesses onboard or generally violating the rules of civilized behavior, (except on a deployment where it sometimes became necessary to blow off a little steam). The BOQ was basically a gentleman's club where quiet and order dominated.

Ed felt comfortable in the BOQ. Maybe it wasn't quite as nice as a modern motel but it felt very comfortable; sort of like a pair of old shoes after a long hike or a hunting trip in the field. He showered and sighed as he relaxed in the single bed allotted for the room. He fell asleep thinking of the bugle call for colors at 0800 in the morning.

The next morning he was up prior to the colors. He showered, shaved and dressed in civilian clothes. "Have to remember that I'm a fricking civilian now," he thought as he shaved. "Got to think like them, bad cess to 'em all," he thought in words that his ancestors from Scotland would have voiced.

Soon he was on his way to the Northwest Orient Airlines home base to make his presence known. He checked in through a number of officious secretaries and front people and finally was told that he was to show up in three days for his first day in "Boeing School".

He expected several schools before he could be allowed to fly the airline's airplanes. The Navy was the same way. You always had to go to school before you flew. It didn't matter what the school's name was, you still had to attend and make the grade. So he had to go to school again. Big deal. He had three days to get squared away before he had to buckle down.

He bought a copy of the Minneapolis Tribune and checked the "apartments and rooms for rent" classified ads. After calling several numbers he hit on a "room" in a house owned by a widowed lady who needed a renter. He checked the place out and it seemed to be very nice. It was near a meandering creek that ran for miles through the southern part of Minneapolis near the airport. It was nice and quiet, didn't require much from him and was economical. The lady who owned the house wished to know if he intended to "cook" on the property and seemed relieved to find out that Ed didn't have any intention of doing so. He assured her that he only wished a place to sleep and study. She told him that he could use her washing facilities if he wished and he was grateful for the offer. It was going to be a nice arrangement.

On a Monday morning at 0800 Ed presented his body for Boeing School. The name was deceptive. Prior to learning anything about the Boeing systems everyone had to submit to a "welcome aboard" lecture from a Northwest "heavy". A "heavy" in Navy language was a senior officer or whatever passed for a senior officer in civilian life. The "heavy" in this case was a senior pilot who had opted to work in the training department rather than to fly the line as other pilots did. Ed soon learned that the "training pilots" seemed to give themselves airs and thought that they were a cut above the rank and file pilots.

The "training pilot" assigned to Kruger's class was a classical example of what he could expect for the rest of his career. His last name was Frederickson and he welcomed everybody aboard by saying, "We all wish that if you people are going to screw up you will do it in your first year because it is much easier to fire you then than after you have become a member of ALPA." ALPA was the Airline Pilots Association and was the "union" that represented most of the airlines except American Airlines that was represented by the Allied Pilots Association. It was telling that Jerry Fredrickson was also an ALPA member but not one of the "friendlies". Apparently Jerry Frederickson was willing to subvert his loyalty to ALPA in favor of the company.

Kruger filed that little homily away for future reference. It was always nice to know who the "friendlies" were and who the "hostiles" were. In his mind Northwest Orient Airlines had just become a "hostile". The battlegrounds were drawn now. Northwest was a nice airline to be employed by but not a particularly nice airline to work for. The pay was good and the time off was excellent but all of the other work rules were onerous. The watchword in your first year was to keep your head down and be careful.

Each Captain who a first year parolee flew with had to fill out a critique sheet on the probationary pilot. There was no recourse on the part of the probationary pilot. He had to submit to whatever whim the captain maintained. One bad report in the first year was enough to axe the career any probationary pilot ever entertained. If you considered that a first year probationary pilot might fly with as many as four or five captains in any one month it becomes readily apparent that as many as sixty reports could be submitted on any new pilot. Any quirk a captain held could result in a poor report on any probationary pilot. It was a shaky system for any first year pilot but it was necessary to overcome the first year in order to fly for any airline.

On the first day of Boeing school a little man who looked like a gnome was introduced to the class of approximately thirty pilots. He said that he was the head of Training Schedules and, as such, would control our lives for the next year. He introduced himself as "Mr. Anderson". The class learned later on that the "Mr" was a title that the little man gave himself. He was generally held in low regard by most of the pilots who referred to him as Andy. He did not seem like a nice individual. Ed was beginning to get used to "not nice people". They seemed to abound onboard this airline.

The senior man in the class reported to the "gnome" and identified himself as the senior man on the basis of seniority as required by Naval regulations. All of the pilots sans one were ex-military and so this requirement was right in line with their expectations. The "gnome" asked what he wanted. Al (his name was Alwin) said that, as the senior pilot aboard, he was aware that he had a responsibility for the rest of the class and requested just what was required of him. The "gnome" told him that he needed only to shut up, study, and pass his tests like the rest of the pilots and everything else would be left up to the Training Department. This was duly reported to the rest of the class.

The classes were dedicated to the normal things any pilot had to learn in order to fly a modern plane. The prospective Northwest pilots had to learn all of the systems of the Boeing 727 plus all of the Northwest procedures relative to their passengers. The school was mundane and boring to most of the military pilots attending. A major part of the school was dedicated to the Federal Aviation Regulations that governed a Flight Engineers job since all of the pilots would be hired as a Flight Engineer, an entry level employee. It was a lousy job as far as a pilot was concerned but it paid very well, the time off was nice and it was a necessary precursor to becoming a Captain.

As regards the flight pay relative to a first year engineer an explanation is in order. A pilot on probation in 1968 could only make $500.00 a month no matter how many hours he would fly. It was termed "probationary pay" by the airline and "slave wages" by the pilots concerned. The pay scale was less by three-quarters what the pilot would normally make in the military and all of the pilots were acutely aware of this and had budgeted for this eventuality. It was a necessary hurdle in the process of becoming an airline pilot. All pilots had to supplement their monthly income from whatever savings they had managed to accrue during their active duty assignments in the military.

The class that Kruger was in was organized, like all classes, according to the birthday of each pilot. Kruger was the second in seniority after Al. The two pilots became comrades and adopted the habit of studying together. Al was a Navy pilot also but he flew A4s off of a carrier. The two pilots fell quickly into the habit of friendly banter common among Navy

Aviators who flew different aircraft with each pilot extolling the relative merits of their planes and missions.

The days passed slowly. The school was boring. Everyone was marking time until they passed the tests given by the company and the FAA that would certify them as Flight Engineers on jet aircraft. After an interminable amount of time the day finally dawned. Everyone was alert at 0800 on the morning of the test. A FAA certified test evaluator showed up with a bevy of tests in a box.

The FAA person was a fat, sleepy-eyed female who seemed to operate on a one-third time schedule. She took the role and handed out the test booklets admonishing everyone not to touch or open the booklets until directed to do so. She then checked everyone's identification in order to assure herself that no one was a stand-in for any prospective engineer. When all of that was accomplished she gave the class a lecture.

"Now I want all of you to listen very, very carefully. When I tell you, you will open your test booklets and begin the test. Do not look at your neighbor's test booklet. Do not attempt to cheat in any way. There can be no crib sheets of any kind. If I catch you cheating you will not be allowed to complete the test nor will you ever, ever be able to take any other FAA test ever again. I mean never, never, never."

The prospective engineers listened in disgust. Who in the hell was this female who presumed to lecture a bunch of pilots in a manner more befitting a third grade school class than a group of professional people? One of Mr. Anderson's underlings in the Training Department happened to enter the room as the FAA personage was finishing her lecture. He paused and listened in awe. Then he endeared himself to the class by telling the FAA woman, "Say, can you wait just a minute and maybe give that speech again? It's so good that I would like someone else to hear it and I'd like to tape it also so we could play it over and over again to all of our classes."

The ignorant woman never even flinched. She had no idea, apparently, that anyone was making fun of her. There was an almost universal urge on the part of the military pilots to attempt to put her in her place but Northwest Orient had attempted several times, in many references concerning the FAA, to convince their new-hires that the government bureaucracy always had the final say in any controversy and that it was prudent to get along with its policies.

When everyone had completed the exam the FAA representative collected the answer sheets and left without any further comment. Several of the pilots simply shook their heads as she departed. Some of the more outspoken pilots made references to what they called her simian ancestors. None of the prospective Northwest Orient pilots could really believe that they had just been treated like third grade children. These military pilots had braved and overcome death itself in flying the missions they had been tasked with while flying with the Navy, the Marines and the Air Force. They were all used to being treated with honor and respect. Now they were treated like children and bad children at that.

"Well, guys, welcome to civilian life," one wag announced.

"I feel like a whore," Kruger said, "but if the rumors about all of the money we will eventually make is true and if we all get the time off we are being promised then maybe, just maybe, it's worth it. I'll never like being a civilian again, though. I feel like I've somehow compromised everything I hold dear but I did it with my eyes wide open. All of this, however, is all shit. I'm still a Navy pilot and don't any of you assholes ever forget it."

"Awwright!" was the shout that greeted his little speech. It was punctuated by attending shouts of, "Navy is pussy! Marines, Ooorah!" and "Air Force is the only way to go!" Kruger grinned. These civilian pukes could posture all they wanted but when the chips were down everyone knew that military people and military thinking would rule the day.

The following days were taken up with classes on everything from weight and balance, meteorology, company procedures and systems to the history of Northwest Orient Airlines. Everyone was anxious to get out of the classroom environment and into flying the line. The classes seemed to go on forever.

Weekends were free for the students. Kruger filled them with study and an occasional drinking bout with his buddy Al. None of the students were flush with money. Northwest had agreed to pay them $500.00 per month. Most of the pilots were married and had to support families on that penurious amount. Kruger and his friend adopted the habit of drinking a cheap beer called Cold Spring. It was horrible but, in the value system then extant Kruger said, "Cold Spring Beer was like bad breath. An old quip had once said, 'Bad breath is better than no breath at all'."

The balance of time was spent on writing to Joanna and attending any movies that looked promising.

One weekend Ed and Al decided to check out the "downtown" area of Minneapolis. They walked around the unassuming areas including the vaunted "Foshay Tower", which Ed thought looked like something that a sophomore engineering student would have designed. Nothing looked as wonderful as the residents touted them to be. Minneapolis residents apparently hadn't traveled much. They thought that their rather small city was the epitome of what any real city ought to be. To call them insular was understating the case, in Kruger's opinion. They finally ended up in a bookstore. Nothing could be safer than a bookstore in the center of town, right?

Wrong! The bookstore was a pornographic shop or a "porn shop" in the vernacular. When they entered the palace of ill repute they didn't pick up on just where they were at first. They were too engrossed in trying to find books that they had an interest in. Little by little they caught on to the atmosphere of the place and when they did they were embarrassed. "God! What if anyone caught them in a place like this? What in the hell could they say?"

"Hey, Al, let's get the hell out of here."

"Damn right. Jesus, this is a fucked up place. I'd hate for anyone to see us here let alone catch us coming out of it."

They headed for the door. A leering, cadaverous looking man smiled at them as they passed him. "Hi, boys, looking for a little action?"

"Get the fuck out of my way, you asshole, or I'll reach down your throat and pull your cock up through your mouth." Al was not going to shirk his fighting stance in this wonderful bookstore in the heart of the learned center of the Midwest. Ed gave him a "thumbs up", glared at the shrinking skinny man and stalked out. They almost ran out of the door hoping not to see anyone that they knew.

They jumped in the car and headed for Bloomington, a south suburb of Minneapolis. "God, I need a drink," Ed said.

"Would you settle for a Cold Spring?"

"Damn right. Six Cold Springs almost equals one Navy Martini," Ed retorted.

They ended up drinking Cold Spring Beer and arguing about what should be done with porno shops in general.

14

The classes drug on interminably. Kruger thought that they would never end. Everyone in the class groused at the never-ending lectures and exams. Each day saw at least one exam and sometimes two or three. It was Northwest Orient's policy to administer an exam at the end of each lecture. The policy not only documented the attendees but insured that they would pay attention instead of falling asleep, the tendency in a warm room after lunch.

In Kruger's estimation if one didn't know better he would presume that the population of Minnesota was 99% Nordic in makeup. He had never seen so many Swedes, Norwegians, Finns and Danes in one spot prior to this. There were even a few Germans. He felt like he was in a foreign country. Probably, he thought, all of these Nordic types had sailed here to the good old USA and had walked through all of this beautiful land until they had found something that looked like home. That was Minnesota, the home of perpetual winter, snow tires, snowmobiles and mosquitoes. All that was lacking, in Kruger's opinion, were polar bears.

There was one redeeming feature in the surrounding countryside. That was the rivalry among the various "Nordic types" that Kruger equated with the quaint notion of virginity among whores. Apparently the Norwegians had the idea that Swedes had the affliction of having heads that were "rounder" than anyone else. They made fun of the Swedes because of this. The Swedes retaliated by accusing the Norwegians of possessing "square" heads. Kruger couldn't tell the difference. Probably it was an acquired bit of knowledge, one an outsider didn't possess. The give and take among the residents was humorous, though, so Kruger just looked on and enjoyed the repartee.

One day an instructor appeared in the classroom while the real instructor was on a break. He looked around, saw that the listed instructor was absent, picked up a piece of chalk and drew a square on the blackboard. Under the square he wrote, "Norwegian haircuts. Five cents a corner." The class broke up in laughter as the real instructor appeared. He looked around and dryly remarked, "Well, I don't think it's that funny."

As time went on Kruger learned to love the dry humor exhibited by the Nordic people. His favorite comic author was a man named "Guindon" who published several humorous books all making fun of the Minnesota people. One of Kruger's favorites was a picture of a guy from the rear. He was peeking out of a closed curtain that covered a window.

The caption said, "Herkimer Olson found a piece of paper in his pocket that said that he had been inspected by inspector number 32. He thinks that it might have happened while he was asleep."

One of the full-time instructors was an old Flight Engineer named Don Abbott. Abbott was a very knowledgeable engineer and knew his stuff backwards and forwards. Years prior to Kruger joining Northwest Orient there had been a battle royal between the pilots and the flight engineers. The engineers were jealous of the large salaries the pilots were drawing and wanted to share in the largess. Flying an airplane looked easy to them especially when the plane was on autopilot so they lobbied for the right to become pilots in their own right and become interleaved into the seniority system. Apparently the pilots had no quarrel with them becoming pilots if they could make the grade, a task few pilots thought possible given the exalted status of a pilot and the superhuman qualities conferred upon that being, but they had a real problem with the seniority issue.

You see, the seniority number is like gold to a commercial pilot. Seniority determines what type of airplane that person can hold and that equates directly to money. The larger and heavier the plane and the more people it can hold determines the pay rate for flying that plane. Senior pilots can bid for that plane as the bidding, like everything else in a commercial airline, is predicated on seniority. Just one seniority number can mean the difference between thousands of dollars monthly to a pilot. Not only that but the annual vacation schedules, the nicer routes, the time off from work all are impacted by the golden seniority number.

The Flight Engineers wished to interleave into the pilot group based on their time of first hire. That meant that some pilots would have to lose seniority, take lesser runs and receive less pay. How dare these upstarts who wanted a piece of the pie? It was war, pure and simple. Each side sought to denigrate the other and apparently there was plenty of ammunition on both sides. When the dust settled some of the Engineers had become pilots, some had flunked out and would have to remain Engineers until the Engineer rating was abolished. Those Engineers who had become pilots could interleave into the pilot group as pilots or as Second Officers.

The Second Officer rating was tantamount to the old Flight Engineer rating. The Second Officer sat at a panel and controlled the plane's pressurization, air conditioning, electrical, hydraulic and any other systems that needed monitoring. In addition the Second Officer had to perform all of the preflight duties required for each flight. His was the number three position, the Pilot and Copilot being the number one and two. The Copilot was officially known as the First Officer with the pilot known as, of course, the Captain.

As far as Kruger could tell there never had been any peace treaty between the old pilots and the old flight engineers. Both sides harbored grudges and probably would until they retired or died, the latter condition each side wished on the other.

Don Abbott was probably a good Flight Engineer. He was a miserable pilot. Kruger had occasion to observe his prowess several times on training flights when the instructor pilot found pity in his heart and allowed Don to fly for a little while. Don was a good instructor, however, and once he had found his niche he was astute enough to stick to it. Everyone liked him. He had a few warts, just like everyone else. His main fault was that he stuttered. He had sought treatment for his affliction and one of the main things he had been taught was that he had to say a "key word" to break the stuttering syndrome. Don's key words were "actually" and "in other words". Sometimes he would use the terms several times in one sentence. Kruger became used to hearing him say, "This is the actually, in other words, circuit breaker." The class broke up one day when Don referred to one of the students named Tom Snyder as "Tom actually Snyder". The name stuck and Tom was forever after called Tom Actually Snyder. Whenever the class got boring the pilots would all try and catalog the number of times poor Don would utter the words "actually" and "in other words". They wrote the numbers down on sheets of paper and compared notes at the break, the winner being the pilot who could document the largest number of utterances.

Don got even with everyone, however, because he administered the Flight Engineers exam. This was the "big final". Regardless of what Northwest Orient called the Flight Engineer he still was a Flight Engineer as far as the FAA was concerned and he had to pass the FE exam. Everyone sweated Don's oral exams and he proved, through his questions, that he still knew far more than the average "puke" did about the aircraft systems.

Eventually everyone in the class passed the muster and were released to the Training Department for aircraft checkouts. The Training Department consisted of primarily three people in the administrative end. The head of the Department was the little weasel known as Mr. Anderson. He wanted everyone to call him by that name but, as he was held in disrepute if not actual contempt by the pilots, he was universally known as "Andy". He was a miserable pup. His second-in-command was a man named Ralph Douglas. Ralph was a very likeable person with a good sense of humor and was everybody's favorite. People always tried to access Ralph whenever they had a question concerning Training.

Kruger was tied into the system like everyone else. There were a few training flights to ascertain his prowess as a pilot and then everything was oriented around his Second Officer qualification. His first year with Northwest Orient seemed to be a year of nonstop testing. The Company wanted to make sure that they were getting everything they paid for. Kruger thought that they were getting a lot more than they had paid for. For one thing they were getting hardened military pilots, people who had survived at least four years of military flying and in some cases a lot more. Then the company contracted to pay those pilots "slave" wages of $500.00 per month while flying them just like their line brothers who were making four to six times their meager salaries. The new pilots weren't stupid and all referred to their wages as slave income. No one quit, however, as the second year and all years subsequent were more than compensation for the meager wages being paid in their first year.

Kruger thought that the job was easy. Most of the other pilots agreed with him. You only needed to pay attention to a few things in a timely manner and then just set back and monitor everything while you conversed with the other pilots and the Cabin Attendants. You also got to eat a First Class meal at meal times. Maybe you weren't flying but the job was nice. In Navy terms it was "Pussy". The term "Pussy" was used to denote anything that was "soft, felt really good, was easy to assess and didn't take much prowess to accomplish". It was the new term for "a milk run".

Kruger graduated from the Training Department to the Line. It was nice to be out of the testing phase all of the time but the pay was still miserable. On one of his first flights he had a Second Officer Training pilot along to monitor his actions. On an approach to one of the fields served by Northwest Orient one of the Cabin Attendants called the cockpit. Kruger answered the phone as was his duty. The Cabin Attendant said, "I don't know what in the hell you are doing with the pressurization on this plane but it's driving us right through the cabin floor." Kruger looked at the Training Pilot in horror. Was he doing something really bad relative to the cabin pressurization? What about all of those passengers who relied on him to make their flight comfortable?

The Training Pilot had heard the transmission and was bent over in suffused laughter. "Pay no attention to those dumb broads," he said, "They don't know the difference between pressurization and "G" forces." The pilot had been banking a lot in order to align the plane with the runway. The "G" forces, of course, became larger in a bank. This was Kruger's first foray with Cabin Attendants. He was later to learn that the company didn't teach the Cabin Attendants anything relative to actual flight. They were only taught those things that would relate to passenger service such as comfort on the plane, how to serve drinks, those things that needed to be learned about evacuation of a plane in case of an emergency and a few items of first aid. They were really "dummies", no fault of their own. The company only taught them what it had to teach in order for them to operate.

On the second flight Kruger was alone and attending the Second Officers panel when the senior Cabin Attendant came into the cockpit. Kruger ignored her as he was brand new to the job and simply embarrassed by being in close proximity with a female. She stood uncomfortably close to him and watched him for a few seconds. Finally she said, "How long have you worked for the company?'

Kruger swallowed and said, "Only three months."

The Cabin Attendant said, "I'm senior to you."

"Great", thought Kruger, "Someone who is fixed on seniority." He said, "Sugar, everyone is senior to me. I'm brand new. The garbage man and the dogcatcher are senior to me. What do you want from me?"

The Cabin Attendant said, "I make more money than you do."

Kruger retorted, "Yeah, I know. So does the dogcatcher and the garbage man and everybody I know." The cabin attendant finally caught on and laughed. She flounced out of the cockpit.

Once again the Captain cautioned Kruger to pay no attention to the CA's. "You'll find out that the less you have to do with them the better", he said. "Most of them are right out of high school and don't know anything about anything."

Kruger felt that his plate was full enough trying to do everything that was required of him as a Second Officer. He didn't have any spare time to devote to the "GIBs" or the "Girls in Back".

Kruger liked flying the 727 but being a Second Officer was not like actually flying. Sure, the time off was great and the pay would be great after the year as a probation pilot but he felt that something was lacking. Most of the pilots were very good but there were some 727 Captains who were less than optimal. One day Kruger had occasion to fly with one of them.

On the day in question the weather was marginal. The 727 was scheduled to fly from Minneapolis to Seattle with stops enroute. Kruger was the Second Officer and he put up with the BS coming from the front cockpit for a bit. When the crew had to shoot an ILS to a minimums approach to the runway at Great Falls, Montana Kruger was as alert as he could possibly be. The Captain was a marginal pilot who had upgraded from a flight engineer some time prior to the time that Kruger had joined Northwest. The copilot was a lickspittle who was a weak pilot and who groveled at everything the Captain said. Kruger figured that they flew with each other simply because no one else would put up with them. He felt ill having to fly with this marginal crew but a schedule was a schedule. During the approach the Captain was flying. Actually the term flying was a misnomer. The Captain was hanging on to the yoke while the airplane did pretty much what it wanted to do. Kruger was amazed at the lack of flying ability and the acquiescence of the copilot who let the Captain get away with it. Kruger's thoughts ran in the order of, "How did this guy ever get to be a Captain in the first place?" and, "Doesn't the copilot want to live? Why doesn't he take the plane away from this idiot?"

Finally, at around 300 feet from the ground Kruger reached forward and shoved the throttles full bore saying, "Let's get the hell out of here." The Captain made the go-around without comment and the crew proceeded to their alternate without any further discussion. Kruger thought, "Holy shit! It's just like the guys up front are in a simulator and I'm the instructor. How in the hell can this airline operate like this? I wonder how many other jugheads are flying like these guys?

Kruger was just getting his feet wet on the line flying as a Second officer on the 727 with Northwest Orient. He was learning that airline flying was nothing like flying for the Navy. The main fly in the ointment was that flight crews had little to say with the day to day operation of the airline, especially where the passengers was concerned. Northwest Orient talked a good line for the passengers but was little concerned about them other than to collect their cash for a ticket. "Passenger service" generally stopped after the cash had changed hands.

On one flight that stopped in Great Falls, Montana a passenger was flying in tourist class and had to deplane at that station. He was crippled in that he had no use of either of his legs. He had boarded at O'Hare in Chicago with the aid of a special wheel chair the airline used that allowed easy access down the narrow aisles in the 727. When the plane landed at Great Falls Kruger called the station and requested another chair in order to allow the passenger to deplane normally.

The whole plane deplaned and no wheel chair had shown up. Kruger called two more times before a customer service agent appeared empty handed. When questioned he said that the station only had one wheel chair and that it was "out of service". Kruger asked how the passenger would be deplaned and the agent said that he would "talk to the passenger". The crew stood by in the first class section while the agent went to the rear of the now empty plane to attend to the infirm passenger.

Suddenly the agent and the passenger appeared. The agent had both of the passenger's legs tucked under his arms and the passenger was "walking" down the aisle, wheel barrow style, on his hands. The sight generated an uproar on the part of the pilots while the Flight Attendants broke down crying at the sight. The pilots offered to make a "chair" with their arms but the agent wouldn't hear about it and the longsuffering passenger kept repeating, "I only want to get off this airplane".

The passenger was deplaned in this degrading style and the agent ignored the caustic remarks directed to him by the irate pilots. Letters to the company about the incident went unanswered.

CHAPTER II

Kruger felt unfulfilled now that he was "flying the line". The company kept him busy enough but he still had plenty of time off and really nothing to do with all that time. He nosed around the twin cities, spent time at the library and attended more movies than he had previously seen in three years. Face it! Civilian life was boring in the extreme.

He gave up and headed for the Naval Air Station that occupied the northeast side of the field. It was a small facility and Kruger soon found the Program Manager who handled the VP pilots. VP was the Navy's shorthand for patrol aviation.

As soon as he entered the front gate of the Air Station and saw the flag flying he felt at home. Damn it, why had he ever left the Naval Service?

Kruger introduced himself to the VP Program Manager, a LCDR TAR (A specialty assignment. TAR stood for "Training and Administration of Reserves") by the name of Chuck Peterson. Chuck was delighted to see a Lieutenant fresh off of active duty who wanted to fly for him. They sat around and swapped tales for awhile and Kruger bared his soul telling the TAR why he had felt that he had to leave active duty. Chuck was sympathetic but he cautioned Kruger, "Don't think that you have left incompetent people behind you. You're going to find that there are plenty of them here. You're going to have to really watch just who you fly with as there are some guys here who only fly a couple of hours a month in order to get flight pay. The rest of the time they are civilians who don't even think about planes. They've been doing that for years and are now so rusty that they are a danger to themselves and anyone else in the area."

"Why do you keep them around?" Kruger was incredulous.

"Why? Because I'm tasked with keeping the Reserve squadrons under my administration filled up with pilots. Most of the pilots who leave active duty don't want to fly any more for the Navy. That leaves the scrubs for me. I guess you could say that I'm just as poor an officer as the ones you left behind but I've got a job to do and this is the only pool I've got to draw on. At least these guys have been trained. My job is to try and bring them up to snuff once again. It makes my day when I get an interested new pilot like you."

"Thanks for the complement but are the guys in the squadrons as bad as you've just painted them to be?"

"Ooooh, yeah." Chuck rolled his eyes and sat back in his chair. "You'll find out soon enough. Just don't let your guard down for a second. Any time you want to fly just let me know. I've usually got a crew lined up who need a plane commander. When do you want to take your PC check ride?"

The reserve squadrons at NAS Twin Cities all flew P2V-5s. Kruger almost vomited when he heard that bit of news. He hated the "dash 5s". They were a conglomerate of bits and pieces. No two were alike. They were also ugly in that they possessed very large wing tip tanks that looked out of place. He checked out a flight handbook figuring that whatever he had to fly it was still Navy and could give him back some of his self respect.

The next few days were busy ones as he flew for Northwest Orient, studied the NATOPS (Naval Air Training and Operating Procedures) Flight manual, and hunted for a suitable home for his wife, Joanna and his daughter, Lori. He had left his family in Jacksonville, Florida while he attended the various schools required by Northwest Orient. Now he had to find something they all could accept while trying to fit it into a budget of $500.00 per month. That wasn't easy.

The next week he scheduled a flight check with the TAR. It wasn't hard because Kruger had just spent the last two years teaching the P2V-7 in VP-30 at Jacksonville NAS. The dash 5 handled a little heavier than the dash 7 and everything was located somewhere else in the cockpit but other than that it was a piece of cake. He didn't even have to drop any weapons or fire any rockets. Chuck mainly was concerned that he could make the take-off, take care of a few emergencies and land OK. He was asked a few cursory questions about the aircraft systems that Kruger answered OK and he was done. Chuck left Kruger to shut down, complete the post flight check and fill out the yellow sheet while the TAR hastened to cut Kruger's PPC (Patrol Plane Commander) papers. Kruger got the feeling that the TAR wanted to nail him down so he couldn't run off.

Kruger's plan worked 4.0. (Under the Navy grading system a 4.0 was a perfect score.) Flying for both Northwest Orient and the Navy kept him as busy as he could wish. One weekend he got to meet all of his squadron mates. The requirements for remaining in a Reserve squadron in 1968 were that you had to attend one weekend a month and go on active duty for training for two weeks every year.

Kruger soon found out that some of the reserve pilots were good, most were average to below average and a few were abysmal. All were nice guys and all were friendly. It was more like a gentleman's club than a flying squadron however. Kruger flew with several of them and each flight left him just shaking his head. He laughingly told one of his contemporaries that some of the pilot's idea of a successful Reserve weekend was one shaky take-off and one shaky landing interspersed with four hours of orbiting the field to make sure that it didn't go anywhere. Each pilot needed four hours of flight time per month in order to qualify for flight pay. Some pilots were not above using their pencil to complete the necessary four hours. After all, flying was a dangerous profession.

One weekend a competent pilot who flew company planes for the 3M Company approached Kruger at "happy hour". This pilot's name was Dick Reebe and he was a good "stick" meaning that he was a good pilot in pilot's terms. He confided to Kruger, "Ed, I know that you are a shit hot pilot right now but, trust me, as time goes on you'll get to be just like the rest of us. You'll be just as shitty as all of us are. It's inevitable. You can't possibly fly the few hours we do and remain competent."

Kruger's response was entirely predictable and was totally expected from a Naval Aviator. "Would you be mad at me if I told you 'bullshit'?" he said.

Dick smiled and said, "Yeah, I know, I said the same thing a few years ago. Just remember that I told you that it would happen and don't be surprised when it does. It may just save your life."

"OK, if it ever happens I'll look you up and thank you for the 'heads up'."

Dick grinned and said, "That's good enough. Just remember, that's all I ask."

Reebe's prediction would come all too true in the near future.

Kruger maintained reservations concerning the prediction. That same day he overheard a pilot telling another reservist that he had to fly a night hop in order to satisfy his annual requirements that specified a minimum number of hours of night and day VFR and IFR. The pilot was complaining that he had tried to shoot several night landings but was somewhat prevented from doing so because the landing lights kept popping the circuit breakers that serviced that particular circuit. The landing lights were powerful and demanded a lot of current in order to operate. The pilot laughingly said that he solved the problem by stationing a crewmember by the circuit breaker panel who would push the breaker in and hold it in for as long as the pilots needed the lights. Kruger shuddered when he heard that and resolved to say something to the Maintenance Officer so that the overloaded wires on that airplane could be inspected.

The problem was that many of the reservists; commonly called "weekend warriors" all had the same lackadaisical, cavalier attitudes toward flight safety. The name of the game here was to accumulate flight hours in order to get paid. Many of the pilots supplemented their monthly income by flying for the Navy. The Navy considered the flight time to be training in order to keep up proficiency in case the pilots were needed for any emergencies the government might deem appropriate. The pilots saw flight time to be a pain-in-the-ass requirement that was necessary in order to be paid. Not all pilots felt this way but enough did that it affected the whole unit's esprit-de-corps. Kruger was appalled but the camaraderie and the company of other Navy pilots kept him coming back. It was like flying with a squadron in World War One in France. All bravado and little real experience.

Kruger was even more appalled when he fell into the same pattern one night when he was requested to take a flight out on a night hop in order to get 4 hours for the crew. He climbed into the old P2V-5 and settled into the pilot's seat. He normally had to familiarize himself with the particular cockpit arrangement on each plane, as no two were alike. Just another thing to chalk up against the dash 5s. On this particular hop he could not find the rheostat that controlled the pilots instrument lights. Try as he might the little switch eluded him. After ten minutes of searching he was ready to call it quits and cancel the flight. Maintenance had gone home long ago and no one else seemed to be any more successful at finding the elusive switch.

He climbed out of the cockpit and called the crew together. When he told them about the problem he watched their faces drop in disappointment. They had all given up their evening in the hope of flying and bringing home a few extra bucks to Mom and the kids. How in the hell could he screw up their plans just because he was so dumb as to not be able to find a fucking switch? He suddenly told them that he had thought of an alternative and to climb aboard. The relieved looks on their faces was reward enough.

Kruger belted in once again and pulled out the little pencil light he kept in the pocket on the left arm sleeve of his flight suit. The flashlight was the right size to hold in your mouth, just one of the reasons for choosing it. He turned the light on and shoved it into his mouth hoping that it was clean and that the batteries were good for a couple of hours at least.

The takeoff was unique in Kruger's experience. He had never before made a takeoff while holding a flashlight in his mouth and trying to read the flight instruments in the light of a bouncing narrow beam of light. It was not his finest moment. Once the gear was up most of the rest of the flight was, as far as Kruger was concerned, training to find the damned rheostat. It only took him an hour. The elusive switch was behind his seat on the left side. He could barely reach it. It was quite apparent that someone who hated pilots had installed the fucking thing that way.

The only good thing that was accomplished that night was that Kruger was known after that as a "can-do" pilot who would do almost anything to complete a four-hour flight for the crew. The flight time for crewmembers was known as "STARPS" or "Supplemental Training and Requalification Procedures" and the name quickly became a noun. Crewmembers would ask if someone wanted to "Starp", in other words did they wish to fly a training flight? Kruger was always amused at the terminology. What would some headshrinker think if they heard a conversation containing the term without knowing anything concerning the verbal shorthand?

Kruger could almost collapse in a fit of giggles at the thought of a psychologist furiously writing on a pad while two Navy people engaged in a conversation concerning Starps.

"Hey, Jack, do you want to Starp this evening?"

Kruger soon learned just which people he could count on for the supplemental training flights and which ones would simply show up and expect to be chauffeured around, doing nothing and accomplishing nothing while they drew their pay from the Navy. Some of the latter were pleasant but ineffectual while others were, in Kruger's opinion, dangerous.

The Reserve program, at that time, was also pretty ineffectual. "Training" in the eyes of the TAR Officer in charge amounted to "flight time". It didn't seem to matter just what you did while you were flying so long as you were in the air. As far as the TAR was concerned the crew who practiced emergencies and IFR approaches trained just as hard as the crew who simply bored holes in the air for four hours. Kruger tried not to create waves as he needed the extra income to supplement the meager income Northwest Airlines grudgingly doled out to its first-year pilots. He used the four hours needed to "Starp" to train the pilots he flew with and adopted a live and let live attitude toward the hole-borers.

One day Kruger got a phone call from the Naval Reserve office. The TAR Officer-in-Charge (OINC) wanted to fly to Washington, DC to check on some orders he was supposed to receive. He needed a copilot and was calling around to see if anyone was available to fly with him. Kruger was happy to comply and replied that he would be onboard in a half-hour.

When Kruger reported aboard, the TAR, Chuck, asked him to preflight the plane and to file a flight plan to Andrews Air Force Base to remain for three hours and return to Minneapolis. He waved Kruger off and returned to the ever-present paperwork he had to do daily.

Kruger shoved off to look at the weather enroute and in the DC area. He found that, due to an aberration in the upper winds the jet stream, a river of air in the upper atmosphere, had dipped down into the United States and was situated around 23,000 feet between Minneapolis and New Jersey. That was pretty low for the jet stream but it afforded a rare opportunity for anyone who wished to fly east as the jet was running at around 80 to 100 knots. That wind could add lots of speed to any plane flying inside it. It would be like boarding a bus and being taken on a free ride.

Kruger filed for Flight Level 250, which was around 25,000 feet. Normally P2Vs flew below 10,000 feet. They were Anti-Submarine Warfare planes and when they hunted subs they flew at 100 to 200 feet. ASW pilots were not used to flying very high. Kruger called Operations and ordered a number of Oxygen masks and made sure that plenty of Oxygen was onboard in the planes system. He preflighted the plane and briefed the crew. Everything was in order for the senior officer.

Kruger rounded up the crew and got everyone onboard. He started the engines and taxied to the Chuck's office. When that officer saw the plane he ran out and jumped into the right seat. "Ed, you taxi out to the duty runway and I'll get the clearance," he said. Kruger called Ground Control and headed toward the runway.

Chuck called for clearance and began to copy the instructions. "Navy 23606, cleared to the Andrews Air Force Base via . . . ." Clearance Delivery read off the route to Andrews as the TAR copied the monotonal drone. When Clearance Delivery got to the altitude assigned they said, "Climb to and maintain Flight Level Two Five O (250)."

Chuck looked astonished as he turned toward Kruger. "What the hell? Flight Level Two Five O (250)? What the hell do those guys think we're flying? 250? Jesus, I'll set them straight."

Kruger grabbed his arm. "Hold on. Don't get on their case. I filed for 250."

"What the hell are you thinking of? 250? We'd need oxygen. Why 250?"

"There's a jet at 230. If we get to 250 we can take advantage of a 100-knot tailwind. It ought to knock off around 2 hours from our flight plan."

"I don't think I've ever been at 250 in a P2V." Chuck looked distressed.

"Relax, the plane has blowers. You've probably never used them but they work just fine." Blowers were superchargers; turbines that packed additional air into the planes induction systems that allowed flight in the rarefied air found in the upper atmosphere.

"Chuck, relax, I've got everything covered." He keyed the interphone switch. "Crew, Flight, pass up another oxygen mask."

When Chuck was handed his oxygen mask he stared at it like it was some sort of exotic animal. In his case it probably was. Kruger suggested that he plug the mask into the plane's system and preflight it. "Do you remember how to do that," he laughingly asked the TAR?

"Just barely", Chuck grated as he fitted the mask.

They began the climb. Initially the plane performed nicely but as the altitude increased it became more and more doggy. Kruger kept the jets running. At 10,000 feet he called for the smoking lamp to be out and ordered the crew on oxygen. Each man donned his mask, took a few breaths while watching the oxygen indicator to make sure that he wasn't just breathing ambient air and settled back for the long ride. Chuck looked in distress. He was a heavy smoker and the use of pure air augmented by oxygen was foreign to his lungs. His eyes looked like saucers. It was clear that he probably hadn't been on oxygen on a flight in many years. He was huffing rapidly.

Kruger laughed, "Chuck, don't hyperventilate so much. You'll use up all our oxygen. If you pass out I'll have to fly and talk to the center all by myself."

As the plane passed 12,000 feet Kruger throttled the engines back to idle and moved the blower lever to "high". The plane shuddered as the big 3350 engines shifted to high blower and then gained new life as the power was reapplied. The climb to flight level 250 was slow. The plane was not designed for high altitude flight. They finally leveled off over Detroit and Kruger only shut down one jet leaving the other to augment the power required to maintain the true airspeed they had filed for. Even using a jet, not normally used in cruise, they would save fuel due to the jet stream pushing them along. Half way to Andrews Kruger shut down that jet and started the one on the other side of the plane in order to balance the fuel. They arrived in the Washington area in record time and as they descended below 10,000 feet Kruger came up on the interphone.

"Crew, Flight, secure from Oxygen. Turn off all masks and systems and report." When everyone was breathing normally and the oxygen system had been secured he transmitted, "The smoking lamp is lighted."

The "smoking lamp" was a carryover from the old sailing ship Navy when ships carried powder for deck guns and no seaman was allowed to have matches or flint and steel due to the dangers involved. Crewmen were allowed to smoke pipes but they could only be lit by the use of a designated lamp hung only in a safe area of the ship for that purpose. The Bo'sun lighted the lamp when it was considered safe to allow the crew to smoke. When it was not the lamp was extinguished and the word was passed that the "lamp was out". The tradition carries over to this day with the singular exception of the old smoking lamp itself.

When the word was passed that it was OK to smoke Chuck tore off his mask and lit a cigarette with shaking hands. He had obviously been nicotine deprived. Kruger laughed at him. "Chuck, you should savor this moment. This is as healthy as you've been in years." Chuck drew heavily on his cigarette and glared at Kruger.

After the plane had been secured and Chuck had shoved off to talk to his detailer Kruger walked into the privy in the Operations Center, called "the head" by the Navy. He was startled when he looked into the mirror. It had been a long time since he had flown in an unpressurized plane on oxygen. His face was an unhealthy pasty white color and he had large black rings around his eyes. He looked like a dead man. He decided that he probably wouldn't repeat the high altitude trick soon.

*   *   *

Flying the line, as the commercial pilot's term for what they do, was interesting for Kruger mainly because it was new, novel and he got to stay in more hotels than he had ever stayed in up to this time in his life. The pilots he flew with were, for the most part, not only superb but interesting to talk to and fun to be with. His job as a Second Officer kept him busy enough. He had to do the exterior preflight on each leg, regardless of the weather. In flight the pressurization, cabin atmosphere and fuel scheduling among the various fuel tanks occupied his attention. He also had to keep up with logbooks, Cabin Attendant flight time sheets and the pay sheets for the pilots. In addition he was responsible for all communications with the company and had to get the weather and ATIS or Air Traffic Information System information for the pilots who were flying. Generally the Second Officer took care of anything that would otherwise distract the pilots who were actually doing the flying while those worthies relaxed and watched the autopilot fly the plane.

One fine day Kruger experienced his first engine failure on the 727. Granted that he was only a Second Officer on the plane and the "real pilots" took care of the emergency. Kruger was monitoring the Second Officer's panel and the takeoff when he heard a loud grinding sound. It was louder than any other sounds he had heard during a takeoff in any plane that he had ever flown in. It gripped his stomach and seemed to go on and on. It happened while the plane was still on the runway just prior to takeoff. Lights flashed in the cockpit and Kruger instantly picked up the emergency checklist and began to read it as he went through his emergency procedures on his own panel. The Captain was flying the plane and he made a takeoff turning downwind as the copilot called the tower and declared an emergency, asking for an immediate return for a landing. The landing was uneventful and the plane taxied up to the jet way again. Amazingly, a television crew was available to film the passengers and those of the crew who couldn't duck fast enough. Kruger thought that the crew performed in a professional manner without any panic at all but a local TV commentator reported that the Captain "appeared shaken". When he heard that the Captain wished that he could only have the opportunity to rip the head off of the commentator. Kruger concurred with his assessment. It was Kruger's first but not his last association with the press.

Layovers were fun. The 727 crews usually consisted of three pilots and three Cabin Attendants. For compatible people the number was ideal. Most of the time all six would go to supper together. If everyone seemed to be having fun the evening was spent at any number of bars and nightclubs available with just enough time devoted to sleep so the crew could function the next day.

When Kruger had been hired he was informed of the myriad rules, regulations and laws he would have to observe if he wished to stay on with Northwest Orient. Ninety percent of the time the company spent on the rules was devoted to two subjects, drinking while on layover and cohabiting with the Cabin Attendants. Kruger had to listen to innumerable lectures about both subjects.

Drinking was absolutely prohibited. It made no difference how long the layover lasted, no amount of alcohol could be imbibed during the time the pilot was on duty, and the company considered "on duty" meant from the time a pilot checked in to the time he checked out.

"Remember, gentlemen, that means no alcohol. None. Not one drink, not one little sip." This was from the Director of Flight Operations. Kruger was reminded of the old term from the UCMJ, the Uniform Code of Military Justice, concerning rape and sodomy, which stated, "Penetration, however slight, is sufficient to complete the offense".

As for the Cabin Attendants, Kruger's class was treated to several lurid stories calculated to scare off any prospective Lotharios. Don Abbott was fond of telling his class, "Re-remember gentlemen, Confucius say, 'He who dip pen in co-company ink, co-company soon f-f-find out." This tidbit of information was treated to groans by the longsuffering class.

Neither caveat was observed by anyone as far as Kruger could tell. He observed both during his first year of probation, not because he was a purist but because he was afraid of being terminated. He had no objection against drinking. Indeed, he had more than held up his end of the bar while on active duty. He felt that he had burned a bridge when he had resigned a regular commission with the Navy and didn't wish to return, hat in hand, begging for another flying job. As for the Cabin Attendants, he didn't wish to become divorced or made a eunuch by having his gonads severed by a dull knife and Joanna, his wife, was quite capable of both actions. Kruger enjoyed the parties but did so sober . . . . and without female company.

Kruger was amazed at how easy casual sex was on the line. Young women who should have known better had liaisons with older, married men all the time. It seemed to him that a lot of the older pilots were concerned that their life was slipping away from them rapidly. Close proximity with a lot of very young, nubile females, most barely out of high school, seemed to augment that feeling. Kruger observed that, in this era, a lot of pilots donned open necked shirts with lots of gold chains showing. A lot of the time those particular pilots were losing their hair and had only the "Nero" look with hair only around the sides of their heads like a halo. Kruger laughingly thought that they were still growing; they had grown right through their hair. The combination of no hair and open necked shirts sporting lots of gold chains was, well, humorous. Kruger said a silent prayer that he would grow old with dignity and not like these guys.

On one of his trips Kruger was flying with an old Captain who always flew with his girlfriend. One of the Flight Attendants apparently took a shine to Kruger and flirted openly. Kruger went along with the flirtation as any gentleman would do but thought that if he was going to cheat on his wife it would not be with a woman like the one that was currently available for him. After the trip everyone went to their rooms in the hotel. Kruger's phone rang and when he answered it the Captain said, "Your presence is requested at a party in my room". Kruger could hear the giggles and general noise of the "party" in the background. He suspected that the Captain was trying to set up a liaison with the Flight attendant that had been flirting with him. He declined the offer as graciously as possible saying that he was tired and wanted to just turn in. The Captain wouldn't hear of it and insisted in spite of Kruger's protestations. Finally the Captain said, "You will get your butt down here and that's an order." At that, Kruger bridled. "Just how do you intend to enforce that order, Captain", Kruger snarled. At that the Captain backed down, sensibly. Kruger went to bed thinking that the freaking civilians on the airline tossed orders around like the English tossed dwarfs.

The next morning the little Flight attendant that had flirted with Kruger buttonholed him. "You really blew it last night, buster", she said. Kruger professed amazement and said, "How did I do that?" The F/A looked at him like he was probably the dumbest pilot on the airline and said, "I shouldn't have to point this out to you but you could have gotten laid last night if you had been a little more cooperative." Kruger again put on his "dumb" face and said, "God, I never thought of that." The F/A sniffed and, turning on her heels, walked away from him. Kruger smile and thought, "Better to let her think that I am the dumbest pilot on the airline than that she had been evaluated and had come up a little short".

The time passed quickly because he kept busy with both his Northwest job and the Naval Reserve. All of a sudden he discovered that he had been with the company for six months. It was time for his six-month interview with the Chief Pilot.

All probationary pilots had to undergo a six-month and a twelve-month interview before they could become members of the Air Line Pilots Association or ALPA. Any pilot could be terminated without cause prior to becoming an ALPA member. Anything could precipitate a termination; attitudes, the way the pilot parted his hair or wore his uniform, a discussion with the Captain that put the Captain in a bad light, an affair with one of the girls no matter how brief, anything at all. Several pilots were allowed to work for a year only to be dismissed at the last moment. This gave rise to the charge among the probationary pilots that the company used pilots as "slave labor" for a year only to discard them at the last minute.

Kruger reported for his six-month interview with a clean conscience. He could think of nothing the company could fault him for. His interview was not with the Chief Pilot but with his assistant. The assistant's name was Don Nelson. He had been a member of SAC with the Air Force. Kruger had heard that he had only risen to the status of copilot in SAC. Kruger had been warned about him. He was a snake, pretending to be a friend to all but he would fink on anyone to the company with the goal in mind of terminating them. Nelson was a perfidious sort. When Kruger entered Nelson's office he shook Kruger's hand and invited him to set down. Nelson then imperiously pretended to study all of the Captains reports on Kruger as if he had never seen the file prior to this. Kruger pretended ignorance and played along with the game.

"So, Ed, it says here that you were a Navy pilot."

"Yes, sir, I was and I am. I still fly with the Naval Reserve."

"Ho, ho, ho. You don't have to 'sir' me. I'm not in the service anymore."

"Yes, sir."

"Well, I don't see anything derogatory in any of your reports, in fact, they are all very good. How do you like flying for Northwest Orient?"

"I really like it, sir. It's interesting and fulfilling. The flight crews are all top drawer."

"I'm glad you're happy here. I think that we will get along really well together. OK, now, the interview is over. You've passed with flying colors. Just relax and let's talk for a while. Is that OK? Do you have anything else important to do?"

"Oh, no, sir. I'd be more than happy to talk with you as long as you want."

Nelson relaxed as he put his feet on top of his desk. He lit a large cigar. He took his time doing so. Kruger would find out that Nelson liked to smoke cigars. They seemed to give him a better aura of importance; at least as far as he was concerned. When the cigar was glowing he puffed on it and said, "OK, now, man to man, I know that some of the flight crews drink a little on layovers." He chuckled, "I'd be pretty dumb if I didn't, don't you think?"

Kruger smiled but remained silent.

Nelson continued, "So just between us guys, have you ever seen anyone drinking on layover?"

Kruger thought, "Boy, this guy wants to make me a fink. He thinks this 'good old boy' attitude is going to fool me. Shit, he thinks that he can put me in his pocket and that I'll tattle to him anytime."

"No, sir, I've never seen anyone violating the company rule about drinking."

"Oh, c'mon now! We both know they drink. All I'm asking for is a little corroboration here."

"Well, I've never seen anything like that and I always go out to eat with the crews. If anyone drinks they hide it from me. I personally think the crews are squeaky-clean."

Nelson shook his head in disbelief. "OK, then, you can go. The interview's over. Enjoy flying the line and I'll see you in six more months."

Kruger left and reported the results of his interview to one of the ALPA reps. The rep commented, "That slimy SOB. You're right; he tries to enlist a bunch of finks and fellow travelers who will rat out their peers so he can fire anyone he dislikes. He's all about control. If he can get something on you he can control you. Watch out for him and don't ever trust him. He's not your friend."

Kruger knew full well the position of the company. He'd been told that straight out on his first day when he had been told that the company hoped that if he "screwed up" it would be in his first year because "it was easier to fire him then". His hope for comradeship lay in his joining the pilot's union, ALPA, at the end of his first year with the company. He figured that membership in ALPA would sort of be like being back in the Navy where other pilots watched your back. Those hopes were dashed when he attended his first ALPA meeting.

CHAPTER III

It was in the 1968-69 time frame and the contract between ALPA and Northwest Orient had become amendable. Under the Railway Labor Act, that law which ruled the transportation industry, an airline's contract with labor could never really end. It could only become "amendable". That meant that labor was not free to strike a company until and unless the government could intervene. The rule was meant to facilitate transportation in the United States so people would not be inconvenienced by work stoppages.

The bargaining process with any union and Northwest was tough. The President of Northwest Orient was Donald Nyrop, a tough old bird who asked and gave no quarter. The pilots had called a meeting to try and figure out a strategy for making Northwest cave in to their demands. Kruger wasn't a union member but as a probationary pilot he was allowed in, the presumption being that he would eventually apply for membership.

During the meeting a Captain stood up and made a suggestion. "Why don't we all just simply call in sick for our next trip? That'd show the company our resolve and get their attention."

Another pilot stood and countered. "If we did that the company would fire all of the probationary pilots. I think there has to be around 250 of them.

The first pilot stood again. "Well, that's their worry isn't it?"

Kruger couldn't believe his ears. Here was a pilot who was quite willing to sacrifice a large number of junior pilots just to make a point. He thought, "That's just great. I should die for you and I don't even know you." All thoughts of camaraderie and watching out for the other guy vanished. This was the real world. This was civilian life. It was truly dog-eat-dog. Kruger couldn't count on either the pilot group or the company. Just another lesson to be learned and filed away.

Kruger was beginning to get the idea that maybe, just maybe, he had made a wrong decision when he chose the life of an airline pilot over that of a Navy Officer. The latter seemed to give a person a lot more pride and self respect than the former could. Early on Kruger had been told, by a Northwest Orient pilot, that the absolute best way to end a career with the company was to leave the plane after the last flight, cut a hole in the fence surrounding the field and creep silently home. He said that a successful career with the company included keeping your head down and doing your job without letting anyone in management know who you were along with not drawing any attention to yourself in any way. Kruger's thought was, "What a way to go through life, being afraid and paranoid of the company you are working for".

Northwest Orient was known for its hard-nosed treatment of labor. It wasn't just tough on pilots; it was tough on Cabin Attendants, Mechanics and Customer Service people. The normal time period for settling contracts was in the vicinity of two years and sometimes longer. In 1969 the Brotherhood of Railway and Airline Clerks struck the company. The company pared its operation down to the most lucrative routes and hunkered in while the BRAC people walked picket lines and generally starved. The pilots, who "firmly believed in the concept of unionization", crossed BRAC's picket lines in an instant to the hoots of the picketer's cries of "Scab".

The company needed only approximately 200 pilots. The rest were laid off for the duration of the strike plus however long it took for the company to generate customers again. The pilots who flew were caustically known as "The Golden 200" by the rest of the pilots. The other employees knew them as "scabs".

Most of the laid off pilots sought temporary work anywhere they could. A jungle telegraph was created whereby any pilot who knew of any number of jobs or any employer who wanted workmen would call all of his friends informing them of the fact. Those friends would, in turn, call other friends and soon the prospective employer would have his choice of up to 50 overqualified people willing to do any work available. It was a good deal for everyone.

Kruger found work loading and unloading structural steel, picking orders in a warehouse, weeding in a nursery and several other jobs, none lasting more than a month. The strike seemed like it would never end.

The first job he had was with a nursery in Minneapolis called Halla's. Kruger took the job figuring that it would probably require some heavy labor. He thought that he had begun to get soft since he had left the Navy and this might be a good opportunity to harden up a little. He was correct. It was a tough job. He learned first hand what it took to wield a hoe for 10 hours a day. Some days he was not allowed to use a hoe. He had to pull the weeds by hand. He arrived home each day dirty, tired and in dire need of a beer. Sometimes he humorously thought, "If this is what flying is like maybe I ought to be a television evangelist. I'd make a hell of a lot more money and I'd have any number of women."

The nursery owner's kid, a strapping man in his late twenties named Dave, ran the nursery. Dave Halla had the dubious reputation of hiring kids from a local high school, browbeating them to the point where they rebelled explosively and then luring them to the back lot where he delightedly beat them up. He was a bully of the first order. He had a pronounced limp from an old injury and Kruger figured that if he had something to prove to all and sundry it was because he felt that he wasn't up to par with others. Dave was in for an enlightening. He didn't know that Kruger hated bullies and delighted in "thumping" them.

One day the foreman told Kruger that he had been selected to run the rototiller. Initially it seemed like a better deal than pulling weeds but after having rocks thrown up against his shins for an hour he changed his mind. He took a lot of ribbing from his pilot buddies working for Halla about running the rototiller but it was still a job. He was required by Halla to clean the machine each evening with gasoline. Hallas had never heard of the EPA. The first evening he quit work 15 minutes early in order to fieldstrip and clean the tiller. The next day he was informed that he would have to work until quitting time and then clean the machine. He told the foreman that he would run the machine and clean it but that he would not clean it on his own time. The foreman was noncommittal regarding Kruger's attitude and left without saying anything. The next day while Kruger was running the rototiller Dave strolled over and said, "Shut off the machine. I need to talk to you." Kruger complied and turned to face the owner.

"The foreman tells me that you have a problem running the rototiller," Dave began.

Kruger knew immediately just what was up. "No," he said, "I don't have any problems at all about anything here. I don't know what you're referring to."

"Sure you do." Dave was smiling in anticipation of something. He seemed relaxed and enjoying himself. "He says that you had a problem with cleaning the machine after you use it."

Kruger took a deep breath and relaxed. He knew what was happening here and was totally prepared for it. He had trained at a military Karate dojo for a few years before he left active duty with the Navy. He was confident and relaxed, watching and alert for any offensive moves Dave might make. Dave was used to pounding on high school kids. He had no idea what he was getting into.

"No, as I said I have no problems at all. I merely stated that I would not clean the machine up on my time. I'll clean it but you'll pay me for my time or, I'll work until quitting time and you can clean it. Your choice. Just let me know what you want to do."

Dave began to suspect that he wasn't dealing with the average kid here. He fully expected complete compliance or, at least, a sulky reticence. His eyes narrowed. It was time to pull out the stops and roll out the biggest hammer at his disposal. "You're kind of a smart-ass, aren't you? Maybe I should just whip your smart ass for you."

Kruger laughed. This was exactly what he suspected. He squared his body and looked directly into Dave's eyes. "I've heard that about you, Dave. I've heard that you like to pick fights with young kids so you can prove how big and strong you are when you whip them. You're welcome to try any time you want to with me. In fact, I'll make it fair for you. I'll allow you the first two punches, free. After that you're on your own. I'll also promise that I won't break any of your bones but I'll hurt you. You can begin anytime you wish and you can use your fists, feet, elbows head, anything at all. We won't be observing the Marquis of Kingsbury rules here and there isn't any referee that I can see. You should know that I don't fight fair. I fight to win. You can start anytime now, Dave." Kruger smiled confidently at Dave.

Dave obviously had never watched or studied sumo wrestling. The sumo wrestlers always had to face off inches from each other. The highly stylized wrestling matches had the wrestlers facing each other a few times before the actual physical bout began. It was well known that the bout was won or lost in those few moments when the wrestlers were facing each other. Each wrestler knew intuitively who would eventually win and who would lose at a result of those face offs.

Dave looked alarmed. No one had ever invited an assault prior to this. Maybe this guy was as good as he seemed. It wasn't worth the pleasure he figured he would have if he could beat Kruger into insensibility and he sincerely had doubts now that he could accomplish that feat. Dave obviously had never followed the Japanese Sumo wrestling crowd so he was unaware of the prevailing thought that any match was won or lost in the first face-offs before any participant had ever touched the other. The bout is always won or lost in the minds of the participants prior to the actual physical contact.

Dave caved in. His face reddened and he turned without comment and left. Kruger never stopped smiling. He started the rototiller again and continued to till the ground.

Eventually the foreman walked slowly over to Kruger. He was kicking dirt clods as he walked and his bearing was like that of a person attending a funeral. Kruger smilingly shut off the rototiller and waited for him. This was as predictable as the sun rising in the morning.

The foreman mournfully announced, "Well, Ed. I've got bad news."

Kruger laughed. "Let me guess, I've just been fired."

"Yeah, I'm sorry but that's the word."

"Don't let it spoil your day. It certainly hasn't spoiled mine. Oh, and by the way, tell Dave that he can clean his own rototiller." Kruger shut off the machine and started walking toward the front gate.

Dave was a slow-learner. He was waiting for Kruger by the gate and couldn't resist one last parting shot. He had an audience. Several other employees were lounging around apparently in order to watch the boss serve comeuppance to a surly worker.

"Let me show you the gate," he crowed as he smilingly reached out to "help" Kruger.

Kruger paused and faced him. "You ridiculously dumb shit; you haven't learned a thing have you? I know my way through the gate and if you come anywhere near me or touch me in any way I'll rip off your head and stuff it up your ass! I'll tell you what, Dave. I'm a fair man. I'll give you the first two punches and from then on you're on your own. Whadda ya say?" He waited as Dave and the cheering section beat a hasty retreat in alarm. No one came near him. He left the gate ajar as he strode through it.

He had worked for Halla for a total of thirty days.

A few days later he got word through the jungle telegraph that a local brewery needed workers in the bottling house. He gathered up three other pilots and they hotfooted it to St. Paul to inquire about work at the Grain Belt Brewery. Yes, they needed workers and yes, they were happy to hire pilots for the jobs.

The Bottle House Foreman was happy to hire Northwest Orient pilots. He had been through this process before and knew that the laid-off pilots would perform any job he wished done without question or complaint. He also knew that this was a temporary situation and that the pilots had no aspirations at all of changing jobs and lifestyles. According to the Brewery Worker's Union a new hire could only work for thirty days after which he had to join the union or leave. None of the pilots would ever qualify for the Brewery Worker's Union, which necessitated resigning from Northwest Orient, so they would never have any union goon facing off with the foreman on account of any odd job he assigned them. The pilots were ecstatic at landing this job. It not only paid well but they were allotted seven "beer breaks" of fifteen minutes each per night according to the Union contract. During those breaks they could consume as much beer as they wished. They also could imbibe before work, during lunch and after work for as long as they wished. All of the beer of any quality and quantity was free for the employees. It was a pilot's heaven.

Kruger's job was breaking down cardboard boxes that empty bottles had been shipped in. There was a system for this. Boxes arrived at his workstation via a conveyer belt. His job was to grab a box and slam it onto a metal probe in order to break the seal on the glued flaps. The box could then be folded and laid onto a pallet.

The metal probe was capped with a round enlarged end and was situated so as to be vertical. Accordingly, the irreverent pilot group christened it "the iron peter".

Other pilots sat on stools and tried to remain awake while they watched bottles of beer float by on a conveyer belt as they looked for faults in the caps or the paper labels. These pilots did not have to work with their hands so they always had a hand with which to hold a bottle. They were always in a state of inebriation. Kruger had one of the more physical jobs so he could not imbibe constantly as some of the others could. He felt like he was pretty low on the food chain but couldn't really complain, as he candidly could not hold any more beer than he was currently consuming.

One night the foreman attempted to train one of the pilots in the art of making a box for the full bottles of beer. Marine Captain and Northwest Orient pilot Dave Good loved his beer and always reported for work inebriated and "in the bag". That fact seemed to not matter to the foreman. Apparently he was used to his workmen being "in the bag". The box machine was pretty much automatic. All the operator had to do was to open the folded box and align it with the machine's conveyor belt.

A "dog" on the belt would then scoop the box up, fold and glue it until it arrived at the end completely ready to be filled.

Other pilots who knew Capt. Good stood by to watch the show while the foreman attempted to show Dave how to make boxes with the automatic box machine.

"OK, now, Dave, here's all you have to do. Open the folded box and wait until that little tit there called a "dog" rolls by. Then you smoothly feed the open box onto the conveyer belt and the machine will do the rest. Got it?"

Dave, beat up cigarette in his mouth, nodded. The foreman stood to one side and Dave grabbed a box and stuffed it into the machine promptly shutting the whole conveyer down.

"No, Dave, you don't have the picture yet. You have to wait until the little tit, see that one right there? You have to wait until it goes by. Then you feed the box slowly onto the belt. Here, I'll show you again. There. See how easy that was? OK, you try it." The foreman didn't count on the fact that Dave was a Marine. Marines only know how to kill and destroy, not create.

Dave shakily grabbed a box and jammed it into the machine, which promptly shut down once more. He shrugged and puffed on his cigarette.

The foreman was unflappable. "OK, Dave, I've got a better job for you. Just step over here and I'll show you." Dave was given a job that required only breathing as an attribute. The Grain Belt Brewery was a wonderful place to work, especially if you were drunk.

The brewery was an equal opportunity employer. One day a Souix Indian showed up as a bottle inspector. His job was sitting near an assembly line of capped bottles looking for things like crooked caps. Of course he was allowed to drink beer while he worked and he soon became so inibriated that he fell off of his stool and couldn't perform his job. He was dismissed for cause (being drunk), no mean feat at the Grainbelt Brewery. The Indian figured that he was being fired because he was an Indian and a rukus ensued that necessitated the services of the St. Paul police. In Kruger's estimation you had to work really hard to be fired from the brewery.

After three days at work at the brewery Kruger was dehydrated. He had been drinking nothing but beer for all three days. He asked one of the brewery workers where the scuttlebutt was. The man just stared at him and it occurred to him that "scuttlebutt" wasn't a civilian term. "Where's the drinking fountain?" he asked.

"Drinking fountain?" the man said, "Why in hell would you want one of those? The beer here is free!"

Kruger eventually found a source of water. He was astounded at the amount of alcohol the regulars employed by the brewery could hold. One man drank a can or a bottle of beer every fifteen minutes during the entire shift he worked. During his lunch break he hotfooted it across the street to a restaurant where he ordered and drank no less than four or five vodka "shooters". Kruger looked on him with awe. How he could still stand up, let alone work, was beyond anyone.

The pilots were in "hog heaven". They could work and drink at the same time. Each evening their shift ended at around 0130. They drove home in drunken bliss. One evening one of the group announced that he was horny. He wanted the group to stop over on Hennipen Avenue and employ the services of one of the prostitutes who frequented the area. Kruger was driving that evening. He vetoed the idea and laughingly drove down Hennipen while the other pilot ranted about what he thought was a diminution of his rights. Eventually he ripped off his trousers and "mooned" the whole strip while the staid Minnesotans gawked in wonder at the gigantic bare ass protruding from the right hand window of the Volkswagen driving down the street.

The brewery was very lenient about the times employees could come and go. Normally everyone would linger on the premises after work until they had imbibed at least two bottles of beer before vacating the area. The regular employees were amused listening to the Northwest Orient pilot's give and take. This was something they had never experienced prior to this time. It was novel so everyone lingered and drank beer after work in order to listen to the banter the pilots offered.

One evening the banter devolved into a joke telling session. Soon everyone was laughing hilariously. Finally one of the "regular" employees told a joke that fell flat with everyone. The joke teller waited for the laughter that usually accompanied the telling while Kruger looked at him in wonderment. Finally Kruger spoke up.

"Does anyone wish to do the honors?" he asked. When he received no reply he turned to the joke teller. "Well, I guess it's up to me," he said. "In the Navy, whenever anyone tells a joke that absolutely falls flat the man nearest to him has to pour a beer on his head . . . like this!" Kruger punctuated his statement by pouring the contents of his bottle of beer onto the man's head.

At first the man just sat there in stunned silence while beer cascaded down over his head and shoulders. Then he gave a shout and jumped up shaking his bottle of beer. He then inverted the bottle and used it as a spray rig, spraying everyone in sight. Whoops erupted as the whole bottle house erupted into a beer fight. When everything calmed down the bottle house was dripping wet and smelled of beer.

The next day when the pilots came to work they were met with a sign on the door of the bottle house. It read, "As of today all employees will vacate the bottle house no later than fifteen minutes after their shift has ended. This goes double for Northwest Orient Pilots!"

One evening Kruger was working with a young man who had just been hired. He had come off of a farm in South Dakota and this was his first real job in the big city. He was a talker; in fact he babbled. Kruger listened patiently to his constant chatter, amused at the wonder the young man had for everything. Eventually the chatter came around to the young man's fellow workers.

"Say, I heard yesterday that there are some real honest-to-god pilots working here. Can you imagine that? Pilots! I can hardly believe that. Imagine working with real pilots."

Kruger tried to make light of the chatter. "I wouldn't make a big deal about working with pilots. They're just like you are. They get up in the morning, brush their teeth just like you do, pee and put on their pants one leg at a time just like you. They're just normal people."

"I don't believe you. They are super people. Just imagine; they can actually fly airplanes."

"Flying planes is no big deal. Don't let it throw you. Flying is just like driving a car or riding a bicycle. Anyone can learn to do it."

The kid stared at Kruger for a few seconds. "My God!" he said, "you're one of them aren't you? You're a pilot."

"Yeah, but like I said, being a pilot is no big deal. I'm just an average guy trying to do an average job. Just like everyone else around here. I'm just another pilot."

The kid stared at Kruger in awe. He looked like he might fall to his knees anytime in worshipful ardor. Kruger was embarrassed at the attention. He tried to make light of the fact that he was a pilot but his companion wouldn't hear of it. It was an uncomfortable evening and when it ended Kruger felt uncomfortable and ill at ease regarding the adulation the young man had paid him. In Kruger's estimation flying was just another job, a nice job, to be sure and one that was very interesting but still just another job. He really couldn't imagine doing anything else but he didn't understand any of the adulation the young man had paid to him.

Ralph Douglas, the "nice guy" in the training department at Northwest Orient, had a job at the brewery. He was used to this sort of stuff, strikes, and had long made a habit of hotfooting it to the Grain Belt Brewery at the first sense of strike information. He had a job of sweeping the floors. He could always be seen with a huge smile on his face as he pushed his broom around, clanking as he did. Ralph clanked because he always had at least two bottles of beer in his pockets that rattled as he walked. Ralph was happy. He had found a niche for the duration. The pilots felt happy for him.

The fun ended after a month when the bottle house jobs evaporated. The foreman apologized as he handed out the pink slips to the pilots. He said that he wished that he could keep all of the pilots on as long as possible as they never complained and would do any job he wished them to do. The pilots were sad to see the job evaporate also. It was one of the more fun jobs anyone could ever ask for.

Kruger found several jobs after that brewery. Most of them were mundane and paid little. He eventually found a job unloading structural steel from boxcars and using it to set up rows of shelves in a warehouse. As usual there were a number of other pilots filling in as necessary. One of them was a young pilot named Ted Swan who had been a Captain flying 727s for as long as Kruger had been working for Northwest Orient. He was one of the pilots who had hired on to Northwest early in his life. He had not been in any military organization and had to wait until his 21st birthday in order to take his Airline Transport Rating. He was used to good times and big paychecks. Ted had been working for ten days and payday was nigh. Ted was happy. Why wouldn't he be? Payday was a happy time. Eventually the foreman came around handing out the checks individually to each employee.

"Payday, payday," Ted sang to himself, obviously happy. When the foreman handed him his check he danced around like a child at Christmas time. He tore open the envelope and looked at his paycheck. His smile disappeared and his eyes glazed over. His face fell and the change in his appearance was so obvious that the foreman paused and stared at him.

"Are you OK?" the foreman asked.

Ted had backed up until a large bundle of rags had halted him. He sat down on the rag bundle. Actually it would be more appropriate to say that he collapsed on the rags. His eyes were glazed and he had a slack-jaw look as if he were in shock.

The foreman was now alarmed and he hurried over to Ted to see what the problem was.

"What's the problem?"

"Is that all?"

"Whadda ya mean, 'is that all'?"

"Is that all there is? Is that all I get? Six days a week and ten hours a day. Is that all the money I get?" Ted had obviously forgotten how the real world turned. He had been an Airline Captain for so long, drawing down the big money for so long that he didn't relate to the real world.

The foreman threw back his head and brayed a long laugh. He was relieved to find that there was nothing wrong that could reflect adversely on him. "Yeah, that's all and you ain't worth even that." He laughed again.

Ted stood suddenly. He had made up his mind. Decision time. "I quit," he announced.

The foreman was alarmed. "What do you mean?"

"I quit. Finito. I'm done. Fuck this job. If that's all I can make I'd rather go fishing." He strode purposefully off.

The foreman followed him in an attempt to convince him that the job was really a very good one. Ted never missed a step. He disappeared in twenty seconds to the tune of general laughter on the part of the other pilots who knew how he felt but who couldn't emulate him as they didn't have the resources a Captain had.

Kruger brought his paycheck home and threw it onto the desk in the family room. Joanna found it the next day and quipped, "A check from Walgreen's." The Walgreen Company owned the warehouse. "Did you turn in some pop bottles?"

Kruger grinned. She still had a sense of humor. She knew that the check represented six days work at ten hours a day. "Good girl," he thought. "Goddamn civilian flying. I should have stayed in the fricking Navy."

Much later he was called back to work. He had been absent from Northwest for nine months.

Chapter IV

The transition back to work was an easy one but it still took a great deal of time. There were lots of hoops to jump through. The FAA wanted to make sure that all pilots were up to speed on the rules and regulations plus current in all respects so that the traveling public would not be inconvenienced. All pilots had to undergo additional training and that took time as the Training Department was swamped.

All of the transitional training and class work was done in seniority order like everything else that concerned the pilots. Since Kruger was at the tail end of the food chain he was one of the last to be trained. He was checked out once again as a Second Officer.

Like most of the pilots in his category his morale was at an all time low. The bills had piled up during his nine month sabbatical and had to be paid. There were a few notable parties thrown, all by Captains with a lot of seniority who hoped to get some back pay as a result of the back-to-work settlement but probationary pilots like Kruger would not be participating in any scheme like that. They still drew $500.00 per month and still had to serve out the year's probation not counting, of course, the time they were forced onto the streets. Like most of the others Kruger hunkered down and tried to keep his mouth shut until he was allowed to join the Airline Pilot's Association. Until that happened he could be terminated for anything at all including the whim of anyone who didn't like what he was, stood for or said. It was prudent to shut up and do the job given to him.

One day Kruger's flight was required to accommodate a jump seat rider on his way to Minneapolis to take a check ride. Unfortunately the jump seat was occupied by one of the older, more senior pilots who had chosen to fly while all of the rest of his comrades were out of work because of the BRAC strike. Those pilots were sarcastically known as the "Golden Two Hundred". They drew down fat paychecks while their peers starved. Kruger wasn't alone in thinking that if ALPA had refused to cross the BRAC picket line the strike would have ended a lot sooner. During this time period the name of the game as far as strikes were concerned was "Attrition", or who could hold out longer. The Airlines had formed a pact called the Airline Mutual Assistance Pact. It provided that any airline that had been struck by any union could draw on its competitors who would funnel money to it based on what its usual revenue was. The companies really couldn't be hurt although they could always alter their balance sheets to "prove" that the unions were anti-business and were really out to harm the companies that paid their wages. The union workers had to make do with tiny sums doled out by their unions and paid based on the workers walking picket lines while the union top dogs basked in the sun and counted their contributed union dues. The actual worker was the filling in the sandwich and took the brunt of the punishment.

The jump seat rider on Kruger's flight wasn't smart or astute enough to simply shut up and ride. He chattered incessantly attempting to justify what he had done to a rather hostile cockpit. None of the pilots were in his corner. Everyone thought that he was an idiot, as did Kruger. The senior pilot was an opportunist. He didn't care anything at all about his fellow pilots. He was generally ignored. Suddenly he pushed Kruger's shoulder to get his attention and croaked, "You can see my position can't you? If I were to refuse to fly guys like you would have taken my job."

That did it. Kruger lost his temper. "That's a bunch of absolute bullshit," he spit out. The Captain looked around in surprise that his heretofore-quiet Second Officer would react like he did. "You expect me to swallow that crap? Save it for some other chump. You're just another fucking opportunist looking for a chance to feather your overstuffed nest. Why don't you just take your big salary, shut the fuck up and leave us peons alone?"

The surprised Captain was silent for the rest of the flight. Nothing was said concerning Kruger's outburst. "Well, that's one way to screw up a good job," he thought. "Any one of those guys in the cockpit can drop a hint to the Chief Pilot that I'm maybe a little unstable. I wonder if the Navy would accept me again." He shrugged. Nothing to do about it now except wait and see.

Nothing ever came of the issue. Apparently everyone thought the same way Kruger did or at least they were sympathetic with the attitude.

That wasn't the only episode that gave Kruger a few misgivings about his new job. A month later he had to fly with one of the most notorious Captains the airline had. In the first week of employment Kruger's class had a visit from a non-probationary pilot; a well-wisher. He surreptitiously dropped off a list containing the names of the worst pilots to fly with. There were nineteen names on the list, which was quickly copied by all of the new pilots. Newer pilots would all be on reserve, which meant that they had to stand-by for any flight that needed them. They could not choose their flights. As they became more senior they would be allowed to bid for whatever line of flying their seniority would allow them to hold. Only then would they be able to avoid the names of the notorious nineteen.

Kruger had been assigned to fly with an overweight Captain named Ray Severson. Ray was a fidget. He tried to do everything in the cockpit as if the plane were only being flown by one pilot. The inevitable result was that he did nothing well. He was a poor pilot and he kept the cockpit at an advanced level of tension because he continually gave conflicting orders as he attempted to do everyone's job. Kruger figured that he had to have been frightened out of his mind at some point or other and his uncertainty communicated itself to the other pilots.

He introduced himself to the other pilots when he arrived at the cockpit. The copilot was obviously unhappy with his lot in life and had little to say. Ray complained nonstop. "All I ever get are reserves," he whined to no one in particular.

Kruger smiled to himself. "If you were a little more human maybe someone would bid your trips," he thought.

The crew settled down to fly. On the taxi out Kruger activated the fuel cross feed valves to feed all engines out of the center fuel tank as he had been taught. Ray heard the clicking of the switches and instantly his head swiveled around to stare at the Second Officer's panel. "What the fuck are you doing?" he shouted.

Kruger figured that this was just another test like he had been facing ever since he had hired on with the airline so he began to explain, "On the 727 and facing more than a few minutes of taxi time in order to maintain the in-flight center of gravity all engines must be manifolded from the center tank . . . ."

"That's just fucking around," Ray shouted. "You put those goddamned switches where they were when you climbed aboard and quit fucking with the fuel."

Kruger sullenly did as requested steaming with anger as he did. "Nothing like fighting with someone who can't fight back," he thought. "I'm correct and he's as wrong as anything but if I argue with him he'll give me a bad report. There'll be better days". He gritted his teeth and kept silent.

The rest of the trip was much the same. When they arrived home in Minneapolis both the copilot and Kruger stalked off the plane without a word to the Captain.

A few weeks later Kruger almost lost his temper again. Well, actually he did lose it but a pilot didn't witness the episode. It all began when he was eating breakfast in Seattle. The Cabin Attendants entered the restaurant later than he did and ordered breakfast, chattering among themselves as they did. Their breakfast had just been served when the Captain marched out of the motel on his way to the waiting limo. The girls frantically grabbed their belongings and were about to bail out but Kruger stopped them. "The Captain said pickup was to be at 0700. It's only 0655. Eat what you can in five minutes and I'll carry your bags out to the limo". The girls thanked him and pitched into their breakfasts.

Kruger muscled the bags out to the limo watched disapprovingly by the silent Captain. Everything went as planned but when Kruger was walking behind the Captain in the terminal the Captain turned savagely on his Second Officer and, pointing his finger at Kruger's face he grated, "Don't you ever let me catch you carrying any of the puss's bags again, you hear me!" Most of the older pilots referred to the girls generically as "the puss".

Kruger flared. His face was red and it was all he could do not to break off the Captain's finger and stuff it where the sun never shines. As a Navy officer he was not used to being talked to in this manner and it seemed to be happening more and more often. He merely nodded thinking that he only had a few more months to go on probation. The Captain turned and walked angrily away.

Kruger sulked all the way home. The Captain tried to mend things several times but Kruger wasn't buying it. When the flight arrived at Minneapolis Kruger called the company for a gate assignment. The company responded with, "Flight 647, gate 04 inbound, gate 11 outbound." Kruger rogered the transmission but was too new to understand what it meant. Before he could ask the other pilots what the message meant the plane arrived at gate 4. The agent who opened the door stuck his head into the cockpit and asked Kruger if he had told the cabin attendants that there was a gate change. He answered, "No", and thought, "OK, that's what the gate control meant." The agent made an announcement and the passengers started to deplane.

Kruger had a number of things he had to do before he left the cockpit. When he was finished he picked up his flight bag and started to leave. A male cabin attendant who had boarded at Seattle stopped him and said imperiously, "Wait a minute, you. Why didn't you tell us there was a gate change?"

Kruger started to confess that he was too new to the company to know what the transmission meant and before he could ask the plane was parked but the cabin attendant cut his answer short. "That's no excuse", he said, "Don't you know that's what we pay you for?"

The effrontery of the smug male cabin attendant finally was the straw that broke the dam of Kruger's anger. Dropping his bags Kruger reached out suddenly with both hands and grabbed the startled cabin attendant by the collar. Lifting him bodily off of the deck Kruger shook him like a dog shakes a rag. Then he slammed him against the bulkhead and pushed his nose against the frightened man's face and growled, "Shut the fuck up. Say another word and I'll rip off your legs and stuff you in the biffy". The "biffy" was the toilet. The cabin attendant was white faced by now. The other cabin attendants were backing up as rapidly as possible least they provoke the anger of this madman. Kruger threw his enemy away who promptly fled. Kruger disgustedly grabbed his bags and left the plane.

"Hoo, boy, you've really done it now. That little fit you just threw has to put the cap on your airline career," he told himself. "Damn!"

Two months later he had his final interview with the Chief Pilot's office. He waited for the axe to fall but miraculously there was nothing adverse in his jacket. Once again the Assistant Chief Pilot, Don Nelson, tried to place Kruger into his hip pocket trying to get him to "snitch" on his fellow pilots but Kruger, alerted this time, had no trouble ducking the issue. Nelson then tried to enlist Kruger into the Training Department but the last squadron Kruger had been in had convinced him that he didn't want to teach anymore. He left the office a free pilot, indentured to no one. The next day he joined the Airline Pilots Association. Now he couldn't be terminated for anything except for cause. His probationary period had been over a year and nine months.

About two months prior to all of this Kruger had been ordered to undergo another check with Northwest Orient. Sometime ago one of the pilots who had always considered himself to be a little better than the rest and who had aspirations concerning the politics of a major corporation, to wit, he wished to be in a management position, had come up with a plan to weed out any prospective pilots who might be marginal. That pilot's name was Bill Hochbrunn. Initially he had been a flight instructor and had always been one of the detractors concerning Northwest Orient. He always peppered his lectures with stories portraying Northwest Orient in the worst possible manner. To the uninitiated he appeared to hate Northwest Orient. That all changed once he had conceived a plan and had sold it to the company. Anyone with half a brain could see that his plan was self-serving. It involved Hochbrunn buying an Aero Commander, a two engine aircraft that could hold several passengers in luxury, and leasing it to Northwest Orient. The idea was for Northwest Orient to give one final series of check rides to the pilots who were about to come off probation before they could join ALPA. Somehow Donald Nyrop, the CEO of NWOA bought the idea. This was a series of check rides to assess the qualifications of military pilots who had not only survived but who had chalked up thousands of hours of flight time. These pilots were the cream of the crop, which was why Northwest Orient had preferential hiring policies concerning military pilots. It really made no sense to make them undergo another check ride or rides after they had been examined extensively for over a year.

Kruger was assigned to undergo the check ride syllabus. The check pilot was another pilot who had an exalted opinion of himself, no mean feat among pilots in general who all considered themselves to be just a little more god-like than the average citizen. Kruger considered the whole idea an insult. He had survived the Navy's flight program, one of the finest in the world, and had gone on to no less than three squadrons, distinguishing himself in all three. Now he had to prove himself all over again. This was not just a check ride but was a whole syllabus about how to fly a civilian plane that had no application to anything he would ever fly anytime. He was pretty disgusted with Northwest Orient.

Kruger put up with the Aero Commander flying without comment. He actually thought that flying the plane was pleasurable. It was easy and fun and if it were not for the fact that it hid a threat to his future he would have actually enjoyed it. He resented the implication that he was not a "fit pilot" and had to prove that fact one more time. He sailed through the syllabus, which was about 4 or 5 flights, all on his own time. He never forgot that the whole idea put future pilots at risk all, in his opinion, because some greedy bastard by the name of Hochbrunn, wanted a better position and an expensive airplane.

*   *   *

Now that the pressure was off Kruger could really enjoy his new job without wondering when the next shoe was going to drop. Even though he wasn't actually flying he was still in a cockpit performing a flying role. He had adopted a series of patterns as a way of performing his Second Officer tasks so most of the things he was responsible for were pretty much routine. He had always thought of his role in his last squadron as an instructor as basically teaching habit patterns so that, in the final analysis when the chips are down, the pilot would revert to his old habit pattern and wouldn't have to think much about what he was doing. He began to look at his job as a series of trips between layovers.

Layovers were fairly short for a 727 crew but those crews were the youngest and newest pilots and cabin attendants. They still had lots of energy and curiosity so the layover periods were divided up into time spent sleeping and time spent having fun. Almost every layover lent itself to a few hours in a local watering hole quenching a thirst that always seemed to flare up as soon as the flight had ended. In 1969 the 727 crews generally consisted of three pilots and three cabin attendants. It made for a good mix and the crews usually hit the road together in spite of the firm edict laid down by Northwest prohibiting any drinking whatsoever during layovers. Both crews and individuals were cautious about their drinking, as the company had been known to hire spies to follow crews in the hope of catching someone imbibing.

Some pilots and crews were more overt than others. Some pilots drank secretly; carrying a bottle around with them and furtively offering to share it with another pilot they trusted. Kruger quickly became initiated into the favorite watering holes at each layover station. His favorite layover cities were Chicago, Washington, DC, Seattle and Miami. His least favorite were most of the cities in the Western states especially the western "cowboy" towns like Missoula, Grand Forks, Fargo and Billings.

Each town had its own flavor and each could be counted on to offer some fun and humor. One night Kruger was drinking beer in Great Falls, Montana when the urge to recycle the beer he had consumed hit him. He made his way to the head and was relaxing at one of the urinals on the wall. He caught some movement to his left with his peripheral vision and glanced over to see a woman in typical cowboy garb with her trousers down to her ankles straddling one of the urinals. As he stared she angrily said, "Whatsa matter? Ain't ya never seen a lady take a piss before?"

Kruger exploded in laughter responding, "Yeah, I have, but never in one of those!"

Washington, DC was fun but tough. Kruger never let his guard drop in cities like that. Like a lot of pilots he carried a small, easily concealable handgun with him. He had been out of practice with his Karate for some time now and refused to think of himself as the weapon he once had been. There were plenty of stories handed around where a pilot had produced his weapon and had prevented a mugging or worse by doing so. Kruger knew of no instance where a pilot had abused his constitutional right to "keep and bear" firearms. There were numerous instances where someone had attempted to enter a pilot's locked room and had been discouraged by the sound of a gun being cocked and the pilot's voice telling him to "come in and meet Mr. .38".

Pilots had long traditionally carried handguns. Since they were totally responsible for the airplane and the passengers it only made sense to have the means to back up their authority. The only time that Kruger had known that the custom had been semi-abused was when some old Captains were talking about aircraft hijacking while sitting around in the lobby of the hotel in Narita, Japan. One old Captain pulled out a long barreled handgun from his flight case and said, "If they tried anything like that with me I would react just like this." He pulled the trigger and the gun discharged with a very loud report. The Japanese have a hysterical view of guns in general. They simply don't like or allow them. As soon as the gun report had sounded you couldn't find a pilot anywhere in sight. They had all disappeared. When the Japanese police showed up the lobby was not only empty but no pilot could be found anywhere.

One night in DC Kruger and another pilot were walking home from one of the local watering holes. Two black ladies were walking toward them. The ladies were skimpily dressed and both were amply endowed. As they neared the two pilots Kruger nodded and said, "Good evening, ladies. Nice night isn't it?" The ladies stopped and engaged the pilots in a little small talk with one lady doing most of the talking while the other sized the pilots up. Finally the more silent of the two broke in with, "Well, do ya want to talk all night or do you want to fuck?" Kruger broke up laughing and courteously told the ladies that they had to call it a night but other than that they would love to engage the two for the evening.

Kruger related the tête-à-tête to the crew the next day. One of the cabin attendants countered with a humorous story of her own about

DC. The girls knew that DC was a dangerous place for flight crews. The company had carefully briefed them about that. They tried to take care of themselves and each other but they were, after all, fresh out of high school in most cases and still had much to learn about the world. As the girl told it she was sharing a room in the hotel in DC with another cabin attendant. Most of the girls had to share a room while the pilots all had separate rooms. They had been "talking it up" as far as crime was concerned in the DC area and both girls were spooked by the time they finally went to bed.

Later on that night one of the girls heard a commotion in the street below. She quietly left her bed and tiptoed to the bathroom where she stood on the toilet seat in order to peer out of the window. When she was satisfied that everything was OK she jumped down off of the toilet seat and walked back into the bedroom.

The first girl making her way to the bathroom had awakened her roommate. The roommate had not seen the first girl but only heard noises coming from the bathroom. The noises sounded like someone climbing in the bathroom window. While the girl was frozen in fear in her bed she heard the "intruder" jump down onto the floor and start walking into her bedroom. As she stared transfixed in terror the intruder suddenly appeared in the doorway. The girl in the bed suddenly jumped up and started screaming and jumping up and down in the bed.

The first girl had just entered the bedroom when an apparition, screaming and jumping up and down in one of the beds, startled her. She started screaming and jumping also. Both girls screamed at the top of their voices and jumped up and down until realization dawned on them. No one ever knocked on the door to inquire if they were OK or not. Just another night in Washington, DC.

Sometimes one or more pilots would overdo the evening's festivities. In cases like that they could be termed to be "hung-over". One morning Kruger shared the crew limo with another crew who looked a little the worse for the wear. They were strangely silent and looked unnaturally white. Suddenly the copilot lifted his Wall Street Journal and barfed explosively into it. One of the other pilots laconically observed, "Well, that's another use for the Journal."

Chicago layovers were always fun. During long layovers the crews were housed in very nice hotels in the heart of Chicago where there were many superb restaurants and "watering holes" where thirsty pilots could quench their eternal thirst.

One evening near Christmas Kruger decided to get a beer at the Billy Goat Tavern in Chicago's underground. It was late and he had decided that a hamburger and a beer would be just the ticket before he turned in for the night. The Billy Goat Tavern was a popular night spot in Chicago and it was crowded with a lot of people who were happy and celebrating.

As Kruger relaxed at the bar he saw an elderly black man who was the "swamper" or the clean up person sweeping the floor in the bar area. For some reason a bunch of merry makers were wadding up paper and tossing it on the floor for the swamper to clean up.

As the white-haired black man passed Kruger he muttered a classical comment that Kruger thought was outstanding and ought to have been inscribed in stone somewhere. The old man said, "Fuck dis place. Fuck dese people. Fuck Christmas and fuck Santy Clause too". Kruger was delighted with his philosophy and left him a large tip.

New York Layovers were something else. New York was in a class all by itself. Individually the people were just like everyone else in the USA but collectively they were very different. Kruger thought that they were humorous and was happy that he only had to interact with them occasionally and not permanently.

Northwest had a contract with the Fugazzy Limousine company. That company was supposed to transport any Northwest crew from the airport to their hotel. The company also transported crews from New York International to LaGuardia airport when the crews had to switch airports in order to fly their next leg. The trip from Kennedy International to LaGuardia was about an hour in terms of the fare for Fugazzy.

The usual driver that Fugazzy put on for the crews was a little Sicilian who was about as wide as he was tall. He was a jolly man who sang and talked incessantly. Kruger liked him.

One day the weather was bad all over the East coast and Kruger's flight was rescheduled several times. Finally, when the crew arrived at Kennedy, crew schedules sent them a telex that said that they were to go to a layover close to Kennedy in order to be rescheduled the next day instead of being transported all the way over to LaGuardia.

The crew took the reschedule in stoic order but when Kruger left the terminal in order to take the scheduled limo he thought that the little Sicilian driver was much too happy in spite of the change that put the crew in a hotel no more than 10 minutes away from the terminal instead of taking them all the way to LaGuardia, about an hour away. Due to the weather and the rescheduling of the crew the little driver had been waiting in the taxi line for over an hour. It all translated into money for the driver.

When Kruger put his luggage into the back of the limo he said to the driver, who was happy and singing, "Did anyone tell you that this crew is going to a hotel nearby instead of going to LaGuardia?"

The driver's face fell and he began to curse. Kruger had been in the Navy a long time and had been convinced that he knew all of the curses that had ever been uttered but he was surprised by the diminutive Sicilian who climbed onto the bumper of his limo in order to gain some altitude. The driver screamed to any passerby who happened along, "Before I take another Northwest crew anywhere I'll cut off three fingers of my right hand and jack off with my left." As the rest of the crew arrived they looked at the driver with amazement. The rest of the New Yorkers who were walking by just took it into context and weren't bothered in the least by the vituperative assaults of the Sicilian driver against Northwest Orient Airlines. Kruger was amused and amazed at the innovative curses of the driver and made sure that he tipped the driver accordingly.

On one of his New York layovers Kruger found out that a local department store was closing. It had advertised that it had a big sale going on and Kruger decided to spend his time observing the locals during a big sale like this one. He showed up 10 minutes before the store was supposed to open and found that he was one of about three hundred customers who crowded the main entrance. When the store finally opened he was amazed at the flow of people that jammed the opening. He felt that if he pulled up his feet he would be carried by the shoving crowd in spite of himself. He was shoved onto an escalator that was prominently situated in a direct line with the front entrance. As he good—naturedly got onto the escalator he was surprised by a man behind him who elbowed him in an attempt to get passed him on his left side. Kruger was surprised as the escalator was crowded. There was simply no place for the guy to go if he had successfully gotten passed him. As Kruger turned to look to his left side he was elbowed once again on his right. He began to get a little irritated as his short ribs had sustained several hits. He thought, "What would a good New Yorker do in a situation like this?" He turned and faced the idiot who was trying to get passed him. Kruger said, "Charlie, if you touch me one more time I'm going to break both of your legs and stuff you inside a garbage can." The startled man actually backed down one step on the escalator. Kruger didn't know how he had done that as the escalator was crowded but he smiled to himself and thought that he had solved the way to treat New Yorkers.

*   *   *

Layovers weren't the only thing the Washington, DC area was notorious for. The River Approach to Washington National Airport was another. In order to reduce noise in the area the FAA had come up with an approach that followed the river all the way to the last bridge prior to the airport. At that point the plane had to be banked sharply to the right in order to align it with the runway. The pilot only had a few seconds until touchdown. It was a very challenging approach and Northwest had dictated that only the Captain could make the approach. Some Captains, after flying with their copilot for a little while, would allow them to shoot the approach anyway if, in the Captain's opinion, the copilot could adequately fly the demanding pattern. The company had dictated that the Captain tell the passengers, via the passenger address system, about the approach, reassure them that the approach was safe and that it was all for everyone's good. It reduced noise in the DC area.

One of the more controversial Northwest pilots was a diminutive Irishman named Harry Muldoon. Harry smoked a pipe incessantly. He was never without his pipe. Northwest had long ago told all pilots that pipe and cigar smoking was prohibited. Harry ignored the edict. Once, while Harry was flying as a copilot, the Captain, tired of the smoke, had grabbed Harry's pipe and thrown it out of the Captain's window while the crew was sitting on the ground waiting for the pushback. Harry stoically left the cockpit and disappeared. Pushback time came and went. There was no copilot to man the cockpit. No one knew where Harry was or why he had disappeared. Finally Harry appeared 30 minutes later than the scheduled pushback time. He had hired a taxi, gone downtown and purchased a new pipe.

When Harry became a Captain he never changed. He still smoked his pipe and was as controversial as ever. One day while flying the River Approach into DC he told the passengers that the only reason he had to "shoot this dangerous approach was because a few fat cat senators wanted to land at National instead of Dulles". Unfortunately for Harry, Senator Gerald Ford was aboard and was offended. He called Donald Nyrop, the president of Northwest and Harry had to fly as a copilot for six months to think about his sins.

Kruger loved flying with Captain Harry. It was a laugh a minute. Everyone loved Harry. It was just his judgment that turned some people off. One day while flying with Captain Harry the plane landed at Washington National. It was supposed to return to Minneapolis that evening and the trip was supposed to end there. Kruger was the Second Officer and, as the plane landed he received a message from the company that said that the crew had been rescheduled for two more days with the exception of Second Officer Kruger who was scheduled for duty with the Naval Reserve the next day. The company could not refuse to release a pilot for duty flying with any of the reserves that had anything to do with the Department of Defense. When Kruger relayed the message Captain Harry exploded. He railed at the company and said that he had bid this particular line of flying in order to attend his goddaughter's christening that was scheduled for the next day. Now he would miss that event. Harry was frothing-at-the-mouth mad. As he taxied in he was told to stop in order to allow an American Airlines plane to taxi in front of him. Harry growled, "Goddamn American, I'll just give them a shot of radar." He turned the radar set on and gave the American plane a few sweeps of the emissions. He hadn't apparently been awake during the lectures on the radar however, as the set would not emit any radiation while the wheels were on the ground. Kruger didn't want to rain on his fun and simply rolled up in laughter. Finally the plane was parked and the passengers were allowed to deplane. Harry expected the ground crew to roll up a set of stairs to the number one door but the crew lowered the aft air stairs for the people to use. Harry grumbled about the tardiness of the ground crew and finally, whipping himself into a frenzy, he popped open his emergency escape hatch. Sticking his head and shoulders out of the window he screamed at the ground crew, "If you'd pull up a fucking set of stairs the fucking people could deplane from this fucking plane."

The ground crew disgustedly pointed toward the aft part of the plane where the passengers were walking toward the terminal looking curiously at the Captain who was cursing at the ground crew. Captain Harry hurriedly got back into the cockpit muttering, "Oh, the people are deplaning out of the aft end." Kruger and the copilot were collapsed in laughter.

A few months later Kruger had an opportunity to fly with Captain Harry again. When Kruger arrived at the plane and began his preflight he met the copilot, Vern Clobes, who smiled at him and said, as he shook Kruger's hand, "Do you know the difference between a Marine and a submarine?" Kruger, suspecting what was up said, "No, but I expect you're going to tell me." Vern grinned and said, "There's no difference. Squids go down on both of them."

Kruger laughed as he said, "Oh, so it's going to be one of those flights, is it?" The term "squid" was universally used by the Marines to denote Navy personnel. Kruger had once asked a friend when they were together in Gitmo (Guantanamo Bay Cuba), what a "squid" was. The friend, a Marine whose call sign was Mofak, told him that a squid was a slimy creature that crawled around on the bottom of the sea and had no backbone. Kruger laughingly tried to tell the Mofak that he should take a course in vertebrate biology but the Marine allowed that it made no difference. All Marines knew full well what a squid was and no biology professor could change the facts. Kruger looked up to the Marine as he had taught Kruger how to fly formation flight in training but as proficient as Mofak was in flying he was lacking in biological knowledge. It made no difference either way. A squid was a squid and that was that.

It was apparent that Vern was a Marine. Later on he confessed that another Marine, Captain "Wally" Walbaum, had found out that Vern was scheduled to fly with Kruger. He had hunted Vern up and had told him "he was flying with Kruger, who was a squid, and that he was to give Kruger a lot of crap".

The contest was on. Vern and Kruger vied to see just who could be the most rotten in their insults. Captain Harry chortled as he listened and finally, unable to stand aside from the festivities, he began to cast darts at first the Marines and then the Navy. Vern and Ed halted their insults and attempted to counsel Harry. "Harry, you really don't understand how this game is played. The goal is to get the other guy's goat. The insults are supposed to make the other guy so mad that he loses his cool. You can't play because you get too mad too quickly. You're better off just listening and enjoying the game. Don't try and participate."

Harry's response was, "Fuck both of you guys. I can handle my own."

Vern looked at Kruger and smiled. Both pilots knew what was going to happen but Harry was a big boy and wanted to play.

Now Harry was one of the all time good people. He faithfully tithed to the Catholic Church. He had adopted a black baby who needed a home. You would have to search very hard to find fault with Harry's life.

Vern finally found an Achilles' heel. He saw a way to get two birds with one stone. He turned around to Kruger and said, "Hey, Ed, what are you going to do when your daughter gets a little older and all of the boys start screwing her?" Kruger just smiled serenely and said, "Well, that will probably never happen because I'm going to put her in a convent and make Harry pay for her education." Harry started to make strangling noises around his pipe.

Vern grinned as he sprang his trap. "She won't be in that convent an hour and the nuns will have her on her back . . . ." Vern described in gory detail just how the sisters would sexually treat Kruger's daughter.

By now Harry was hyperventilating as his pipe turned cherry red. He gargled as he tried to alternately talk and smoke. Vern and Kruger doubled over in laughter. The plane was completely forgotten. Kruger beat the Second Officer's panel in his mirth. Vern had tears flowing down his cheeks. The Center wondered if Northwest 606 had a problem, as they apparently could not communicate except in gasps.

The plane finally arrived at Minneapolis. The pilots were drained. They just wanted to get off of the plane and rest their stomachs, which were aching from laughter. As the Captain taxied into the gate area a black ramp signalman attempted to wave the plane into the gate. He had ignored the edict that ramp signalmen had to have signal wands in order to legally wave the plane in. It was broad daylight and he saw no real reason to have wands in his hands when his hands were readily identifiable.

Captain Harry stopped the plane. He muttered around his ever-present pipe, "Look at that gorilla. All you can see are eyes and teeth. Why doesn't he have wands?" Harry opened the side window of the 727, stuck his head and shoulders out of the hatch and screamed, "Get some wands."

The black signalman shouted back, "They ain't no wands here. I can't find any."

Harry had jerked back into the cockpit. He was again muttering to himself around his pipe. "No fucking wands! Why the hell not? Isn't this the main base? Goddamn!"

The signalman, seeing Harry withdraw into the cockpit thought that everything was OK. He once again began to wave the plane into the gate.

Harry became apoplectic. His face became bright red, as did his pipe. Once again he jammed his torso out of the cockpit window. By now a number of passengers had stopped at the large windows fronting the runway to look at the spectacle unfolding. Harry ignored them.

"Goddamn it, I told you to get some wands, you idiot." Harry was intractable.

"I done tol' you, they ain't no damn wands here." The signalman could be intractable too.

Harry, by now, couldn't even talk. He gargled. Jumping back inside the plane he released the brakes and cobbed the power by shoving the throttles full forward. "I'll show your black ass," he muttered among curses.

The 727 leapt forward. The signalman abandoned his post and ran headlong for the safety of the terminal. Kruger and the copilot were impotent with laughter. Tears ran down their cheeks and they pounded their knees with mirth. Harry realized, suddenly, that the plane was about to hit the terminal. Passengers, more astute than the Captain, were running down the concourse in an effort to get away from the runaway plane. All of a sudden Harry realized what was about to happen. Without reducing power he applied maximum braking. The 727 lurched to a halt and, as it did, there were a series of bumps emanating from the cabin as the 727's passengers fell down in the aisles. The passengers, as always, had ignored the PAs about how to stay in their seats until released by the cockpit and were standing in the aisle when the brakes were suddenly applied. The interphone rang frantically as the Cabin Attendants tried to tell the cockpit about the mayhem occurring in the cabin.

Kruger was positive that he was about to have a heart attack as he was having trouble breathing due to all of the laughter. Vern was resting his head on the yoke as he too gasped for air while holding his stomach with both arms.

The plane finally arrived at the jetway leading to the terminal. The engines were shut down and the crew attempted to get the passengers to their feet and off the plane. As they deplaned they unanimously threw glaring looks at the Captain. Ed and Vern were reduced to groans.

"Goddamn crew," Captain Harry muttered. "If I can only stay out of the Chief Pilot's office this month I'll have it made." He glared at his copilot and second officer. "I figure you assholes owe me a whole can of tobacco. I must have used up at least that much puffing on my pipe due to being pissed off at you guys."

Another humorous incident happened with Captain Harry while Kruger was flying with him. The crew had a long layover in Miami and ended up early one morning in the room of the senior flight Attendant. She had been flying with Northwest a long time and possessed a very large "chest". Harry was seated on the bed next to her while the rest of the crew was scattered around the room in various places. During the conversation that was ongoing Harry reached over and caressed the lady's large breast. She laughed and said, "Harry, you old goat, I think that if you had a chance at me you'd actually take it." Harry said something risqué and the Flight Attendant said, "I'll fix you Harry." She began to rock back and forth. The bed they were setting in began to knock on the wall. As the bed kept up the metronome thump, thump, thump the Flight attendant started to moan, "Harry, Oh Harry."

Captain Harry gave up the struggle and ran down the passageway yelling, "I did not", like some second grade kid.

Captain Harry was a lot of fun. He was also competent. Some of the Captains Kruger flew with were neither. One notable senior Captain who was still flying the 727 was a prime example.

This particular Captain's name was Don Mark. He was, in Kruger's opinion, the prime example of why airline pilots had to retire at age 60. Captain Mark had several short circuits in his gray matter. In Kruger's opinion he should have retired at age 30. Kruger had bid a trip sequence that had him flying with Captain Mark for the whole month. It was going to be a long month.

The Captain began the trip by telling his crew that he had just undergone training in the DC-10. Kruger asked him why he hadn't opted for the training earlier. The Captain was senior enough to have been one of the first pilots trained. The answer was that the Captain wished to "make absolutely certain that he wished to fly the new airplane before asking to be trained in it". Kruger had been around long enough to know that the answer meant that the Captain's response was proof that he was apprehensive about the checkout and wanted to talk to several contemporaries who had already undergone the training before he took his chances. Northwest's policy concerning checkouts was that if a pilot bilged or failed any checkout he was immediately terminated. The term "terminated" in civilian language meant that he was fired.

Captain Mark had finished the classroom portion of the DC-10 checkout but had not yet completed the flight checkout. Prior to this time he had flown the 727 for years. Make that many years. He should have known the 727 better than most pilots. He also should have been an excellent pilot with all of his years in the cockpit and his experience. As the month wore on Kruger watched Captain Mark's flight prowess with something approaching awe. In fact it was hard for Kruger to believe that an inept pilot like the Captain could remain in a flight status let alone operate as a Captain.

On this particular flight the crew was supposed to operate from Minneapolis to Atlanta to Miami. Kruger's apprehension started as the flight leveled off in cruise after leaving Minneapolis. The Captain wished to make the normal announcements over the PA, welcoming the passengers aboard, telling them about the weather enroute, mentioning the route and the sights that may be seen, etc. This particular flight was being flown aboard a 727-200, the "stretch" version of the 727. Both airplanes were similar but the newer -200 had a few added niceties and changes to the cockpit that normally would alert any pilot to the fact that he was flying the newer version that was 20 feet longer than the old 727-100. Only a pilot who was either brain dead or totally oblivious would fail to notice which version he was in. Captain Mark fell into that category.

The 727-100 had a telephone handset located behind the center consol that was used for the cabin PAs. In order to use it one had to remove the handset, press a button located near the stowage place for the handset and talk into the set. The -200, on the other hand, had a microphone hotwired into the PA system in addition to the normal handset that was now used to talk to the cabin crew. This difference was covered at length during the normal checkouts on the -200.

As the flight reached the cruise level the Captain removed the handset and began to feel around for the "button". Kruger, who was watching all this asked, "What are you looking for, Don?"

"The damned button. Where in the hell's the button?"

Kruger answered, "This is a 727-200, remember? There's no button on this plane." He picked up the microphone. "All you have to do is to talk through this."

The copilot watched incredulously as the Captain retorted, "The hell you say. I don't believe you." He unbuckled and got out of his seat to look at the back of the center consol. When he had observed that Kruger was correct he climbed back into his seat muttering to himself. The copilot looked at Kruger who just shook his head. This was a Captain that would bear watching.

The Captain chattered all the way to Atlanta about the DC-10. He told his crew all about its systems and its idiosyncrasies. He was so caught up with his description of the DC-10 that he paid little attention to the operation of the plane that he was supposed to be flying. His copilot and Kruger, his Second Officer, had to repeatedly call his attention to the clearances and the operation. Luckily the weather was optimal; it was CAVU (clear and visibility unrestricted) and approaches to Atlanta were not a problem. The flight was cleared for an ILS approach to one of the west runways.

Kruger took care of the Second Officer's panel as he had been taught to do. He set the pressurization, balanced the fuel load and set the fuel feed up for the landing sequence, checked all of the systems and recorded any readings that were necessary. He then swiveled his seat around to face the front of the cockpit in order to observe the approach to back up the two pilots flying. He immediately saw that the Captain had his VOR (Variable Omni Range) approach plates out and had set his navigational radios to the VOR frequencies. A quick check on the copilot proved that he had the correct plates displayed and the correct frequencies set.

"Say, Don, We're cleared for an ILS approach. You've got the wrong plate displayed and the wrong frequency set in your radios." Kruger punched the copilot on his shoulder as he told the Captain this in order to make sure the copilot knew what was happening. The copilot looked over to the Captain's approach plates and did a double take.

"That's OK. I'm doing this off the VOR" was the Captain's answer. Kruger had never heard of something like this but the copilot remained silent and all of the planes in front of them could be readily seen. Kruger decided to remain silent but to watch everything the Captain did and to react if it appeared that the plane would ever be in extremis. The approach and landing were uneventful. As they rolled out on the runway Kruger decided to ask several of his contemporaries if they had ever encountered anything like this. Maybe this was just one of the strange things airline pilots did.

When the plane was stopped at the terminal Kruger kept an eye on the Captain. He saw him thumbing though his approach plates. Suddenly the Captain stopped and remarked to himself, "Well I'll be damned. There IS an ILS approach on that runway."

Kruger told the copilot what he had just observed and remarked, "I don't know about you but I think that guy has a wide spark gap in his brain. I'm going to watch him like a hawk. I'd appreciate it if you did also." The copilot agreed.

They got to Miami without incident but in Kruger's opinion Captain Mark was not fit to fly large commercial jets. That opinion was reinforced on the next trip when they were once again flying a 727-200 and the Captain again removed the handset and began to feel for the "button".

"What are you looking for, Don?" he said.

"Damn it, I can't find that button again. I had a problem with it on the last flight, too."

"Are you talking about the PA button".

"Damn right I am. What other button would there be back here?"

"I thought we covered that subject last flight. There isn't any button on this airplane. This is a 727-200. The button you're looking for is only on the -100. Remember?"

Once again the Captain said, "The hell you say!" He again got out of his seat to see if Kruger was correct or not. Kruger resolved not to fly a trip with Captain Mark again if he could help it.

You see, pilots are pilots. They are like any other group of professionals. Some are excellent, some are bad but most are just average pilots trying to do an average to slightly above average job. The excellent and the bad pilots stick out like a sore on the end of one's nose. Everyone knows about them. Whenever one of the average pilots was privileged to fly with one of the really good ones it was a good month. Flying with one of the bad or one of the intolerable ones was a whole year rolled up into one month. Really bad operational pilots always flew with reserve pilots since no one would choose to bid their trips. Those trips always went very junior which meant the reserve pilots flew them. But in the final analysis all pilots are graded the same. Pilots are not allowed the levity of doing a job well 60% or 70% of the time. Pilots have to do their job well 100% of the time. If they don't the result is a massive loss of life. Of course the traveling public knows nothing about any of this.

Most of the Captains, indeed, most of the pilots working for Northwest Orient were fine gentlemen, friendly, competent and humble enough to get along with just about anyone. A few were self-important and pig headed. One of the latter types generally ignored his Second Officer as a matter of course. He was of the old school that held that any pilot in the cockpit other than the Captain was redundant, that the copilot wasn't needed and the Second Officer was beneath notice. Kruger almost had to fly with him one day. After doing the pre-flight inspection, usually referred to as the "walk around", Kruger had entered the cockpit and had seated himself at the Second Officer's panel. The pilots went through the start sequence and got the OK from the ground crew to release the brakes prior to the push back. Just as the 727 began to move there was a sudden and very large thump. Kruger immediately said, "I think we just hit something". The Captain turned around and said in a tired, bored voice, "Naw, you're too new. When you've been around as long as I have you'll be able to recognize when the tow-bar pin breaks. That's all that was. Nothing to get excited about."

About that time the interphone activated and the mechanic on the large tug pushing the plane back said disgustedly, "You might as well set the brakes. This plane ain't goin' anywhere now."

The Captain grabbed the hand mike in alarm and yelled, "Why not?"

"The crew bus just ran into the right wing. I knew that bus driver couldn't breathe and pick his nose at the same time. Now maybe people will listen to me."

Kruger left the cockpit after the passengers had all deplaned to be rerouted to other planes. The right wingtip had been mangled for about two feet from the tip. The Captain never referred to the incident again in front of Kruger, the new guy who didn't know anything.

Early one morning Kruger was awakened by the telephone ringing. He sleepily answered it only to hear a female voice saying, "The Aero Commander is on time today." Kruger had to think about that for a few seconds. As the fog of sleep cleared he realized that some crew scheduler had erred and thought that Kruger was still on probation and needed a check flight on Hochbrunn's plane. Kruger's sense of humor kicked in and he immediately said, "What's the going pay rate for flying the Aero Commander?" The scheduler was confused and didn't know how to answer so Kruger helped her out a little. He said, "I'm not on probation now and am on increment pay so before I show up to fly that plane I want to know what the company is going to pay me for doing just that."

The now confused scheduler said, "Why, I don't think anyone gets paid for flying the Commander."

Kruger said, "Ah, so, if I am not going to be paid for flying it them I guess I'll have to decline the honor. Get someone else to fly it."

"You mean that you aren't going to show up for the flight today?"

"You got that right, sugar. If there's one thing that Northwest Orient has taught me in the last year or so it's that if it doesn't pay then screw it. I'm a quick learner. Get someone else to fly the Commander today."

The confused lady said, "Well, all right, I'll let the pilot know that you aren't going to show today."

"Do that and by the way . . . ."

"Yes?"

"If the Aero commander is going to be on time tomorrow please don't call me and let me know about it, OK?"

As he hung the phone up he sighed and said, "God, that felt good."

Interservice rivalry did not cease just because the pilots were flying for a commercial airline. Navy and Marine pilots all thought that they were each much better than the other service guys and both service pilots looked down on Army pilots but not nearly as much as they looked down on Air Force pilots better known as the "Air Farce". As for the Air National Guard, well, the less said the better. Mostly the rivalry was in fun but there was always just that tiny little proud bit of truth to all of the mud slinging. The 727 Second Officer's seat was situated in front of the panel that housed all of the gages, switches and dials needed to monitor and control the systems onboard the aircraft. At the base of the panel there was a small desk with a hinged top. Inside of the desk were all of the necessary forms needed for the flights progress. Taped to the underneath side of the desk a small quip of one kind or another could normally be found.

One day Kruger opened the desk and found the following, "I'd rather be a dog in a whore's back yard than a Second Lieutenant in the Air National Guard". Kruger stopped laughing when he ran out of breath.

Kruger did his time in the reserve slot just like any other pilot. His self-respect was recouped when he finally got off of his probationary period. As a non-probationary pilot he was allowed to join the pilot's union, the Airline Pilot's Association or ALPA. Now if he was to be terminated it could only be for cause and not on the whim of any Captain. One day he was called up to fly with his old nemesis, Captain Ray Severson. This was the same Captain who had told him to "put those fucking switches where they were when you got into the cockpit . . . ." Kruger determined to enjoy the flight regardless of Ray Severson.

He was conducting his preflight when the copilot, a Japanese-Hawaiian kid named Lee Ozawa, came aboard. Lee looked at Kruger for a few seconds and then began with, "You poor fucker, do you know who we are flying with today?" Apparently Kruger appeared too relaxed to him.

"Sure I do. We're flying with a Captain called Severson. I believe his name is Ray Severson."

"Yeah, that's right but do you really know him? Have you ever heard about him? Have you ever flown with him?"

"Sure. I know all about Ray Severson. I've flown with him."

"Well you sure look relaxed for a Second Officer who knows the prick. Do you know how he flies his planes and how he treats his crew?"

"Yep, I sure do. I also know that I just got off probation and that I don't have to take any shit off Captain Severson. I don't know about you but I intend to relax on this flight and if the Captain doesn't like it he can file a complaint about it. We can all go take a flight check and see who flies according to the way the company wants a flight conducted."

Lee digested this for all of three seconds and then said, "You know, on second thought, this might just be a real horseshit flight for Captain Severson."

The flight progressed. It was supposed to fly to Washington, DC via several stops enroute and return the same day. The weather in the DC area was marginal. It was good enough for most pilots but Ray seemed threatened by it. He was nervous as a cat creeping around a pack of hound dogs. He continually attempted to do everything in the cockpit as if he didn't have any crewmembers. He insisted on monitoring the Second Officer's panel and, as a result, missed a number of things he should have caught as a pilot.

The flight was given a holding clearance by the Washington sector. Things were backing up around Washington. Kruger called the company and gave them an update on the flight including the hold so they could send information on the flight to several of the stations that were concerned with the flight. Ray ignored the flight controls and turned to Kruger.

"Who are you talking to, Goddamnit?"

"Why, I'm giving the company the holding report, just as the manual says I'm supposed to do."

"D'ja ever think of checking with the Captain first? I mean before you called the damned company?"

"Why would I do that, Captain? All of this is supposed to take the pressure off of you pilots. Do you want me to do something outside of the standard operating procedures? If you do you will have to write it all down on a piece of paper. I'll do anything you want me to do within reason but you will have to document it all first. Do you want to do that?"

"Hey, goddamn it," the copilot hit the Captain on the shoulder. "We just got a clearance from the center."

"Wha! What did they say?" The Captain was obviously out of his league.

"I dunno," the copilot answered as he flew the plane. It was his leg and he was flying while the Captain was supposed to handle the communications. "I'm flying the fucking plane. You are supposed to handle the comm."

The Captain called the center and tried to straighten things out. The flight looked like a screwed up mess to anyone listening in. The copilot and Kruger smiled at each other. Things were not going too well for Captain Severson.

Somewhere, sometime the Captain must have had the crap scared out of him by fuel starvation or something that had to do with the temperature of the fuel. At the altitudes the planes flew at the fuel could freeze in the lines and starve the engines making them shut down, not something that anyone wished to happen. The temperatures at those altitudes could reach a minus 48 degrees below zero. Kerosene Jet-A, the fuel the Northwest Orient jets used, started to freeze at minus 53 degrees. Captain Severson insisted on the Second Officer applying fuel heat to the fuel feed regardless of the temperature. Normally fuel heat was applied only when the fuel temperature dropped below a set figure as measured by the monitors in the fuel lines. When the temperature dropped below that figure the Second Officer was supposed to apply fuel heat to each engine feed, one at a time. This was accomplished by the positioning of a toggle switch for each engine. Each time a toggle switch was activated a "click" was heard. There were three engines on the 727. Ray expected to hear three clicks. Kruger delighted in clicking each toggle in turn followed by flicking the interphone toggle, which produced another distinctive click. Ray would always whip around and stare at the Second Officer's panel to see if he could find the source of the fourth click. Kruger would pretend ignorance and would refuse to acknowledge the Captain's concern. Ray never asked as to the source of the mysterious "click" but would continue to stare at the panel much to the delight of the other pilots in the cockpit with him.

The flight was cleared to a lower altitude and given an airspeed to fly in an attempt to schedule it in with other planes. As they descended the center requested that they expedite the descent as they had conflicting crossing traffic. The copilot rogered the request and Ray panicked. "Why did you tell them we could do that?" he asked.

"Can't you comply with the clearance, Captain?" the copilot asked. "Do you want me to fly the plane?"

"Everybody knows you can't slow down and descend at the same time," Ray whined.

"I can," his copilot retorted. "Want to see me do it?"

"Goddamn it," was the only answer the now red-faced Captain could manage as he fought the controls. The copilot turned and grinned delightedly at Kruger who responded by clicking more switches causing the harassed Captain to almost break his neck turning to look at the Second Officer's panel.

Things were backing up on the deck as the weather deteriorated. Several of the flights in the area were issued holding clearances. Kruger's flight got such a clearance and the copilot rogered for it. Kruger flicked his VHF communications switch and called the company, giving them an update on the flight's progress.

"Who are you talking to? What the hell are you telling them?" Ray was near panic for sure now. Sweat popped out on his forehead. Kruger looked at the Captain's junction box and discovered that Ray was listening to every frequency that was tuned into the various radios the aircraft had on. "I wonder how in the hell he manages to keep things straight with the welter of information he's getting all of the time," Kruger thought. The answer was obvious. All you had to do was to look at Ray and you could see that he was entirely out of his league. He looked like he was having an increasingly hard time keeping up with things. He was attempting to run the whole show all by himself instead of letting his crew share the workload. It wasn't working and his crew was having a wonderful time letting him dig a hole that he was about to fall into.

"I'm giving the company our holding clearance like I'm supposed to," Kruger answered.

"D'ja ever think about checking with me first?" Ray gargled.

"Why would I do that? Standard Operating Procedures clearly call for the report to be made. Do you want me to go against SOP? Hell, Captain, I'll do anything you want me to do but I guess you'll have to write it down for me so I can answer the company when they call me in to ask me why I did an end run around SOP. Wait a sec. Here's some paper to write on. All you have to do is write down what you want me to do and I'll do 'er. Hell, I'm here to help you." Kruger was having a field day. Ray's face was fifteen shades redder than normal and he was beginning to hyperventilate.

"Hey! Watch your airspeed," the copilot yelled. "You're supposed to be entering holding. The FAA says you should be at your holding airspeed two minutes prior to entry. Do you want a flight violation? Have you figured out your holding entry yet?" Ray chopped the power roughly and looked like he wanted to throw up. He grabbed a chart, tearing it in the process. He looked like he wanted to cry.

"Jesus, I'd watch how you treat the plane, Captain," Kruger said. "I know I'm only the Second Officer but the people back aft can feel how rough you are on the controls. I'm sure it doesn't give them much confidence in our ability to fly, with you jerking the controls and the power levers like that."

The flight progressed and finally got on the ground. By now the Captain had given up on micromanaging the cockpit and refused to talk to his crew other than to shout commands like "gear down" and items like that. His crew relaxed. They had made their point. Maybe Ray would slack off on his crews from now on.

Two weeks later Kruger was notified that he would be entering training as a Second Officer on the Boeing 707.

Chapter V

The Naval Reserve Squadron Kruger was affiliated with was going to get new airplanes. Everyone was excited. The TARs were ecstatic. No more crummy airplanes. The first ones were supposed to arrive in a week. They were P2V-7s, the same models that Kruger had flown for the last four years.

The first time Kruger showed up for a STARP after the new planes were delivered he discovered that a new TAR officer had arrived with them. He was a likeable guy and seemed a little more thorough than the last TAR had been. He asked Kruger if he wanted to go on a training hop. Of course the answer was yes. A training hop in a P2V-7 was a piece of cake to a pilot who had just gotten off of active duty instructing in them. He suited up and let the TAR walk him around the plane, explaining the preflight to him.

The TAR put Kruger in the left seat and let him do the start, run up and take off. As they flew the TAR explained the various systems to Ed who quietly listened as though he had never heard any of this before.

"Let's tune in the ILS frequency at Minneapolis and let me check something," the TAR said. When this was accomplished the TAR swore, "Damn, it's doing that in this plane, too. Maybe it's the station that's screwed up."

"What's the problem?" Kruger asked.

"The damned FPDI (Flight Path Deviation Needle) Needle is swinging all over the place. Just look at it."

The FPDI was an instrument that allowed a pilot to fly a course selected on the VOR or Variable Omni-Range. It allowed flight through clouds and weather without reference to the ground. The needle in the instrument showed the pilot just how far right or left of course he was and how to correct to get back on course. In the present case the FPDI needle seemed over-sensitive. It was swinging all over the place.

"Relax," Kruger said. "It's supposed to do that."

"It is not."

"Sure it is. When you tune in an ILS frequency the instrument is four times as sensitive as when you tune in a VOR frequency. It allows you to more closely fly an ILS course down to minimums."

"Bullshit!"

"We've got an aircraft handbook onboard, haven't we? Hand it here and I'll show you."

The TAR rummaged in his flight bag and produced the thick book. He handed it to Kruger who turned, from long practice, to the page that explained the system. Kruger handed the book back to the TAR saying, "I've got the plane". The TAR read incredulously. He then put the book away and looked long and hard at Kruger.

"How in hell did you know that?" he challenged.

"Oh, I've flown this type of bird for the last four years. The last two I instructed in it in VP-30".

"Damn!"

They continued to fly only now the roles were reversed. Kruger became the instructor and the TAR became the student. They went over several of the aircraft systems with Kruger explaining each. Several times he had to prove his points by reference to the aircraft manual.

When they finally landed the TAR stalked into his office with Kruger in tow. He growled at the secretary, "Write Kruger here up for a PPC check right now. He knows the damned plane better than I do." A PPC was the same thing as an aircraft commander or a pilot in command. The term actually meant Patrol Plane Commander and meant the pilot was not only in command but was adept in the art of hunting submarines, dropping any of the several weapons the P2 carried, offensively mining enemy harbors, running any of several types of patrols and becoming the on-scene commander in any tasks that required coordination between surface and subsurface warships. Kruger returned home happy with the TARs assessment.

Flying with what Kruger privately referred to as the raggedy-assed militia was now actually fun. The planes were newer and better maintained. Maintenance was easier since all of the planes were alike. Crew chiefs didn't have to hunt around for systems anymore. Pilots were now assured that whatever switch or button they reached for would actually be there and the pilot would not have to hunt for it. Kruger rapidly became the squadron's check and training pilot. And he didn't have to fly with a pencil flashlight in his mouth at night ever again.

Summertime was the ideal time for the squadron's two-week active duty period. The pilots had been notified that they would be flying to Rota, Spain to work with one of the deploying squadrons there. The reserve squadron would pick up tasks and patrols from the deployed squadron. By doing so the in place squadron would have a little breathing room and the reserves would benefit from the hands-on flying.

One week prior to the deployment Kruger was called into the program manager's office. "Ed, I'm assigning you to crew number 6. You'll fly as the third pilot/navigator with LCDR Zussman as the PPC and LT Jankowski as copilot."

Kruger couldn't believe his ears. He was clearly the most checked out pilot in the outfit and the program manager had just told him that he would be flying with two of the squadron's least proficient pilots. Zussman was OK but Jankowski was known to most of the squadron's pilots as "Wedge". Kruger had been told that he was called Wedge because a wedge was "the simplest tool known to man". Alternatively he was known as "the Polish gustlock". A gustlock was a wooden device that was only used to keep the plane's control surfaces from blowing about in the wind when the plane was tied down on the ramp. If that wasn't enough Lt. Jankowski was confrontational and abrasive. He didn't get along with many of the other pilots and had few friends.

Jankowski also flew for Northwest Airlines. He was senior to Kruger and was widely known as an abrasive person who was so confrontational that he had few friends or pilots who supported him.

One incident at Northwest epitomized Jankowski's intractability. During a normal flight on a NWA 727 Jankowski was flying as a copilot. During the takeoff checklist as the plane taxied out one of the challenges was "start levers". The copilot was supposed to ensure that the start levers were locked in the forward position by pushing them toward the forward position. The start levers were actually the controls for the fuel system. They allowed fuel to the engines. Instead of pushing the controls toward the locked and "on" position Jankowski always persisted in pulling them toward the "off" position. When questioned about this odd behavior he said, "If the engines are going to be shut off we need to know that while we are on the ground". Efforts to persuade him that it was not necessary to "shut off the engines" fell on deaf ears. Jankowski was intractable.

On the day in question Jankowski shut down the engines during the taxi out while responding to the check list. The irate Captain had him removed from the flight and he had to explain himself to the Chief Pilot. He showed up for the interview dressed in an old suit that looked like a World War II hand-me-down. When asked what he was doing he responded, "The Captain I flew with doesn't fly by SOPA (Standard Operating Procedures)". Of course Jankowski's reasoning didn't convince the Chief Pilot but that didn't change Jan's thinking one bit.

When Kruger had blown up in the program manager's office over his latest assignment the TAR hastened to explain. "Ed, I know you're good. That's why you're going to have to fly with this crew. None of the other pilots know anything about the plane. I have to have someone on that crew so we won't lose the plane and crew somewhere along the way."

"Then why am I flying as navigator instead of PPC?"

"Both of the other pilots are senior to you. I can't very well put you in ahead of them."

"The hell you can't." Kruger argued with the TAR for a half an hour but got nowhere. The TAR was intractable. It became apparent that Kruger either had to accept the assignment or drop out of the reserve program. He gritted his teeth as he agreed to fly in the position assigned to him all the while telling himself that "it was only two weeks".

"OK, I'm glad to hear you're onboard with this one. I don't know what I'd have done with that crew if you hadn't agreed. Now I'm going to have to ask you to take Jankowski out and run him through some training exercises. Give him some single engine landings and a few emergencies. I don't think he's very up on his procedures."

Kruger did a slow burn as he left the office to look up Jankowski. "Jeezus, that's insult on injury. I not only have to fly junior to the dumbshit but I have to teach him how to fly in the bargain."

The two pilots were soon in the air. Kruger was appalled at how little Jankowski knew about the plane. He ran the other pilot through as many emergencies as he thought Jankowski could assimilate. When Lt. Jankowski complained about the workload Kruger replied, "It's my sweet ass up there with you, damn it. I want to know you can handle the plane if it decides to come apart out over the north Atlantic while I'm in the tube navigating." That had actually happened to Kruger when he was on active duty in his second squadron. He had been on the lead plane flying to Sigonella, Sicily when the port engine blew up. The crew finally made it to Argentia, Newfoundland only to crash on the runway. And that was with competent pilots.

Kruger worked Lt. Jankowski for 2 hours. Finally he took the plane from the sweaty pilot and said, "OK, Jan, give Minneapolis a call and tell them we're on a straight-in for landing."

Jankowski stared at Kruger for a few seconds and then said. "We're at 8,000 feet just a few miles from the runway. How are you going to land from here?"

"Never mind, Lieutenant, just make the call."

Jankowski called the tower and assured them that the plane could make the runway if cleared to do so. When they were so cleared Kruger said, "OK now, Jan, pay attention. I'll show you what the plane can do."

He closed the throttles and brought the nose up to rapidly lose airspeed. When the speed was low enough he dropped the landing gear and selected full flaps. He then opened the bomb bay doors. With all of that drag on the plane he lowered the nose and the aircraft plummeted like a stone. Lt. Jankowski was obviously nervous about the rate of descent. He said, "I don't think this is safe."

"Relax, Jan, this is the only way to get down in a hurry. The only other way is to stall the plane and crash. Watch and learn." Kruger estimated the distance to the runway at three miles and they were rapidly approaching 3,000 feet. He closed the bay doors and opened the jet clamshell doors allowing the jets to spool up. When the jets were spinning at 25 % he turned off the fuel boost pumps and ignited both jet engines. The plane was still dropping so he selected ten degrees of flap to slow the rate. As the runway approached he scheduled the flaps in order to land with 30 degrees. The throttles were still closed.

Lt Jankowski was used to flying Northwest Orient's 727s. All jets land with power on the engines. Jet engines have a fuel control instead of a carburetor like engines have on propeller planes. A carburetor supplies an instantaneous power response to throttle movements. The jet fuel control operates much slower taking into consideration density altitude, temperature and air flow hence the need to carry power to avoid a premature landing due to low power selections. Jankowski reached for the throttles on short final.

"Ah, ah, ah. Don't touch a thing. We're going to dead-stick this beast on the runway in the first thousand feet." Kruger had the approach and landing all figured out in his head. The plane squeaked down just as he had planned. He applied reverse pitch on the props on rollout and turned off at the Navy ramp. "How d'ya like them apples, Jan?" he smiled.

"I still think that was unsafe." Lt. Jankowski was unconvinced.

"Well, Jan, that's the difference between you and I. I know this plane inside out. I know its shortcomings and its capabilities. Don't forget that while we're on deployment. If I tell you something about the plane I don't expect any arguments. OK?"

A few days later 10 crews lifted off from the Naval Air Station, Twin Cities headed for Rota to the muttered prayers of the TAR who sought divine aid in getting his charges to their destination. The planes and crews would remain over night or RON at Brunswick, Maine and Lajes, Azores before reaching Rota. The route was familiar to Kruger who had been there before. As he navigated using the periscopic sextant, the Loran and the drift meter he thought back to the last time he did this. That time was harrowing as the plane had split an oil line freezing the engine and uncoupling the prop. The plane had barely reached Argentia, Newfoundland before crashing on the runway there. P2Vs had a bad habit of losing parts and coming unglued at inopportune times. Kruger was slightly uneasy thinking that he was the only pilot onboard who knew how to navigate and the only one who really knew the plane itself. He was sustained in the sure knowledge possessed by most Naval Aviators that there was absolutely nothing he could not overcome.

Periodically he would be called to the cockpit to assure the two pilots sitting there that there was nothing wrong with the plane. He was like a walking encyclopedia to those worthies, available on call to solve any problems that arose. After explaining the system in question to them he was then summarily dismissed to the dark recesses of the "tube" to attend to the navigation so the plane would arrive at the planned destination while the pilots enjoyed the sunshine and the pleasant sights over the north Atlantic. Each time Kruger held his tongue and did a slow burn. It would avail nothing to rail at the two toads in the cockpit.

A fourth pilot had been assigned to the crew to help Kruger with the navigation. He was a handsome young Lieutenant who had never flown P2Vs prior to this. It was expected that Kruger would try and check him out in whatever spare time there was during the deployment. He worked diligently on the navigation while the toads up front in the cockpit asked a bevy of questions about the whole process interrupting sun observations and plotting. Kruger had set up a watch bill so that the two navigators would trade off tasks with one officer plotting while the other took fixes using the sun and the Loran. The system was working but both navigators were kept busy as it had been a long time since they had practiced their navigation skills.

Lt. Jankowski was being himself. He asked constant questions regarding where they were insisting the navigators supply him with positions. Kruger ignored him but the other Lieutenant tried to navigate and furnish the abrasive Jankowski with as much information as he thought he required.

"Nav, pilot, where are we now?"

"Just a sec, pilot, we're working on a position right now."

"Don't you know where you are?"

The navigator was busy plotting. Every time he had to answer the pilot he had to lay his pencil down and pick up the hand mike. It was irritating. "Yes, I know where we are but I'm a little busy right now plotting a fix. I'll get to you in a sec."

"Do you want to fly a wind star?" Wind stars were flown by altering heading 60 degrees for two minutes to observe the drift on the drift meter. At the end of the two minutes a turn of 120 degrees would be flown for another two minutes followed by a turn to the original heading. By observing the drift of the plane on each leg the navigator could determine an accurate wind.

"I don't need to fly a wind star, I know the damned wind. If you'll leave me alone I can plot this fix."

"If you know the wind you can fly anywhere and not be lost. Are you sure you don't want to fly a wind star?"

Kruger watched and listened with amusement. Obviously the pilot was getting to the navigator but the dumb pilot apparently couldn't see it. All of a sudden the navigator remove his headset, slammed it down on the navigation table and cupping his hands around his mouth shouted at the cockpit, "You goddamned dumb Polack, will you shut the fuck up and let me navigate?" Kruger doubled over with laughter as the navigator was of Polish extraction also. In fact Kruger appeared to be the only officer onboard who wasn't Polish.

Apparently it worked, as Lt. Jankowski remained silent for the rest of the day.

The prayers of the TAR were answered as ten planes landed successfully in the Azores. Kruger could have sworn that the same old men were on hand to carry the bags to the BOQ just as they had done six years earlier when he had landed there with VP11. The next morning, bright and early, the same ten airplanes were winging their way to Rota.

It was with nostalgia that Kruger saw the Pillars of Hercules appear on the radar and soon they touched down in Spain.

The squadron quickly fell into the routine of a deploying detachment. Daily flights were laid on patrolling the western Mediterranean and the approaches to that body of water. Throughout the two-week period Kruger stayed in the tube navigating. Not once did the pilots offer to trade places, perhaps because they couldn't navigate, but that possibility didn't make his position any more palatable. The only satisfactory time he had during that time was when the crew didn't have to fly a patrol. At those times Kruger was scheduled for training hops with the pilots who were not yet proficient on the plane while the other pilots on his crew relaxed in the warm Spanish sunshine. VFR flying in Spain was fun. Kruger was scheduled more than most of the other pilots but he loved it and loved flying as he had been used to fly in the last squadron that he had been in.

One morning as Kruger was reporting for breakfast he heard a loudspeaker page a "Lt. Sheedy". Kruger immediately found the bank of telephones that served the pages and soon saw an old friend, Frank Sheedy, pick up one of the phones. Frank had been one of the Lieutenants in VP 11 that Kruger had known and had been one that was the brunt of a joke as the squadron had deployed to Guantanamo Bay, Cuba. The squadron had several Philippino stewards who had a difficult time pronouncing the letters "d" and "s". Accordingly, every day someone in the squadron would page LCDR Sheets and Lt Sheedy. The resulting page over the loud speaker would make most of the officers double over in laughter as the page would come over as "LCDR Shits, Lt Shitty, you hab telepone calls at extension tree-pipe cerro".

Kruger pounded Frank on the back as he shook his hand but Frank was busy. He had a job of trying to round up all of the officers attached to one of the carriers that were in port as that ship was scheduled to sail shortly on short notice. Frank said, "Ed, I can't talk to you right now but go in the annex where breakfast is being served and see if you see anyone there you know."

Kruger did as he was bid and saw another old buddy, the Air Intelligence Officer from VP 11, Lt Jack Thoren. In VP 11 he was always known as "Rosy" Thoren, the name stemming from a time when "Rosy" had caught what is commonly known in the Navy as "the clap" while he was on a deployment in Rota, Spain. Rosy had never lived that name down. Kruger immediately yelled, "Hey, Rosy" and approached his old friend. Rosy appeared somewhat perturbed as he said, sotto voice, "Hey, hey, knock off that name. I'm known as Jack in this squadron. I hate that fucking name."

It was too late. The damage had been done. The Lieutenant next to Rosy said, "Rosy? What's with the name Rosy?" Kruger gleefully told the tale of Jack's foray with the ladies of the night and his christening of the name "Rosy". The Lieutenant was delighted with the tale and immediately started to spread it by saying, "Rosy Thorn, it fits."

Rosy was, by now, holding his head in his hands and moaning, "Goddamn it, another squadron with that fucking name." Kruger patted him on the back and said that he would see him in a few years when he had reported to another squadron. It was simply amazing how small the world was to a Naval Aviator. You could run into old friends anywhere in the world.

One day Kruger was setting on the approach end of a runway in Madrid. He had been told to "hold short due to landing traffic". The local weather was fog below 2,000 feet and VFR above that. As he sat waiting on the traffic he was amazed to see a World War II German Heinkle two-engine plane appear out of the fog. It was complete in all respects with green and black camouflage and black German crosses on the wings and fuselage. It was eerie; just like looking backward in time. Kruger watched open-mouthed as the German plane touched down and rolled out. He keyed the mike and asked the tower about the apparition he had just seen. The tower explained that The Battle of Britain was being filmed in England and that many of the old planes were being flown in to be filmed there. The sight was one Kruger would always treasure; just another incident offered to a pilot but denied to desk-bound unfortunates.

During a stand-down from duty on a weekend Kruger and a few other officers attended a fair at a town near the Naval Station. La Fairia was a gala affair with several of the great wine producers offering free drinks at the several tents they had erected for the occasion. Most of the fair attendees were relaxed and happy especially after the application of a few glasses of port or brandy. Kruger was happily enjoying the crowds when he felt a tug on his sleeve. Looking around he saw a sad-faced little lady holding an infant in her arms. When Kruger looked at her she used one hand to gesture toward the infant saying, "Por favor, Senor, por la nina". (Please, sir, for the baby). Kruger wasn't used to beggars and instantly coughed up a few pesetas for the mother. She thanked him and glided away.

Kruger continued to make the rounds at the tents and twice more he was approached by several of the ladies with infants begging for money in the same way. (Por favor, senor, por el nino). Someone had told him that the ladies were gypsies who always attended fairs in order to beg for money. Finally Kruger had his sleeve tugged for the fourth time. He looked a little closer to the pair this time as the gypsy woman asked for something for the child. Each time he had been tapped for money the lady looked a little older. This time he was sure that the lady was a grandmother. He looked a little close and discovered that the infant was the same one that had been passed around from woman to woman in the effort to separate him from his cash. Kruger laughed at his discovery and said, "Now just a minute, Grandma . . . ." His reaction started a bevy of laughter from the various gypsy ladies that had been handing the infant around from person to person as they begged from him. Kruger started laughing also. He said, "Ah, you guys got me this time." Apparently the gypsies understood English as they redoubled their laughter and nodded their agreement. It all contributed to the good time at the fair.

All too soon the active duty period was over and the squadron was, once again, on its way over the Atlantic. This time the route would be via the Azores and Newfoundland on the way to Brunswick.

When they landed at the Azores Kruger was certain this time that the little man who appeared and wanted to carry their baggage was the same one that had done the same task many years ago when he had been here while on active duty. The crew retired to the BOQ and the enlisted quarters and got a good night's sleep. The next day Kruger had said that they would go to the package liquor store in order for anyone who wished to purchase a case of wine to take back home. Wine from the Azores or Spain was unbeatable and cheap.

Lt Jankowski was a teetotaler and didn't hold with drinking. He objected to the delay in allowing the crew to buy a cheap case of wine but Kruger told him to stuff it. He sulked aboard the crew bus.

The crew all bought cases of Rose Matteus. When they made their way back to the bus they found Lt. Jankowski sitting in the number one seat with his feet stretched across the aisle. The crew looked at Kruger for guidance. Kruger boarded the bus and kicked Jankowski's feet snarling in German, "Stand at attention when I come on the bus, you pig".

Jankowski had spent some time as a child in a Polish DP camp. His parents had been killed by the Germans. When Kruger, knowing this, said what he had said Jankowski blanched and said, "You want to watch that, Kruger." Kruger said, "OK, then act like a human being and I'll treat you like one." Jankowski always excelled in animosity.

The weather was excellent until they reached Argentia. As always, the weather in that area was IFR. After spending the night at the Navy base the squadron sat on the end of the runway awaiting takeoff minimums. Fog blanketed the area. The station's Meteorology Department, known universally as "weather guessers", had a prognosis of the fog "burning off around noon". Everyone knew that the "prog" was merely a guess at best and a hope at worst. Fog was a way of life at Argentia, Newfoundland.

Kruger's crew had looked at the weather and the pilots had determined that it was below their personal minimums. In other words the sky was not bright blue. Accordingly they asked Kruger if he would like to fly in the left seat today. Kruger had retained his Navy Green Instrument Card that allowed him to take off and land in zero-zero conditions if the operational conditions dictated. They even offered to put the junior navigator in the right seat for takeoff. Kruger thought that the decisions were shortsighted. Normally you would want the best pilots in the cockpit when the weather was marginal. He had no argument with himself in the cockpit but having the junior navigator in the right seat was really dumb. The pilot had never checked out on the P2V and had never even had many more than a few training hops in it. Kruger didn't argue with the two pilots who heretofore had hogged the cockpit. If they didn't think they were proficient enough to make the takeoff in marginal weather then far be it from him to argue with them. As for the other pilot, Kruger figured that he could handle anything that was thrown his way considering his two years in the RAG, the training squadron for P2Vs.

Kruger's plane was the first one on the end of the runway. The fog was pea soup thick. The plane sat ready for takeoff awaiting the signal from the tower that the visibility was good enough to make a takeoff run. The jets were on line and eating up fuel at a rapid rate. The big 3350 engines were snarling and constantly trying to load up the spark plugs with carbon; something they were prone to do at idle power settings. When the recip plugs were loaded up they would never produce the power needed to make a successful takeoff.

Kruger sweated and cursed the weather. Periodically he ran the recip engines up to high power on order to burn off the carbon that was always trying to foul the spark plugs. He kept up a running dialog with the tower and the weather guessers. He kept looking at the fuel gages and figuring the probable fuel needed to get to his destination with the necessary fuel reserves on board. The plane was burning a lot of fuel setting there. They had been at the end of the runway for fifteen minutes now. Kruger had to decide whether to go when the weather cleared or to go back to refuel. He also kept up a running dialog with the crew to let them know what was happening.

The ceiling rose and lowered. The fog was thick and maddening. It seemed as if it never was going to lift. Kruger contemplated scrubbing the takeoff and trying it again the next day but the weather would probably be the same the next day also. Then, too, there was always the consideration that his crew had civilian jobs that they had to attend to in the next few days. The considerations about what the crew had to do had to be tempered. The old syndrome called "get home-itis" had killed more than one Naval Aviator as they allowed their judgment to become clouded by the urge to get home as quickly as possible. He continued to sweat and watch the weather, which lifted and lowered in a very frustrating manner.

Kruger's plane had been on the end of the runway for a half an hour when the tower called and said that the weather was finally lifting. He alerted the crew for takeoff and sat listening. Finally the tower called and said that he had takeoff minimums. He called for the final items on the takeoff checklist and asked if everyone in the cockpit was ready to go. When he got an affirmative answer he ran the recips up to full power and popped the brakes. The big plane leapt forward as if it, too, was anticipating the takeoff. Kruger scanned the instruments. Everything seemed to be OK. He settled down to scan the airspeed and the runway as necessary for the takeoff.

The takeoff run seemed to take forever. Kruger had an uneasy feeling about the whole run but couldn't pin it down to anything. He was busy trying to keep the plane on the runway. The fog made things difficult on the takeoff run. He could only see things for about a hundred feet in front of the plane. No one could see the end of the runway. Finally the airspeed gage said that the plane could fly. Kruger horsed the plane into the air. It felt sluggish, like it didn't want to fly. It wasn't accelerating like it normally did. Instead of climbing Kruger leveled off at 100 feet and screamed at rooftop level over the dependant's housing at the end of the runway.

Why wasn't the plane accelerating? Kruger couldn't figure it out. It sure didn't feel like any other takeoff he had experienced. Something was wrong. He could feel it in his bones but couldn't put his finger on the problem. He looked around. Gear was up. Bomb bay doors were closed. It wasn't drag that was slowing them down. What the hell was wrong? The 3350s were generating as much power as they could be expected to generate. Something was wrong here. What? He didn't dare to suck up the flaps until he had adequate airspeed. He continued at 100 feet in order to get the planes airspeed up so he could clean the plane up.

Kruger knew that there were hills and mountains all over the area. Here he was flying in a pea-soup fog in an unfamiliar area in unforgiving terrain. He was sweating profusely as he tried to figure out what was wrong with the plane while scanning his instruments and trying to stay out of the hills that surrounded the airfield. His brain was in overdrive trying to figure out just what was wrong. Obviously something was amiss. What the hell was wrong?

The plane wasn't accelerating or climbing. It streaked over the housing section at 100 feet generating lots of noise but little power. "Wake up, assholes," Kruger muttered under his breath as he continued to try and find the problem. It had to be drag. What the hell else could it be? Why was the plane so sluggish? If it wasn't drag then it had to be . . . .

Power! Goddamn! The fucking jets weren't on line! The unchecked out copilot didn't know enough to run the jet throttles to 100 % on the takeoff roll and Kruger had been too busy to catch it. The copilot was still sitting in his seat looking straight ahead. Kruger screamed "Jets" as he slammed the throttles full forward. He almost broke the hands of the Plane Captain who was wondering what was wrong just as Kruger was doing. Kruger's yell of "jets" had jarred the Plane Captain who had reached for the throttles at the same time. As the jets responded to the throttle movement the plane leapt forward. It also began to climb. They quickly climbed to a safe altitude and cleaned up the plane. Kruger hadn't dared to lift the flaps prior to this. The aircraft felt normal with the addition of the extra power and the climb out was uneventful except for Kruger sweating profusely and swearing occasionally in frustration.

The crew didn't seem to be aware that anything untoward had happened. The off duty pilots were blissfully snoring in any number of cubbyholes found on the plane. Kruger could not get over what he had just allowed to happen. He had allowed the plane and the entire crew to be placed in extremis because of a lapse in his attention span. A small thing, but one that could kill just as effectively as a missile. He was devastated. The pilot who had talked to him early on, Dick Reebe, had foretold this and had warned him. He had been too pigheaded to listen and for that he would never forgive himself.

Kruger berated himself all the way across the Atlantic. He had a large amount of humble pie to eat and it took some time to digest it all. He had to finally realize that he was just another pilot, just like any other and subject to all of the foibles and mistakes that any other pilot was exposed to any day of the year. He wasn't invincible. He was just another pilot. He felt small and ineffective. Just another pilot. A JAP. Just another fucking pilot.

The squadron landed at the Naval Air Station at Brunswick, Maine. Kruger felt nostalgic as he gazed around at the familiar surroundings while the crew deplaned and was only interrupted by a well-known voice that challenged, "Where the hell have you been? I haven't seen you for years." It was the omnipresent customs official, Tony, who had charge of, among other things, the Naval Air Station.

"Goddamn, Tony! You haven't changed at all. You're just as ugly as always. How the hell are you?" Kruger was pounding Tony on the back as Tony reciprocated enthusiastically. The dust flew.

"This your crew?" Tony challenged.

"Yeah, that's them. They haven't had time to buy any contraband. Probably wouldn't know how to define the term if they had to. Say, remember the pilot in Eleven that tried to smuggle in those wooden plates from Haiti?"

Tony was laughing. "Yeah. George, I remember him. He was a nice guy; just a little too smart. We sure cured him, didn't we?"

George Silberstein had tried to smuggle a few wooden plates from Haiti in from a deployment to Guantanamo Bay, Cuba. A radioman had asked George if it was possible and George had told him to put the plates in the classified communications bag assuring him that no one would look in the bag. When Tony had asked what was in the bag George had told him that it "was classified and he couldn't look at it".

Tony accepted the challenge and the issue finally involved the squadron Commanding Officer who ordered George to allow Tony to peer into the bag. As he said, "Goddamn it, George, Tony isn't going to read anything in the bag. He just wants to see inside it." As soon as the bag was opened the contraband was apparent and Tony slapped a large fine onto George pronouncing him "a smuggler".

Tony let George sweat for two weeks and then lifted the fine. As he said, "George is a good man. He's just a smartass and needed to sweat a little." On the next deployment Kruger cornered Tony and reminded him of George's sin. "Let's pull a fast one on him," Kruger suggested. "I'll stencil "Secret" on one of his bags and you give him a lot of shit over it."

"Super! Do it. Do it." Tony was enthusiastic. He loved a joke as much as any of the pilots.

Kruger waited until George was occupied and did as he had suggested. Tony kept an eye on him and as soon as the deed had been done Tony announced in a loud voice, "Whose bag is this labeled secret?" George took one look and almost fainted. It took months before he would speak to Kruger.

Now Tony waved at Kruger's crew. "Tell them to pack up. I don't need to see anything here. I know you wouldn't let them smuggle anything."

Kruger thanked the customs official and they reminisced for a few minutes more before the busy customs man had to look at other crews. Two days later Kruger was back in Minneapolis and home.

*   *   *

Any proficient pilot could have foretold that the squadron had a bevy of pilots who couldn't find their ass even if one of their hands was placed on it. Kruger was appalled at the lack of knowledge and the cavalier attitude some of the pilots had. The TAR knew all about the lack of professionalism on the part of the reserve pilots and welcomed the expertise Kruger brought to the squadron. Kruger saw his role in the squadron as one of an instructor rather than simply a check pilot. He constantly tried to correct any bad habits or habit patterns the pilots may have picked up on the way. Kruger became known as the pilot who would not give a down on a check ride but who would work for hours with a pilot to correct any deficiency that pilot may have adopted.

One day the entire cadre of Navy people were called to muster by the TAR OinC. The Naval Air Station at Twin Cities was going to be closed. The Navy had determined that they were going to reorganize the Naval Reserve based on the concept of "the youngest, best qualified" idea. According to this concept the youngest, best-qualified Plane Commander would get plane number 01. The next best pilot would get plane number 02 and so on. When the Navy had run out of Plane Commander slots they would work on copilots. After the copilots came the TACCOs and then the Navigators. It was part of an idea to cull the non-functioning pilots and TACCOs in favor of people who could perform. The Navy had assessed the Reserve program and had decided to alter the concept of the Reserves. Instead of maintaining a cadre of pilots for some future unknown situation it had been decided to use the Reserves to augment the active duty squadrons and therefore it was impingent on the Navy to furnish competent flight crews in order to accomplish that mission. Marginal pilots and crews would no longer be tolerated.

When the massed group of officers was formed the TAR OinC explained the concept to them and then read off the names of the few officers who actually had orders to the Naval Air Station, Glenview, Illinois. It seemed that the NAS, Twin Cities was going to be pared down substantially and that all squadrons were going to be sent to operate out of Glenview, a Naval Air Station several miles north of Chicago's O'Hare field. There were only about a dozen officers who had orders to Glenview. The rest of the unfortunates had to get to Glenview on their own dime and try to wrangle a billet based on their own expertise and persuasive powers. It was not a nice plan.

Kruger was one of the few officers who had orders. He thought about the offer for a few days and then told the TAR at Twin Cities that he did not wish to accept the orders. He thought that commuting to Glenview was too much of an imposition. The Navy would simply have to do without his talents. The TAR obligingly said that the Navy would miss his expertise and leadership but would somehow manage without him. End of conversation, dismissed.

Kruger thought about his decision at length. He didn't like severing his ties with the Navy he loved so much but then he had made the decision to fly for a civilian organization. The Navy would have to take a back seat this time. Besides, he was making a lot of money now that he was off of probation with Northwest and really didn't need the Naval

Reserve to augment his paycheck. Lots of other pilots had told him that he wouldn't need the Reserve once he started to make the "big bucks". He decided to throw his lot in with the airline.

But somehow Kruger's decision didn't set well with him. The airline paid well, the time off was very nice and the company of other pilots was nice but something was lacking. He had observed the Northwest Captains, at least the older ones, as lacking any leadership qualities. They were empty "yes-men", willing to do anything the company wished without any thought about the ramifications that were sure to pop up. The concept of "passenger service" was a myth. Kruger had watched with horror as a customer service agent had pointed to the runway and had yelled, "GO", to a Captain who had offered to delay the flight so that a few more meals could be boarded for the passengers who had been shorted meals. The Captain meekly complied.

Something was missing here. Kruger wanted desperately to belong to a unit, group or company that would give him some pride in the belonging. Northwest Orient obviously was not the ideal outfit to fulfill this dream.

Then the other shoe dropped. ALPA initiated a "withdrawal of services" from Northwest due to a failure in the negotiating process. Kruger was involved in a strike once again.

It was disgusting. The company played every card they could in an attempt to get the pilots to cave in and sign a substandard contract. Northwest had always been known as a hard-nosed negotiator. Northwest was also known as a "cheap" company, known for not paying its bills or at least paying them very late. It was a policy laid down by the President, Donald Nyrop, known by his employees as Donald "Dry Rot". Northwest paid for TV and newspaper ads in a vain attempt to get the public on the company's side. The company put what it called the "pilot's pay scale" in the paper in an attempt to show what penurious, cheap, greedy, avaricious, materialistic sons-of-bitches the pilots really were. The public was not swayed. It had been here before and had weathered numerous strikes called down on Northwest. In fact, the company was known by the tongue-in-cheek name of "North Worst Arrogant" by the traveling public.

ALPA had always been a strong alliance of pilots. Pilots were the last bastion of independence. Gather 77 pilots in a room and ask for an opinion and you would get 100 different ideas. ALPA somehow managed to corral the independent knot heads and got them to all march in step together . . . . usually.

Most of the striking pilots walked the picket lines and received "strike pay" for their efforts. Some of the more enterprising pilots circulated flyers offering to walk the picket line for those who didn't want to do so or those who thought that walking a picket line was below their dignity. Of course the pilots walking the line had to be paid for their services. One pilot, Gar Bensen, an innovative soul, advertised "Rent-A-Picket" for hire. Gar was even more junior to Kruger and, as such, had weathered more time off duty as the result of strikes than Kruger. Being a survivor like most pilots, Gar had come up with a number of ways to earn enough money to keep body and soul together and, by the way, pay his mortgage in order to keep his home.

Kruger had a problem. He had just signed a contract for a new house in an upscale area south of Minneapolis and desperately needed cash. Strike benefits wouldn't pay the tariff at all. He needed additional income.

Businesses in the Minneapolis area were all too familiar with Northwest Orient strikes. They weren't about to hire any pilots on a long-term basis because they knew that a pilot wished only to fly. They knew that as soon as the strike was over the pilot would inevitably go back to flying, his first love. No one would hire a pilot for anything but cheap, temporary help. Kruger needed something else.

He nosed around what was left of the Twin Cities Naval Air Station to see if there was anything he could wrangle in the form of a job, any job. Maybe the Navy could use him in some way he hadn't thought of yet. He hit pay dirt on his third day of nosing around. There was an opening for an officer for two weeks in Glenview in a paper-shuffling billet. Kruger was desperate. He would accept orders for the two weeks.

Arriving at the Naval Air Station, Glenview, Illinois, Kruger was happy if not ecstatic. The NAS was a WWII holdout; everything in or on it was old and rather rundown. It was located in an affluent area north of Chicago that salivated over the land the Air Station was situated on. The various newspapers in the area mounted weekly attacks on the Air Station. The main complaint was safety and noise. The Air Station was constructed many years prior to the advent of the many houses surrounding the field but that seemed to have no value in the arguments against the Navy. The nicest thing possessed by the Air Station was the golf course, another item coveted by the civilian populace that surrounded the military bastion.

Kruger checked in to the NAS in a familiar manner that tugged on his heartstrings. He found himself again wondering just why he had ever left the Navy. Civilian airline flying didn't seem so damned red-hot just now. He found the building and the office where he was supposed to work and reported to the Officer in Charge.

The job was dreary and boring in the extreme but it was still a job and it paid more than strike benefits. Kruger gritted his teeth and settled down to his desk job. One of the few perks on this job was a whole hour for lunch. Kruger wasn't up to the usual lunch at the "club" that included the usual few martinis so he scouted the area for something to do after his two-week stint was over. He found himself in the hangar housing the Anti-Submarine Warfare/Patrol area of expertise. Summoning up all of his courage he approached the office of the TAR in charge of ASW flying. Kruger introduced himself and was surprised that his name seemed to ring a bell with the TAR.

Commander John Lynch was a "take no prisoners" type officer. He was effective and abrasive. He gave no complements and there were no soft corners on him. He got the job done . . . end of comment.

"Kruger, huh? Yeah, I remember your name. You were the sterling officer who never showed up here after orders were issued for you. Yeah, I remember you real well. What the fuck do you want?"

"Well, Commander, I want a job, simple as that. If you need pilots I can fill that need. I'm good; you can try me out anytime. I'll be a good pilot for you."

"Oh yeah? Well, you quit on us once so why should I take you back now? As far as I care you can take a flying leap. I don't want you. I won't use you. Go away. Go fuck yourself."

That's a hard commentary to follow. Kruger had no answer for the Commander so he turned, without comment, and left. He thought about the Commander's evaluation of him and figured rightly that no amount of rationalization would sway him. It was time to trundle out the big guns.

Kruger's next stop was the Training Officer for the Naval Air Station. This officer outranked all of the TARs on the station who administered the various squadrons based there. This officer was also a Commander albeit a very senior one. Kruger requested and was granted an audience with the Commander.

"What can I do for you Lieutenant?" the Commander asked.

"Sir, I'd like to fly for the Naval Reserve. I'm a Naval Aviator with thousands of hours of flight time. I've served in three squadrons and my fitness reports are very good. My last squadron was VP30, the training squadron for P2V7s where I instructed in both ground classes and flights."

The Commander riveted Kruger with a fixed stare for a few seconds. Then he said, "You should see John Lynch. He's the Program Manager for the P2s here on base. He will give you a billet."

"Commander, I saw Commander Lynch. He doesn't want me."

"Why not? What did he say to you?"

"Well, sir, he advised me to go fuck myself."

The Commander chuckled. "Sounds like John Lynch alright. Why would he tell you that?"

"Sir, he told me that because I originally had orders here to Glenview and I threw them away. I opted not to come to Glenview."

"Well, John has a point. Why should we allow you to fly for us now when you tossed us away prior to this?" The Commander was kind but resolute.

"Because, sir, I'm a better pilot than any other you've got here. I'll prove it. Stack me up with your best. I'll out fly him hands down. Not only that but I've just come out of VP30 as an instructor. I know the P2V7 inside out. Make me prove it . . . . Sir."

The Commander leaned back and took a long look at Kruger. Then he took a deep breath and said, "If I let you back in will you agree to go to the training squadron and train the other pilots?"

Kruger was elated. A job was a job. "Absolutely," he said without hesitation.

The Commander bent over his desk in a posture of dismissal. "OK. Go tell John Lynch I said you were to go to RTU-60. He's not going to be happy with you. You not only went over his head, you were successful. That sticks in anybody's craw. If you can put up with it you can have the job."

"Thanks, Commander. You won't regret it."

"I already regret it. I've got to have lunch with John and I'm going to have to listen to all of his complaints about you."

Kruger left before the Commander could change his mind. Damn! He was happy. Screw Northwest. He was back in the Navy, well, sort of.

Kruger waited until after lunch to present his body to Commander Lynch. He thought that there just might be the slightest chance that the good Commander would be a little mellower after lunch providing, of course, that the wardroom had served something good this time.

"Kruger! You conniving, son-of-a-bitching asshole! You can't even follow orders. I told you to go fuck yourself and you ended up by fucking me instead."

Obviously Commander Lynch hadn't mellowed all that much. Kruger stood silently at attention while the Commander circled him as he chewed him out. There was no use trying to defend himself. He really didn't have any defense anyway. Everything Commander Lynch said was true. In his place Kruger felt that he probably would do the same things the Commander was doing although he doubted that he could come up with as many adjectives as the Commander was using. Finally Commander Lynch had to come up for air. He stood glaring at Kruger who meekly said, "I know how you feel Commander but I will promise you that I'll work hard for you and in six months if you feel that I haven't produced in a satisfactory manner then I'll drop out of your life." The Commander turned and, without any more words, walked out of the room.

Kruger went right to work. He gathered up all of the training folders on all of the pilots and went through them looking for evidence of check rides, weaknesses, training hops, anything that would tell him how the pilots were performing. From his past experiences with the reserve program he suspected that more than a few were just skating and were marginal at best. He found more proof than he had wished for. He had his work cut out for him.

Things were looking up. Kruger had a more or less permanent room in the BOQ and lived at the Naval Air Station in Glenview. He got home about once every two weeks but managed to send money home and pay the bills. He was kept too busy to miss his family and, in all fairness, his absence was more like Navy life than civilian.

At first Kruger was treated with suspicion in his new squadron. The pilots felt that he was there to make their life hard and to wash them out. Kruger not only gave check rides he also lectured on the aircraft systems. After two years in the P2 RAG (Readiness Air Group) he knew how to make the systems easy to understand and palatable to pilots who were more interested in flying than in the mechanics of their planes. Pilots really only became interested in a system when that component of their plane malfunctioned. Usually by then it was too late to study. Kruger could combine a check ride with an instructional hop. He never gave a simulated emergency without explaining how to trouble shoot the system and either remedy it or manage without it. He began all of his check rides by explaining that he would never give a down. If the pilot had some weakness in an area they flew until that weakness was ironed out. Pilots began to look forward to flying with him.

Kruger was not what was known as a "Santa Claus". A "Santee Claws" was a check pilot who overlooked deficiencies. Kruger found those deficiencies and corrected them but he never failed any pilot. With hard work and long hours the training jackets were all in order and soon all pilots were current. The program managers relaxed for the first time in a long time.

Six months went by in no time. The Northwest pilot's strike was settled and pilots began to be recalled. Pilots in Kruger's seniority were the last to be recalled due to their low seniority. Kruger continued to fly with the Naval Reserve. Upon reflection he found that the job not only paid the bills but also gave him a lot of satisfaction.

The Naval Air Station at Glenview, Illinois was not in the league of an active duty station but close enough for him to feel at home. Like most Reserve Air Stations the buildings appeared shabby due to a lack of funds. The Reserves were at the tail end of a long line of "needs" when it came time to allocate the resources allotted to the Navy. Kruger looked on life there as a type of deployment much like the style of life he had lived when he had been on active duty. Viewed in that light Glenview, however shabby, was much nicer than Guantanamo Bay, Cuba, Soudha Bay, Crete, Sigonella, Sicily or Keflavic, Iceland or even Midway Island and, as in most deployments, the camaraderie was excellent.

For the most part the Reserve pilots worked hard at their job. Like any pilot they intuitively knew that the more you knew about your plane the better your chances of survival. Flying was much safer now than it had been, say, in 1930 but flying, as the old saying goes, was inherently unsafe. The more you knew about everything the longer you lived. Thus the Reserve pilots tried very hard to comply with all of the safety regs and notices, all of the standard procedures and all of the little hints and nudges any of the instructor pilots wished to impart. There were exceptions.

Joe Olzinski was a case in point. Joe was a likeable guy and had, after all, made the grade to become a Navy pilot. Not only that but Joe had flown S2Fs off of carriers proving his survivability if nothing else. Joe did have a few faults, which were immediately apparent to his peers. Chief among these was the tendency to stutter when the going got rough. He also had few social graces and was known to pick his nose and examine the residue left on his index finger prior to wiping said finger anywhere convenient. Joe was not invited to many dinners with his companions who had appropriately named him "the Polish Gustlock".

Joe had achieved notoriety by surviving a catapult launch off of a carrier in an S2F, a twin engine anti-submarine plane. His number two engine had immediately indicated that it was on fire and Joe, in his excitement, had feathered and shut down the number one engine resulting in his landing in the water in front of the carrier. Luckily he narrowly missed being run over by the carrier. He remained a Naval Aviator but his record showed his tendency to react without thinking.

Joe was up for an annual check ride in the P2. Kruger read and reread his training jacket and shook his head. This was going to be challenging. The morning of the event the two aviators met, briefed and proceeded to the plane. Kruger watched Joe go over the aircraft preflight, brief his crew and then climbed into the P2 after him. Joe took the left seat, as was normally the case in a check ride. Kruger acted as his copilot.

Joe started both engines without incident, no mean feat with the big 3350s, which were cantankerous and would backfire or afterfire any time during the starting procedure. Sometimes the backfires were severe enough that the exhaust stacks were blown clear off of the engines. All too soon the crew was aboard and Joe was taxiing out to the duty runway. Kruger handled the radios and kept notes on the progress of the flight on a kneeboard. Joe got an engine "cut" on takeoff, simulating a loss of power on that engine. He handled it OK but was very nervous. Kruger waited until they got to 5500 feet and told Joe that he would take control of the plane. He then said, "Joe, you look a little tense. This isn't what you'd call a normal check ride. If you've talked to any of the other pilots you know that you can't possibly fail here. I know you're a pilot. That fact isn't in doubt. I know you can do everything I ask you to do with the plane. Maybe you won't do it 4.0. If not I'll let you know where your weakness lies and we'll practice until you've got it right. OK?"

Joe nodded but didn't appear to be any more relaxed. Kruger gave control of the plane back to him and the flight progressed. Joe could do just about everything required on a check ride but he was rough around the edges. Kruger remembered an incident a long time ago in one of his squadrons where the CO gave him a down on a check ride for Patrol Plane Commander. When pressured the CO had said that Kruger "wasn't smooth enough" giving rise to the name he was known as for the rest of the time he was in that squadron, "Smooth Ed".

Joe did pretty well handling a loss of an engine emergency. He also could do OK when it came to ditching and bailout drills. One of the more important emergencies a P2 pilot had to remember was a "runaway vericam". The vericam was, in actuality, a "flying tail". It was part of the elevator system and gave an instantaneous response to the elevator during flight. The only problem with the system was that it had a design flaw that allowed it to "run away" putting the plane in a situation that was very nearly uncontrollable. There had been many "fixes" to the system resulting in very few runaways but if it happened it could still kill you. The pilots had to know the emergency procedures for the runaway and had to know them cold. There would be no time to research the system if a runaway happened especially, in accord with Murphy's Law, it happened at a critical moment of flight. The procedures were different for a runaway up and a runaway down vericam. If the pilot forgot them and applied the wrong procedure it exacerbated the emergency to a point where the plane would be uncontrollable and would result in a crash even with adequate altitude to affect a normal save. Joe had to demonstrate that he could handle a runaway vericam.

The way an instructor would give a runaway vericam was to switch the system from the normal to the emergency system without the pilot's knowledge and then toggle the vericam either up or down. The pilot would feel the elevator pressure and try to counter it with the normal system; the button on the pilot's yoke. This would not work, of course, since the normal system was inoperative having been switched to the emergency one. The pilot would then immediately reach for the emergency system. If the check pilot wished to see the whole procedure he would then tell the pilot that he had just switched to emergency and it "didn't work" so the whole procedure would have to be augmented. This meant that for a runaway up vericam the pilot had to reduce power, drop 30 flaps, roll the plane 30 to 45 degrees to allow the nose to fall through and, as level flight had once again been established, add power sufficient to keep the plane flying level once again. For a runaway down the pilot had to reduce power, drop 20 flaps and add power once he could control the plane.

The P2 had what is called fowler flaps. These flaps would extend aft of the wing making the wing effectively wider for up to 20 degrees of flap movement. That gave the wing a lot more lift and would always cause the plane to nose upward as the flaps extended. From 20 to 30 degrees the flaps would "droop" causing not only a greater wing area but also a drastic change in the camber of the wing. This caused the nose of the plane to drop. If the pilot forgot his procedures and lowered only 20 degrees of flap with a runaway up the plane would pitch up to an uncontrollable attitude, stall, crash and burn. Reason enough to remember the procedures.

Kruger initiated the emergency at 6500 feet. He quietly switched the vericam to emergency and began to toggle the elevator full up. Joe felt the pressure on the yoke, analyzed it correctly and reached to switch the power to emergency. Kruger switched back to normal immediately before Joe could reach the emergency toggle so that Joe found the switch in the normal position when he touched it. Joe switched to emergency and began to run the vericam back to normal. So far, so good. Joe then apparently forgot that he was running the vericam down and continued to run it all the way down. Kruger almost swallowed his tongue in an attempt to not laugh at the spectacle of Joe giving himself an emergency. Joe knew the procedures because he correctly analyzed the problem as an uncontrollable runaway down vericam. He knew that he needed 20 flaps but had excitedly begun to stutter. Like most people who stutter he had adopted a few "trigger" words that hopefully would break the stutter syndrome. Joe's trigger was "here".

"Here . . . . here . . . . here". Joe rolled his eyes as he attempted ineffectually to ask for 20 flaps. Kruger was in knots as he strangled to keep from laughing as he watched the poor pilot give himself more down vericam all the time while he tried vainly to ask for the proper flap setting. Joe could not even let go of the yoke in order to reach for the flap lever himself as he was using all of the muscle he had to try to keep the plane flying as the plane dove for the ground.

Kruger struggled to keep a straight face as he asked, "What do you want, Joe? Flaps? How many?"

"Here . . . . here . . . . here . . . mmmmm". Joe was trying really hard to get the idea across.

"30 flaps, Joe? Want 30?"

"MMMMM . . . . here." Joe was emphatically shaking his head. He definitely did not want 30 flaps. His hand was still on the emergency toggle, which, by now, had run the vericam to the full stops.

"What, Joe? Want 20?"

Joe nodded his head so vigorously that Kruger thought he might get a whiplash. Kruger selected 20 flaps and as the plane became more flyable he said, "You can let go of the emergency toggle now, Joe. Good job. That's the first time I ever saw anyone cooperate so well in giving themselves an emergency.

The rest of the flight went well. Joe passed his annual flight check and retired to the BOQ to change out of his sopping wet flight suit. His self-imposed emergency had made him sweat enough in one hour to make him need to replenish his body fluids. The accepted method of doing this for aviators always had been and always will be copious amounts of beer.

Kruger's six month self inflicted probation period with Commander Lynch was up. He met the crusty Commander in the BOQ bar one afternoon for an assessment of his progress. The good Commander sized him up for a few seconds and finally said, without any smile, "Well, you did what you said you would. Good job. You are as good as you said you were but I still don't like you. I'm still waiting for you to go fuck yourself but meanwhile I'll buy you a beer."

Kruger was happy. He still had his Navy job and Commander Lynch liked him regardless of what the old curmudgeon said. All was well in the world.

Well, almost. Kruger had been saddled with a Plane Captain who was a Navy Chief Petty Officer. The thinking here was that the Chief, being very senior and having been around the Naval establishment for a long time, would be an asset to the main training pilot, Kruger. That was not the case. Chief Schleigh was a nice guy but was spectacularly ignorant of the systems of the plane he flew on. Kruger had a double task; teaching the Chief and checking and teaching the pilots in the squadron.

One day while training one of the pilots Kruger had simulated a hydraulic emergency in order to show the pilot how the systems of the plane could be operated manually by positioning hydraulic pistons on the main hydraulic panel in the nose wheel well. The redundant systems would allow operation of the flaps, the gear and the trim systems for the ailerons and the elevators. Chief Schleigh was asked to operate the pistons manually.

The Chief entered the nose wheel well and spent an inordinate amount of time there. He finally appeared in the cockpit saying, "Can't be done", meaning that the information that Kruger had told the pilot was incorrect. Kruger had to leave the cockpit, climb down into the nose wheel well and show the Chief how to operate the system. He was disgusted about the whole incident and disgusted at the Chief who had long quit learning and was merely content to be chauffeured around in the P2 in order to collect his flight pay. As soon as possible Kruger swapped the Chief for another Plane Captain who could actually help out.

*   *   *

Kruger was recalled to Northwest. He was, once again, a second officer on a 727, just like when he had first been hired. He was disgusted. Northwest felt that he should be grateful for his job and thought that the Naval Reserve was an extraneous appendage. Whenever Kruger wished to go on extended active duty the paperwork he had to fill out for Northwest had the clause that read, "This is a request for leave to serve with the Reserves. Duty with the active reserves is subject to the needs of the service with Northwest Airlines." Kruger knew that statutory law mandated that Northwest had to allow reservists to serve regardless of the needs of the airline. He always crossed out the "request" and stated on the form, "pursuant to public law this will serve to inform you that I intend to take orders to active duty in the Naval Reserve on the following dates." No one ever quarreled with him over the wording but Kruger still wasn't happy with the whole concept. He knew that there were other reservists who believed that the company could prevent them from going on active duty. Accordingly he looked up a Veterans Administration official and laid the problem at their feet. The official said, "Is Northwest up to that crap again? You can tell them or tell your union that if they don't allow any reservist to go on active duty anytime they want to I'll see to it that they never get another mail contract from the government again."

It was about this time that Northwest lost a plane. The flight was a 727 flown by only a crew of pilots in a "ferry flight" that was to preposition the plane. It was in the Boston area and was in IFR conditions with rain and snow. The pilots were chatting like all pilots do as the flight conditions were not all that bad at the time but they suddenly ran into icing conditions. The Captain called for the icing systems to be activated and for some unknown reason the copilot turned off the pitot heaters. It was one of those moments of inattention that kills. As the pitot probes that give information on airspeed and altitude iced up the indicated airspeed seemed to be increasing rapidly. That was not the actual case but at night and in IFR conditions the pilots reacted as if it was. As the airspeed indicators seemed about to reach the maximum speed allowed the crew pulled off power and pulled the nose up to an alarming attitude. The plane stalled and fell off spinning. In a high tail airplane like the 727 a power off stall and spin is extremely hard to recover from and the plane impacted the ground with the crew still trying to recover from the "high speed" situation. All aboard were killed.

It was a sobering time for Northwest people. As soon as the Flight Recorders and Cockpit Voice Recorders were analyzed all pilots had to attend briefing classes on how to fly the plane with no inputs from the airspeed and altitude indicators. They were taught to fly using the "seat of their pants" and subtle indicators like the pressurization indicators and the attitude indicators along with the ambient noise levels that were louder at higher airspeeds.

Up to this time all of Kruger's training with both the Navy and Northwest Airlines had emphasized relying on the aircraft instruments and ignoring the "seat of the pants" feelings that would give a pilot vertigo. Now he had to rethink all of that training in the "gee-whiz" instrumentation in lieu of what his body was telling him about the conduct of the flight. It was akin to asking a modern warrior to throw away his state of the art rifle and pick up a club instead. Still, it was using any and all of the information available to a pilot in the goal of preserving life and the airplane. It would bear lots of thought.

All pilots were also castigated for the conversations the dead pilots had just before they had died. Like most pilots the conversations had been about sex, the opposite sex and a few risqué jokes. The sanctimonious senior pilot who took it upon himself to berate the rest of the pilots was well known for his foul mouth but to hear him preach to the rest of the pilots one would think that he was as pure as snow. It was all most of the pilots could do to stand to stay in the room as he pontificated. His name was Frederickson and he was a matter of extreme disdain by the pilot group.

Kruger continued to fly for the Navy any time they needed him. He not only attended the regular drills required of a reservist but he put in as much extra time as he thought he could get away with and still keep a happy home life going. Other Northwest pilots asked him why he persisted in flying for the Navy. In their words they said, "Sooner or later, Ed, you'll find that you really don't need the Navy anymore." Kruger couldn't disagree with them more. The Navy had come through for him time after time. He wasn't about to bail out again. He liked flying for the Navy, always had, always would.

'The Glenview Naval Air Station wasn't just home to Naval Aviators. There were several squadrons of Marines based there also. In Kruger's opinion the Marines gave color and life to the Air Station that otherwise would be lacking. On duty they were all business. Off duty they were fun loving and uninhibited, far more prone to outlandish behavior than the average Naval Officer.

Kruger had made several friends with Marines from both an A4 and a helo squadron. Since they never flew together their comradeship was always limited to the Officer's Club. The presence of alcohol in its various forms in the Club always enhanced the tendency of the Marines to exuberance and made them more innovative than usual much to the delight of Kruger and several other Naval Officers. Rowdy Marines were much more entertaining than the usual, run-of-the-mill bands the Club Manager could come up with.

The Officer's Club was a thorn if the side of the Commander of the Air Station. It had run at a deficit for some time in spite of anything the Club Manager or the CO tried. No one ever asked Kruger just what he thought relative to the club's lack of fiscal health. If he had hazarded a guess it would have been a lack of clientele, high prices, bad entertainment, ineffective management and skimming on the part of the bar keeper. The club was really the only common meeting ground for all of the officers who worked on the Station.

The Club Manager was a retired Chief Petty Officer who insisted on smoking cheap cigars and who was married to a fat, overbearing German woman. Both entities gave themselves airs and seemed to work hard at being as obnoxious as possible. The officers who frequented the club avoided each of them as much as possible. Kruger thought that the patronizing attitude of the retired Chief was especially reprehensible.

The man acted as if the club was his and his alone and the officers who frequented it were barely tolerated guests. The added insult of smoking a foul smelling cigar in the club spaces without so much as a by your leave was almost more than Kruger could stomach. He christened the Chief with the name of "The Pig" to the amusement of the other officers who immediately referred to him only by that name after the christening.

The barman was a civilian black man who adopted an easygoing patronizing attitude toward the patrons he had to serve, probably as a result of his association with the Pig. The barman's name was Algee and that he was tolerated to a much greater extent than the Pig was probably due to the fact that no one would accept any grief from him at all. Algee would push only so far and no farther. In that respect he was much smarter than the Pig. He knew when to back down and so was tolerated by everyone.

The Officer's Club was a cross on the back of the base Commanding Officer. It never made any money and rarely broke even. In all fairness that fact could not be laid at the door of the club manager, the Pig. Even on the occasions the club brought in some entertainment the draw was simply not enough to pay the tariff. A few of the station officers would occasionally bring their wives to dine there and spend part of the evening but the club really needed at least four times that amount of patrons to pay the bills. The reservists who flew for the Navy used the club to relax in and to imbibe greater or lesser amounts of alcohol as the occasion demanded. Most of the time a greater amount was usually required and the participants were prone to becoming rather rowdy as the evening wore on. The fact that both Marine and Naval Officers occupied and used the same spaces did nothing to ameliorate the rowdiness.

All Navy Officer's clubs were ubiquitous in owning a ship's bell, usually salvaged from some ship that had been consigned to the scrap heap. The bell would occupy a place of honor on the bar itself and was lovingly polished and maintained. A whole cadre of customs had grown around the club bells and all officers rigidly enforced those customs. Anyone who rang the bell voluntarily had to buy drinks for anyone present in the bar at the time of the ringing. The choice of drinks was left entirely up to the many observers without consideration as to cost.

Ringing the bell in a crowded bar could well-neigh bankrupt the person so unwise to do so. Another strictly observed custom was applied to anyone who dared to enter the bar "covered", that is to say, with a hat or cover still on their head. The first person to see the covered officer enter the bar would launch themselves over to the bell and ring it several times. The miscreant would then be speedily captured and forced to buy a round for everyone. The sinner would rarely repeat the mistake.

One Saturday evening the club was packed. It was a regular drill night for several squadrons and the pilots of Northwest Airlines were on one of their frequent strikes against the airline. Since they had nothing else to do and since the drill would put a few dollars in their pockets there was heavy attendance. Some of the more junior Northwest pilots had heavy hearts just contemplating a long strike and wondering where they would come up with the necessary operating funds that would pay all of the recurrent bills their families had obligated them to pay. One such poor soul wandered into the bar with his cover squarely atop his head. His mind was far removed from his body trying desperately to solve the weighty problems confronting him. He actually got three steps into the bar before one of the several thunderstruck pilots watching him could react. No one could really believe their eyes. This wasn't a newly commissioned Ensign. This was a full Lieutenant who had been around long enough to know better than to pull such a stunt, such a cardinal sin, such a travesty mocking the well established Naval custom.

A Lieutenant whose reflexes were several microseconds faster than any of the others started shouting, "Ring the bell! Ring the bell! Ring the fucking bell!" Some other mobile officer grabbed the bell's clapper and started ringing it like it had not been rung for several years. The poor soul who had left his cover on actually looked around to see who was so unfortunate as to have caused such a ruckus. Then, as realization dawned on him he glanced upward once as if to confirm to himself that he was the causative factor. A look of shock and dismay came over his face as he saw that he was the sinner and stood to lose an inordinate amount of money if he had to buy drinks for everyone in the crowded bar. As the mass of pilots surged toward him he turned suddenly and sprinted away in panic followed by several howling pilots. He was like a greyhound after a mechanical rabbit. No one was able to keep up with him let alone catch him. Kruger silently cheered him on, hoping that he was able to get away unscathed. A Northwest pilot on strike could ill afford to pay for all those drinks.

`The Marines were a constant and unrelenting source of humor for the pilots who frequented the bar at Glenview. Kruger loved watching their antics and took the grief they gave all Naval Officers with good humor. It was a normal way for hard working, hard playing pilots to blow off steam and only the self-important prig would take offense.

One Saturday evening the club had booked a small four-piece band to entertain the officers and their ladies. A few of the Marines from the Marine helo squadron had started a little early to celebrate. A favorite football game was offered on the communal TV in the bar and the Marines, five in number, were thoroughly enjoying themselves watching the game and drinking an occasional beer. They were bothering no one. They had made sure that their flights were scheduled early and had worked their tails off in completing them. Now they were playing.

Sometime after the fourth (or was it the tenth?) beer one of the stalwart helo pilots observed that the jukebox located in the bar area was not in use. Accordingly he obtained change from the bar and fed numerous coins into the machine. He selected a few choice tunes and settled back to listen in comfort. His buddies were more interested in the game than in any music the more introspective Marine wanted to hear. The game was in the fourth quarter and things were getting heated up. The Marines were also getting heated up and occasional roars were heard. The music lover was therefore forced to turn up the music. He had experienced this problem at some prior time and knew exactly how to proceed. He pulled the jukebox away from the wall and turned it up using the small knob on the back of the machine. He was forced to repeat this several times in order to hear his choices of tunes, most of which sounded like they had originated in a small mountain area of West Virginia.

Inevitably some senior officer took offense at the noise level emanating from the jukebox. Also, inevitably, the senior officer had to be a Naval Officer. The Commander had entered the bar in the company of three other people, two of which were female, and had observed that the noise from the jukebox coupled with the TV was interfering with what he was saying to his friends. Since a Commander's observations and comments are normally extremely interesting and important it seemed that the correct thing to do was to attenuate the noise from the offending jukebox. Unfortunately he chose to do so by summarily pulling the plug on the box without a by-your-leave, effectively cutting off all noise whatsoever.

Once the music-loving Marine realized that his beloved arias had been shut off he did what any innovative Marine would do. He sought the reason for the sudden silence. He discovered the sabotage immediately and being a peace-loving person he didn't seek revenge but merely re-plugged the machine back in and fed more change into it. In all fairness he did turn the volume up all the way, quaintly referred to in Naval terminology as "two-blocking" the volume, that quaint name referring to the sailing ship custom of hauling on the block and tackle attached to the sails until the two blocks or "pulleys" were touching each other signifying that any further movement would be impossible. Being an astute person he realized that a saboteur was afoot so, to prevent a reoccurrence, he enlisted the services of two of his buddies to stand watch over the machine. They were standing guard when the Commander arrived on scene again to do away with the din emanating from the jukebox. Of course, an argument erupted as the Commander refused to recognize the rights of the person who had fed the money into the machine to listen to what he termed music. The Commander became insulting and said something about "hillbilly noise passing as music". This remark was offensive to the Marines who considered "hillbilly country" to be the last bastion of freedom in the United States. The arguments elevated in both pitch and volume and threatened to drown out the jukebox noise. Things were rapidly coming to a head when the little four-piece band arrived on the scene.

The bandleader saw immediately that his combo would never be able to compete with the jukebox so he adroitly bypassed the Marine guard, who were engrossed in defending their rights against the Commander, and pulled the plug on the machine. The sudden silence was so deafening that it got the attention of the Marines who, warriors that they were, abandoned the non-threatening Commander to fight on a more serious front. One should know that Marines always advance toward the sound of fighting or gunfire. As the band set up for their performance the Marines each grabbed a chair and sat directly in front of the band with their knees touching the knees of the band members. They were hard to ignore but the bandleader, being wise in the ways of nightclubs, did his best to do so. He counted off for his combo, "Ah one, ah two, ah three . . ." and started to play. Just as the first notes of the band began the Marines jumped to their feet in unison and began to count cadence as if they were on a drill field. Their strident voices rang out, "Harrall-Ep Two Three, Arrell Ep Ri Lep, Harrall-Ep Two Three . . .". They completely drowned out the band. The combo members stopped playing and looked to their leader.

"OK, guys, OK. We give up. What do we have to do to get you to leave us alone?"

The Marines were men of action. They immediately had an answer. "You got to play the 'Marine Corps Hymn'," was the only option. The bandleader nodded and turned to his combo who played the Hymn. Everyone in the club was required to stand as the Hymn was played. No shirkers were allowed. In all fairness by now no one was willing to throw themselves into the path of the Marine juggernaut now that it had begun to roll. After the Marine Hymn everyone applauded and sat down. The bandleader thought that enough penance had been paid so he started to introduce the combo members. He was immediately interrupted by one of the Marines, apparently the one from West Virginia who was still smarting from the slights of the Commander.

"Naw, Y'ain't done yet. Y'all got ta play the Yaller Dog Blues".

The bandleader didn't agree. He tried to ignore the Marine. No one had ever explained to him that that particular feat was very nearly an impossibility. He tried to speak into a wireless microphone but the Marine he was trying to ignore took it away from him and, using the band leader's face as a lever, seated him unceremoniously into his seat. Then, with the mike in his possession, the Marine mounted the small platform, faced the audience and shouted into the mike.

"Y'all know why they cain't circumcise Squids?" he shouted.

"No, why?" his buddies all roared.

"'Cause there ain't no end to them pricks," he shouted back.

There were gasps from the females present and roars from the males, most of whom were Naval Officers or "Squids" to the Marines. Here and there were heard sounds of laughter from those "squids" who were open minded enough to appreciate the Marine humor. All thoughts of the little combo had evaporated. The Marines had the high ground.

The club manager tried to amend things but they had deteriorated to the point of no return. Most of the couples were leaving, the band had already packed up and the Marines and the remaining squids were engaged in a friendly but raucous give and take as each sought to refresh their drink orders. The manager panicked and called the Officer of the Day.

Kruger was delighted with the turn of events. Once again the Marines had jumped into the breach and had turned a boring evening into an aviator's delight. He was discussing the events with another aviator when the Assistant OOD showed up. This officer was a very young Lieutenant junior grade who possessed "coke bottle bottom" thick glasses. He was tasked with the job of either calming the Marines down or removing them from the club. Both tasks were akin to Hercules cleaning out the Aeolian stables. The term "impossible" comes to mind. When Kruger left the club the little Ltjg was standing at attention while a Marine in civilian clothes read him the riot act. Each word the Marine spoke was punctuated by punching his index finger forcibly into the chest of the AOOD.

"Who (poke) the hell (poke) do YOU (poke) think you are? YOU (poke) can't kick ME (poke) out of MY (poke) club and if YOU (poke) want to know MY (poke) name it's MAJOR (poke) JACK (poke) SMITH (poke) and furthermore FUCK (poke) YOU (poke)."

The diminutive AOOD was totally cowed. He stood at attention and kept saying, "Sir, why are you abusing me like this? I was sent here to see you out of the club. It's not my idea, Sir." The AOOD was also outnumbered. The rest of the Marines had surrounded him and punctuated the Major's finger pokes with growls and loud "Yeah, what the Major said!" Kruger walked away shaking his head in amusement. He loved these rough and rowdy guys.

The club continued to be . . . . well, the club. Kruger was observant and found that the bartender was stealing from the club. He was doing so by bringing his own bottle of whiskey or vodka and pouring out of it. Then he would pocket the money the bar charged for a drink. He kept the bottles under the counter and poured from them whenever he thought no one was looking. Kruger got an audience with the station Commanding Officer and informed him of his findings. The CO sighed and told Kruger, "Yeah, I know he's ripping the bar off. Thanks for telling me anyway." Kruger left wondering just what hold the bartender had over the station. The incident merely cemented Kruger's dislike for the club in general. It seemed to occupy an inordinate amount of time and effort relative to its position in the Naval Air Station.

CHAPTER VI

Kruger was in class again. It seemed that flying was one classroom after another. This time it was a systems class on the Boeing 707. The 707 was an old airplane. It was soon to be replaced with newer planes but for now it was the biggest plane Northwest had and so was the highest paying plane a pilot could fly. Kruger went through the sequence of classroom studies, simulator flights and finally airplane flights culminating with a flight check and an oral quiz. Finally he was released to the line as a line pilot.

The plane had its own unique flight patterns and layovers. Since it was a long range plane Kruger got his fill of layovers in Anchorage, Alaska, Seattle, Washington, Miami, Florida, New York's Kennedy airport and Dulles in Washington, DC. It was much less hectic than flying a 727 as the legs were longer and there was plenty of time to get ready for the next approach and landing. Kruger was flying as a Flight Engineer on this plane initially.

A few months previously the pilots had endured a long strike against Northwest. When the strike was over not all of the pilots were rehired. The pilot's union, ALPA, took a poll in order to find out how many of the pilots would contribute some money toward funding those pilots until they could get back on board once again. The majority of the pilots voted "yes' but there were a few penurious ones who didn't want to contribute anything to the unfortunate few who were currently out of a job.

One day Kruger was on a plane that had been dispatched with no autopilot. Normally every plane flew on autopilot since it was usually more comfortable for the passengers and it actually was more efficient and thus less costly for the company. Sometimes it was necessary to dispatch a plane without one due to backups in the engineering and repair sections of the company. This was one of those days.

Commercial pilots have gotten lazy over the ages and do not like to fly without the autopilot. The crew Kruger was with was no exception. As soon as the plane was at cruise altitude the Captain turned to Kruger and said, "OK, Second Officer Kruger, you and I are going to trade seats. You are going to fly this plane until we get to our destination." Everyone was cognizant of the prohibition against anyone but the Captain occupying the left seat. Nevertheless, Kruger moved to the left seat and flew the plane by hand. He also had to keep track of the Second Officer's panel since the Captain was enjoying himself and didn't really know how to schedule the systems like Kruger did. Everything went well and when they got near their destination they traded seats once again and the Captain landed.

On the next leg the copilot, Jack Harless, pushed his seat back and said, "My turn", expecting Kruger to trade seats with him since this was his "leg". Kruger grinned at the Captain and said, "Your turn what?"

Harless said, "Aren't you going to fly for me on this leg?" Kruger replied, "Nope, you can fly your leg all by yourself. You probably need the experience anyway."

Harless was what was known by the rest of the pilots as a FLAP. As previously described, that meant that he was a non-military type. Harless had also refused to chip in for the pilots who were still on the street.

Harless thought that Kruger was joking with him. He said, "You mean you are going to give up a chance to actually fly instead of sitting in the Second Officer's seat?"

Kruger replied, "Hell, Harless, I'm military. I've probably got more pilot time than you have. I don't need the time."

Harless disgustedly said, "You did it for the Captain; why not for me?"

Kruger said, "I won't fly for you because you're a cheap screw. You won't chip in for the laid-off pilots, most of whom are military and friends of mine." The Captain was, by now, thoroughly enjoying the give and take and was laughing at Harless.

Harless complained and griped and finally said, "OK, I'll contribute on the next go around."

Kruger grinned and said, "Why should I trust a cheap screw like you to keep your word? When you get a notarized statement from ALPA certifying that you have contributed I'll fly for you; not before."

Harless griped the whole trip but had to fly anyway whenever it was his leg. Kruger didn't feel sorry for him. He had always been overly impressed with himself.

Harless seemed incapable of telling a joke unless it was pointed at someone. He delighted in telling jokes to the Flight Attendants making Kruger the butt of those jokes. On one flight two Flight Attendants were taking a break in the cockpit. Harless was, as always, being a "funny man" and telling jokes at the expense of Kruger who ignored hm. Finally Kruger said, "Say ladies, do you know what a FLAP is?" Harless got a little red in the face as the girls giggled and said that they didn't know exactly what a FLAP was although Kruger suspected that they did. He said, "Well, you see, most military pilots have named guys who were not in the military that. It translates roughly to 'Funny Light Airplane Pilot'. I've cleaned it up a bit for you."

Harless was quite red by now as he gritted his teeth and waited for the punch line. Kruger smiled and continued, "Do you girls know that Harless here is a FLAP?" The girls laughed and said "No". Kruger finally administered the coup-de-grace by saying, "That's why we all call him 'Flap Jack'." The girls were openly laughing by now and Harless was silent for once. He was known as "Flap Jack" for the rest of the trip.

Harless was a young civilian pilot. He had never been in the military and had been treated to the wonderful experience of being hired onto a large airline early on. He cut a wide swath among the Flight Attendants and was not above bragging about his sexual conquests with the young impressionable girls who were just out of high school. He finally married a beautiful young lady and the marriage seemed to be a "made in heaven" one except that Jack couldn't seem to keep his trousers zipped up when it came to the girls. He jumped in and out of bed with any and all and had no commitment to anyone. The Flight Attendants soon figured him out and had contempt for him although that attitude was lost on him as he continued to try to entice anyone he could into his bed.

Some of the Flight Attendants, in an attempt to get revenge on Jack for his foibles, told his new wife about how they had jumped into bed with him but she refused to believe any of them. Finally, another pilot sweet-talked her into his bed and she, feeling guilty, confessed to her husband. Kruger was flying with Harless on his next trip after the confession.

Harless was openly vociferous in his denunciation of his wife. He told Kruger that he was going to divorce her. Kruger laughed at him and said, "Go ahead. What you'll do is to make about a hundred other pilots happy as hell. They'll all thank you for freeing her for anyone else to grab her. What you don't realize is that you are married to a beautiful, wonderful young lady who fell for someone's enticement, just like you have been doing for years to all of the other Flight Attendants. She probably did that because you were off running around with some other lady and not paying any attention to her. I'll guarantee that a lot of other pilots will pay lavish attention to her. She won't be hurt and will have more attention than you can imagine. You are more stupid than anyone I have ever met. Go ahead and divorce her. You'll end up paying for all of her dates for years and a lot of pilots will be ever grateful to you."

Harless blinked and said, "What do you think I should do?" Kruger said, "I would buy her a dozen red roses and send them to her on your next layover along with a nice note that said that you love her more than anything and that you understand why she did what she did." There followed a long conversation about the double standard and what Harless had been doing for years while he was married to his wife.

On the next layover Harless reported that he had done exactly as Kruger had suggested. As far as Kruger knew the marriage continued.

*   *   *

The pressurization on the 707 was unique as far as Kruger was concerned. The air was compressed by a combination of turbo-compressors called "TCs" and engine bleeds. An engine bleed was a system of robbing the engine of air that was normally used for combustion and thrust to keep the plane in the air. The turbo compressors "packed" air into the system without stealing it from the engines. There were TCs on engines 1, 2 and 3. Engine number 4 had only a bleed. Any engine could be "bled" to use that air for pressurization and air conditioning.

The "lower 41" area was an area containing most of the electronics and electrical items necessary for the operation of the plane. It was accessible from the cockpit by a trap door that allowed a pilot to drop down into the "hell hole" in order to affect any repairs that became necessary. Since the lower 41 contained a lot of electronics it was normally hot. In order to cool the area off Boeing had installed a fan that operated whenever the pressurization/air conditioning was not functional, as on the ground. Unfortunately the fan operated too well and would evacuate the air in the cabin when the plane was on the ground and the pressurization was not being used. That meant that the cabin pressure would shift into the negative millibars and passengers would feel an unpleasant pressure change on their ears. To allay this, the Flight Engineer/Second Officer would pull the circuit breaker to the evacuation fan prior to shutting off all of the TCs and engine bleeds. When the plane was docked at the ramp the ground crew would open the lower 41 door in the bottom of the plane. Then and only then could the Second Officer reset the circuit breaker allowing the fan to operate and cool the hellhole without the unpleasant pressure bump assaulting the ears of the passengers.

The Second Officer always conducted the preflight that was necessary before each flight. One of the crucial things on the preflight was to ensure that the hellhole hatch located on the lower part of the fuselage was open. This was so that the sequence on the start of engines and the pressurization operation would ensure that no pressurization "bump" would be felt by the passengers. On the airplane pushback the engines would be started, the evacuation fan circuit breaker would be pulled, the hatch would be closed by the ground crew and the TCs would then be placed on line after which the evac fan CB would be reset once again. It was always done this way and, because of this, Murphy's Law was set for operation.

On one of Kruger's flight patterns he was the Second Officer on a Boeing 707 that had the ability to monitor the outflow valves along with the TC input. This particular plane was a snap for a flight engineer since there was plenty of information displayed on the Second Officer's panel. On pushback Kruger went through his normal pattern and soon had a TC online in order to pressurize the plane for takeoff. As the air source came online Kruger saw a slight pressure bump as he expected to see. The big plane made the takeoff and was soon climbing rapidly to altitude. Kruger saw immediately that something was wrong. The cabin was climbing at the same rate as the plane, around 5 or 6000 feet a minute. It was uncomfortable on the ears to Kruger who was used to fast rates of climb. He could imagine that the passengers were upset with the rapid climb rate.

He scanned the engineer's panel. Obviously something was wrong but he couldn't see just what. He placed another TC online. It had no effect. In desperation he placed a third TC and finally an engine bleed online. As he tried to troubleshoot the system a warning horn began to honk. The Captain turned to him and asked, "What the hell is that horn? What's it mean?"

"Level off, level off!" Kruger blurted. "If you don't all of the oxygen masks will drop." At 10,000 feet cabin altitude a warning horn would sound and at 12,000 feet all of the passenger oxygen masks would drop out of the overhead and the Flight Attendants would make sure that each passenger had a mask on and was breathing oxygen. It wasn't a scenario Kruger wanted to contemplate.

The Captain cleared the level off with the center and the plane leveled at 10,000 feet. He turned to Kruger and asked, "What's the problem?" Kruger told him and said, "I can't figure out what's wrong. I'm putting air in the cabin but I can't pressurize."

The Captain shook his head and said, "Well, go over the checklist again. Maybe you missed something." He turned around dismissing Kruger. In desperation once again Kruger grabbed the checklist and began to read. When he got to the pressurization and air conditioning system he read, "packs . . . . PACKS!" He had neglected to turn on the packs.

The packs were the series of air exchangers, heat exchangers and air cleaners that pack air into the plane's cabin monitored by the outflow valves that allow the plane to become pressurized. This allowed the plane to fly at altitudes of up to 39,000 feet while the cabin was maintained at a comfortable 5,000. The control toggle switches for the packs had not been turned on.

Kruger quickly flipped the three toggles to the "on" position and the plane immediately pressurized. The problem was that Kruger had not turned off any of the air sources prior to pressurizing. The cabin went from an ambient 10,000 feet to around 1,500 feet in about three seconds. Kruger winced as his ears equalized. He felt sorry for the civilian passengers who weren't used to pressurization changes of this magnitude.

The cockpit door popped open and an irate Flight Attendant appeared. "What the hell is wrong with the pressurization?" she rapped. Kruger tried to explain but she flounced out of the cockpit slamming the door behind her in an expression of what she thought of Second Officers who screwed up the pressurization. Kruger shook his head. Sometimes you win and sometimes you lose. Kruger felt like the dumbest goat around as a result of his screw up.

One day Kruger's plane was redispatched to a station that a 707 never operated out of. A 727 had become inoperable and the passengers had to be taken out by the next plane available, which was the 707 that Kruger was on. Kruger paid particular attention to the operating procedures as they landed on the strange field. During the preflight Kruger noticed that the ground crew had not opened the hellhole hatch so he opened it as per operating instructions.

When the passengers were aboard and the engines were started the push back was accomplished. On taxi out Kruger noticed that when he placed a TC on line there was no noticeable bump in the cabin pressure but he ignored it except to notice it. The crew obtained clearance and made the take off without incident. Kruger immediately saw that something was wrong. The cabin was climbing just as fast as the airplane. Something was obviously wrong. Kruger alerted the rest of the crew and kept working on the panel. He soon had 3 TCs and a bleed trying to pressurize the plane but nothing seemed to work. The cabin was still climbing at the same rate as the plane, a clear indication that the plane was not pressurized. Kruger could hear the air coming into the plane but nothing would pressurize it. He thought, "You dumb shit! You did it again." He reached for the pack switches but they were already on.

At 10,000 feet the cabin warning horn sounded. Kruger shouted, "Level off or the masks will drop." At 10,000 feet cabin pressure the horn would sound. At 12,000 feet all of the oxygen masks would drop out of the cabin overhead for the passengers. The Captain leveled off and notified the center.

"What the hell's wrong?" the Captain asked.

"I don't know," Kruger replied. "I'm putting all of the air I can into the plane but it's all going out just as fast as it's coming in. There must be a huge leak somewhere."

"Well, where the hell is it?" the Captain asked.

"Damned if I know," Kruger answered. He was still smarting over the last time he had screwed up the pressurization. "Are there any openings shown in the copilot's enunciator panel?" The copilot had a panel near his right knee that showed any of the openings on the plane. The copilot punched his "test" button. One of the little windows was blank.

"If a light is burned out on the enunciator panel is it blank when I test it?" the copilot asked. Normally the tiny light rectangles would either show or "enunciate" a hatch or hole in the airplane or, if the little window was not being used, it would show a straight line indicating that it was not in use. The window was never "blank".

"Damn, it has to be the hellhole door," Kruger said. "It's the only hatch that was operated other than a passenger door on that last landing. The annunciator window is burned out."

"What can you do about it?" the Captain asked.

Kruger immediately said, "Shove your seat forward. I have to get down the hellhole door to the lower 41." The Captain did as he was asked and Kruger dropped down into the bowels of the 707. It was dirty and he tore his shirt in the process. He walked aft and immediately saw the problem. The lower 41 external hatch was open. The ground crew had not closed it as they had not been trained to do that on the 707, an airplane that they had never been trained to service. Air roared through the hatch propelled by the 3 TCs and the engine bleed. It was an awesome sight. Kruger could see the small landscape 10,000 feet below, the tiny houses, the miniscule cars. The hatch was two and a half feet on each side. Kruger could feel the inexorable pull of the air through the hatch propelled by four large engines.

He popped back up through the flight deck hatch and stood with only his chest and head exposed. "It's the hellhole hatch. It's open. We can't possibly pressurize with it open."

"Do you want to dump fuel and go back and land?" the Captain asked.

Now think about that a little. The Captain has all of the information available concerning the problem. He is the Captain of the airplane; the person who is totally in charge of the situation. And now he asks the most junior pilot on the flight deck as to what he wishes to do about the problem.

"We'd have to dump thousands of pounds of fuel," Kruger replied. "I think I can close the hatch if the copilot will catch the pressure bump when the hatch slams shut."

"Are you sure?" the Captain asked. "You know we don't furnish parachutes on these flights."

"Yeah, I can get a pretty good handhold on a stanchion down there. I don't think I'll get spit out of the plane."

"OK, if you're quite sure," the Captain replied. He relaxed and continued to fly the plane on autopilot. The copilot unbuckled and sat in the Second Officers seat. Normally the plane's outflow valves would control the pressurization making the interior of the plane comfortable but now the large lower 41 hatch was overriding the smaller outflow valves and controlling everything. The plan was for the copilot to monitor the outflow valves and try to control the large pressure "bump" when the hatch was closed by Kruger. The hellhole hatch was five times the size of the outflow valves.

The Captain held the plane at 10,000 feet while Kruger crawled into the lower 41 space. The closer he got to the open hatch the more he could feel the pull of the air leaving the ship. Kruger made sure that he had a good hold on a substantial piece of the plane as he made his way aft. The inexorable pull of the airflow increased with each foot as he slowly made his way toward the yawning open space. The roar of the air flowing through the hatch and the pull of the air was mesmerizing. He could make out the tiny figures two miles below the plane and shook his head to keep from being mesmerized by the panorama below. He took a deep breath and leaned over the large hole trying to ignore the roar of the air pulling everything out of the plane as it screamed outside. He fumbled and found the latch that held the hatch open and finally released it making sure that he had a firm grip on a stanchion.

The hatch suddenly released, popped closed twice bouncing against the air flowing around the plane and then slammed shut. Kruger winced and opened his mouth coughing to equalize the sudden pressure pop as the plane pressurized at altitude. The poor copilot didn't stand a chance. He hadn't turned off any of the TCs and Kruger hadn't thought to tell him to do so. Three TCs and an engine bleed pumped a huge volume of air into the plane all of a sudden and the cabin went from 10,000 feet to around 1800 feet in about two seconds. Needless to say it was painful on the ears of everyone in the plane.

Kruger climbed back into the cockpit. Both of the other pilots were shaking their heads and using the Valsalva method of clearing their ears and Eustachian tubes. Kruger grinned and said, "Well, if anyone on the plane had any problems with their sinuses they sure don't now." The cockpit door slammed open and a Flight Attendant shouted, "Now what the hell is wrong with the pressurization?"

For some reason Kruger thought that the whole thing was humorous. Maybe it was because he had just done something very exhilarating; something that few other pilots would have done. He had risked his neck in order to save the company a few thousand gallons of fuel and plenty of time that all translated into money. He knew that he would never get as much as a handshake for his pains but the rush of doing something like he had done was its own reward. He was still laughing when he told the Flight Attendant, "Nothing is wrong with the pressurization. It's working just fine. Couldn't you feel it?" The Flight Attendant's slamming the cockpit door said mountains about just what she thought about the whole thing. The whole incident was totally ignored by Northwest Orient Airlines.

The 707 was the senior airplane on the Northwest system and, as such, the senior pilots all flew it. Kruger had long been amused by the old Northwest saying that a "good trip" was when the Second Officer found a ten dollar bill, the copilot got laid and the captain had a bowel movement. The saying said wonders about the relative ages of the three. Kruger liked the long trips on the plane and especially he liked the flights to Alaska. He liked flying with one pilot in particular, Austen Lytle. This pilot had told the same old jokes for years and the Flight Attendants all knew them. Normally they would finish the punch lines for him while he clucked in disgust. He had flown the route for so long that he had copied all of the center frequencies down and had them all on a small card that he kept in his top pocket. When he thought that the copilot wasn't looking he would pull the little card out of his pocket, glance at the next frequency and then, a few minutes later, would tell the copilot, "In about a minute now the center will tell us to change to frequency 124.6." He always hoped that the copilot would be impressed with his phenomenal memory but the copilot, having been briefed by another pilot in advance, would just grin and nod. Let the old man have his fun. Austen used to don a Mandarin hat and stick an opium pipe in his mouth when he was parked at Anchorage. The deplaning people could look into the cockpit and see their captain who, by now, looked like a Chinese junky. Austen thought that it was a lot of fun.

The meal service on the Alaska flights was superb. Reindeer steaks, Eggs Benedict, prime rib, caviar, Champaign and all the trimmings. It was a meal or two fit for a king. There was always much more food than the passengers could eat since Northwest Orient, at that time, boarded enough food for selections for everyone. When the passengers were satisfactorily stuffed and the Flight Attendants had eaten they would bring up all of the food that was left for the pilots. Kruger smiled one day when a Flight Attendant came to the cockpit and saw the pilots sitting amid copious amounts of food with the plane on autopilot. She took the scenery in and said, "I could be a pilot too, just like you guys. It doesn't look all that hard."

Flying with the senor pilots took certain patience. Some of those guys were very good; some were very bad. Most of the bad ones were Midwest farmers who had stumbled into flying a long time ago. They had been flying as Captain for so long that they had forgotten their past and now thought that they had the answers to everything. They were victims of their own public relations and believed everything they heard about the omnipotence of Captains.

One winter night Kruger was flying with a crew over the northern portion of the United States. It was long after midnight and the Northern Lights were making a spectacular display in the northern hemisphere. The three pilots stared in awe at the display and finally the Captain said, "I wonder what makes that?"

Kruger answered, "It's due to a magnetic disturbance in the ionosphere."

The Captain looked back at the Second Officer in disdain, "The ionosphere? That's way up there isn't it?"

"Yes, sir, it's almost in outer space."

"Well, that's just plain bullshit. We're here at 37,000 feet and you can readily see that those lights, whatever the hell they are, are below us."

Kruger remained silent. He figured that the Captain wouldn't listen to any argument about the curvature of the earth or how the "lights" were thousands of miles away. There was no way you could educate a man who had made a statement like that. The earth was flat and that was that. Kruger remained silent and the Captain remained smug in his vast knowledge.

The older pilots, especially the Captains, were sensitive about their hearing and eyesight. That fact wasn't surprising considering that their eyesight and hearing was paramount to their continued employment as a pilot. They were so protective of their facilities that it was amusing. One of the Captains that everyone liked used to wander down to the flight office at O'Hare. He would ask for something, say "hello" to everyone and finally pick up the telephone.

"Say, can someone patch me into Minneapolis?" he would ask.

The crew who manned the O'Hare station all knew the Captain and they all knew that he needed his glasses (that he seldom wore) to see. Everyone in the O'Hare office would grin and finally someone would say, "Just dial the number. It's 656, wait for the dial tone and dial 343-2254."

The Captain would turn red and say, "Can't someone just patch me in?"

"We don't have time. We're all too busy." Everyone would be looking at their desks trying to hide their grins.

Finally the Captain would grumble, "Awright, awright, goddamn it." and fumble for his glasses. Once they were on he could see to dial the phone number. When he had done so the massed assembly at O'Hare would all burst into laughter. The Captain would usually grin, as he knew that he had been outwitted. It was all good fun.

The lack of hearing was pretty easy to hide. Most flight physicals stressed sight and not hearing. Some of the older Captains were pretty well stone deaf. Kruger flew with one who was well liked around the system but who relied on his cockpit crew to give him cues to what was going on around him relative to sound. One day a Flight Attendant came into the cockpit. She was what is popularly known as an African-American female. She breezed into the cockpit and professionally asked, "Good morning, gentlemen. My name is Babs. May I get you anything to drink?" There were the usual requests for coffee and a few pleasantries were exchanged. Babs slid smoothly out of the cockpit.

As the flight attendant left the Captain turned to the Second Officer and said, "Stabs? What the hell kind of name is that?" Kruger rolled up into a ball laughing at the thought that the Captain had harbored the idea that black people all carried a knife or a razor. That thought had been extant for decades; in fact Kruger had grown up in an era where the idea was taken as gospel. In questioning the old Captain Kruger ascertained that he did, in fact, believe that all black people carried some sort of a knife. Kruger assured the Captain that he did, in fact, carry a knife and always had and that he, Kruger, was not black. That fact did nothing to relax the Captain who observed, relative to Babs Afro hairdo, that going to bed with her would be "like sticking it into a brillo pad". Kruger laughingly told the Captain that he didn't have to worry about going to bed with the flight attendant.

The 707 was being phased out rapidly. It was being replaced by the DC-10. Kruger had a choice of being a DC10 Second Officer or a 727 copilot. He opted for the copilot's seat and, again, had to go through training for the right seat on that aircraft. The training period was pleasant as it was done in the airplane. Simulators were not up to par as yet and did not fly anything like a plane. They were mainly used as procedures trainers during this period. Kruger was posted to a motel in Kansas where a few instructors and a few 727s were kept in order to train copilots and new Captains. The pay was nice and the duty was optimal. Salina, Kansas was a target rich environment for predatory pilots looking for pretty women who, in turn, were looking for adventure and excitement. Airline pilots offered all of that and more. Kruger felt sorry for the girls in "fly-over country". They didn't stand a chance.

After Salina, Kruger was posted to Miami, Florida for training. What could be nicer? The weather, motel, nightlife and flying were all superb. This was what flying for the airline was all about. The instructors were more like friends than instructors. They were professional but still more like military pilots than civilian types. Why not? They had mostly only been out of the military for a few years and identified more with the military than the civilian field. Kruger felt entirely relaxed with this environment and wondered sometimes, just why he had ever left the military. He never felt completely comfortable in this civilian field. He missed the camaraderie and the discipline of the military. This flying with ex-military pilots was comfortable and pleasant.

One evening Kruger and one of his classmates, a superb pilot named Jon Wood, decided to do a little bar hopping. They wandered along a strip in Miami and soon found a nice bar that looked clean and inviting. They wandered in and ordered a beer. After a few pulls on their beer and a few cursory comments they started looking around. A few civilians were watching a lewd movie on a large screen deeper in the bar. As time passed the movie and the comments of the civilians watching it became disturbing. Finally Kruger made a comment to the bar tender who expressed surprise. "Don't you guys know you're in a gay bar?" Kruger and Jon looked at each other and sat their beer down. They left to the tune of shouts of, "Hey, you're leaving early". Once on the street Jon said, "Jesus, Kruger, you always go to bars like that?" This devolved into a regular Navy spat involving regular Navy terminology. Civilians ran for cover and mothers sheltered their babies. The night was a complete success.

Kruger was coupled later with an ex-Navy pilot who flew fighter-bombers on active duty. Jim Karg was an excellent pilot and both Jim and Kruger flew with a senior instructor pilot with Northwest. Jim was senior to Kruger so he always flew first. Since each pilot undergoing training flew for two hours by the time Kruger flew the heat emanating from the Fort Lauderdale area, where they were training, had made the air surrounding the area unstable and the result was a bumpy, turbulent flight. This wasn't an ideal time for flying precision ILS approaches to Fort Lauderdale International Airport.

Kruger concentrated on flying the instrument approaches but wasn't happy with the results. The instructor remained silent but Kruger got the impression that he wasn't too happy with the approaches either. On one approach the instructor said, "The weather for this approach is 200 feet ceiling and ½ mile visibility. Shoot the approach like you would on line." He placed a large piece of cardboard in front of Kruger so as to obscure his visibility. Kruger knuckled down and concentrated on flying the instruments. When the airplane was down to 200 feet the instructor called "200 feet" and shut up. Kruger was expecting the instructor to tell him when to break off the approach. The instructor was expecting Kruger to execute the missed approach procedure at 200 feet. There was no communication between the two pilots. Kruger was quite comfortable flying at 200 feet. As an Anti-submarine Warfare pilot he normally flew his plane at 200 feet and often went down to 100 feet or lower. This was not the name of the game here but Kruger didn't realize it and the instructor didn't communicate it. When Kruger flew in the Navy the name of the game was "get aboard". The instructor called, "I've got the plane"; a call that usually signaled that the pilot being trained had somehow screwed up. Kruger was crushed. He did what he normally did and went over the approach in detail. He realized what the instructor pilot wanted but by this time it was too late. They flew in silence to Miami and home.

Once they got home the instructor turned to Kruger. "I'm not going to give a down to a Navy pilot who has carrier qualified. I hope you've learned from this and will "go around" the next time you get to minimums and nobody says anything." Kruger finally realized just what the game was here. It hadn't been discussed prior to this time but he finally knew that at minimums if no one said anything the premise was that no one had the field in sight and the presumption was that the plot flying should execute a "wave-off" in Navy terms or a "go-around" in civilian terms. Now that he knew the parameters of the game he could play it as well as anyone. A "go-around" was mandatory anytime no one said anything during an approach at minimums. He wouldn't repeat this mistake. A week later Kruger was a qualified copilot and was on his way back to Minneapolis.

Kruger never forgot the checkout or the instructor who forgave his screw-up during a training ILS approach. He had cut his teeth on Navy GCA's and thought that the name of the game was to "get aboard". He now knew that he had to rethink all of his ideas and adhere strictly to the FAR rules. The old rules about getting home and debriefing were out of the window. The name of the game now was to fly by the rules and to fly safely.

*   *   *

Kruger had been attending collage while he sat on reserve as a copilot. He had long been interested in biology and interviewed with the head of the College of Bioscience at the University of Minnesota. When he presented his case the professor said that he could take any courses he wished either for credit or to audit the courses after Kruger told him that he only wished to gain more knowledge and had no intention of competing with the college kids for employment. Kruger alternated between animal and plant biology but finally settled on non-vascular plants with emphasis on marine algae.

He had subscribed to a rather obscure publication that attempted to keep all bioscience majors tuned to what other disciplines were doing. One day he read that a professor from the University of South Florida had written about a marine algae (seaweed) that contained a very useful phycocolloid. It was called Eucuma isoform. The colloid it contained was used in just about everything we wear, eat or use. It was a solidifying agent and was used in anything that was not pure liquid. Currently it was only obtained from the Sulu Sea in the Philippines but E. isoform grew in the Florida Keys.

When he read the article and reread it several times he had a brainchild. What if he moved to south Florida, got dive qualified, bought a boat and found where the stuff grew? He did some research and found that no one else had even thought of doing something like that. He called the professor who wrote the article and that learned gentleman said that he couldn't understand why no one had done just that. Kruger thought that he knew the answer to that. How many people with money and time subscribed to a relatively unknown publication like the one the article appeared in?

Kruger broached the subject to his wife who was all for moving to south Florida, never mind the idea of some crummy seaweed. Kruger found a dive instructor who ran a dive shop in the Minneapolis area and contracted for a private, intensive course in scuba diving. The instructor made sure that Kruger was well checked out throwing a lot of emergencies at him and making sure that he could operate under pressure and the occasional thing that could go wrong. Kruger was tasked with diving to the bottom, shucking his gear, ascending to the surface and diving again to re-don all of his gear. He was subjected to harassment in donning and doffing his gear under water. It was still winter in Minnesota and Kruger passed his "final" check by diving in a local lake during a snowstorm. By that time he figured that he could handle just about anything that the gods threw at him. He had told the dive instructor that he planned on diving alone, something that was severely frowned upon by all divers. Kruger had no partner and his wife would have nothing to do with his plans.

Things worked pretty well as planned and six months later Kruger had a new home in Naples, Florida. He lost no time in finding, buying and outfitting a 32 foot boat that he could live aboard temporarily.

In 1976 drug running in south Florida was rampant. It was a fairly common practice for the drug runners to hijack a suitable boat, kill the people who were aboard, use the boat for two or three runs from larger mother ships offshore and then scuttle the boat. Just about every boat chandlery in the whole area had circulars wanting to know the whereabouts of several boats and crews that had mysteriously disappeared. Kruger did his homework and armed himself with a sawed-off 12 gage shotgun loaded with number two buckshot (he thought that the dispersion pattern for that load was optimal over the 32 foot length of his boat), a 30.06 rifle loaded with armor-piercing ammo and a .357 Magnum sidearm.

Early one morning he headed south from Goodland, Florida, a small fishing village located on an island just southeast of Marco Island. The marina owner where he was birthed was awed by his plan to navigate by dead reckoning using the winds, currants and occasional visual lines of position as he neared the Florida Keys. Most of the fisherman in that area wouldn't get out of sight of land. Kruger would be on the open sea for about 7 hours on his run to Marathon in the Keys.

The weather was fine and the winds light. The twin engines purred along without any problems. Kruger had calculated the fuel required and knew that he would have an adequate reserve when he reached the fueling docks at Marathon. He soon lost any radio station except a few that only featured Spanish speaking announcers. He did have a good radio that he could use to call the coast guard if he got into trouble.

After a run of 7 hours he could finally see East Cape off of the tip of Florida. It was getting fairly late in the afternoon so he looked for a good place to anchor for the night. He was headed into shoal water and didn't relish running at night. He was soon anchored with two anchors and plenty of anchor rode. He made sure that he had anchor lights on and went below to cook dinner. After he had eaten he settled into bed in the forepeak bunks.

Late in the evening he woke up. Something was wrong. He couldn't put his finger on just what was wrong but all of a sudden he was startled by the realization that his boat was not peacefully rocking in the waves any more.

He rocketed out of his bunk, grabbed a floodlight and went on deck. He found that the boat had dragged anchors and that he was firmly stuck on a mud bank near Florida Bay. Kruger went below, got his navigational Polaris, compass, binoculars and charts and soon had plotted his position based on the navigation lights he could see. He then consulted the tidal tables he had the foresight to carry aboard and found that the 12 hour tide would not be sufficient to float him off the bank. It would take the 24 hour tide to accomplish that. He called the Coast Guard to confirm his calculations and they confirmed what he had found. They asked if he needed a tow and he declined. He figured that his 24 hour layover would be punishment for not properly anchoring or setting a watch, even if there was only one man aboard. He went back to bed but didn't sleep well.

Early the next morning he arose, had breakfast, shaved, showered and tried to keep busy doing "ship's work". He went over the side and waded to the end of the mudbank setting his largest anchor there so that he could kedge off with the first tide float. Live and learn.

He kept one eye on the clock and the other on the tide as he worked. Several boats sailed by and Kruger could imagine the people aboard them laughing at the dummy who had gone aground. His boat was canted at an awkward angle that left no doubt that Kruger was trying to sail over a mud flat. It was humiliating.

Finally, the tide started flowing in the right direction and soon Kruger could rock the boat as the water under the hull increased as did the distance between the hull and the mud. Finally Kruger decided that the boat could float and he went forward in order to throw the anchor line that was attached to his "kedge" around his anchor winch. He threw the winch in gear and was soon happily being winched toward the edge of the mud flat. His engines were running fine and as he approached the kedge he went forward once more lifting the anchor from the mud and stowing it. Moving aft to the wheel house he looked around to make sure that everything was OK, engaged the double props and the boat started to come up on the step as it rapidly moved off of the flat.

Kruger was puzzled at a loud buzz that he heard as the props engaged. Looking around he saw, to his horror, that the anchor line for the anchor that he had obviously forgotten was rapidly disappearing over the fantail. He quickly disengaged the props and stopped the engines. He took a deep breath and assessed his situation. He had forgotten the other anchor and the rode or the line to the anchor. When he engaged the props they had caught the anchor line and had wrapped it tightly around the prop shafts. There was only one fix to the problem.

Kruger suited up in his dive gear. Going over the side he submerged and slid under the boat. Claustrophobia instantly set in as the space under the boat was tight and he could have easily gotten stuck. With no one to help him he would have run out of air and suffocated. Good enough reason for the diving rule of never diving alone. Kruger drew his diving knife and started sawing at the large rat's nest of line. Adrenalin made his breathing rate increase and very soon his regulator began to "honk" as that was the audible signal that he was on his 300 pound reserve.

He surfaced, re-boarded his boat, changed air bottles and was soon over the side and under the boat once more. The sun was setting and Kruger really didn't want to cut away anchor line in the dark under his boat. He soon had freed the prop shafts and was happy to get out from under the boat.

As he re-boarded once more and stripped off his dive gear he thought, "Can anything else go wrong?" He thought about it, looked around once more, started the engines, engaged the props and was quickly on the plane as the boat flew over the surface of Florida Bay. In very few seconds he heard a banging noise. Paranoid by now he quickly shut down and made a circuit of his boat to find the source of the noise. He soon found that he had neglected, in his haste to leave the mud bank, to haul up his dive ladder. The water in his wake had hammered it against the hull destroying the $300 teak ladder. It was in shambles and totally unusable.

Kruger was completely angry with himself. He had made so many dumb mistakes and now he couldn't complete his diving survey as there was no easy way to get back aboard the boat once he had gone over the side since his boarding ladder was trashed. His diving trip was effectively scrubbed.

Evening was fast approaching and Kruger didn't want to steam for over 7 or 8 hours home in the dark so he headed for a deep section of the Gulf. When he had found approximately two fathoms of water he anchored once more. This time he had to bend a new line onto the anchor that had lost its rode due to the props. As night fell he was below deck making his dinner and preparing to go to bed. He was tired from all of the things that he had to contend with the day before. It was pretty apparent that he was a babe in the woods when it came to small boat operations away from shore. Kruger had only a candle lantern for illumination below deck as he was constantly afraid of running out of battery charge. Without batteries he couldn't start the big V-8 engines that powered his boat.

It was dark as ink when he heard and felt a bump against the hull of his boat. It felt substantial, like a log hitting his boat or something like that. It bore examination.

As Kruger cracked the hatch to the deck a little and peeped out what he saw made the little hairs on the back of his neck stand on end. A boat was alongside his. It was totally dark and just as silent. There were two men aboard it and one of them was tying a line to his lifelines. They had made no noise, no loudhailers or horns to alert Kruger that there was someone who wanted to speak to him or who wished to board his boat. This was simply not done in these waters with the drug runners around that populated this area. Kruger's adrenalin topped out as he realized that modern-day pirates were trying to board him.

Donning clothing was the last thing on his mind. Kruger grabbed his sawed off shotgun, kicked the hatch open and rolled out onto the deck. It was easier to roll out as the deck was several steps up a ladder from the cabin. Kruger was ready for war. He was naked as were his Celtic ancestors who fought naked. The only thing missing was the blue woad his ancestors coated themselves with. His roll ended up in the scuppers on his knees with his shotgun shoved rudely underneath the man's chin who was tying up to his lifelines. Kruger growled, "Say who the fuck you are or I'll blow your damned head off."

The surprised pair on the other boat immediately had their hands in the air as they yelled, "Jesus, don't shoot. Don't shoot. We're just fishermen."

Kruger didn't relax one tiny bit. He held the shotgun steady and he said, "Why are you tying up to my lifelines? Why didn't you hail? Why are you dark ship?

The man who had been tying up to Kruger's boat began to babble, "We are drift fishermen. We have a net that's drifting down onto your boat. All we wanted to do was to move you out of the way so we wouldn't lose our catch this evening."

Kruger glanced around. He saw no little lights that would normally be attached to a drift net. He kept the shotgun trained on the two as he growled, "Bullshit."

So far the man who had been behind the wheel on the other boat had remained silent but he watched Kruger with an intensity that told Kruger that he was probably the one to watch the most. Kruger never took his eyes off the pair but he finally said, "OK, get this line off my boat. Move out away from me. Start your engines and move out. If I hear your engines cough even once or if you make a move toward my boat I will open fire on you. When you get out of shotgun range I will put something a little heavier on you. If you appear at any time to be a threat I will sink you and you will have to swim ashore if you can." At that time they were about two or three miles offshore and it was dark.

When Kruger had thought about a scenario just like this he had decided that he could open fire on and kill anyone who he considered a hostile. Now that it had actually happened he found that he couldn't shoot the two who had their hands in the air. It seemed like murder to him. Make no mistake; if the two had made any overt moves that seemed threatening Kruger knew that he wouldn't hesitate to kill them. He knew, for a certainty, what they wanted and he knew that, given the opportunity, they would have killed him but for right now they were no real threat so he let them go. Much later on when he related the incident to a few Marine friends they were unanimous in their assessment that Kruger should have killed them both. As one Marine said, "Hell, Ed, them assholes will just do that to some other poor puke. They ought to be given the deep six". Kruger figured that he was right but he, Kruger, wasn't the executioner this time. The Marine said, "Just remember; if you have to shoot someone empty the gun 'cause you're going to have to clean it anyhow".

The two pirates did as Kruger asked, exactly. He had the firepower. When their boat moved someway away Kruger grabbed the 30.06 rifle and trained it on them until they disappeared in the night. When he couldn't hear their engines any more he rapidly pulled up his anchors, started his engines and moved smartly away from his old position. He knew from listening that the pirate's engines were diesels and probably couldn't match his 350 V-8 gasoline engines. Nevertheless, he wasn't going to chance another onslaught. He ran toward the Keys in the dark.

He heaved to about three miles north-west of Marathon and dropped anchor once again. He tried to get some sleep but his adrenalin levels wouldn't seem to calm down. Early the next morning at dawn he was up and running toward Marathon to fuel up.

As he ran he saw another boat that looked a little familiar. As he neared it he could see that it was the pirate's boat. He could also see that he was right in his assessment about the relative speeds of the two boats. He rapidly drew alongside the pirates and, with his loudhailer, ordered them to heave to.

By now Kruger looked like Pancho Villa. He had his sidearm on and his shotgun cradled on his right hip. His 30.06 was by his side near the wheel. The pirates heaved to as ordered. Kruger, using the loudhailer asked, "Where are you headed?" The answer was to the fuel docks at Marathon. Kruger's Navy training took over as he said, "Carry on. I'll follow you."

The two boats entered the Marathon River and soon were tied up to the fuel docks. While Kruger was readying his boat one of the pirates, the one that had the shotgun shoved under his chin, strode over to Kruger's boat. He appeared cocky. The sun was shining and there were lots of people walking around now. The pirate said, "Mister, you scared the shit out of us last night".

Kruger looked at the pirate boat. It had no nets, no fishing gear of any sort. He turned to the pirate and said, "I know exactly what you two assholes were up to last night. I remember what you look like. If you ever try something like that on me again or on anyone around me I will kill you without thinking about it. You had your last chance last night. Now you are on borrowed time." The pirate walked off without any comment.

Kruger fueled up and headed home. As he approached the Coon Key light on his way to Goodland he had a few thoughts about his last three days. The first one was that he ought to stick to flying planes instead of driving boats in waters that harbored pirates, mudflats and other things that befell novices. The second thought was that the last three days proved that his old assessment that advocated that the closest you came to death the more exciting and full life was. Danger was exhilarating even while being scary. All in all he was happy to go home, shower and have a stiff drink. His wife was disinterested in his adventure.

Chapter VII

Flying copilot was a breeze. The Second Officer always made the preflights called "walk arounds" so Kruger was now spared having to brave the winter weather outside. He did make out the flight plan, which the Captain had to sign, but that worthy gentleman rarely lowered himself to actually check the figures trusting his subordinate to get it right all of the time. Kruger had developed a well-rounded sense of survivability by this time so he wasn't as cavalier as some of the Captains. He took the job of filling out the flight plan seriously and actually worried over the fuel figures, something a few of his peers didn't take the time to do.

Most of the pilots trusted the Flight Dispatchers who worked for Northwest to catch any "mistakes" in the fuel loading. Flight Dispatch existed to ensure that the flight was conducted entirely within the guidelines of the FAA rules and that included the fuel loading along with the fuel reserves carried in order to keep from running out of kerosene in inclement weather. Most of the pilots figured that the Flight Dispatchers knew more about fuel requirements for a flight than they did so they trusted the Dispatch section to keep them safe. Kruger trusted no one where his life (or his sweet ass, as he put it) was concerned and he made absolutely sure that the fuel was adequate on all flights he flew on. Some of the Captains felt like he did and actually checked the fuel. Kruger looked up to these pilots but discounted anything the others proclaimed. Kruger had looked into the Flight Dispatcher's job and had determined that they not only concerned themselves with the FAA rules but also were very concerned with the bottom line; profits for the company. If any plane carried a little more fuel than was actually required it ended up costing the company more or less. Flight safety had nothing, really, to do with the whole concept. Kruger, as the pilot, thought more in terms of flight safety and getting to some destination without running out of fuel due to some unforeseen circumstance. Kruger had been there before and knew all about unforeseen circumstances, known in the military as "shit happens". Kruger preferred to trust his expertise rather than some guy who sat in an office and didn't have anything at risk except his reputation.

Northwest Airlines published a "Bible" of flying procedures called "SOPA" or "Standard Operating Procedures, Amplified". All pilots were required to adhere to the SOPA procedures and the semiannual check rides ensured this. Some of the older pilots were either incapable of following SOPA or were too stubborn to do so. Most of these guys were on the 727 simply because they were too apprehensive to check out on anything newer or larger. There weren't too many of them and they were well known on the line.

Kruger figured that he could fly with just about anyone. He also refused to be intimidated in any manner now that he was off of probation. One day he found that he was paired with Carl Vandyke. Carl was odd in that he rarely allowed a copilot to fly any leg. Carl also refused to use the autopilot. He was a leftover from the barnstormer days. Kruger thought that he was amusing.

Earlier on, when he had been a 727 Second Officer, he had been called up to fly with Carl. The copilot on the flight had been a "flap" or a "freaking light airplane pilot" (to clean it up a little) and had been anxious to fly. Carl ignored him and flew every leg of a three day trip. Each time Carl violated SOPA he explained to the copilot why he did so. Of course that did not excuse what Carl did but that made no difference to him in the least. Finally, on the last leg of the last day, Carl hit the copilot on the shoulder as the plane took the duty runway and said, "Is the trim set OK for you? Why don't you take her home?"

Now you had to know Carl's idiosyncrasies. Most Captains split the flying down the middle, giving half of it to the copilot. With Carl you never knew if you were going to get to fly or not until he asked you if the trim was set OK. The trim he referred to was the setting of the horizontal tail. This was computed by the Second Officer and depended on the weight of the aircraft. This information was passed to the two pilots via a form called an OP-300, which also listed the aircraft weight and the various speeds the aircraft needed in order to accomplish some of the maneuvers during the take-off roll and the first section climb sequence. Carl would completely ignore the trim setting and would set what he thought was appropriate on the vertical tail.

The copilot was overjoyed at being allowed to fly and immediately took the controls. The takeoff was accomplished and as soon as the flaps were up the copilot trimmed the plane up and engaged the autopilot. As soon as Carl saw this he took the controls and disengaged the autopilot saying, "OK, if you don't want to fly the fucking plane then I will." The copilot immediately began to protest while Carl simply ignored him.

Kruger was laughing uncontrollably by this time. Finally the copilot turned to him and, red-faced shouted, "What the hell is so damned funny?"

Kruger managed to gasp, "Man, you have got to be the dumbest copilot I've ever seen. Here Carl has tried to teach you how to fly for almost four days and you can't even get to three thousand feet." By now tears of mirth were coursing down Kruger's cheeks. The copilot turned around and refused to acknowledge anyone for the rest of the flight. Carl never even blinked or let on that he had heard Kruger.

Now when Kruger drew Carl Vandyke for a Captain it didn't bother him in the least. The flight was from Minneapolis nonstop to Atlanta and nonstop return. Karl did his usual thing and hand flew the plane to Atlanta. Kruger ignored the Captain's flaunting of SOPA and the flight was uneventful. On the return leg Kruger was surprised by Carl hitting him on the shoulder as they rolled onto the runway and asking, "Is the trim set OK for you?" Kruger laughed as he glanced at the trim wheel and said, "Oh no, Carl, you aren't going to suck me into that one. I know you set the trim to suit yourself." Carl laughed as much as he ever did, more of a snicker than a laugh, and said, "Dammit, you want to fly or not?"

Kruger said, "Sure, Carl, I'll fly it if you want me to". They began the takeoff roll. Carl watched Kruger like a hawk. Kruger ignored him and refused to touch the autopilot. They flew for about an hour when Carl said, "Here, let me take it for a minute" Kruger relinquished control of the plane and Carl frittered with the trim for a few seconds, turning the trim wheels as he did. Finally he said, "OK, take her now. How's that feel?"

Kruger had trimmed the plane up prior to Carl taking the control wheel. Now he took the wheel and felt the trim forces on the plane. As he had suspected, Carl had screwed up the trim so the plane felt logy and took more attention than it should have. Kruger grinned and said, "Why, Carl, that feels about as shitty a trimming up as anything I've ever felt but if you want it trimmed that way I'll fly it that way." Carl grinned and snorted, "Oh, hell, trim it up any way you want to." The rest of the flight was pleasant. Kruger felt that there were several ways to handle a curmudgeon and the dumbest was to get into an argument with him.

Carl finally flunked a check ride and elected to retire early rather than admit that he had been wrong. Kruger was sorry to see him go.

Several months later Kruger had an opportunity to fly with another outstanding example of some of Northwest's finest Captains. Mel Christiansen was an old flight engineer that had made it to the pilot ranks in spite of all of the vituperative missiles that had been thrown at him during the old fight over who could and could not fly. He was a weak pilot but a pilot nonetheless. He knew his shortcomings and tried to live with them. One of the shortcomings was the inability to handle more than one task at a time.

In actuality no pilot could do more than one task at a time. In fact no human could either. The human brain cannot do more than one thing at a time. What pilots had learned to do was to concentrate on doing each task in very small bits and then rapidly move on to another. Pilots called it scanning. Psychologists called it encapsulating. It called for intense concentration. What it boiled down to was the ability to do a mini-task quickly, drop that task and move rapidly on to another one. To the uninitiated it appeared as if the pilot was multi-tasking or doing several things all at the same time. That was far from the truth. Multi-tasking is a misnomer. There is no such animal. Some pilots were better at it than others. Mel did not excel in this regard.

Once again, the flight was scheduled to go from Minneapolis to Atlanta and return. It was nonstop each way and Kruger was the copilot with Christiansen as the Captain. On this flight there was a check airman who was along to give the Second Officer a line check.

Mel flew the first leg as was usual. The flight was uneventful to Atlanta. Coming out of Atlanta Kruger flew and Mel handled the radios. Things started to come apart as soon as the plane had lifted off and the gear was coming up. The tower handed the plane off to departure control and Mel started talking on the hand mike. In order to not become distracted Mel would look out of the left windshield, thus divorcing himself from anything that was going on inside of the cockpit. Kruger thought it a little odd but didn't give it much thought.

As the plane climbed it was necessary to "clean it up" or bring the flaps up. On the 727 the flaps were retracted in three stages. The takeoff was made with 15 degrees of flap. When the gear was up and as the airspeed increased the flaps were retracted to 5 degrees. As the speed increased more the flaps were lifted to 2 degrees. At 2 degrees some of the leading edge flaps retracted. It was necessary to ascertain that all of the leading edge flaps at 2 degrees were up before retracting any more flap as it was possible for the plane to roll a lot if the leading edges came up unevenly. This was accomplished by a blue light that would illuminate when the appropriate leading edge flaps were up. Then and only then could the final flaps be raised.

As the plane climbed out Kruger called for "flaps 5". Mel was busy talking on the radio and looking out of the left window. Kruger called for flaps 5 once more and then, getting no response, he lifted the flap handle to the 5 degree position himself. Mel heard and felt the change in attitude and power on the plane. He broke off talking and pointedly looked carefully at the flap setting and power settings. He actually leaned over and almost put his nose on the flap lever in order to make his point nonverbally. Kruger ignored him. Mel was disproving, obviously, and wished to make a point. Mel said nothing but the atmosphere in the cockpit could be cut with a knife.

The airspeed continued to increase and Kruger called for "flaps 2". Mel carefully and slowly reached over and lifted the flap handle to 2 degrees. He was very deliberate about it in order to make some sort of point. Kruger could hardly keep from laughing at the extremely serious face on the part of the Captain. The airspeed continued to increase and suddenly the Center called the plane. Mel once more turned to his left and talked to the Center, completely ignoring the plane. Kruger called for the flaps up; "Up on the blue". Nothing happened. Mel was completely divorced from the operation of the plane. Kruger called, "Up on the blue lights" once more. Still nothing happened.

Kruger lifted the flap handle to up and pulled the power back to a "quiet EPR" setting. EPR was "engine pressure rating" and was simply a way to measure the power rating of the engines. Quiet EPR was mandated in order to alleviate any complaints about noisy airplanes on takeoff. The plane continued to climb in a clean configuration. Suddenly Mel stopped communicating and blew up. He screamed, "This is a two pilot airplane. I'm here to help you. How can I help you if you insist on doing everything yourself?" Kruger just shrugged and said, "You were busy talking. Apparently you can't talk and do anything else. That's OK by me. I can fly this fucking plane all by myself if I have to. And one other thing. This is a three pilot plane. You apparently forgot the Second Officer. Help out all you want but I'm not going to screw up the flight profile because you can't talk and chew gum at the same time." The flight check pilot just shook his head and Mel settled into a three hour sulk. Kruger flew the rest of the flight in silence.

Some time earlier Kruger had occasion to fly as a Second Officer on a 727 that had no APU. The APU or auxiliary power unit was a very nice perk on the 727. It allowed the crew to use power when the engines were shut down in order to air condition the plane and to power any of the various systems that made sitting in a plane that was on the deck tolerable. Occasionally the APU would become inoperative and since it did not stop a flight as such it was shunted to the back line in the schedule of maintenance that NWA considered important.

When a 727 crew flew a plane without an operative APU each station was notified in plenty of time so they could cope with the problem. Normally the APU was use to start the 727 engines. The APU furnished both air to spin up the engines and the necessary electric power to strike off the igniters that fired up the jets.

Jet engines rely on a flame front that is self sustaining once the engine is started. It's pretty amazing to consider that a jet functions on fuel sprayed into a combustion chamber in order to sustain a flame that is further fed by air pumped into the chamber by a system of rotors that pack air into the engine. Nothing else is needed. All ignition systems are turned off once the engine is started. As long as fuel and air is fed into the engine it keeps on producing power.

On the occasion that Kruger flew the 727 without an APU they landed at Midway. When they taxied to the terminal the crew kept the number two engine on line. Doing so allowed the crew access to electrical power and air, both needed to sustain comfort in the plane and to start the engines once the plane was needed to fly to another destination. If an APU was not available the station had to have both an auxiliary power unit and an air start machine. Midway had neither. The station manager asked the crew, via a radio, to shut down all engines since he didn't like the noise the number two engine was making. The crew tried futilely to convince the station manager that they would not be able to restart any engine without the power from the number two. The station manager was adamant. He wanted the number two shut down.

Finally the Captain said, "Screw it. He wants it shut down, OK, we'll shut it down". The shut down was accomplished without incident and passengers were deplaned and reboarded.

The time came to push back and depart. The push back mechanic called, "Release the brakes, cleared to start". The Second Officer (Kruger), who was in communication with the ground crew said, "How are we going to do that?" The confused mechanic replied that they ought to start the way they usually did and when told that they couldn't do that he sought advice from the station manager. That extremely knowledgeable person came on the radio and told the crew that he was absolutely sure that they could start the engines if they would only give it a little thought. He further told the crew that he had called Minneapolis Maintenance Control and they had informed him that the crew could, in fact, start the engines. It was, of course, a lie.

The crew delighted in the predicament of the station manager. Any time an obstinate, pig-headed person gets caught in a situation that is completely his fault it's a time to celebrate. The Second Officer radioed that he could start if the station could find 30 elephants. Of course the station manager wanted to know just what he meant by that and he said, "Well, we've checked out the air needed to spool up the engines to sustain a start and we've found that it would take either one air start machine or 30 elephants".

Finally the passengers were bussed to O'Hare and the crew was released to a local motel until the station could truck an air start machine into the airport. Kruger was amazed that any person in power in any position in NWA would ignore the information available to him in making command decisions. This kind of situation would be repeated many times during the time that Kruger was aboard the sinking ship called Northwest Orient Airlines.

Kruger still had lots to learn regarding his position as a copilot on the 727. Sure, he could fly the plane well but there was a bundle of items that the company wanted their pilots to accomplish that Kruger still had to assimilate. One of these items was the series of events that covered flying a minimums approach. The SOP said that once the decision had been made to "go around" (Kruger's name for this was a "wave off") it had to be followed. Kruger was still thinking in the mode of "get aboard" like he had always been when he flew in the Navy.

One day he was flying with a fairly new Captain when he had to shoot a minimums approach to Cleveland. The Captain had confidence in Kruger's flying as he had been with his copilot for more than a few days and had occasion to observe him on several approaches. It was

Kruger's leg and he flew the approach right down to the minimums of 200 feet.

When the Captain called, "minimums, no contact" Kruger added power and began the missed approach procedure. All of a sudden the Captain, who had been looking outside the airplane, said, "There it is". Kruger looked out of his scan and saw the runway as they passed over it. His Navy training took over and he immediately chopped the power and muscled the plane onto the runway. He immediately went into reverse thrust and stopped the plane with no problem. When he finally looked at the Captain that worthy was white faced and looked stricken. Kruger suddenly realized that he had just violated a cardinal rule of the airline. Sure, he got onboard but, in doing so he had upset the Captain a lot. The Captain had never been in the military and had no idea why Kruger had done what he did. The fact that the Captain's call of "there it is" had triggered Kruger's response was not mentioned. Kruger apologized for the approach and vowed never to do that kind of thing again. He realized that he had almost given the young Captain a heart attack and he also realized what the rules were meant to accomplish. "When in Rome . . ." he thought and vowed not to repeat that particular stunt.

It was about this time that the country of Rhodesia was in a civil war with a lot of terrorists. Kruger was particularly interested in the war and followed it avidly. One day one of the male flight attendants said that he had come from Rhodesia. Kruger spent every layover picking his brain relative to the country and its problems.

The Captain noticed Kruger's preoccupation with the male flight attendant and began to rib him about it. He said, "Hey Kruger, are you coming out of the closet? I'm going to tell all of the other pilots how you spend lots of time with one of the male flight attendants". Kruger said, "OK, asshole, I'm going to get you for that." The Captain allowed as how Kruger couldn't do anything to him and continued to tease Kruger.

On the next layover in Cleveland Kruger went to the nearest drugstore and bought a package of condoms. The next morning he unrolled one and snapped it into the Captain's suitcase while the Captain was having coffee. The condom hung out of the suitcase showing about four inches including the protruding tip. It could not be mistaken. The Captain walked the length of the Cleveland terminal dragging the condom behind him. He was oblivious to the grins of passengers as they passed him.

When they boarded the plane the Captain finally found the offending condom. He appeared in the cockpit red-faced and said, "You guys won't believe what I found in my baggage this morning". Kruger grinned at him and said, "Let me guess. You dragged a rubber the length of the Cleveland terminal, right? I told you I'd get you." The Captain wouldn't speak to him the rest of the flight.

A good friend of Kruger's related the story about how he had a long layover at Kennedy airport in New York. The layover was actually around four hours so the Captain decided to take his crew into New York and buy them lunch. They hired a cab and were soon in Times Square in the middle of the city. They didn't know where to go so they approached one of New York's finest, a cop, and said, "Officer, can you tell us where to have a nice lunch here in the city?" The cop looked the Captain up and down and then snarled, "Read the fucking signs."

It was an education of the first order about how to conduct yourself in New York.

It was about this time period that a bunch of Northwest pilots decided that it would be a good idea to buy Virginia a car. Virginia was the "check-in" lady that all crew members had to see as they checked in for their flights. She was a very nice person, affable and cheerful and a friend to all with a phenomenal memory for names. A quick poll of the pilot group found that a good majority of them agreed and the necessary cash was quickly collected and a car was purchased and presented to an astonished and grateful check-in lady.

And that was when the law of unintended consequences kicked in. The office that housed the check-in lady also housed a bevy of crew controllers; those persons who assigned trips that were not filled on the open board. The controllers were miffed that no one had thought them good enough to buy them a car. After all, weren't pilots richer than kings and really didn't know what to do with all of their money and didn't deserve it anyway? What was so good about old Virginia? The gift of a car created rancor that existed for months and really never disappeared.

Then the other shoe dropped. Virginia got religion. She had long seen pilots and flight attendants pair up on trips and, with her new found morals, suspected that they were involved in a (gasp) carnal relation. Virginia began to call the pilot's wives and inform them of the activities of their husbands. Of course no proof was ever offered but then none was ever needed. Everyone knew that pilots were immoral son-a-bitches and several pilots were handed their hat, asses and overcoats in the form of divorce proceedings.

Kruger was amused when he flew with a Second officer who protested loudly about Virginia and wanted to know if he could get his contribution for the car back.

CHAPTER VIII

Kruger liked flying for Northwest Orient Airlines but his heart was still with the Navy. He attended all of the required monthly training days and volunteered for any additional days he thought that he could get by with, considering his family that was stuck in Minneapolis. Northwest was not a problem even though they tried to bully their pilots into requesting a leave and then denying it. Kruger had early on made that ploy indefensible by alerting both the Navy and the Veteran's Administration to the ploy the company tried to run.

Kruger still adhered to the agreement that he had struck with Cdr. Lynch. He maintained his position as a training officer in the squadron. It wasn't a particularly notable position but it was a "billet" and, as such, was as good as gold, especially during those times when the pilots of Northwest Orient decided that a withdrawal of services, otherwise known as a strike and happened too often, was on. The nice aspect of the job was that he could correct any of the bad habit patterns that he had observed among the various pilots that he flew with. Kruger became known as a hard taskmaster, one that would book no compromises but one that would take as much time as possible in order to bring the pilot being checked up to standard.

The old P2V-7s were rapidly being phased out of service. Most of the really good mechanics were being sent to the Navy's school for flight engineers on the P3, the newest anti-submarine platform the Navy had selected to replace the P2. That left the "scrubs" to maintain the planes. The results were predictable.

Kruger spent more and more time at the air station for a number of reasons. One, he liked flying for the Navy more than he liked flying for Northwest. Two, he liked the money he made flying for the Navy and he liked the security attendant with all of that. He had found out the hard way that security was non-existent at Northwest. Finally, the squadron needed him to train the newer pilots, as much as it galled to admit that fact. Kruger didn't rub that fact in whenever he asked for additional duty and the squadron didn't acknowledge that fact whenever it called him to ask him if he would agree to go on active duty to train some new guy on the planes. It was enough to know that he was needed and had a good job with the squadron. Most of all, the flying was good. And it was fun. God, it was fun.

The Officer's Club was, as always, a royal pain in the ass for the CO of the Naval Air Station. The main problem was the lack of people who would attend the club on any given night. The "O" club traditionally came up short when it came to funds. Not that it was a bad club, mind you, but it had some shortcomings in terms of who could attend and when. On some weekends it was hopping. That was when all of the squadrons were in attendance at the Naval Air Station. On other weekends the place looked like a morgue. The fact that the bar tender continually "ripped off" the station didn't help at all.

Finally the Commanding Officer tried to solve the problem by instituting a new Club Manager. Kruger wasn't in the lofty think-tanks that decided things like this so he never knew just why the new manager was selected. He only knew that the selection was not a good one. The new manager had been a Blue Angel. For those of you who are not conversant with the Navy's advertisement programs, the Blue Angels are the crack aerobatic team flying the most advanced aircraft the Navy has. The "Blues", as they are known, fly all over the United States, putting on air shows for the population in the fond hope that some youngster will see the light and wish to become one of the most talented persons on earth; a US Naval Aviator.

All well and good, except that sometimes the Blue Angel pilots begin to believe their own public relations stuff. That's when things begin to go awry.

The first thing to "go awry" was when the Club Manager fired Algee and instituted a civilian bar tender in his place. OK, sure, Algee was ripping the club off but there are lots of ways to correct that problem to, as the Marines put it, "adjust his behavior". The new bar tender looked and acted like a Mafia hood. He didn't belong in a Navy Officer's Club any more than a pig belongs in an upscale salon in New York's finest areas. Kruger instantaneously disliked him. It became a synergistic accounting as Kruger also disliked the Club Manager, the way the Club was being run and the Club's bar tender.

Kruger decided to boycott the club. He announced his intentions at a squadron meeting and his announcement was generally met with catcalls. As time went on Kruger's non-attendance at the club was noticed and people began to take note of it. One night a few friends decided to find him as he had been absent from the club for several nights. They found him in the lounge reading a book and drinking a beer from the beer machine that was located in the basement.

"Hey, Kruger, what the hell are you doing out here? Why don't you come into the bar with the rest of us?" Kruger explained the reasons why he was doing what he was doing to them and they complained, "Well, godamnit, why don't you just buy some fucking beer and carry it into the fucking bar and drink it in there with us?" Kruger admitted that there was really no fucking reason why he couldn't do just that and he proceeded to buy several cans of fucking beer from the fucking machine and carry them into the fucking bar.

Once in the bar Kruger popped one of the cans of beer and proceeded to drink it from the can to the hoots and catcalls of several of the squadron pilots.

Kruger had not been sitting at the bar for very long until the bar tender came over and said to him, "You can't drink that here at the bar."

Kruger looked at the scruffy bar tender and raised an eyebrow. "What do you mean by that?" he said.

"I mean you can't drink that beer here."

Kruger smiled and said, "I don't know what you mean by that. I'm drinking this beer without any problems so far as I can see. If you leave me alone I'll drink the damned thing completely. I don't see the problem. Maybe you can explain it to me.

The bartender simply picked up his telephone and called the club manager. This was exactly what Kruger was waiting for. Soon the perfectly coiffed Commander showed up, was apprised of the problem by the bartender while Kruger sipped his can of beer pretending that all was well in the world, and approached the offender. The Club Manager was smiling as if he had just won the lottery. That, of course, was something else that Kruger couldn't stand about the man. He was a political body, more concerned about his image and how he looked to his seniors than he was about how he did his job or how efficient he was. Kruger had always been scathing in his scorn for officers of that type.

The Club Manager put his arm around Kruger's shoulder as if they were two long lost buddies. "Good evening, Mr. Kruger, how are we this evening?"

Kruger simply raised an eyebrow and responded, "Got a mouse in your pocket, have you?"

"I don't understand."

"You used the word 'we'. Since you are alone I figured that you must have another entity on or about your person. Either that or you are speaking like the old kings used to speak, in the plural instead of the singular."

"I was simply asking how you were," the Commander said. Kruger noticed that the Commander's face was becoming flushed. "Well and good," he thought.

"In that case I guess that the appropriate response is that I'm just excellent and enjoying myself immensely."

"I'm glad to hear that," the Manager said, "but I have to tell you that you can't drink that can of beer in here."

"Damn, there seems to be an echo in here," Kruger said. "I could swear that someone just told me that. I guess that I would be guilty of repeating myself if I said that I really don't see a problem involved in drinking this beer. In fact, I've already drunk half of it and, if left alone, I'm quite sure that I can get the rest of it down without any problem." Kruger turned on his best smile for the Commander who, by now, was what was known as "tight-jawed" as his eyes narrowed in his perception that he was being "tweaked".

"Ed, I can't allow you to drink a can of beer in here. It gives the wrong impression and the club needs your participation in drinking only beverages that are served by the bartender."

"Ah, two thoughts here, Commander. One is the use of first names. Excellent. We are now buddies, I guess. Ed. I love it. The second thought is that I could swear that you used the words 'can't allow' in reference to my use of my club. Correct me if I'm wrong here but I'm under the impression that as an officer attached to this base this is my club. You, on the other hand, are simply the manager of this club. I should be giving orders to you and not the other case, don't you think?"

"At least allow me to pour the rest of your beer in a glass."

"Oh, I don't think so. I happen to like the taste of beer in a can rather than in a glass."

"Ed, I think that you are trying to make an issue of this."

"Commander, I think that I've already done that."

The Club Manager, by now not perceptibly friendly, gritted, "What will it take to get you to get rid of that can?"

Kruger finally turned serious. He set the can down and turned toward the Club Manager. "Well, Commander, as I see things you have three choices. One, you can order me out of my club and I'll go but I'll make one hell of a scene and I'll bring the whole thing up to the Commanding Officer of the Naval Air Station. Two, you can try to put me physically out of my club if you're feeling feisty tonight. Three, you can just go away and let me drink my beer in my club." Kruger smiled at the Manager.

The Club Manager, by now showing no discernable evidence of friendliness gritted, "Why don't you just drink your beer?"

"Why, thank you, Commander, I will," Kruger said but by this time he was talking to the Commander's back.

The next thing the Club Manager tried was to open the Officer's Club to civilians. The way he did this was to rent the club to groups of civilians who had not been able to find facilities elsewhere. The whole idea was, of course, met with disdain and scorn by the entire officer cadre. Civilians did not belong in a club with military officers. The two groups were like oil and water. Neither one understood the other. Moreover the Officer's Club was a place where hard-charging military men could unwind from whatever tasks they had been handed. It was akin to placing a good boxer who adhered to the rules laid down by the Marquis of Queensbury in a room with dirty street fighters and telling them to enjoy themselves. The idea was doomed to failure.

The first episode came about when a party for twenty ladies booked the club. The ladies were seated around a large circular table when Kruger and several other Navy Officers entered the room after flying all day. It was still early and Officers were still allowed to be in flight gear. After 1700 hours Officers had to be in the uniform of the day or appropriate attire. The ladies had a large chaffing dish filled with Swedish meatballs placed in the center of the table. They were in earnest conversation and largely ignored the pilots. They had turned on the large juke box and were listening to some contemporary music.

Lt. John Sears was watching the group as he drank his first beer of the evening. John was what you might call one of the most unattractive pilots the Navy had onboard. He had a bad skin condition and his hair looked as if he had been scalped and the hair put back on at an angle. To add to the entire picture John was a chain smoker and his breath was something that a komodo dragon could brag about. John was taken by the group of young, beautiful ladies.

John finally said, "I guess that I'll amble over and ask some of those ladies if they would care to dance." He stumbled over to the group in his sweaty flight suit that had not been laundered for a week. Leaning down to place his face (and his breath) in close proximity to the faces of the ladies he asked if any of them would care to dance. The lady to which he was closest turned blue and averted her face as she vainly tried to wave away John's noxious breath. The ladies were unanimous in their refusal to dance.

John then valiantly said, "Well, if none of you ladies would care to dance would you mind if I had a Swedish meatball?" The assent was unanimous. Anything to get this strange apparition to kindly go away.

Once John was given the "go-ahead" he went into action. He pulled up the right sleeve of his flight suit and dipped his entire hand into the bowl of meatballs. He then began to noisily gulp the meatballs as red gravy dripped down his arm and off of his elbow onto the table. The good ladies looked on in abject horror. When John had gulped the last meatball he belched noisily and thanked the ladies. They were still staring at him as he made his way back to the group of pilots who, by now, were suffused with laughter.

The second episode happened when a large group consisting of businessmen and their wives booked part of the club. Again, the rest of the club was open to the officers. The club manager didn't have the authority to close the club to the pilots. As the evening wore on the businessmen congregated in one corner leaving the wives to their own devices in another. One of the prettier women curiously prowled the wardroom, looking at the several squadron plaques and artifacts that were on display there. She was especially taken by the ship's bell on the bar.

"Look, look, watch her, she's gonna ring the bell," one of the officer's whispered. The pretty lady ran her hand over the bell's smooth surface. She read the caption chiseled on the bell. She snapped the bell with her perfectly polished fingernail as the watching officers held their breath. Finally she reached under the bell and, catching the clapper she struck the side of the bell, which gave off an alarmingly loud peal. The bell's loud ring was echoed by the equally loud collective cheer from the assembled officer group.

The attractive lady was immediately surrounded by approximately 30 officers. She was not only attractive and polished but was also very poised and self assured. She smiled at the officers who were, by this time panting, and waited for them to speak to her.

Finally one of the officers said, "Lady, you rang the bell so you've got to buy the bar. It's an old Navy tradition."

The lady was unflustered as she smiled and said, "I'm sorry gentlemen but I simply don't have enough money to buy each one of you a drink."

One of the officers pushed to the front of the group and leeringly said, "That's OK. We can make other arrangements."

The lady continued to smile as she softly said, "Surely you don't expect that I'll sleep with all of you."

Another officer growled, "No, pick three and all the rest will go away." The lady thought that was hilarious and laughed as her husband came to her rescue. Kruger had to admire her. She had all of the officers eating out of her hand. She was cool and collected. He allowed as how she had "one-upped" the military with grace and dignity.

The inevitable finally happened. The bar tender, who looked like he had been hired from a Teamster publication that tried to place uneducated microcephalics in a job, was terminated and Algee, the old bartender, was reinstated. Kruger was actually glad to see Algee back even with his thieving ways. Algee immediately adopted his old ways, probably thinking that the club couldn't function without him. The Officers generally ignored him.

One evening the club was sparsely populated. Kruger was present along with several Marines. Algee decided to close the bar since it wasn't making much money. He announced that he was closing up and gave the reason. Kruger figured that Algee had cause to do what he wished and said, "OK, serve up one last drink and close up." Kruger was the senior officer present in the bar at that time.

Algee decided to be obstinate and said, "No, baby, I ain't gonna serve no mo' drinks this evenin'. I gonna close up an' that's it."

Kruger retaliated by saying, "Now Algee that sounds like a challenge. I'll pay for the drinks. All I'm asking you to do is to serve up one last round and then you can close."

"No, baby, I ain' gonna serve no mo' drinks this evenin'."

"Algee, stop with this "baby" shit. I'm not your baby. Serve the last round, OK?"

"Naw, suh, naw, I ain' gonna."

"OK, have it your way." Kruger slid over to the ship's bell and rang the clapper to the tune of cheers from the Marine contingent present. Algee immediately exited the area and ran off. The Marines surrounded Kruger and demanded, "OK, Commander, you rang the bell so you have to buy us all drinks."

"Hey, guys, no contest. I'll buy you drinks but as I see the problem it's not getting me to buy the drinks, it's getting the bartender to serve the drinks. Do you guys think you can find him?"

The Marines immediately split off into several scouting units. This was what they had been trained for and they excelled at it. It wasn't long before one of the scouting squads produced the bartender. They had him by the scruff of the neck and the seat of his pants. His feet were futilely scrabbling on the deck as he had been lifted several inches off of the ground and carried by two Marines who were grinning from ear to ear.

"Here's your bartender, Commander," they crowed.

"Place him behind the bar and let him serve drinks," the Commander said.

The Marines unceremoniously tossed the hapless bartender over the bar, growling as they did so, "Goddamn it, serve the fucking drinks."

Algee picked himself off of the deck and immediately called the Command Duty Officer to complain about the treatment he had just received. Kruger listened with glee as the CDO said, "Well, as I see it a Navy Commander rang the ship's bell and offered to buy drinks for a contingent of Marines. I think, under the circumstances, that you ought to serve the drinks and then you can close the bar like the Commander told you to do."

Algee took the drink orders and served them but, in so doing, he cast several aspersions on the US Marine Corps in general. The Marines reacted as could be expected by tossing chairs into the bar and through windows and generally trashing the whole area as they had been trained to do. Algee fled the area, fearing for his life, probably one of the more astute things he had ever done in his life.

When the fog of war had lifted the Command dictated that the Marines involved could not enter the bar for six months so Kruger was forced to make beer runs for the sinners via the coat room for the time period dictated. It was more pleasant in the company of the marooned Marines than most of the other Officers in the bar.

The VP squadrons were slated for an inspection by the Commodore. That title was given by the Navy to an officer who was the head of a wing of squadrons. Normally the "Commodore", a title that was normally only given during war time, was allotted to a Navy Captain who commanded a "wing" of squadrons, that is to say, a number of squadrons.

All of the VP commands were given the instructions as to what to do and what to wear during the inspection. All officers were to wear nametags.

Kruger figured that nametags were demeaning. He thought that any commanding officer of any worth would know the name of all of his people and would not need nametags. Accordingly, he never had ordered one and did not wear one. The Executive Officer ordered him to "get a nametag". Kruger did exactly that. He ordered a nametag that said, "Naemtaag". When he put it on his uniform he told everyone that he was a Dutchman and that was his name. The squadron loved the joke and went along with it.

During the inspection by the Commodore the Executive Officer made a cursorily inspection of his own before the Commodore inspected the ranks. As he stood in front of Kruger he said, "Kruger, what the hell is that on your uniform where your nametag is supposed to be?" Kruger said, "Sir, that is my nametag, Sir." The XO said, "Get that thing off of your uniform before I shove it up your ass." Kruger said, "Yessir", and complied with the order.

When the CO and the Commander got to Kruger in the inspection line the CO said, "Kruger, why the hell don't you have a nametag? I could have sworn that you had one earlier." Kruger said, "Sir, The XO made me take it off." The CO said, "Why would he do something like that?" Kruger said, "No idea Sir".

And the game went on.

When the Commodore inspected the work spaces in the hanger he came on one space that was labeled "WETSU". Now most work spaces were numbered by numbers as in W120. All of the enlisted men in the workspace were lined up at attention and when the Commodore said aloud, "What is WETSU?" all of the men shouted, "We Eat This Shit Up!" The Commodore loved it. That was what esprit de corps was all about.

CHAPTER IX

Flying the 727 was fun but the real reason Kruger had signed on with the airlines was to maximize his income and the time away from the job that the airlines offered. Accordingly he opted to fly, once more, on the DC10 as a Second Officer rather than as a copilot on the 727.

The flying was undemanding in the extreme. The pilots that Kruger flew with were, by and large, wonderful guys but sitting on the Second Officer's panel was anathema to the perishable skill of flying an airplane. It was a tradeoff.

A lot of the Captains on the DC10 were, of course, very senior pilots and, as senior pilots are apt to be some of them could be crotchety. One day Kruger found himself onboard a flight with one of the more crotchety ones. This Captain prided himself on not speaking to any pilot below the rank of copilot, which meant that he rarely spoke to the Second Officer. Kruger figured that he could put up with just about anyone, especially if no conversation was required. They got along fine until the first leg of the flight ended in Winnipeg, Manitoba. It was early spring in the United States but spring had not arrived as yet in Winnipeg. One of the Northwest rules was that after a certain early spring date the pilot group could forgo their blouses or coats and opt to fly in the short-sleeved shirt uniform. The Captain was supposed to set the example and the crew was supposed to follow suit. This Captain opted to wear the short-sleeve uniform and as soon as the copilot saw that he removed his blouse and placed it in his suitcase. Kruger didn't do so since he had to do the preflight walk around and, as the weather was still pretty nippy, the blouse was warm and comfortable. No one mentioned a thing until the three crewmembers were walking from the plane to the terminal. It was cold in Winnipeg and Kruger was glad that he had kept his blouse on. The Captain and the copilot were walking side-by-side leaving Kruger to follow behind them. On the way to the terminal the Captain leaned toward the copilot and, in a sotto voice said, "One of us is out of uniform". Obviously the message was intended for Kruger but it wasn't addressed to Kruger who immediately responded to the winds, "Maybe he thinks one of us gives a shit". The Captain, startled, glanced over his shoulder at Kruger but continued walking without any comment. The night continued without incident.

The next morning Kruger arrived at the airplane, started the APU, initialized the INS navigation units, warmed up the plane with the air conditioning systems and powered up the Flight Attendants service areas. He then got the Air Terminal Information Service or ATIS information and wrote it down on a piece of paper that he taped to the forward console for the pilots so they didn't have to do that little chore. He accomplished the preflight walk around. When he arrived back in the cockpit the other two pilots were sitting in their seats prepping for the flight. Kruger sat down in the Second Officer's seat without comment. The Captain reached over and removed the ATIS from the consol where Kruger had taped it. Holding it he leaned over to the copilot and said loudly enough for everyone to hear, "On the next layover we'll have to take the Second Officer out and buy him a grease pencil so he can write the ATIS in big letters so we can actually read it". The term "Second Officer" was said in a tone of voice that suggested "Asshole" was what was really meant.

Hearing this Kruger left his seat without comment and walked back into the cabin where the Flight Attendant auxiliary suitcase was kept. Once there he opened the case and removed a grease pencil and a tray liner, which was used to line the large serving trays the FAs used. He wrote the ATIS in very large letters on the back of the liner, which was approximately one foot by two feet dimensionally. He wadded up a large amount of tape and stuck the wad on the back of the new "message pad". He then walked back to the cockpit and, without comment; stuck it on the forward console. The new "ATIS" obliterated most of the instruments on the forward console including the radar unit. The Captain and the copilot were both silent for about 10 seconds. Then the Captain leaned over to the copilot and said, "Whatever you do, don't piss him off". Kruger exploded with laughter and even the dour old Captain smiled proving that he did have a sense of humor after all.

Kruger by now was commuting from his home in Naples, Florida. On one of his commutes he was in the first class section of a 727 when there was a delay due to some sort of a mechanical glitch. Kruger settled down with one of his ubiquitous books and decided to weather the delay without any complaints.

He had been reading for a little while when he heard the couple in the seat in front of him talking. The female was very drunk and whined,

"Why aren't we going anywhere?" Her longsuffering husband said, "Barbara we will go when the fucking pilot decides to go". She continued to complain and finally the plane pushed back and was underway. As the plane taxied out it was bumpy. Kruger heard the husband say, "Aww, Goddamn it Barbara, you just dumped your drink all over me". She retorted, "Well, if the pilot would just hold the plane steady that wouldn't happen." It went on and on. Kruger was happy that he didn't have to put up with any female like that but he was also happy to listen to the comic conversations of his fellow passengers.

Northwest had always had a policy of no alcohol on any layover, regardless of the length of the layover. Irrespective of that policy most of the pilots and Flight Attendants imbibed anyway. Most of the forbidden drinking was low key and caused no problems or incidents at all. Nevertheless, some pilots were paranoid about the policy, thinking that they were under constant scrutiny and spying. Those pilots were usually closet drinkers and were constantly tense due to their guilty feelings. One day Kruger flew with a Captain named Steve. He was a nice guy who smoked a pipe but was so nervous that Kruger kept a close eye on him. At the first layover Kruger thought that Steve could use a little loosening up so he said, "Say, Steve, the copilot and I are going to have a beer at the nearest watering hole. Would you like to join us"? Steve did a double take that almost snapped his neck. He stared at Kruger for a few seconds and finally said, "Oh, I don't drink on layovers but you guys go ahead. I won't tell".

"Won't tell?" Kruger said. "Steve, if I thought that you were going to "tell" I'd break both your legs and stuff you in garbage can". Kruger walked off as Steve stared at his back.

When Kruger told the copilot about the incident the copilot said, "God, I can't believe you told him that. You know, he drinks all of the time. He's a closet drinker".

"Fine by me as long as he can still fly. He looks uptight as hell to me and that's why I invited him along thinking that he could use a little loosening up but I think that a guy ought to know what's in store for him if he is going to fink out on another pilot."

The incident was never commented on in any of the future flights Kruger had with Steve.

Passengers were sometimes a problem on some of the flights. Some of them just couldn't seem to realize that they had bought a pass for a ride on an airplane and not a massage, foot rub, access to a slave and a four course meal served without regard to anyone else onboard. Kruger called them "prima-donnas". One day the senior Flight Attendant asked him if he would talk to a passenger who insisted on talking to "the Captain". Kruger made his way back through the cabin and found the irate passenger. The plane was on the ground at the time.

He asked the passenger if he could help him. The passenger, who had a heavy accent, said, "Are you za Captain?"

"No, I'm the Second Officer."

"I vill talk to you anyvey."

"OK, what's the problem?"

"Za Stewardesses here do not know how to cook. Za food iss badly prepared."

Kruger's eyes sought the overhead. "Boy," he thought, "Where do we get them?"

"Well, sir, you have to understand that the Flight Attendants don't really cook the food. It's already prepared and cooked. It's served in large containers in order to keep the food warm. All the girls do is to dish it up and serve it to you."

The nutcase thought about this for a minute or two and then came back with, "Ziss airplane iss unsanitary. Za toilets are too close to za kitchens."

The passenger was upset because the biffy between the first class section and the economy section was close to the first class food area.

"Well sir, we don't design the planes. We just fly them. I think you need to talk to McDonnell-Douglas about the design of this plane."

"OK, but I am going to write to Mr. Ralph Nader about ziss plane."

"That's OK by me. You can certainly do that. Anything else?"

"Yes, ziss airplane comes in from all over za vorld bringing in germs into za United States. I am going to write Mr. Nader about zat also."

"Hoo boy," Kruger thought, "We've really got a winner here." He said, "While you're writing to Mr. Nader there's something else you should mention to him."

"Oh, yes, Vat iss zat?"

"Now not too many people know this but I'm going to tell you. Do you know that the Flight Attendants don't wash their hands after they go to the toilet? I'm sure that Mr. Nader would like to know that too."

"Really?" The nutcase was really interested now. "I vill certainly tell him zat. Sank you".

"Oh, you are certainly welcome." Kruger went back to the cockpit chuckling as he did so. He couldn't wait to tell the lead Flight Attendant about the nice conversation he just had with Mr. Nader's friend. Her comments couldn't be printed on or in any media and they were directed at the passenger in question, Kruger, Mr. Nader, the airline and its passengers and anyone else in the general area. Kruger was reminded of the old black man in Chicago who said, "Fuck dis place, fuck dese people, fuck Christmas and fuck Santy Claus too".

Airline passengers in general were solid citizens; calm, courteous and easy to get along with. Some were miserable and deserved to be relegated to those who had to use their feet to travel. One such miserable person was the cause of a Flight Attendant coming to the cockpit in tears. She said that a passenger in first class had been very demanding and abusive and had finally thrown a cup of coffee on her because she had not been swift enough to refill his cup. Kruger told her to go back into the cabin and demand his ticket stub so that the crew could identify him. She did so and reported back to the cockpit saying that the passenger was very contrite and apologetic. He did not want to show his ticket stub. Kruger said that if he didn't wish to do so then he could answer to law authorities when they landed on a charge of assaulting a flight crew member. He finally gave the flight Attendant his business card that identified him as the president of the Prudential Insurance Company. He was apologetic and contrite enough that the Flight Attendant did not wish to pursue it any further.

On another flight a passenger in the tourist section wanted to smoke an evil smelling cigar during the taxi out. The Flight Attendant told him that he had to put the cigar out and he did so but as soon as the plane was airborne he lit up once more. The Flight Attendant reported to the cockpit for help.

Kruger left the cockpit and headed aft. He soon saw the passenger, an elderly man, who had hunkered down between the seats so he was out of sight, huffing on his evil smelling cigar. Kruger thought that it was humorous because the smoke from the cigar along with the smell was wafting over the whole area somewhat like the old Indian smoke signals. Kruger tapped the guy on the shoulder and gestured for the cigar, which was produced reluctantly and that was the end of the story. Kruger reflected that no matter how old you were sometimes you reverted to thinking like a three year old.

Then there was the time that a Flight attendant reported to the cockpit with the information that a passenger in the First Class section refused to stow his baggage under the seat in front of him. The plane was ready to take off so Kruger rushed out of his seat and hurried back to the area that the passenger was in. As he approached the area he saw a passenger who appeared somewhat rattled. He pointed to the passenger and asked the Flight Attendant, "Is this the guy?" The passenger hurriedly shouted, "I'm not the guy. I'm not the guy. He's back there." Kruger looked back of the passenger and saw another passenger trying to hurriedly trying to stow his gear. Kruger marched back to the main problem and as he did the passenger said, "I'll be good. I'll be good", like a three year old. Kruger gave him a lecture on how he was costing the airline a lot of money in time and how he had inconvenienced the other passengers by being a selfish, uncaring prick. Most of the other passengers chipped in with cat calls in regard to the dummy who wouldn't stow his luggage.

Kruger was always amazed at how his passengers thought that they had purchased a ticket that accorded them perks as if they had slaves in the guise of airline employees instead of simply a seat in the conveyance that took them from "A" to "B".

Once when Kruger had to "deadhead" or simply ride in one of Northwest's planes in order to get to a destination he was seated in the center section of a DC-10. The plane was filling up and suddenly a stern lady plopped her gear in one of the window seats and opened the storage locker above her seat. She saw that it was full and she began to pull some of the stored luggage out of the locker saying, "Who put their luggage in MY storage bin?" Kruger was amazed at the effrontery of the woman who thought that she had a dedicated storage compartment over her seat. In all actuality the storage bins were "first come, first served". The woman succeeded in bluffing another passenger by dumping all of his belongings into his lap making him have to stuff his gear under his seat. The woman then said loudly to the person seated next to her, "My name is (whatever) and I am a lawyer."

When Kruger heard that he turned to his copilot and said loudly, "Do you know what a trench full of dead lawyers is?" When his copilot said, "No", Kruger said, "It's a good start". The female lawyer just stared at him.

*   *   *

One of the several flies in the ointment was the so-called security system the airlines had in place. As the Second Officer, Kruger had to board the plane first in order to start the Auxiliary Power Unit or APU, enter the appropriate data into the INS units for navigation, power up the electrical systems for the Flight Attendants to heat up the food for the passengers and start the air conditioning systems prior to the passengers being boarded. Kruger could not board the aircraft even though the people servicing the toilets or biffies could do so. Access depended on having a code number that was keyed into a security lock in order to open the door leading to the plane. Kruger complained to the station managers but was told, "If we gave you access to the plane we would have to give everyone access to it." Kruger thought that the statement was idiotic but had learned long ago that a fight with the local bureaucrats was futile. Accordingly he carried a book and merely sat in an area that was closest to the plane and read until someone would finally find him and let him on the plane. The plane could not go anywhere until he had accomplished his preflight and everyone knew it. If the plane pushed back late it was not his fault or the fault of any flight crewmember. Meanwhile Kruger could read his favorite book in the interim time.

Winnipeg, Manitoba was one of Kruger's least favorite layover spots. It was cold and stark. The hotel was primitive according to American ideas and it was far from any city or place where you could relax. One day Kruger was paired with a young copilot named Gary Barr. Gary had never been a military pilot and was young, single and good looking. He cut a wide swath among the Flight Attendants.

When the crew got to the layover hotel they lined up to check in with the front desk. All three pilots had lots of time on this particular layover and were discussing where to go to relax. One of the ladies at the desk asked what they were talking about and when she was told that they were trying to find a place where "the action was" she said, "There's plenty of action right here in the hotel". Thinking that she was talking about the swimming pool area the pilots snorted. The hotel didn't even have an adequate bar where they could "relax" with a beer or two. Finally the pilots decided to call it a night and retired to their rooms.

When Kruger got to his room his phone was ringing. When he answered it he heard a soft female voice that said, "Hi, are you looking for a little company this evening?" Kruger laughed and said, "Oh sweetheart, you've got the wrong guy. I'm married (a lie) and don't really need any company. The guy you really want to talk to is named Gary. He's single, a young handsome stud and makes one hell of a lot more money than I do. He's in room 354." The lady thanked him and hung up.

The next morning the copilot was bleary eyed and complained that he got little sleep as his phone rang all night as some girls kept trying to entice him into a party.

The DC10 seemed to be cursed at times. Pilots were prone to say, at those times, that the plane seemed to only want to do its own thing; "Well it does that sometimes". On one trip as the crew docked the plane at its destination, the external crew charged with opening the hatch that allowed the passengers to exit the plane could not do so.

The cockpit crew sat in their seats while the Flight Attendants griped incessantly about how the passengers could not get off of the plane. Kruger had called maintenance several times with no effect. Finally he got up and walked back to the hatch that "could not be opened". As he did so he was the recipient of several dark looks from passengers who really wanted to get on with things and didn't wish to stand in the aisles while maintenance screwed around with a door on the airplane.

When Kruger got to the hatch he looked out of the small window port and saw the maintenance people working to get the door open. It had remained closed for about 10 minutes after the plane had parked at the dock.

Kruger banged on the hatch to get the attention of the external crew that had been working in order to get the hatch open. He motioned for them to get away from the door. The maintenance people, who by now knew what Kruger was up to, began shouting, "Don't do that! Don't do that!" Kruger shouted, "Stand away from the door" several times. Knowing what Kruger was going to do the external crew stood far away from the door.

There are several ways to open the DC10 hatches. They can be opened hydraulically in the normal mode or they can be blown open in the emergency mode along with the deployment of the escape chutes. Alternatively they can be blown open with the assistance of an air bottle that opens the door, bypassing the hydraulic systems and not deploying the chute. This was what Kruger was going to do. The maintenance people didn't want him to do that because then they would have to replace the air bottle; more work for them to do.

When the external crew was well away from the plane Kruger positioned the levers accordingly and blew open the door. It opened in a half of a second. There was a loud cheer from the passengers who deplaned with smiles on their faces. The maintenance people grumbled about his action but he said, "Guys, it's all about customer service. Our passengers don't want to stand in the aisles with their fingers in their asses while we "fix" the damned airplane so they can get off of it."

It was about this time period that an American Airlines DC10 crashed after a takeoff at O'Hare International. All DC10s were grounded as a result. Kruger was called one evening and asked if he would deadhead to Seattle and fly on a DC10 in order to get it back to Minneapolis in order to be inspected. Kruger agreed and found himself on a crew composed of an obese ex-Marine pilot named Stanley Kegal who was flying as the Captain and a copilot named Leonard Jankowski who was known as the "Polish gust lock" by most of the Northwest pilots. Kruger had experience with both pilots and sighed when he found out just who he was going to be flying with. It was going to be a long trip. It was an unbeatable crew.

The crew got together in Seattle. It was late at night and the terminal was empty. All three pilots were in uniform. They proceeded to the security checkpoint area and placed their bags on the checkpoint belt monitored by three rather obese female security agents who appeared totally disinterested in the whole affair. None of the agents said a word as the pilots walked through the security arbors after showing their airline identifications. Kruger and the Captain passed through OK but Jankowski rang the buzzer. The security agent nearest to him silently motioned for him to back up and re-enter the arbor again. Jankowski took off his hat and placed it on the belt, thinking that it might have set the buzzer off and reentered the arbor. Once again he entered the arbor and, once again, he set the buzzer off. This time Jan took off his overcoat and placed it on the belt to be x-rayed. This scenario was repeated several times as Jan slowly field-stripped himself as several trains that ran to the field side of the terminal passed by.

Kruger, in disgust, attempted to reason with the security people. He approached the female that appeared to be in charge and said, "Ma'am, why don't you just let the man go through the checkpoint. He's shown you his ID. There are only three of us crewmembers and we have to pick up a DC10 and ferry it back to Minneapolis. The Captain and I can vouch for him. He's the copilot".

The security person so addressed simply silently turned her back on Kruger, refusing to even answer him.

Kruger figured that there was always more than one way to skin a cat and get attention so he shouted, "Hey Jankowski, if you didn't pack that .38 maybe they would let you pass".

A female police officer who was arguably even fatter than any of the other security agents waddled over and, approaching Kruger, said, "I'm afraid I'm going to have to see your ID".

Kruger responded, "Oh hell, lady, don't be afraid. I'll show you my ID. All you had to do was ask".

The cop's face got red and she grabbed the proffered bifold that contained Kruger's military ID in one side and his Northwest ID in the other.

As she began to write in her notebook she asked, "Do you know what you just said, Mr. Kruger"?

"Hell, yes, lady, I know what I say all of the time. How about you?"

By now the red had spread to the cop's neck. She persevered, "Just how long have you worked for Northwest, Mr. Kruger"?

"Why sweetheart, that's none of your fucking business".

By now the cop couldn't talk. She turned the bifold around and attempted to fish Kruger's military ID out of it.

"Ah-ah-ah, get your fucking fat fingers out of my ID case and leave my military ID alone".

By now the cop could hardly contain herself. She silently thrust the ID card holder toward Kruger who snatched it just as abruptly. By now Jankowski had divested himself of whatever offending article the machine didn't like and had been allowed to redress and stand to wait for the next train. Kruger silently joined both of the other pilots and they flew back to Minneapolis without further incident.

When Kruger finally entered crew schedules the next morning he reported to the Chief Pilot's Office saying, "You are going to want to talk to me sooner or later so we might as well get this over with right now" The Chief Pilot was a little surprised but looked though his in basket and finally said, "OK, this is probably what you are talking about. Tell me about it". Kruger did so.

When he was through the Chief Pilot laughed and said, "Didn't Stan Kegel give you any backup?"

"No sir, and I didn't ask. I didn't need any."

"OK, I don't like those people either but the next time try and be a little more congenial." Kruger just smiled and left the office.

*   *   *

Every Northwest pilot had to undergo an initial physical by the Mayo Clinic prior to being hired. After they were hired they had to undergo additional physicals every two years in addition to the FAA physicals they had to take. Most of the pilots resented the Mayo physicals as they took a lot of time the pilot group was not paid for and were a threat to a pilot as most other physicals were. The pilot group suspected that Northwest got a special insurance rate for making their pilots go to the Clinic and that the Clinic was using the pilot group for some study or other without the permission of the pilots. Nevertheless, the pilots were coerced into going to Mayo whether they wanted to or not. It was that or be fired for insubordination.

Most of the Mayo doctors suspected that all of the Northwest pilots were alcoholics. The doctors were well aware of the policy that Donald Nyrop had instituted concerning the absolute prohibition against any alcohol usage on any flight regardless of the duration of the layover and the obstinacy of the pilot group who were mostly hard charging, hard drinking military pilots who were going to drink regardless of any edict laid down by any tin-horn non-military CEO. A war of sorts ensued between the doctors of Mayo and the pilots of Northwest Airlines who loved fighting and were not about to be ordered about by doctors who, in the pilot's opinion, were only there to do away with their jobs.

One of the pilots refused to fill out the lengthy questionnaire that Mayo gave all pilots to fill out prior to their physical. When the doctor assigned to him tried to question him in order to fill out the form the pilot asked, "Do we have a doctor-patient relationship?" When the doctor asked why he wanted to know that the pilot said, "Because it makes a difference about what I tell you, you stupid shit." Of course there was not a doctor-patient relationship between the pilot and the Mayo doctor because the physical was ordered by NWA, paid for by NWA and the attendance of the pilot group at the Mayo Clinic was not voluntary.

One of the pilots, when asked, "How is your sex life?" answered, "Hey doc, it's just great. How's yours? Got any pictures of your wife? Got any sexy stories to tell me. Maybe we can both cork off while we relate what we do while having sex."

Another pilot when asked, "Do you drink?" said, "Well, no, not much, not all the time. What I usually do is to buy a whole case of Jim Beam and drive over to Wisconsin, check into a motel and drink the whole damn thing before I go home a few days later. Then I'm OK for a month or two." He reported that the doctor listened open-mouthed until he was finished and then realized that he was being tweaked.

Kruger loved tweaking his particular doctor, a little rotund man named Hogston. Dr. Hogston was a prissy person who was very impressed with himself. He was authoritarian and self important. Kruger initially refused to take the chest X-ray that Mayo "required" and when asked why he refused he told the doctor that he had talked to a PhD Radiologist who had told him that the exposure to a prophylactic X-ray was ill advised. Kruger asked, "Why doctor, are you suggesting that x-rays are good for me? If I am not sick should I take that X-ray? I thought that all of that radiation was cumulative. Are you telling me that it's not the case?" Hogsten was red-faced and had no response. He said, "Well, I'll have to note your refusal on your physical." Kruger said, "Note whatever you wish. It's not my physical. I didn't ask for it. I was ordered here for you guys to give me one by NWA."

Kruger always hated being led to the head of the line of very sick people in order to get a damned physical for NWA while the sick people had to wait for him. It was degrading to do that and see the sick watch him go to the head of the line. He hated NWA for putting him in that situation. And he hated the Mayo doctors for prostituting themselves to NWA for money.

A Navy Doctor had once told Kruger that the three most over-rated things in the world were sex with your wife, Mom's home cooking and the Mayo fucking Clinic.

One NWA pilot was on reserve and as such had to be on call for the crew schedulers to assign him a flight any time. He missed a Mayo Clinic appointment three times because of being called up for a flight. Mayo then called NWA and told the company that Mayo suspected that the pilot was an alcoholic because he refused to show up for a physical.

One day Kruger had to get a Mayo physical. He went through all of the tests and finally had to see Hogston for the evaluation. When he approached Hogston's office he kicked the door open which slammed against the wall. Then, having announced himself he strode into the office with authority and said in a loud voice, "Well, I see that you have put on weight the last time I saw you!" The surprised doctor said, "That's not true. I weigh the same as I did when I got out of Med school." Kruger said, "Well, you ought to exercise and take care of yourself. Your weight is concentrated around your middle. You look horrible!" The good doctor took offence at being tweaked and shortly ended the evaluation.

Another Mayo doctor braced a pilot by saying, "You are one of the hostile ones, aren't you"? The pilot responded in the affirmative whereupon the doctor said, "What are you afraid of?" The pilot said, "I'm not afraid of you, you asshole. I've flown in combat and have been shot at. You don't even measure up a little bit to that. I simply don't like you. You are not my first choice as a doctor, in fact, you aren't my choice at all." The doctor was white-faced when the pilot walked out of his office.

CHAPTER X

Now that the DC10s were grounded pending an inspection of the fleet Kruger needed a new job. Northwest asked him what he wanted to do and he opted to fly the 727 as a copilot again.

Kruger checked in with the training department and they asked him if three warm-ups in the simulator plus a check ride would be OK. Kruger figured that was sufficient in order to get him back in the swing of things, that is, actually flying once again. Flying is a perishable skill and the longer an aviator goes without actually practicing that skill the rustier that pilot gets.

On Kruger's first warm-up he met a former Flight Engineer, Wally Weber, who had been flying as a 727 Captain. When the 747s came on line Wally had opted to fly on that plane as a copilot since the pay was pretty comparable to that of a 727 Captain and there was little responsibility. Now he wished to fly as a 727 Captain once more and had to undergo the same sort of checkout that Kruger was engaged in. After the introductions had been accomplished the prospective Captain told Kruger that he had some difficulty in his warm-ups but said that the check/training pilot had told him that he could probably pass the check ride. He asked Kruger if he would help out in any way possible during his check, which was scheduled that morning. Kruger told him that he would do so but said, "I can't overtly help, of course, since the check pilot wouldn't allow that but I can give you some hints. If I see anything awry I'll either put pressure on the yoke or kick the rudders. If you feel anything like that you should look around to see what you are doing wrong. Wally agreed and the session began.

Sessions in the new simulators are conducted just like the actual airplane; in fact, if you didn't know better you would swear that you are actually in a plane. The simulators are suspended in the air on hydraulic pylons and operate in three dimensions just like the plane. In order to get inside of them you have to enter via a gantry that is pulled away from the simulator when the engines are started. Pilots have to wear their seat belts as some maneuvers could throw them out of their seats. The check rides are conducted in seniority order so the Captain always gets to go first.

On this particular session the regular check pilot had called in sick so the head of the training department, Ed Johnson, had to substitute for him. Ed was a very fair man but could be sharp-tongued at times. It didn't help that he had just come off of a regular flight and had been shanghaied into conducting the check ride. Ed was tired and really needed to go home and rest but the old "needs of the service" intervened and he was now committed to four more hours in the simulator plus extra time for the paperwork that was a requirement.

Wally was briefed to make a takeoff and climb to 5000 feet. He proceeded to do so with Kruger watching him and making the required calls as they approached the cleared altitude. Northwest mandated that a callout had to be made two thousand feet prior to the cleared altitude and again at a thousand feet prior in order for the pilot flying to keep from flying through or "busting" the altitude.

"Two to go", and then, "4 for 5 thousand," Kruger called. Wally didn't change power settings, attitude or rate of climb. It looked like he was hypnotized. Kruger realized that he was going to bust the altitude and climb right through it so he surreptitiously pushed forward on the yoke. Wally felt the forward pressure and responded by hauling back on the yoke with the result that the aircraft had climbed to 6000 feet before the check pilot laid his chin on Wally's right shoulder and said, "I won't accept that you son-of-a-bitch". Wally must have had a fragile psyche as that statement decimated him. He absolutely stopped flying. He couldn't have done anything correctly after that in spite of Kruger's help. Given a normal ILS approach to a landing with no emergencies, a rarity in the simulator, Wally crashed the plane. It was a miserable performance. Kruger was appalled. Finally, after two hours of what could only be termed "flogging about" instead of flying, the crew took a short break. Wally was wringing wet from sweating. The simulator was cold, as always.

Now usually the Captain is allowed to go home early at this juncture and the check pilot rides in the Captains seat and acts as the Captain for the copilot's part of the session. That didn't happen today. Kruger thought that portended a bad omen for Wally.

When they got back into the simulator it was Kruger's chance to show what he could do. This wasn't a check ride for him so he enjoyed the workout. He was put through a series of stalls, engine cuts on takeoff, engine-out approaches to minimums with a landing and a number of in-flight emergencies. He enjoyed the flying even if it was only in the simulator. When the session was over the Check Captain handed Kruger a piece of paper and said, "It would be just a waste of time and money to run you through more simulator time. If you have no objections I'm going to call this your check ride and you can go fly the line. Is that OK with you?" Kruger said, "Sure, I don't have a problem with that". The Check Captain then turned to Wally and said, "I'll see you in the airplane. See to it that you do a lot better there than you did in the simulator."

If a pilot received a "down" or a flunking check ride in the simulator he had one more chance to redeem himself by flying a better ride in the actual aircraft. If he couldn't do that he was history as far as being an airline pilot was concerned.

Kruger shook his head and thought, "So goes the war". He was released to the line and was a pilot once more.

Flying on the 727 was about as much fun as you could have with your clothes on as far as Kruger was concerned. It was a small plane as far as commercial aircraft was concerned and the crews were junior, young and full of energy and fun. The legs were short, the landings were numerous, you were always either in or around the weather and, at that time, the crews were together for the entire trip. Trips usually lasted for three or four days. It was real airline flying compared to flying on the 707 or the DC10, which meant one takeoff and one landing with hours of boring flying behind the autopilot in between.

The normal crew complement on the 727 was three pilots and three or four Cabin Attendants. Layovers were usually short but there seemed always to be enough time to party with your crew. Sometimes the trip schedules allowed for a long layover at one of the preferred cities. The crews had to bid for trips and "lines of flying" each month. Your seniority dictated whether you could hold the preferred lines or not. Every pilot had their own preferences as far as layover spots were concerned. Some pilots liked the western towns as they loved to fish and generally tramp that area. Kruger was catholic in his preferences but generally liked Seattle, Washington, DC, Miami, and Chicago. He only tolerated the western and mid-western cities and despised Canadian towns.

Sometimes one of the flying lines would offer a two day layover in Chicago. Most pilots figured that was a boring place and would shun that schedule but Kruger loved it. Since he was attached to one of the reserve squadrons at Glenview Naval Air Station, located just north of O'Hare field, he could "double-dip" and fly for the Navy while on a layover with

Northwest. It wasn't "legal" as far as the airline was concerned but it was a good way to spend the "downtime" on a long layover. One month he did just that.

There were several pilots at Northwest who flew for the Navy out of Glenview. One of them was named Garfield Benson. He was known as "Gar" by everyone except one of the Navy wives who called him "Lt. Filth Mouth", proof indeed that he was a stalwart and competent Navy pilot. Gar would always bid the same long layovers at Chicago that Kruger did and, since there was a gap in their seniority numbers they could bid for the same trip with Kruger flying as the copilot and Gar as the Second Officer.

One month it happened exactly in that manner. Kruger had bid the trip with the long Chicago layover and was called that evening by Gar who asked him if he was up for flying with the Navy during that time period. Kruger said that he would be happy to do so and Gar scheduled a plane and crew for that time period.

When they got to Chicago after the flight Kruger and Gar rented a car and shoved off for NAS Glenview. It was late in the day and the flight with the Navy crew was on for the next day. The two Northwest pilots repaired to the Officer's Club like any self-respecting pilots would. The evening progressed like anyone would expect with the addition of several other Navy pilots reporting onboard and meeting the two pilots in the club bar. Finally everyone decided to catch some chow and one of the pilots, Jim Lipe, agreed to drive. That was probably not the best decision of the group as Jim was a two-fisted drinker and could put most of the other pilots under the table easily.

The pilots sought a Chicago landmark called Hackney's that boasted plenty of onion rings and beer along with some of the best hamburgers in the Midwest. After an evening of stuffing themselves and imbibing more than a little beer the happy group attempted to find the Naval Air Station once again. It was slightly difficult since things tended to be rather blurred at that time in the evening but they pressed on with resolve and great glee. When they found the main gate of the air station Jim attempted to navigate past the Marine guard who didn't really know whether to salute the officer's sticker on the front bumper of the car or shoot the rowdy rabble that almost ran over the guard, mainly because Gar had suddenly placed his hands over the eyes of the driver, Jim, shouting, "Guess who?" Jim, in trying to "guess who" had their hands over his eyes almost ran down the Marine guard who, understandably, took offense at the assault and called the Command Duty Officer. By this time the group had dismounted from the car in the parking lot of the Bachelor Officer's Quarters, commonly called the BOQ. There were several catcalls and doubts cast on the ability of Jim to actually drive the car and this caused Jim to try and prove his driving ability by running down his detractors. As the officers giggled and ran from tree to tree, trying to gain access to the BOQ without being run down by Lt. Jim Lipe, the driver plowed large divots in the golf course that abutted the BOQ parking lot. Kruger, along with most of the officers felt that it was in their best interests to go to bed before someone took real exception to the damage done to the Glenview Golf Course. Jim Lipe was, by this time, immune to suggestion as he gleefully spun his tires on the green grass that had been carefully tended by those who value the game of golf.

The next morning saw an army of investigators scrutinizing the golf course and Jim's car. Jim was called to account and he testified that, as he was a very benevolent person, he had given numerous keys to a great number of officers in order for them to use the car whenever they wished and that he could not be held accountable for the sins of those nefarious officers who sought to abuse his bounty. After the normal tooth brushing and copious amounts of coffee Gar and Ed Kruger set out to fly their P2V.

The crew was mustered and finally the plane was airborne. The flight was over Lake Michigan and the TACCO ran the crew through the normal drills for submarine hunting. After about four hours the plane reported over "point Oboe for landing", entered the pattern and landed. Gar and Ed filled out the necessary paperwork and left for the hotel provided by Northwest for their layover. After a much needed night's sleep they were fresh and ready for duty the next morning. A perfect ending to a wonderful layover and schedule.

Kruger prided himself on his flying skills. He was well aware that he was not a "natural" pilot or one that seemed to have an easy time flying. On the contrary, he had to work hard to accomplish what he envisioned was good flying. He thought of himself as an average pilot although, like pilots have always been prone to do, he was not above telling anyone who wished to listen that he was the best of the best. Accordingly, he always ran each flight, each landing, each odd occurrence or emergency through his mind after the fact in order to see what he could have done to make that flight better. He knew of pilots who were lackadaisical about their flying and was disdainful of them. Those pilots tarnished the image of pilots in general, a cardinal sin in the minds of most good pilots. He prided himself on a smooth landing although he knew that the landing was not only the culmination of the flight but, in most cases, the easiest part of the flight. Irrespective of that, most passengers and all of the Flight Attendants graded the pilot on his landings and on nothing else.

Kruger had always said that he could do "slow rolls on the approach", make a smooth touchdown, and the passengers would consider him to be an above average pilot even though the other pilots would have to change their underwear after the event. That having been said he tried to give the passengers what they wanted; a smooth landing.

One month Kruger picked a line of flying that one of the training pilots picked. That pilot was a young Captain who was well liked and respected by everyone. Like most instructor pilots he had to fly the line every once in a while in order to keep up his flying skills. There is a wide gulf between instructing on an airplane and actually flying it. Flying is a very perishable skill and it doesn't take long to become "rusty" at it. Pilots have always realized this and even a month away from flying while on a vacation can dull the flying skills of anyone. The instructor was not immune to this syndrome and, as he had not flown the line for some time, he was a little "rusty".

As usual, the Captain and the co-pilot traded off "legs" of flying. The usual set-up was for the Captain to fly the first or initial leg of the day and then to trade off. This meant that the pilot doing the flying would make the takeoff and the landing and any flying in between. The pilot not flying would handle the communications. In this instance the Captain made consistent "hard" landings due to his lack of currency on the plane. Kruger, on the other hand, made very smooth landings and made it a point to tease the Captain regarding this by critiquing the Captain's landings in an unfavorable light. The Captain took the ragging in a humorous manner and tried vainly to emulate Kruger's smoothness. He was singularly unsuccessful in this regard throughout the whole month. Kruger amused himself by commenting on each of the Captain's landings.

"Oh, is that the way I'm supposed to do it? Damn! I never got that impression when I went through training. Maybe you ought to show me just how to land this thing. Obviously I can't do it like a training pilot does it." He kept up a dialog like this while the longsuffering Captain sweated and tried vainly to make a smooth touchdown.

Now a copilot has to document at least three landings in the month that he has his annual flight check. This saves the airline the expense and time of having to allow him to make his three landings as mandated by the FAA in a special flight. In the present case this was the month that Kruger had to have the Captain that he was flying with document his landings for the training department.

On the last leg of the last day of the flying for the month Kruger pulled out his training file and handed it to the Captain saying, "Well, I guess that you won't have much of a problem signing this chit considering how I landed this plane the whole month". He was grinning as he said it. The Captain took one look at the training chit and a large grin spread on his face.

"Oh, my! So you have a flight check ride coming up next month! I'll be looking forward to that. You can be sure that I'll try my best to be your check pilot and I'll give you the same benevolent consideration that you've given me this whole month".

Both pilots broke out in laughter after the Captain had said this. It was all good fun and just about every pilot had learned to accept humor of this type. People who possessed a "thin skin" in this regard rarely made the grade of becoming a pilot as the instruction was always presented in a harsh manner, especially for those pilots who obtained their training in the military. The best pilots were the ones that could laugh at themselves.

One month Kruger bid a trip sequence that had him landing at Madison, Wisconsin a few times. Madison had decided to resurface the main runway that month and so all planes had to land on the shorter runway as that was the only one available. Landing on the shorter runway was much more challenging than landing on the main or normal one.

The day had been a long one and had involved several takeoffs and landing sequences. Madison was the last landing of the day and it was Kruger's leg. He lined up in the landing configuration looking directly into the setting sun. There was no good landing aid for the runway like an ILS and the sun was blinding. Kruger sweated his way through the landing sequence but was unable to finesse his way to a smooth landing considering the short length of the runway. After all, the main objective was to stop the plane on the runway and making a smooth touchdown involved landing on a long enough piece of concrete in order to allow for the necessary light touch and finesse. As a contrast, landing on an aircraft carrier is a controlled crash, by definition, and normally involves a three-G touchdown, which would panic most airline passengers. The landing was a "hard" one. On the landing rollout the Captain picked up the PA microphone and announced, "That was not me; that was the copilot", to the tune of laughter from the passenger cabin.

Kruger took all of the ribbing in good humor and that night bought several tubes of Preparation H from a local drugstore. The next morning he handed out the tubes to each Flight Attendant onboard saying, "I figure that I'm responsible for any anal affliction like hemorrhoids that you may have as a result of the landing I made here last night so I'm trying to make amends by furnishing you girls with this remedy". The humor made up for his lack of smoothness the night before.

It was around this time period that Northwest Orient Airlines decided to change its name. Someone, somewhere along the line had decided that the term "Orient" was distasteful to the citizens of Asia so the company name was changed by the simple expedient of dropping the "Orient" art of the name. Henceforth the name of the airline would be simply "Northwest Airlines". Kruger privately thought the name change was unfortunate. The old name brought up images of pirates, the South China Sea and exciting flying, the things that had prompted Kruger to begin his flying career in the first place.

As for the "girls" in back, their collective name had been changed several times. Originally called "stewardesses", they had morphed from Cabin Attendants to the current Flight Attendants. The old name "stewardess" came from an earlier era of travel, that of ships. Onboard a ship the steward took care of all of the passenger needs including attending to the monetary aspects of it. The steward was a respected position. On board modern aircraft that position had devolved into one that was primarily concerned with serving food and drinks. The Flight Attendants desperately tried to get the public to acknowledge that they were crucial to the safety of flight and especially if and when it came to the evacuation of the passengers in case of an emergency. It was an uphill battle as the traveling public persisted in seeing them as sex objects. The design of their uniforms aided in this perception and that was directly the fault of the company itself.

A flight attendant came to the cockpit and tried to make the point that she was responsible for flight safety. She argued with one of the pilots that she was hired primarily for flight safety and the emergency deplaning of the passengers. The copilot cut to the chase by saying, "How many emergency evacs have you done?" The F/A said, "None". Then the copilot said, "How many martinis have you served?" Thereby making his point that the F/A was a defacto drink server and not a flight safety person.

The Flight Attendants had to keep a ships logbook similar to the one that the pilots had to keep. Perusing the log was a fun thing for some of the pilots since the F/As didn't have the experience the pilots had flying and the language used by the pilots was new to them. These logs were kept onboard the plane and were used by maintenance.

One day a F/A had a "gripe" concerning the interphone between the pilots and the Flight Attendants in the cabin. It seems that the chime that rang to alert the F/As was weak and couldn't be heard readily. The senior F/A wrote up the gripe as follows: "Captains dong is weak and sometimes does not function at all". The ink was not even dry on the logbook when the write-up was sent all over the world to any station that NWA serviced. The Flight Attendant was instantaneously famous. The write off was 'Captains interphone serviced".

Flying the 727 was, by and large, fun. Since it was the junior aircraft in the fleet that Northwest maintained it was staffed by the junior pilots and flight attendants. The schedules, at that time, ran parallel so that the schedules for the pilots were the same as the schedules for the flight attendants. That meant that the FAs (Flight Attendants) flew the same schedules and days that the pilots did. It was a setup for a scenario where a flight attendant could engage in a situation with a pilot who might or might not be married. Casual sex was rampant. What can you expect when you pair a bunch of young males with rampant gonads with a bunch of young females with raging hormones? The politically correct Military hasn't come to grips with that as yet. The layovers were, in a word, wonderful. One wag of a pilot said that since he had been associated with a lot of very young Flight Attendants he had to learn what kind of wine went well with peanut butter and jelly sandwiches.

Kruger was scheduled to fly with a Captain and a Second Officer who had planned to take their girl friends along on the trip that had a long layover of a day and a half in Miami. It was winter in Minnesota and the idea of a long layover in Miami sounded nice especially if a "significant other" was along to help cheer things up. Both pilots were nice guys and friendly. The fly in the ointment was the Captain's paramour was not his wife. He had doctored up a company pass for dependants and had listed his girl friend as his wife. He was as nervous as a cat creeping around a room full of German Shepherds. The girl friend sat in the passenger area beaming on "her Captain" who she could see through the large glass windows in the terminal. The Captain was distressed, as he had found out that the trip was oversold and dependant's passes would probably not be honored. The Second officer didn't have to worry as his girlfriend was one of the Flight Attendants on this particular flight. The Captain could see all of his plans flying away. He continually left his seat in the cockpit running out to the service podium to check the seating arrangements. The plane was filling rapidly. Finally, in the last few seconds before the plane was released and the pushback started he ran out of the cockpit saying, "Don't let them push us back yet."

Kruger thought, "Fat chance of that. We can't very well go anywhere without a Captain." Suddenly the Captain appeared in the cockpit with his girlfriend. He pointed to the jump seat and said, "Sit there and buckle in". He then jumped in his seat just as the crew chief said, "Release the brakes". He popped the brakes off and as the ship started to roll back the crew chief said, "Clear to start."

Kruger and the Second Officer sat with their mouths open. What the hell to do now? Do we fink on the Captain or go along with the farce? What the Captain had done had just violated about a million rules and laws. The Federal laws clearly stated that civilians were not allowed in the cockpit and Northwest rules mandated something like drawing and quartering for an employee who screwed around with passes. Kruger took a deep breath, glanced at the Second Officer who shrugged and paid inordinate attention to the Second Officer's panel, and started the engine start sequence.

The cockpit door suddenly opened and the senior Flight Attendant said, "Who is SHE?" pointing to the civilian in the jump seat. The Captain snapped, "She's FAA." The Flight Attendant slammed the door and Kruger thought, "God, it gets worse. That floozy looks like an FAA official about like I look like a Philippine whore." I wonder if any of us are going to come out of this with a whole skin?"

Suddenly the Second Officer said, "You guys need to listen to this." Kruger and the Captain toggled their radio switches in order to listen to the Second Officer's radio. Another flight that was pushing back at the same time had called our flight on "Second Officer common" or frequency 123.4, a frequency that no one else monitored. That flight said,

"I thought that you guys ought to know that the Customer Service Agent running your flight saw what you did. She's highly pissed and will more than likely call the company and report you. Just thought you would want to know. Have fun."

The Captain's face dropped. He looked sick. Kruger felt sorry for him but thought, "What the hell did he expect? That was about as blatant a screw up as I've ever witnessed." The flight progressed without further incident but was much quieter than flights of that type usually are. The layover in Miami was nice. The sun shown, the sand was warm, the beer and the martinis were cool and peace reigned over the earth. The girlfriend was happy and chattered a lot but the Captain was gloomy and looked like he was going to throw up at any time. Kruger felt sorry for him. It wasn't going to be pretty once he was back in the land of the perpetual snow and cold.

The flight home was subdued. The Captain took his penance like a man and didn't lose his job, a miracle in itself. Among other things he lost all of his free pass privileges for about a year or so. Kruger wondered how he was going to explain that to his wife. Kruger analyzed that flight like he did all others. "What have we learned on this flight?" he asked himself. The answer was obvious. "Don't let your little head think for your big one." That answer wasn't original to Kruger. He had heard it long ago from an enlisted friend in the Navy. It was as true today as it was back then.

On another trip the Captain was flying with his girl friend. The alliance had apparently been going on for some time. The Captain was not above bragging about his "conquest" and soon the other pilots in the cockpit were apprised of all of the dirty details about the affair. Both the Captain and the Flight Attendant were married to other people but that little detail didn't figure into the whole equation.

The Flight Attendant was solicitous and liked to talk to the Captain over the interphone. Unfortunately for her and the Captain she had no knowledge about how the aircraft systems were made up especially the communications system. She would call the Captain over the interphone and talk "sweet" to him.

The first time it happened Kruger motioned to the Second Officer and they both flicked up their interphone switches in order to hear what the Flight Attendant was saying to the Captain. They grinned as the F/A said, "Dale, I love you. Do you know that you are super in bed?"

The Captain turned beet red and said, "Hey, the other pilots can hear what you are saying."

The F/A said, "Oh, I don't think so. I think that you're just shy. You don't have to be shy with me, lover. You are a super lover, do you know that?"

Kruger and the S/O silently laughed as the Captain turned redder, if that was possible. He tried vainly to silence his girl friend who wouldn't hear of it. She continued to praise him for his "bedroom acrobatics" much to his embarrassment. His crew members delighted in his discomfort. He continued to try to convince his girl friend that the other cockpit members were listening.

Finally the F/A asked, "Ed, Jim, are you listening?" Neither pilot answered. The Captain continued to try to convince the F/A that others were listening but his words fell on deaf ears.

After a number of minutes of soupy, sexual dialog Kruger finally keyed his mike and said, "Can we stop all of this interphone sex shit and just carry on with the trip?" There was an intake of breath on the interphone and then silence. The F/A had a hard time facing the other pilots for the rest of the trip much to their delight. The Captain just doggedly continued on with his alliance.

On one other trip the Captain had been dallying with one of the F/A s the whole night and had little, if any, sleep that night. When he reported for the flight he looked a little less than optimum. Kruger decided to keep an eye on him.

On the taxi out to the runway Kruger glanced over and saw that the Captain had fallen asleep and was "hanging in his shoulder harness". Kruger had limited steering on the 727 with his rudder pedals and steered the plane to the duty runway. When he got there he punched the Captain's shoulder and said, "Hey, you've got to steer us onto the runway. I can't do that." The Captain roused himself and they soon were aligned with the runway. When they were cleared for takeoff Kruger was super alert, watching the Captain constantly. At liftoff the Captain seemed to be sound asleep once again so Kruger calmly took over command of the flight and made the takeoff himself. He continued to fly the plane and do all of the communications by himself. He did this until they got to their destination. He then flew the approach and, as they neared the outer marker on the ILS approach the "Captain" woke up and said, "Well, I guess that I had better make the landing". Kruger relinquished the controls but continued to watch the Captain's progress. The landing was average according to what Kruger had observed previously. As far as Kruger was concerned the best way to ensure the safety of the flying passengers was to be cognizant of the abilities of the other pilots and to jump in whenever he was needed. The myth of the invincibility of the Captain was just that. They were mostly just the same nose-picking guys as the rest of the pilots. They attended to the same bell curve as everyone else. They were all "Just Another Pilot". Kruger had no problem flying with other pilots like this. As he had told the Captain who shouted, "This is a two pilot plane. How can I help you when you insist on doing everything by yourself?", "I really don't need any help. I can fly this plane all by myself." One of the Captains Kruger had flown with said, "I really think that you are in charge of the plane no matter what seat you are in." Kruger had replied, "I'm always and have always been in charge of every plane I've ever flown in no matter what my title has been. When it comes to safety and survival I have no peer." The Captain said, "I guess I believe that."

Another time Kruger was flying a plane on an approach to Cleveland. The weather was marginally VFR in a lot of haze. The Center asked if Kruger's plane wished a visual approach. That took the Approach Control off the hook as the pilots were then responsible for the approach and landing. The Captain, who was doing the communication while Kruger flew, said "Affirmative" and they were on their own. The Center asked if the NWA plane had the field in sight. The Captain told them that he had but Kruger did not and said so. He objected and the Captain said, "You're doing just fine. Just keep on this heading." They continued while Kruger searched in vain for the field. Finally the Center said, "Northwest, what are your intentions?" That was an immediate alarm. For the Center to say that was akin to saying, "Northwest, it appears that you have your head up your ass. Will you please tell us what you are doing?"

The Captain tried to appear nonchalant and said, "What are you trying to do, Ed, get us lost?" Ha! Trying to get us lost! Kruger had been flying a heading the Captain had pointed out to him. Now the Captain had divorced himself from the problem and was trying to dump the cause of the problem into Kruger's lap. Kruger, no stranger to blame letting, reacted immediately. He switched his automatic direction finder (ADF) to the inner marker of the ILS system for the runway he was supposed to land on and quickly turned to follow the needle that was pointing 30 degrees to his right. He had already tuned the radios so the response was immediate. The landing was without incident but Kruger never forgot the whole scenario and never again accepted a "visual approach" without following his navigation aids

There is really no way to see for yourself the might and power of Mother Nature other than to experience it first hand and up front. Kruger had always figured that the best way to do this was to fly. One day his 727 was following another 727 by about three miles in trail. The center had spaced them that way and was vectoring them around thunderstorms. Now the average citizen doesn't give much thought to a thunderstorm other than to seek shelter when it's raining. Not so pilots and mariners who know full well the power of one of those creations. The average thunderstorm is fully capable of ripping parts of the airplane off and spitting it out. Cells within the storm contain updrafts and downdrafts that can be hundreds of feet per second next to each other. The resulting sheer effect is stronger than any metal we know of. Most pilots, that is, most intelligent pilots, will give thunderstorms a wide margin. Passengers gripe when pilots detour around large thunderstorms by hundreds of miles translating to time spent airborne. What the hell do they know? They gripe even though the pilot has delivered them to their destination a few minutes late but all in one piece. If they only knew . . . .

On this particular day Kruger was entranced by the contrast between what he had thought was a rather large airplane and the thunderstorms, which were much, much larger. The storms towered up to around 45,000 feet and made the 727s look like tiny toys as they maneuvered around the gigantic storms. The 727s looked like Tinker Toys against the backdrop of the storms. It put things into stark perspective. Kruger would always remember that picture whenever he had thoughts about his own importance in the world.

On another day Kruger was handling the radios on a flight from Washington, DC to Cleveland. The center was busy as always and had vectored Kruger's plane head on into a large thunderstorm. This storm towered to altitudes of 50,000 feet or higher. Normally the higher the tops of the storm complex the more power it possessed. Kruger called the center and told them that he would not accept the vector due to the storm. The center responded that due to traffic Kruger's plane would simply have to comply. Kruger then said, "There is no way I'm going to fly into that storm. If you can't give us a corrective vector we'll just set up a holding pattern right here until you can give us a better heading." The center screamed and bawled but Kruger told the Captain, "Might as well go into a hold right here because I'm not about to fly into that thing and you aren't either." The Captain laughed and started a turn into a left hand pattern. Another flight called and offered the advice, "Center, I don't blame him. I wouldn't fly into that thing either." Finally the center buckled under and gave Kruger's plane a better vector that took them far enough away from the storm to be safe.

Northwest Airlines finally adopted a policy of avoiding thunderstorms by one mile for every knot of wind at the higher altitudes. What that meant was that the NWA planes would avoid the storms on the downwind side by up to 150 miles when the jet stream was sailing along at 150 knots, a normal occurrence.

Kruger had a layover in Miami. He liked Miami a lot since it was close to his home in Naples. He decided to have a beer in a local watering hole named Big Daddys. Of all the pilots flying for Northwest Airlines most were ex military. The civilian pilots were jealous of the training the military pilots had undergone and were vociferous in their condemnation of the military pilots. The military pilots all called the civilian ones FLAPS for" Fucking Light Airplane Pilots". The civilian pilots called the military pilots "FEMS" for "Fucking Ex-Military".

One of the military groupies was a Captain on the 727 that Kruger liked to fly with. He used to talk the talk about military things like he was ex-military. On one trip Kruger was flying as the Copilot when the Second Officer asked the Captain what branch of the military he had served with. As far as the Second Officer was concerned the Captain had been in the military based on his talk and his slinging around several phrases and terms that he had gleaned from talking to people who had really served. Kruger turned and smiled at the Second Officer. Then he took out his pen and drew a line under the flap handle that was labeled "FLAP". He terminated the line with an arrow that pointed to the Captain. The Second Officer collapsed in a paroxysm of laughter when he realized that the Captain was a flap. The Captain shook his head and called Kruger an asshole.

On this particular layover in Miami Kruger had gone to Big Daddy's and ordered a beer. It was in the afternoon and the bar was pretty well empty. Kruger was enjoying his beer when a guy sitting next to him offered to buy him another beer. It's a real oddity when any man asks another man if he can buy him a beer. Most males would think the guy offering a drink was gay. Kruger declined as he didn't, on rule, want anyone to buy him a drink. The guy kept up chatter and said that he had flown "Spads". Kruger alerted on this as the A5 was called the Spad in Vietnam. It was known in the Naval Establishment as the AD. Kruger talked to the man for several minutes and found that what he was referring to as the Spad was actually a three winged airplane. He was referring to a WWI plane. Kruger figured that he was an oddball. Finally Kruger asked if he was a Naval Aviator. When he said "yes" Kruger produced his retired Navy retired card and asked if the guy's card looked anything like that. The guy looked at Kruger's ID card and a large tear ran down his face. Kruger figured that he was mentally deranged. He paid his bill and hurriedly left the bar.

Trips to a local bar during layovers was always dangerous. Northwest had a "no alcohol" policy any time a crew member was on duty. "On Duty" meant from check in to leaving the crew bus at the end of the trip. Pilots would drink anyway any time they wished but it was always a chancy thing.

On one layover in Madison, Wisconsin Kruger had gone to a local bar with the other pilots. He was enjoying a quiet beer at the bar, which was populated with a number of graduate students from the local university. A female who appeared to be a grad student kept glaring at him as if she was very irritated with him. Kruger was confused as he did not know nor had ever met the lady and had not spoken to her. As she glared at him he finally lifted his beer to her and said, "Good evening". She suddenly shouted, "What makes you narcs think that you are better than the rest of us?" Kruger left the bar rather than try to convince the lady that he did not work for the Bureau of Alcohol, Tobacco and Firearms.

On another layover in Great Falls Kruger and the copilot wanted to have a quick beer and go to bed. It had been a hard day and the weather in Great Falls was cold and snowing. Kruger put on his uniform coat since it was colder than a woman's liberation's lips after an argument with a damned male entity. The copilot was dressed the same way. The two pilots shivered their way to a local bar and were relaxing, fully dressed with their coats on at the bar. The coats were Navy blue in color. Suddenly one of the local denizens spoke up and said, "You two guys aren't fooling anyone. We all know exactly who you are."

Kruger's blood ran cold as he thought that the company was going to find out that he and the copilot were drinking. He coughed and said, "OK, you've got us. Who are we?" The local said, "Hell, anyone can tell that you guys are undertakers. There must be a convention here in town." Kruger relaxed and laughed as he said, "Well, you figured us out really quick. We will have to get another costume the next time we come here won't we? I have to tell you that you are really quick on figuring out who we were. Congratulations."

Northwest Airlines was run by an old curmudgeon named Donald Nyrop. Nyrop insisted on vetting any and all monetary amounts that were expended by the company. The company was known for paying its bills late or not at all. Nyrop had instituted a policy of not feeding any pilot or flight attendant who was deadheading to fly a trip. He figured that those people were being given a pass and didn't deserve any food even though they were on duty. Accordingly their passes were stamped "No meal authorized"

The pilots were used to this "second class citizen" status and when deadheading, would flash their passes to the FAs in order to make them aware that the pilot did not deserve a meal. One day a Northwest Captain, Thomand O'Brian, was deadheading in tourist class in uniform. He was in seat 23 C in a 727. That seat is next to the aisle. As the FA walked up the aisle with a load of four trays of food she tripped and deposited the whole load into Captain O'Brian's lap. O'Brian, nonplussed and always of a good sense of humor said, "I'm sorry m'dear, but I can't accept this. Y'see here on this here pass issued by NWA. I can't accept any food but thank you anyway."

Sometime later on a new CEO named Lapinski took over the reins of NWA. He was flying in first class with a Northwest pilot who was deadheading in order to pick up a trip when the meal service was commenced. As everyone but the pilot was served Lapinski asked the pilot why he wasn't eating. The pilot said that he wasn't because he couldn't and showed Lapinski his pass stamped "meal not authorized". Lapinski evidenced surprise and ordered the F/A to give the pilot a meal. As soon as he had arrived back at the general offices he changed the policy to include pilots on duty in any capacity. The old "meal not authorized" was summarily canceled.

CHAPTER XI

Flying the 727 remained fun but Kruger had to acknowledge that he had left the Navy in order to make a lot more money than he could make flying for the Navy and the time that he had to spend flying for Northwest was much less than he would have had to fly for the Navy. In addition he would have much more time away from the job to do whatever he wished. He couldn't escape the fact that flying in the larger planes that Northwest flew would improve both factors. He finally sighed and asked for an assignment again as a DC10 Second Officer now that the DC10s had been certified as safe for flying once again.

Flying as a Second Officer on the DC10 would not only mean more money but more time off and some really nice layover spots. It was a tradeoff but then leaving the Navy for the airlines had been a tradeoff also. He went through a fast checkout and was soon on the line once again.

The time off as a result of flying as a DC10 crewmember actually made flying for the Navy Reserve much easier. Since the DC10 schedules were fairly long they left a lot of off time that could be used to fly for the Navy. Kruger used that time to the maximum. Flying for the Navy was still a lot more fun and interesting than flying for the airline.

Kruger had been the NATOPS or training and check officer for a long time. He had promised the Naval Station Training Officer that he would stay in this billet and he had kept his promise. A good friend, John Sears, coveted Kruger's job and had often expressed a desire to replace him. Any job gets stale after a long time and Kruger's job as NATOPS was no different. Kruger had a long discussion with the Program Manager and had recommended Sears for the position. Finally the Manager agreed and John was given the new job. It was like a new toy for a little kid. Sears gloried in his new job.

John was an anachronism. He had left the Navy with no clear goals. He had not attempted to be hired with any airline but knocked around instead, existing by flying for the Navy Reserve as a regular job. Kruger could never figure out why John had left the Navy in the first place. John was junior in rank to Kruger but was competitive nonetheless. Much earlier Kruger had flown with John in the P2 and as they were being vectored by approach control in the Glenview area they were in and out of cloud cover. Kruger had put John in the left seat and John was flying with Kruger as the copilot/backup pilot. Suddenly, as the plane flew out of a thick cloud cover Kruger saw a DC9 from O'Hare approaching on a collision course at the same altitude. Knowing the competitive attitude of Sears and knowing that if he, Kruger, put any pressure on the yoke that John would counter it culminating with a fight for control of the aircraft Kruger simply said, "John, dive, now." John did so and the DC9 passed overhead. Kruger immediately called approach control to advise them as to what had just happened and to complain. The flight continued to a landing at Glenview and as they landed the tower called, "O'Hare is calling and wants you to give them a call by phone as soon as possible." Kruger responded, "I don't want to talk to them. Tell them that I just don't want that near miss to happen again. If they can promise that I'll be happy." The tower said they would be happy to do so.

Kruger discussed the incident with Sears and John agreed that if Kruger had pushed the yoke that he, John, would have reacted like Kruger had figured with the result that a midair collision would have resulted. John concurred.

Lt. Sears was very proud of being the NATOPS Officer. It was as if he had just put on another stripe. One evening Kruger was in bed in the BOQ (called Splinterville by the pilots) when John bumbled into the next room. John was pretty well oiled and was trying to smuggle some female into his room. The walls (bulkheads) in the BOQ were thin and every little noise was transmitted to at least the next three rooms. John's female friend was giggling nonstop. John was very concerned that she had to understand that he was a "training pilot" and he mentioned that fact about every five minutes. It was all Kruger could do to keep from laughing as he realized that John was more concerned about bragging on himself than getting the lady in his bed. John was so drunk that he soon fell asleep and failed to finish the mission that he had obviously started out to accomplish.

As was the usual case with Northwest Airlines, the Airline Pilots Association called a strike against the airline due to an inability to come to an accord in labor negotiations. Kruger was, by now, used to this. Other airlines called Northwest the "Cobra Airlines, willing to strike at a moments notice." As soon as the strike was called Kruger called the Naval Reserve at Glenview and asked if there were any schools available. He lucked out as an ASW (Anti-Submarine Warfare) school was being hosted by the Naval Air Station at Willow Grove, Pennsylvania. Kruger called up John Sears and the two signed up for the course.

Kruger picked up Sears at the Naval Air Station, Glenview. It had been decided that Kruger would drive since he had the better car. The trip to Willow Grove (called Willy's Grave by pilots) was non-eventful and the two pilots signed into a local motel, bypassing the Naval Station's BOQ, considered to be a "slum" by the pilots. The Naval Air Station was not known for its cleanliness.

On the first day of the school the two had breakfast at the BOQ. It was a pretty horrible meal and, during it, Kruger asked for the coffee carafe. Another pilot said, "Take a look at my coffee cup before you ask for any coffee." Kruger looked and saw a large cockroach in the pilot's cup. He said, "Why don't you get another cup and pour yourself more coffee?" The pilot said, "I poured that roach out of the carafe." That did it for breakfast then and in the future.

The school was classified Secret. No documents could be removed from the classroom. Any "homework" had to be done in the security area. Kruger and Sears were the only aviators in the entire class. The rest of the class was made up of Surface Warfare Officers like Destroyer and Cruiser Officers. The class was interesting especially when a submarine officer was the guest lecturer and talked about ASW in relation to helos and dunking sonar.

Most of the other officers did a lot of extra study after class. Kruger and Sears did their study at a local bar. When the final test was given Sears got the highest score in the class and Kruger followed up with the second highest. The rest of the officers were highly irritated at the shakeout. How dare the damned pilots score so high without any extra study at all? Both pilots acted like pilots have always acted. They said, "Well, What can we say? Pilots are, after all, superior in every way. We feel the pain of the Surface Warfare Officers but we really can't do much to help. We consider it to be genetic." I'm happy to report that both pilots escaped with whole skins.

During the school Kruger discovered a club that advertised a cover charge that covered all the beer you could drink. That evening he and Sears drove to the club and checked in. After the cover charge all you had to do was hold your mug over the bar and it would be filled. Kruger and Sears were soon well on their way to absolute drunkenness.

Kruger became besotted while Sears tried to find a female companion. Unfortunately for him, most of the females present were much too young for guys of Sears' age. Sears struck out.

Kruger finally had enough beer and wanted to go home. He looked for Sears without any results and finally decided that John had hooked up with some young chippy, probably blind with a reduced sense of smell, and had shoved off. He decided to find his car and leave. More than likely John would call him in the morning and ask for a ride.

As Kruger approached his car he saw a strange thing. There were two legs sticking out from under his car. Upon further investigation he found that John had somehow become so inebriated that he had rolled under Kruger's car and had passed out. Kruger saw his legs just in time before he drove over them on his way home. Since the legs were sticking out from the right side of the car only the habit that Kruger had of "preflighting" his car or walking around it prior to getting in it saved John from losing his legs. He resurrected John and got him in the car. Then he drove home to the motel and tumbled Sears into his bed. The next morning Sears was unrepentant as always and as befits a good Naval Aviator. After drinking copious amounts of coffee the two drove back to Glenview without incident.

NAS Glenview hosted an august group of Naval Aviators called the Grey Eagles. These were some of the earliest Navy pilots. One morning in summer the sun was just coming up. The birds were waking up and the day promised to be very nice. Kruger was in bed dozing. His BOQ window was open and he could hear the early morning noises as he slowly awakened. Two of the Grey Eagles who were early risers were camped just outside of Kruger's window and were relating some of the things they remembered from their flying days. Kruger was delighted to eavesdrop on the reminiscences of these old warriors. One of the stories concerned a flight where the aviator had run out of gas.

"I was on a flight to Chincoteague in an NCN (A Navy float plane). I was flying along the beach using contact navigation when my engine stuttered and quit. I made a dead stick landing on the beach. The landing was pretty good and nothing appeared to be broken on the plane, which was a few feet from the water on the sandy beach. I figured that I had run out of gas so I hiked a few miles until I found a farmer who had a gas pump for his machinery. He loaned me a few gallons and I tanked up. He even helped me dig a trench for the floats and we muscled the plane into the water. I climbed aboard, started the engine, waved to the farmer and took off. I got to Chincoteague OK, just a little late."

Kruger loved hearing the tale. He marveled at the ease of flying on the part of the old pilot, the relaxed atmosphere, the matter-of-fact handling of the emergency and the solution, which was about as innovative as anything he had ever heard of. It was a different era of flying and tugged at the nostalgia in Kruger.

The Navy always used an airlift in order to round up the military men and officers from their various homes in the Midwest and present them to the Naval Air Station, Glenview, Illinois for service during the drill weekends. The airlift was usually run by the Military Airlift Command or MATS and the planes used were DC6s or 7s. Occasionally the Marines were pressed into service since they flew the C19 or, as the Navy termed it the "dollar nineteen". All of the planes had a given number of seats and when they were full anyone left over had to go via commercial air if they wished to drill at Glenview. The airlift caused several problems, of course.

One of the first problems occurred when a junior officer sought the help of Kruger. This officer was not well liked but was competent in his job nonetheless. His complaint was that an officer more senior to him had bumped him from the airlift by boarding at the last moment and, approaching him said, "I've never liked you so I'm going to take your seat. You are ordered to leave the plane now." Kruger listened and said, "OK, it will never happen again. Leave it to me."

Kruger looked up the officer in question. He described the incident and asked if it had occurred as the junior officer had described it. The officer he faced told him that that was an accurate account of the incident. Kruger then laced the officer with a scathing ass-chewing saying that his action was not in any tradition of the Navy, that he had used his rank to beat down a junior officer and that if he ever did something like that again he, Kruger, would see that a general courts martial was convened in order to revoke his commission and wings. The frightened officer assured Kruger that he would never repeat an incident like that again.

Kruger didn't trust the Marine "Dollar 19s" so he didn't regularly take the airlift. He took one of the Northwest planes to Chicago instead and hitched a ride on a taxi to Glenview. Occasionally he did ride the airlift when the DC 6 or 7 was scheduled.

One Sunday evening Kruger and another officer, LCDR Grey Snobbes, along with several enlisted men were waiting on the DC6 in the Operations Office of Glenview. The OPS office was like a regular airline terminal in that people would wait there until their plane arrived after which they could board. All of the officers and enlisted men waiting on the plane were off duty. They had put in a full days work and were tired. Kruger left and shortly arrived with a few six-packs of beer which he handed out liberally to everyone waiting on the airlift. As he did so he thanked them for giving up their weekend for the Navy.

Kruger had just downed a large gulp of beer when he heard a loud roar. The Operations Duty Officer had seen one of the enlisted men drinking his beer. He was screaming at the man when Kruger intervened. Kruger said, "Just what is the problem here? Why are you bracing that man?"

The Duty Officer said, "He is drinking in a working area. This is a working area. He cannot do that."

Kruger looked around and saw fear on the faces of the men that he had given the beer to. He saw, also, that LCDR Snobbes had hidden his beer near his seat and had not intervened at all. His immediate thought was that Snobbes was a weak Officer who would not stand up for his men.

Kruger got between the enlisted man and the OPS Officer. He directed the man to sit down and told him that he was in no trouble. Then he faced the OPS Officer, who was of a rank the same as Kruger. He said, "I gave the beer to these men. They are not on duty and are awaiting the airlift. You have no right to brace them. If you think that you have observed an infraction of some rule you bring that up with me and not the men under me. Is that quite clear? The Ops Officer blustered in an attempt to salvage his pride but Kruger would not back down. Kruger said, "If you think that my assessment of this incident is wrong then bring it up with the Commander of this Naval Air Station. Otherwise, leave my men alone and attend to your job."

The OPS Officer grumbled but left. Kruger looked at the relieved faces of the men he had given the beer to and said, "Relax, guys, drink your beer and make sure that you throw the cans in the trash so no one has any complaints against us."

During the whole time LCDR Stephen Grey Snobbes said nothing, nor did he finish his beer. Kruger figured that he had taken the measure of LCDR Snobbes.

An amusing incident occurred concerning Grey Snobbes. Grey was employed by Northwest Airlines. One of the Second Officers that Kruger flew with related the following incident concerning Grey.

A couple of crews from Northwest had a layover in Chicago. They all went to supper together and were "well oiled" when they came home to their hotel, the Ambassador West in Chicago. The Second Officer said that Grey was pretty drunk and had taken a fancy to one of the Flight Attendants. He was in the lobby trying to coax her into his room. The lady was reticent.

Now you have to realize that Grey was a large man and was normally loud whenever he spoke. In the Navy he was known as "Boomer" because of the loudness of his speech. In addition, Grey had a very pronounced southern accent stemming from his home in southern Georgia.

According to the Second Officer, Grey had taken hold of the Flight Attendant's arm and was pulling her toward his room. As he did he "boomed" "C'mon girl" in a very loud voice. The lady in question only giggled and resisted the tugs on her arms.

Finally the uproar got sufficient that someone in the hotel called the police thinking that a rape was in progress. When the police arrived on scene Grey released the lady's arm and fled to his room. The lady, thus released, staggered backwards and ended up upside down in a laundry basket left by the cleaning ladies. The Second Officer said that Grey had to go home and "make love to his fist". At the end of the narrative Kruger was laughing was so hard that he could hardly breathe

During the summer Glenview Naval Air Station decided to resurface the principal runway. It was the longest runway Glenview possessed. The next choice and the least used was a very short runway that ended with a lot of civilian houses directly in line with the runway. The plan the Air Station intended to use was to make all pilots use the short runway during VFR conditions. When the weather turned bad the pilots were to shoot a GCA approach to the long runway to be broken off at minimums circling to land on the short runway. Most of the pilots didn't like the plan but had no choice in the matter.

The first incident happened when LCDR George Schuttes tried to fly in IFR conditions. George was a very nice, likeable guy but his regular job in civilian life was as a school teacher. The only flying he ever got was on his one weekend a month at Glenview supplemented by his two week active duty period once a year. That was really not enough flying in order to maintain any real sort of proficiency.

George's Plane Captain was an older enlisted man; also a very nice guy but a little short on grey matter. The Plane Captain was not one of the few chosen to attend the Navy's P3 Flight Engineer School. After takeoff George was to fly around Lake Michigan and the immediate area while the ASW crew practiced their hunting techniques assisted by electronic black boxes aboard the plane that simulated an enemy submarine. The flight was scheduled for four hours. At the end of that time George had to shoot the GCA approach in marginal weather, circling to land on the short runway. Kruger decided to keep an eye on the marginal pilot.

In reconstructing the incident later on it was determined that the Plane Captain had to use the relief tube at some time during the flight. The relief tube was simply a tube the crew used to urinate in. The liquid waste was vented overboard in the vain hope that it would evaporate before it hit the ground or, it was hoped, would at least become a fine mist that no one would even notice if it landed on them. Aviators have long discounted any responsibility for peeing on lesser hominids.

A Plane Captain on the P2V is not the same thing as the Plane Commander. The Plane Captain is sort of like a Flight Engineer only not as technically trained. The Plane Captain is responsible for fueling the plane and ensuring that the engines and systems are capable of operating efficiently.

The Plane Captain was obese and insisted on wearing the full array of his Mae West survival vest along with the parachute harness that was used with the chest pack parachutes carried on the P2. It made for a very bulky crew member.

The P2 had a mass of circuit breakers along the port side of the flight deck. The breakers were used for the wide array of electronic gear onboard along with all of the electrical components used to fly the plane. Enroute to the relief tube the Plane Captain found himself "hung up" or caught on something. Instead of backing up and finding what was holding him he bulled his way ahead. What he had snagged was the circuit breaker for the propeller reverse circuitry. In the present case he had ripped the CB completely out of the panel where it fell unnoticed to the deck.

His task completed the Plane Captain regained his post in the jump seat in the cockpit. He neglected to inform anyone of his snagged gear.

When the four hours were up George ran through the approach check list. One of the items on the list was the challenge "circuit breakers". The response was for the copilot to look back at the circuit breaker panel to see if any popped circuit breakers were apparent. When a CB popped due to some overload it would show a line of white that was only apparent when the breaker was not properly seated. During the approach check list the copilot did not see any white lines so he assumed that all of the CBs were seated. No one could foresee the Murphy's Law in progress now. The CB that controlled the prop reverse was completely missing so no white line was apparent at all. The crew figured that everything was OK so they plodded onward.

George shot the approach OK and circled at 300 feet to the short runway. Kruger was outside watching his approach and landing. He saw George land long, not something you really want to do on a short runway. George was trying to make a "soft" landing. Again, not something you really wanted to do on a short runway. When the P2 touched down it was very close to the middle of the runway. Kruger saw the jet engines dump fuel on touchdown.

Now every approach in the P2 was mandated to be a four engine approach. The jets were to be on line in case they were needed. The big 3350 recips were the primary power suppliers. NATOPS mandated for the copilot to cut the jet engines on touchdown. When the jets were cut they dumped about a half gallon of fuel out of each engine fuel control. The fuel dump was readily apparent. When George touched down the copilot dutifully changed the plane from a four engine machine to a two engine one as far as a wave off was concerned.

The prop reversing system on the P2 rotated the props into the reverse position. The system used different sets of throttles but both sets only distributed avgas into the engines. Without the prop reverse electrical system either set of throttles only furnished avgas to the engine, which functioned like any other engine and sped up according to the amount of gas furnished to it.

George realized that he had touched down long and got on the reverse throttles immediately. When he pulled the reverse throttles in order to slow down he saw, much to his horror, that the plane sped up instead of slowing down. In fact, it sped up so much that he was very soon airborne again. As Kruger watched, fascinated, George flew over the houses at the end of the runway just over stall speed since he only had two engines active. The noise level in those houses must have been enormous.

George was in a dilemma. Here he was, involuntarily airborne, with his throttles in the reverse prop position instead of the normal position. George desperately wanted to add power and climb in order to gain more altitude but he was afraid of touching the throttles. He really did not want the props to go into reverse while he was airborne and had not, as yet, figured out just what went wrong. He called the squadron maintenance officer and asked for a little help. Maintenance had a more relaxed view of things, especially because they were not in the plane and the situation didn't affect them as much as it did the frightened flight crew. Finally Maintenance figured that if George had enough altitude and airspeed it wouldn't harm anything for him to close the reverse throttles and activate the normal ones. George did so with much trepidation and was soon flying normally. The landing was accomplished without any prop reversing and subsequent examination of the incident uncovered the causes thereof. A notice was circulated to all flight crews explaining in great detail what not to do when you became involuntarily detained while moving about the plane, especially when in the vicinity of the circuit breaker panel.

Another incident happened while the long runway was being resurfaced. Kruger was a witness to this one also since he had adopted the habit of watching the pilots land on the short runway especially when the weather was not optimal. Once again a marginal pilot landed long on the short runway and Kruger saw the jet engine fuel controls spray fuel as the copilot cut both jet engines as per NATOPS. This time the pilot flying realized early that he had landed long and cobbed the power on the recips becoming airborne once again. Once more the plane barely cleared the houses at the end of the runway and disappeared in the murk. When the plane had touched down approach control was notified and they gave the all clear for the next plane in a holding pattern to shoot the approach. That plane was being flown by the very large, very loud pilot that hailed from Savannah, Georgia appropriately named Grey Snobbes. Grey was a likeable but very loud and opinionated officer who did not suffer fools lightly. He was making the approach in the approved manner and was about to touch down on the short runway when he saw another P2 approaching the runway on the opposite track at his altitude. It was enough to jump-start a calm pilot's heart. Grey erupted and made a hasty waveoff and a wild right turn to avoid a mid-air collision while calling the tower and accusing them of "fucking him" by setting him up for a midair collision. The tower vacillated between cautioning Grey against using profanity on the air and trying to defend themselves from the charges.

The pilot who caused all of the commotion did not know what to do after he had made the waveoff. He should have called the tower, received a change of frequency to approach control for vectors to another approach and made another attempt at a landing. Instead of doing that he simply did what is known in Navy terminology as a "whifferdill" or a 90 degree turn followed by an immediate 270 degree turn which is supposed to put the plane on the exact opposite track back the way it came from. Of course he did this in IFR conditions, something that is frowned upon by any yardstick you wish to measure it by. What he intended to do once he saw the runway on the opposite heading in the landing pattern is up to anyone's conjecture. It is enough that he gave Grey, the crew and the tower all adrenalin surges sufficient enough to require copious amounts of ethyl alcohol at the club that evening in order to calm down.

Kruger had always thought that the policy of cutting the jet engines on touchdown was idiocy. The ostensible reason for the policy was to keep FOD (foreign object damage) to a minimum. It was advertised that the jets, being shut down, would not suck up any foreign items into the engine thereby damaging them. In actual fact, closing the jet engine throttles dumped the fuel control of fuel and activated a countdown time period of 60 seconds while the jets purged themselves of fumes. By that time the plane would have slowed and turned off of the runway. Then, and only then, would the jet pod engine doors close to prevent the ingestion of FOD. What the policy did, in fact, was to change the plane from a four engine platform into a two engine one thereby derogating its ability to immediately takeoff once again safely. It did nothing to prevent the ingestion of FOD. Kruger had just witnessed two incidents that gave credence to his idea. The system though, once in place, had enough inertia that nothing Kruger could say would change the current thinking about how to fly the plane. Policy, once instituted in the Navy, was like policy in government. Once instituted it was never changed.

One day a circular arrived from high up on the food chain of command. It dictated that all pilots would have a letter of designation placed in their individual jackets ("jacket" being the Navy term for "record"). The designation letter would tell anyone just what designation the pilot possessed, that of being a PPC, a PC, a copilot, a navigator or whatever. The CO, being a very thorough man, complied with the circular. When asked what he was to do with the officers in the squadron that had not, as yet, checked out in anything on the P2 and therefore had no designation he solved the problem by the simple fact of having a letter of designation placed in that officer's jacket designating him as an undesignated pilot. It was a wonderful way to generate more useless paperwork. Kruger figured that the CO was well on his way to flag rank.

During one drill weekend the weather was bad. All of the pilots had to file IFR clearances and fly accordingly. When it came time to get back aboard NAS Glenview the weather had gotten much worse and several planes had to go to an alternate until the weather lifted, probably the next morning.

One of Kruger's friends was still airborne. He was the last plane to attempt to try to get back aboard the air station. Kruger was in the Officer's Club and heard John Sears go overhead twice as he took a wave off each time due to the ceilings being too low. Kruger figured that John would probably spend the night at Gus Grissom Air Force Base to the south in the next state. He was surprised to see John order a beer about an hour later.

"John, what happened? Did the ceiling lift? I heard you go over a couple of times and figured that you were headed for Grissom."

John said, "I landed at Palwaukee and took a cab over here." Palwaukee was a civilian field to the west of Glenview about three miles away.

Kruger slowly set his beer on the bar and said, "John, you can't land a P2 there. The runway isn't stressed for it. If you had checked the flight information manual you would have seen that."

John looked startled and said, "My copilot said P2s land there all the time."

"Who was your copilot?"

"Gar Benson."

"Ah, shit," Kruger said, "Damn it. Gar just wanted to get home. He sure snowed you. You are the first P2 to ever land there. The CO is going to have your ass."

John was silent for a few seconds and then said, "OK, you've got to help me get the plane home first thing tomorrow morning after the weather clears."

Kruger laughed and said, "Oh no. You aren't going to rope me in on that particular screw-up. You signed for the plane and you have to bring it back home. You can't shift that off on anyone else."

John cajoled the rest of the evening trying to get Kruger to agree to help him fly the P2 from Palwaukee to Glenview. Kruger was adamant. He didn't want to get involved in this particular flail.

The next morning at 0500 Kruger was awakened by a banging on the door of his room. It was Lt. John Sears. Sears was suited up for flight. He said, "C'mon, asshole, be a buddy and help me get the plane back home before anyone knows where it is." In a moment of weakness Kruger finally said, "OK but it's still your plane. You signed for it and it's yours until you get it back on the line here at Glenview. I'll ride shotgun for you and handle the radios but it has to be clearly understood that it's your bird." Sears readily agreed and once Kruger had brushed his teeth and suited up the two started to leave the BOQ. They were stopped by the squadron Executive Officer, LCDR Jerry Lamden. The Exec said, "Good morning, guys. I overheard your conversation last night and I know what John did and what you are both up to." Kruger gritted his teeth and thought, "Well, John's in the crapper now." The Exec continued, "I happen to need four hours of flight time this month in order to get my flight pay. I'll conveniently overlook what you two culprits are going to do if you put my name on the yellow sheet and get four hours on the plane before you come home. Of course, I won't go anywhere near that plane. It's going to be sufficient that my name is on the pay sheet."

Kruger thought, "Jesus, in for a penny, in for a pound. Not only am I going to be involved in flying a plane that has landed illegally at some field but I have to be involved in falsifying the yellow sheet too. Ah, well, a lot of pilots before me have crashed and burned. I won't be the first. I wonder what courts martial groups give guys like us?"

John agreed to do as the Exec wished without even asking Kruger's opinion about the whole thing. Kruger began to feel like the whole thing was gaining momentum leading toward some dire result that boded no good thing for him. Have you ever heard of a slippery slide?

John had already shanghaied a plane crew. They were waiting at the hangar. They got the duty driver to drive them to the other field. It only took about a half an hour for the whole trip. By the time they got to the plane the sun was just breaking above the few clouds that remained from the storm of last night. The Plane Captain had to do his own preflight and, as he did, John and Ed went to the field operations office and got a cup of coffee. That accomplished they went to the plane where John did his own preflight. Then they all crawled into the plane and started the engines, hoping that the big 3350s wouldn't wake anyone up. They soon taxied to the nearest runway and took off.

Palwaukee Field had no fuel for the P2 so they only had the fuel that had remained aboard when John had landed the night before. It was far short of what would be required for a four hour flight as the Exec wanted them to get. When Kruger pointed that little bit of info to John he said, "Screw it. I'm going to land as soon as possible at Glenview and just log four hours. The longer we are airborne the greater the chance that someone in the squadron will wonder what the hell we are doing flying at this hour. We aren't exactly on the daily flight plan."

Kruger took a deep breath. Could anything get any worse? Now they were going to falsify a flight log for time. Kruger had known squadron Commanders who condoned that because of a tight budget but he, personally, had never been a proponent of "pencil" flight time. He had never falsified any time. Still, it was on John's head since he had to sign the yellow sheet certifying the flight time. Kruger told himself that he couldn't be held to blame for something that John did.

They finally landed after a total flight of 18 minutes. John taxied the plane up to the flight line and shut it down. He thanked his skeleton crew and they all retired to get some breakfast.

The next morning the squadron CO put out a call for LCDR Kruger and LT Sears to report to his office at their "earliest convenience", Navy talk for "get your asses here right now". The two culprits reported as requested and when they entered to office the CO threw the morning Glenview paper on his desk. As he did he said, "Would you two assholes like to enlighten me about the story on the front page of this paper?" The front page showed a very large picture of Kruger and Sears climbing into the wheel well ladder of the P2. The caption read, "Huge Navy bomber lands at Palwaukee, a first for the field."

Kruger thought, "Well, I should have known." The P2 landing at Palwaukee just had to be news. Someone had notified the newspaper and a news photographer had hurried to the field in time to get a good picture of the two Navy Officers climbing into their plane. Kruger just shook his head.

Lt Sears, adept in the art of survival, obfuscation, escape and evasion, blurted, "LCDR Kruger was the senior officer on board." Kruger grinned and said, "Well done, John. That took some fast thinking. I'll get you for that." Then he said, "Yeah, John's right. I was senior and know better." Then he briefed the CO about the whole episode, omitting the bit about the Exec's part in the adventure. He figured that the whole shitaree didn't need any escalation. He then said, "Whatever you do to us should not include the enlisted crew. They were just along for the ride. I would expect them to be given full credit for the whole four hours. If they aren't then you can forget me for any further flight tests or things like that, that is, if I still have a job with the squadron."

The CO ragged on them for some time. There's nothing like a good ass-chewing to make the chewer feel good about getting a lot of incipient hostility off of his chest. In addition giving a good ass chewing early in the morning was like drinking at least three cups of navy coffee and aided immensely in waking one up. Both culprits stood at attention the whole time. Neither were requested to go away since both were pretty integral to the operation of the squadron and the CO had to perform as close to optimal as possible. He finally told both pilots to get the hell out of his sight. As they left his office Kruger was positive that he heard the CO laugh out loud.

The Naval Air Station had long been a whipping boy for the local newspapers because of the noise the planes generated operating out of the field. The city of Glenview had long been salivating over the area occupied by the Naval Station especially the golf course owned by the Navy. I didn't matter one iota that the Naval Station had been there long before any of the homes that had been built adjacent to the runways and the areas next to the Naval Station after the fact. The clamor in the local papers was ongoing and vociferous. Kruger's CO was political enough to complain about it so Kruger said, "Would you like me to solve the whole problem?" His CO said that he would like to see just exactly how Kruger would do that as no one had, as yet, been able to placate the local paper.

Kruger said, "Give me permission to try and I'll make the problem go away." The CO readily gave Kruger permission and carte blanch to go ahead.

Kruger's CO then told the station CO, Captain Merchant, what he was up to. The Captain said, "That officer of yours is going to screw up everything. This is a very sensitive issue. It has to be handled with kid gloves." Kruger's CO probably wanted to rethink and re-plan everything but, knowing Kruger, he figured that it was too late.

He was correct. Kruger had already contacted the editor of the Glenview paper and had offered to allow him and any photographer to ride on a P2 task out of Glenview to assess, for themselves, exactly what the Navy squadrons were trying to accomplish. Kruger said, "All constraints are off. You can observe and report anything you wish. The Navy won't try to influence anything you print. You will be on your own. All we wish is for you to see the truth about what is happening on the base in your community."

When the CO of Glenview heard what Kruger had promised the news people he took a deep breath. He said, "They are going to crucify us. That officer (Kruger) has shoved it right up our ass." He told Kruger's CO, "If we come out of this with a whole ass I'll buy you a steak dinner."

As it turned out the news people were impressed with the flight and the mission. They took a copious amount of pictures and the write-up in the paper was complementary; the first one in months. Captain Merchant was overjoyed and bought Kruger's CO a steak dinner. Kruger didn't get even a handshake over the whole issue.

The P2 was rapidly being replaced by the P3. The active duty squadrons had already transitioned to the P3 some time ago. It was now time for the Reserve squadrons to follow suit. The Navy took most of the best P2 Plane Captains and had sent them to a six-month school for Flight Engineers on the P3. It was an exceptional school and not one for lazy or non-motivated people. It was a good opportunity for the people sent to the school but the downside was that the squadron was left with the "scrubs" or the guys who had not made the cut for the Flight Engineer's school.

Kruger continued to fly the P2 but now did so with a heightened sense of awareness and survival. The mechanics who were servicing the existing P2s were not the top of the line and bore watching and oversight. Kruger redoubled his efforts at the preflight sequence and inspected the yellow sheets, the record of flights and maintenance, carefully.

One day Kruger was supposed to take a training Plane Captain and a pilot who needed to check out in the P2 from Glenview to the Naval Air Station, Bruinswick, Maine. Everything went as published, the preflight was accomplished and the crew was buckled in. Kruger had checked the weather and had determined that a cold front was rapidly approaching the Naval Air Station. He figured that, with a little luck, he could get the flight off the deck and on its way before the front hit Glenview.

Kruger put the pilot in training in the left seat. The training Plane Captain was in the jump seat. Kruger got the clearance and the current weather. The front was bearing down on Glenview rapidly. Kruger figured his chances of beating the front before it reached the airport was good so he briefed his pilot, started the jets and got clearance to go. The P2 started the takeoff roll.

Everything went OK right up to 300 feet. All four engines were on line and producing plenty of power. Suddenly there was a fire warning light on the number one recip (the 3350 engine on the port or left side) accompanied with a lot of banging noises and fire belching out of various places. Kruger immediately said, "I've got the plane" and initiated the shutdown-feather procedures on that engine. The jets were all producing maximum power so things were not so bad until, at 800 feet, the port jet fire warning light illuminated and the exhaust gas temperature gage for that engine pegged. Kruger thought, "Oh, shit! Two engines on fire on the same side. What the hell is going on here?"

Both training people were frozen in place. Obviously Kruger could not count on them. His training reflexes from VP30 took over. He executed part of the recip engine and the jet engine shutdown procedures from memory since the other two guys couldn't even talk by now let alone read any checklists. As he continued to climb to 1600 feet (1000 feet above the terrain) and called the Glenview Tower with a Mayday he went through the climb, the approach and the landing checklists from memory. He had little time to complete most of all of the checklists due to being a "little busy" trying to stay airborne and VFR.

The Mayday call came from World War I. It was French in origin and was from the French words m'aidez (Help me). Whenever a Mayday call was heard all stations would automatically cease transmitting and would standby to aid the station in distress.

Kruger turned downwind at 1600 feet and, again from memory, since the other pilot couldn't be relied on to even find the checklist let alone read it, ran through the approach and landing checklists, scheduling the flaps and gear as he turned to final. The weather front was rapidly approaching and he had to incorporate that in his calculations also.

Doing everything from memory, scheduling the flaps and gear and watching the weather along with talking to the tower occupied a lot of attention. On final Kruger overshot the runway. By the time he got the big plane lined up it was no longer possible to affect a safe landing. Kruger made a waveoff.

In Navy terminology a waveoff was a missed approach. The name came from the Landing Signal Officer (The LSO) on a carrier who called the landing by each plane. If a plane was "in the groove" and aligned appropriately the LSO would give a "cut", which was a green light on the fresnel lens that the Navy pilots called the "meatball" and which allowed them to land on the carrier. If a landing could not, in the opinion of the LSO, be effected then the LSO would trigger a series of red lights on the lens or the meatball and the pilot would "wave off", a term that remained from World War II and the old straight deck carriers where the LSO used wands that resembled paddles and would wave them over his head in the classic "wave off" or go around procedure.

Now a waveoff is normally not a bad thing. It's normally much better to fly around and make a landing another time than to screw up a botched approach. That's with all engines operating and in good weather. Kruger had none of these things going for him. With two engines out on the same side the plane is stressed as is the pilot who is trying to sustain flight. The application of a lot of power (needed to keep the plane in the air) on one side means that the pilot has to trim a lot along with the application of lots of rudder in order to keep the plane in balanced flight and flying. In addition to all of this was the factor of being at a low altitude, which, in itself, is a dangerous thing since there isn't enough airspace for error. Then factor in the bad weather. It was not a good day.

Kruger ran through all of the checklists again from memory and turned downwind once again. As he did so he punched into a line of rain that made the air look like they were submerged. He was IFR and could not see the runway. He computed the time needed to reach the end of the runway, dropped the gear once more and turned to the runway heading. He began his descent and, miraculously, saw the runway dead ahead. He chopped power and made a landing. As he ran down the runway he was flanked by Navy MB5s, which are large fire engines. When he was stopped the MB5s surrounded him and started shooting fire retardant into the port engines. The port recip had not been feathered so the fire chief asked Kruger, by hand signals, to put power on the recip. That way the fire retardant would be sucked into the engine. As the MB5s shot fire retardant into the engine the engine shot the retardant behind it for about a quarter of a mile. It was spectacular. One of the MB5s tried to get closer to the port engine. It drove up very close to the plane. A fireman grabbed an auxiliary hose from the front of the MB5 and attempted to get closer to the fire in order to fight it. The driver of the MB5 didn't see him and drove the big rig closer to the plane, hitting the firefighter and knocking him to the ground. The firefighter tried to get to his feet but could not do so since the retardant was slick and he could only scrabble on the deck. As he tried to regain his footing the MB5 hit him again, knocking him further toward the big props being turned by the big 3350 engine.

Kruger, in disgust, feathered the engine before the firefighter could become entangled with the prop. When the fire was out the tower called and asked what Kruger wished to do. He said that the wanted to taxi back to the ramp the squadron owned and was given permission to do so. When he was at the ramp and shut down the Plane Captain, who had not uttered a sound the whole time, finally said, "Sir, what are we going to do now?" Kruger laughed and said, "Well, we'll probably find out what is wrong with the engines, fix them and go ahead with the flight." The Flight Engineer trainee thought about that for a minute and said, "Sir, you'll have to go without me." Kruger laughed again and reassured the Plane Captain that no one was going anywhere until the plane had been looked over very carefully and the he, Kruger, had made sure that the plane was safe.

Kruger continued to fly with the Navy and by now most of his flying was done in order to check out new pilots on the P2V, which was a dying animal. P3s were being phased in rapidly and the newer squadron pilots who had been flying the P3s instead of the P2s were in training for the newer planes.

One day Kruger had a "new" pilot to train. The pilot was a very good Navy pilot but had, prior to this time, flown the carrier based S2F plane. Kruger had placed him in the left seat and they were supposed to do a series of touch-and-goes at Glenview Naval Air Station. Kruger had briefed the other pilot extensively and didn't give much thought to the flight since the pilot was competent and could fly as well as any Navy pilot. It was an easy flight.

After takeoff Kruger had briefed the pilot to turn downwind at 1000 feet. The pilot did exactly that. Kruger began to chatter the instructor's chatter about flying the pattern but something was bothering him. The plane seemed to be a lot lower than usual. As they flew Kruger called the tower and asked for an altimeter check. When given that information he checked the plane's altimeters and they checked out OK. What the hell was wrong? Kruger had flashbacks about the time he had almost lost his plane in Argentia, Newfoundland one stormy day when he had forgotten to check on the power up of the jets during takeoff. He couldn't place his finger on what was wrong but he knew, he just knew, that the damned plane was lower than it ought to have been in the pattern that he had flown numerous times. He wracked his brain as the pilot being checked out flew the pattern.

Then it hit Kruger. The pilot had been briefed to fly the pattern at 1000 feet and that was exactly what he was doing. The problem was that Kruger had meant 1000 feet above ground level (AGL) and the station elevation was 600 feet. That meant that the plane should have been at 1600 feet in order to be 1000 feet AGL. They were flying at 400 feet AGL (above ground level). Kruger confessed that he had "stepped on his dick" in making that mistake and suffered the egg on his face. The new pilot climbed to 1600 feet and everything looked good once more. Kruger contemplated that it didn't take much to make one look like a goat when it came to flying, especially when one was a JAP (Just Another Pilot).

* * *

The P2V was a dinosaur. The squadron had been ordered to attend a P3 school in the NAS Patuxent River, Maryland. The school was set for two weeks and, since it interfered with the usual routine of VP30, the training squadron that was supposed to train the Reserve squadron VP60, the squadron had to accept school at night after everyone had gone home. Kruger's last active duty squadron had been VP30 in a detachment in Jacksonville, Florida. He knew the attitude of the squadron as it related to the Reserves in general. It was not a favorable one even though the Navy had reorganized the Reserves to interleave with the active duty squadrons in an effort to take up some slack for the active duty outfits. The Reserves were the Reserves and that was that. Why waste time and effort on lepers?

The officers struggled to stay awake during the classes which were taught by Navy enlisted men who were experts in the nuts and bolts of the engines and systems of the P3 but who were not experts in instructing. Kruger moaned when a Navy Chief traced all of the electrical leads and systems from start to finish on the P3. "What", he thought, "could we possibly gain by knowing what wires go where on the plane? We're pilots, not electrical technicians." Most of the other classes were much the same. Apparently VP 30 simply threw any and all instruction at the Reserve squadron without any regard as to what was really needed in the way of operations concerning the actual flying of the P3. It was an obvious way of getting rid of the troublesome Reserves as quickly and as easily as possible. Kruger thought about his tour in VP30 and how he and a few other Lieutenants had revamped the entire training syllabus for the East Coast VP squadrons because the more senior officers couldn't be bothered by considering mundane things like a training syllabus even though that was the primary reason for the existence of the squadron. This was just one more hoop the pilots had to jump through in order to fly the P3. Kruger was ashamed of VP30.

Patuxent River was pretty much a test and training Naval Air Station. Oh, sure, it had some operational planes but VP30 dictated the attitude of everyone on the station. One morning several officers were sleepily walking to the main BOQ where breakfast was being served. The fact that the Officers had been up all night listening to training lectures didn't compute when it came to the normal plans for the day at Pax River. Meals were served at the usual time without regard for sleepy pilots. It was a cool day and several of the officers had their hands in the pockets of their uniform trousers, a custom frowned upon by the military. Suddenly a car pulled up next to them and an officer yelled at them from the car. "You would make better looking Naval Officers if you didn't have your hands in your pockets", he shouted. The officers so assaulted asked, "Who is that asshole?" It was like being back in the Naval School of Preflight once again instead of being Officers of the rank of Lts and LCDRs. The pilots were insulted. The offending Officer was a full Captain (Navy) with the title of FASOTRAGRULANT. That translated into the Fleet Aviation Supply Office Training Group, Atlantic Fleet. The Captain was the CO of that group. It became apparent that the Captain was singularly impressed with himself. He lived in the BOQ, a fact that typified him as an aberrant officer since no Navy Captain Kruger had ever known lived in such squalor. Navy BOQs weren't all that bad but were pretty much for very junior ranks and temporary living arrangements. The good Captain also liked to dress in tailored and pressed battle dress fatigues with an Australian hat with one side pinned up. Obviously he thought that he was a natty dresser. When one officer asked, "What the hell is a FASOTRAGRULANT?" Kruger offered the answer, "When you're in your garden and you turn over a rock and a squirmy thing with a hundred legs scurries out from under that rock looking for a hiding place; that is a FASOTRAGRULANT."

The squadron held a kangaroo court to decide what punishment the Captain should be given. The Captain was tried in absentia since it was deemed that he probably would not recognize the authority of the court and thus would probably not attend. He was, of course, adjudicated guilty of conduct unbecoming of not only an officer but also that of a normal human being. It was determined that punishment was appropriate but left the punishment up to the executioners who were chosen by popular acclaim. The executioners chosen were LCDRs Jerry Pfennig and Ed Kruger.

The rest of the court recessed to the solace of the TV and their beer while the swat team fanned out to locate the car belonging to FASOTRAGRULANT. Once found, Kruger pulled all of the spark plug wires and rearranged them in random order. Pfennig removed the rotor from the distributor cap and threw it into the next county. Their task completed the pair repaired to the BOQ and the next beer once again.

Soon the assembly of officers watching the television in the BOQ heard a car in the parking lot give off a series of loud bangs and explosions. One of the officers offered the opinion, "I guess he knows by now that sanctions have been imposed." Approximately a half hour later another series of explosions occurred. The same evaluator offered another opinion. "I guess he hasn't figured it out yet." Finally the officers repaired to bed giving FASOTRAGRULANT the opportunity to solve the vexing problem of just why his car wouldn't function the way it was supposed to function. Perhaps the car had its hands in its pocket.

The next morning most of the officers in training were nursing hangovers at breakfast. Copious amounts of coffee seemed to be the proper remedy. While LCDRs Kruger and Pfennig were coaxing breakfast down they heard a series of loud bangs in the adjoining parking lot. An officer at the same table said, "Still hasn't figured it out. I guess he must be a slow learner." That garnered a few smiles from the assembled officers. It was much more important to sober up and feel OK than to worry about some dumb Captain who couldn't figure out the firing sequence of his own car.

One of the officers involved in the training syllabus stopped by the breakfast table and said, "I sure hope you guys wore gloves last night.

That Captain is highly pissed and he has a fingerprint team going over his freaking car." Of course this little bit of intelligence didn't do any of the various hangovers any good. The officers thought it prudent to cast off and spend their weekend in Washington, DC.

The weekend was a fun time. Sunday evening found the assembly of officers in the BOQ lounge watching the television and nursing a beer or two. Things were calm and beginning to wind down when they heard another series of explosions from the parking lot. One of the officers said, "Geez, wouldn't you guess that the dumb SOB would hire a cheap mechanic to put those sparkplug wires where they ought to go?" It was too weighty a problem to solve so everyone went to bed so as to be fresh for the next week of boring school.

The next week lasted for a month, or so it seemed, but finally the squadron was deemed to be adequately trained on the P3 and was released to their home base. Most of the officers gave a prayer of "Thank God" and left the Naval Air Station with few regrets.

Notwithstanding the P3 School the squadron still flew the P2. For the astute pilot that was a noticeable event. Most of the really good plane Captains had been trucked off to the Navy's P3 Flight Engineers School. It was a very good school, albeit very demanding. Graduates of that school were extremely knowledgeable and the P3 crews depended on them a lot. The maintenance people left to maintain the old P2s were not the top of the line and any pilot who valued his life realized that fact and scrutinized the plane they were to fly with a jaundiced eye.

Kruger's loss of two engines on takeoff was a classic case in point. Another episode revolved around a plane that Kruger was to fly that failed the propeller check on the engine run-up prior to the takeoff. Kruger had taxied back to the flight line and had "griped" the plane. He told the crew to stand by until the maintenance people could find the problem, hoping that it could be repaired or fixed shortly. Soon one of the mechanics approached him and told him that the electrical connection to the propeller governor had a short in it because the connection assembly threads were stripped allowing the connection to become loose and sloppy. He said that a new connection would have to be spliced into the system. Since he was talking about many wires Kruger figured the fix would take about a half of a day if not more. He told his crew to stand down and changed into his uniform from his flight gear.

About a half hour later a mechanic told Kruger that his plane was now "up" and ready to fly. Kruger questioned him at length and received no good answers to his questions. Accordingly he boarded the plane and climbed onto the wing via the observation hatch on the flight deck. From there he climbed out onto the engine nacelle, straddled the engine and leaned over to peer into the top of the big 3350 radial engine. What he saw horrified him. The electrical connection to the prop governor had been wired onto the governor by a jury-rig that had nothing to do with proper maintenance procedures. It was obvious that the threads were not holding the connection in place and only the wires were doing so. Kruger "downed" the plane in disgust and refused to fly it until the proper maintenance fix was accomplished. So much for trust in the maintenance division.

Kruger continued to fly but with much more caution as concerned the planes themselves. After a tour in the readiness air group, VP30, Kruger had adopted a renewed survival instinct based on his estimation that most of his flight students were actively trying to kill him. It was one thing to teach someone how to fly. It was quite another to teach him how to use his plane as a weapons platform and to actively use it to fight. That could kill you since the fledging combat pilot could make any number of mistakes that could kill everyone in the general area. Those survival instincts surfaced now that he had to fly planes that were maintained by less than perfect people.

One night the BOQ caught on fire. One of the VP pilots, Chris Hanks, used to shave at the small sink that was furnished in each of the BOQ rooms. The light over the sink in Hanks' room was always tilted for some reason. Chris would always straighten the light before he shaved. What he didn't realize was that the loose connections on the light were chafing the wiring, which was almost as old as World War II. Eventually the wires developed a short and that developed into a fire. Chris reported that he smelled smoke when he entered his room and immediately investigated it. The BOQ was very old and was built of wood. Chris felt the walls and determined that the wall over his sink was hot. He ran to the nearest fire alarm and pulled it. The alarm was deafening.

When Kruger heard the alarm he jumped out of bed and pulled on his pants and shoes. He grabbed his "bail out kit", the small kit that he kept for emergencies just like this, and headed out the door. As he entered the passageway he saw another officer sleepily looking out of his door and asking another officer who was running down the same passageway what the problem was. That officer shouted, "It's a fucking fire, you fucking idiot".

After the fire was extinguished the damage was assessed. It was determined that only three rooms were ruined. One belonged to a friend of Kruger's who had just been recalled to Northwest Airlines after a lengthy furlough. The next time that Kruger had occasion to visit the training facility that Northwest maintained he saw the "owner" of the room, Dave Good. Dave was a Marine officer. When Kruger saw him he was sitting at a table in the company cafeteria making months of changes in his manuals. Piles of paper were on the table before him and more were strewn around his chair. Kruger approached him saying, "Hey, Dave, has anyone told you that your BOQ room at Glenview burned up along with all of your flight gear?"

Dave took the information in stride. Ever-present cigarette in his mouth he squinted up at Kruger and said, "No shit?" That was the extent of his alarm. Dave was about as unflappable as you could get.

*   *   *

The Day finally arrived. The last P2 was to be taken to the graveyard. A special Ferry team had been flown to Glenview to fly the aging plane to its final parking spot. Ferry pilots were supposed to be checked out in all planes but proficient in none. Everyone who was attached to Navy Glenview turned out to watch the departure of the old war bird. Kruger was no exception. He had flown the P2 for a long time and had a lot of memories of the bird.

The P2Vs were being flown out of Glenview in order to make room for the transition to an all P3 fleet. Navy pilots called "Ferry Command Pilots" were chosen to fly the planes to whatever destination they were assigned. Usually the Ferry pilots would review the Natops manual for the airplane they were to fly on the way to the station they had to fly from. It usually worked OK, but not always.

The pilots who were to fly the plane had read most of the NATOPS manual but, in their defense, it was a very large manual with a lot of information to adsorb. As the massed assemblage watched, the P2 took off from the south runway at Glenview. Sometime during the takeoff at about 500 feet the pilot in the left seat wanted a little more elevation from his seat. Activating the little lever on the right side of the seat only released the brake holding the seat in place. It made the seat bottom out if you were seated in it. In order to gain more height the pilot had to grab the hand-hold located atop the front windscreen and take pressure off of the seat. The Ferry pilot intuitively knew that he had to take pressure off of the seat but he chose the wrong handle. He reached for the large red handle immediately over the pilots head.

The P2 is a maritime bomber. As such it is configured so that it can sustain a ditching if it has been damaged enough to prevent any further flight operations. It has a large 16 man life raft in the port wing that is activated by a large red handle located over the pilot's head. Pulling the red handle opens a large panel at the top of the port wing and deploys the raft that inflates as it deploys. The Ferry pilot pulled the handle and the raft operated as advertised.

As the assembly watched the raft deployed, inflated and wrapped itself around the tail empennage of the P2. This prevented the pilot from using his rudder or his elevator. It was panic time. The pilot called a Mayday and tried to turn back toward the airdrome.

Now you have to place yourself in the pilot's seat if you can. He is not really conversant with the plane and had sustained an emergency that prevents him from climbing, descending or turning with any real effect. He is looking for a place to land, any place at all. He is flying a plane that has a large "spoiler" on the left wing that was generated by the deployment of the life raft while the right wing was the only thing that sustained the lift that kept the plane in the air. A "spoiler" spoils lift. The plane desperately wanted to turn left. The spoiler was the portion of the wing that had opened allowing the deployment of the raft. It stuck up at a 90 degree angle to the top of the wing effectively "spoiling" any lift generated by that wing. It took full right placement of the yoke just to keep the plane upright. In this case the pilot could only make left turns and had set himself up to land on a runway that had large Xs painted on each end. An X painted on a runway means that the runway is closed for any number of reasons. As the pilot approached the end of the runway the tower was transmitting an endless litany of "don't do that, don't do that". The pilot continued the approach until, at about 300 feet, he finally looked at the runway and saw a large number of maintenance trailers parked on the runway. People were running away from the trailers. He rammed on all of the power he could get out of the engines and made a waveoff. In doing so he sustained such a high angle of attack and nose attitude that the plane became relatively slow and the raft fell off of the tail empennage into the neighborhood housing area. When the raft fell off the pilot had the use, once more, of the entire tail, the rudders and the elevators. He finally made an approach and landing to the main runway at Glenview. When the plane was finally parked on the ramp the pilot exited the plane and told everyone that he was done for the day. He then repaired to the Officer's Club for a much needed libation in honor of the Gods of Fools and Aviators.

When Kruger saw the panorama unfold in front of him he held his breath until the plane had finally landed. His heart was pumping at four times the normal rate. When the flight crew was safe his "funny bone" became apparent once more. He ran to the nearest telephone and called the public number for the Glenview Tower. When the tower answered he asked for the duty officer. He knew the duty officer that was on duty that day. When the DO came on line Kruger adopted a voice that was like that of an old man. He shrilled, "What are you goddamned Navy people doing? One of your airplanes just dropped a big thing in my back yard. It screwed up my flowers and I'm going to have to clean up the whole fucking mess. I want to know if you assholes are going to pay for this mess."

The harassed Officer said, "I'm sorry, Sir, but I'm very busy right now. Please call back very soon". He hung up.

Later on that evening he ran into the officer that he had ragged on. He told him what he had done. The officer laughed at the call and said that he had been inundated with calls that day. He acknowledged that Kruger had "hammered" him and promised to get even as soon as possible.

The P3 was the plane that everyone flew now. Kruger tried to compete with John Sears about who could check out on the P3 first. Sears won because he didn't have any other job. Kruger had to fly with Northwest and so he was constrained by time. When Sears got his P3 PPC designation he lorded it over Kruger who took the ribbing with humor, as a good Naval Aviator ought to do. The Navy, once more, worshipped the new plane and made every pilot try to do the same. It was just a plane, for God's sakes! Why couldn't the Navy see that?

The Navy dictated that plane Commanders like Kruger had to have 300 hours in the P3 before they could take a PPC check. Kruger buckled down and decided that he would do the 300 hours. He flew as a copilot for all of the younger pilots who had flown the P3 on active duty. They didn't think like the old recip engine pilots. The tactics for combating submarines were different. Kruger could accept that. The nuclear submarine could outrun and outthink an old P2. The real rub was that the "new generation" of P3 pilots disregarded weather completely. A thunderstorm was entirely capable of ripping the wings off of any airplane current technology could build. P3 pilots thought nothing of flying into a giant thunderstorm.

Kruger felt like he was nearing the end of an era in respect to his career with the Navy. He had flown in three squadrons in his eight years on active duty and three more in the Reserve Navy. He had attained the rank of Commander and was now engaged in checking out in a new, to him, airplane. Things were changing fast. The old tactics he had learned in hunting submarines had long gone by the wayside. Submarines were now very fast and very quiet. Anti-submarine warfare that had once been of top concern to the Navy seemed not to matter all that much anymore. The current crop of "newer Naval Aviators" seemed to have a different set of values from the older aviators like Kruger. Perhaps all seasoned pilots felt like Kruger now felt about younger pilots who seemed to take a lot more chances with fate than Kruger could remember having done. Was this old age creeping up on him? Who knew? Kruger had long been leery about trusting the judgment of the P3 pilots who didn't mind at all flying through thunderstorms. Kruger had always been very careful not to fly in those weather patterns that had the capability of tearing airplanes apart and spitting them out of the cloud mass. There was so much energy contained in those towering clouds that nothing man had made up to now could withstand it. Maybe this was how dinosaurs had felt just before their demise.

One of the pilots who had flown P3s on active duty and was thus checked out in them wanted to spend a few days in Brunswick, Maine. He knew that Kruger had been based there and asked him if he wanted to accumulate a few hours in the plane by flying as his copilot. Kruger was happy to do so as he always loved the area. As an afterthought he asked a couple of his Marine friends if they wanted to go along. They, too, were happy to have the chance to go to someplace better than Glenview.

The weather enroute was stormy. As the P3 flew at 23,000 feet they encountered a few thunderstorms. Kruger, who was flying as copilot, called the center and asked if the controllers could vector the plane around any cells they happened to see on their radar. The center tried but their radar is not tuned to see much weather as it's functionally used to see planes. The PPC of the P3 didn't seem to be particularly bothered by the weather but Kruger knew that large thunderstorms could be airplane killers. The up and down drafts in a mature thunderstorm consisting of numerous cells in close proximity to each other possessed enough shear energy to rip a plane in half. Kruger picked up the plane's crew microphone and ordered the crew to buckle in and standby for rough weather. The two Marine officers remained standing in the cockpit.

The plane suddenly hit violent turbulence. Everything not tied down in the cockpit flew around the area. The flight instruments could not be read. A Styrofoam coffee cup on Kruger's yoke was thrown out of the holder and disintegrated. Kruger thought that the windshield had blown out due to the liquid that suddenly covered everything. He had initially grabbed the yoke with both hands but the movement of the plane was so violent he had no chance to control it manually. He let go of the yoke with his left hand to grab the throttles but when he did so his hand became a flying object also. He was unable to control his arm due to the heavy "G" forces that fluctuated between positive and negative "Gs" rapidly and he never laid a hand on the throttles. The Marine officers flew between the overhead and the deck landing on both with enough force to break bones.

The turbulence lasted for about 15 seconds but seemed to go on forever. When the plane became controllable once more Kruger saw that they had been thrown 6,000 feet higher than they had been cleared for. He called the center and declared an emergency giving the center his new altitude. He quickly looked around the cockpit to see if anything was broken. Both Marines were on the deck. One looked at Kruger with eyes as big as saucers and said, "Is it over?" The plane seemed to be flying OK and the Marine struck Kruger as funny. All he could do was laugh. Actually the laugh was a way to rid himself of his highly charged emotion. He was alive whereas a few moments ago he was sure that they were all soon to be dead. Upon introspection Kruger would confess that laughter was the normal way that he would ever rid himself of tension. A call from the after station of the plane sobered him up. One crew member had not buckled in and had been thrown against a crew bunk breaking his back.

Kruger used the emergency declaration to re-file an immediate landing at the military base in Dayton, Ohio. Once there, a medical team removed the injured crew member. An inspection of the plane showed it to be airworthy but it had lost the forward radome and the skin of the plane was pockmarked by hail. It was decided to press on to the Naval Air Station in Brunswick where the P3 could be repaired. All other crew members plus the two Marines were OK except for a few bruises.

They were in Brunswick for three days while the P3 was repaired. The PPC received a message before they left Brunswick directing them to pick up the injured crew member in Dayton and return him to Glenview. They landed at Dayton and the crew member was placed aboard immobilized in a steel gurney.

On the flight to Glenview there was a fire warning on the number two engine. The crew immediately went through the fire/shutdown checklist, firing a fire retardant bottle into the engine. The warning persisted and a second bottle was fired into the engine with no apparent effect. Again an emergency was declared and the center wanted to know if the crew was going to bail out. Kruger wryly told them that they couldn't very well do that and leave the crew member strapped in the steel gurney nor could they attach a parachute to him. Their only option was to land immediately. This was accomplished and an inspection showed no fire. After everyone's heart had settled down they boarded the plane once more and finally landed at Glenview with no further stomach acid producing incidents.

One day Kruger flew as a copilot for a young P3 pilot as they flew from Glenview to Minneapolis to pick up a few crew members for their monthly drill period. On the way to Minneapolis they skirted a big thunderstorm. Kruger made note of it and kept track of it on one of the weather channels on the UHF radio.

On the return trip the Plane Commander decided that skirting the thunderstorm was too much trouble since it had grown extremely large and going around it would take a lot of time and avgas. He opted to punch through the big storm. Kruger advised against it. He tried to tell the young PPC how dangerous thunderstorms, called CBs by the Navy and the weather people, were. The PPC wouldn't listen to him. He was interested in landing at Glenview and relaxing at the Officer's Club with a beer.

Now you must realize that a Plane Commander in the Navy is the sole judge and commander about whatever is done aboard his aircraft. He is the Captain of the ship, literally. No one can supersede him except his immediate commander, his Officer in Charge or Commanding Officer. As they entered the big CB Kruger came online on the interphone and told all crew members to buckle in as they were going to experience a lot of turbulence. The PPC continued onward, apparently without much thought. Suddenly the plane was caught up in turbulence that tossed the plane around like a ball in a Jai-Alai game. The PPC hung on to the yoke like a bulldog without comment. When they had exited the CB Kruger turned to the PPC and said, "I've asked a lot of your contemporaries what they think of your flying abilities and they pretty much say that you are a good pilot but you like to fly into thunderstorms. Do you know what I think about all of this?"

The young PPC blinked several times and said, "What?"

Kruger shifted in his seat and said, "I think that you are a piss poor pilot. You don't have the brains to fly an airplane and if it were up to me you wouldn't. I warned you about that thunderstorm and you flew into it anyway. You put your plane and crew into harms way. That is unforgivable in my opinion. I'll never fly with you again and I'll make sure that everyone knows it. Any questions or comments?"

The PPC said, "The All Weather Flight Manual says that, if you have to penetrate a thunderstorm, you should so it in the lower third." The P3 had penetrated at around 23,000 feet.

Kruger said, "Do you have any idea how high that CB was?"

"Probably around 40,000 feet."

"That damned thing was 75,000 feet. I checked it on a weather channel. It was a mammoth system, fully capable of ripping the wings off of your puny little airplane."

The PPC thought about it and said, "Well, if it was 75,000 feet then we were well within the one-third lower part".

Kruger just stared at him and finally said, "You don't have the intelligence to be a PPC. That publication you just quoted was published around 1950. It's as seriously out of date as you are. When I get back to Glenview I'm going to tell that little bit of info to the Program Manager. Also, if I ever have to fly with you again and you try to fly into a large CB I'll personally put my survival knife as deep into your chest as possible. You, sir, are simply too dumb to be a PPC."

The P3 pilots persisted in disregarding large weather systems like giant thunderstorms. One day, during an all officers brief the duty officer told the pilots that CDR Kruger would not countenance flying in thunderstorms. He made it sound like Kruger was a Prima-Donna who was afraid of flying around weather. At this Kruger stood up and said, "Well, gentlemen, I want to be on record as being afraid of large thunderstorms. I say that due to long experience and a lot of observation and study. Anyone who is not afraid of thunderstorms is an abject idiot in my estimation. Those weather systems are quite capable of tearing any airplane into small pieces and have done so historically. If you don't acknowledge that fact then you have no business being a pilot. The airlines know that and dictate flight one nautical mile downwind for every knot of wind at altitude around thunderstorms. I want to be on record right now as saying that I will absolutely put my survival knife into the chest of any PPC that tries to fly into a thunderstorm while I'm aboard his plane. When I'm checked out in the P3 I'll do my best to see that any pilot that flies into a thunderstorm will lose his wings. Any questions?" There was silence. The officers, knowing Kruger, knew that he meant everything he said.

It was time for the squadron's two week deployment. This would be the first time the squadron would have operated as a unit with the P3. The Navy dictated that the deployment would be at the Naval Air Station, Bermuda. The op-order called for a six plane detachment so half of the squadron would operate out of Glenview and half would be stationed in Bermuda. After one week the two units would swap places in order to give a varied amount of experience to each half.

Kruger was assigned to a crew as a copilot since he did not have enough time in the plane to check out as a Plane Commander. His crew arrived at Bermuda late one afternoon. The place had not changed at all since Kruger had been there years prior to this. It reeked of British spit and polish even though Bermuda had opted out of the Commonwealth some time ago. As soon as the plane had been secured the crew shoved off to their respective watering holes. The Officers went to the Officer's Club which was attended by a proper British gentleman in Bermuda shorts who was the bar tender. Kruger couldn't help but remark on the difference between the Brit and the bar tender at NAS Glenview, a surly black man who looked down on his customers. "I could get used to this" was his thought.

There were some Canadian crews in the club and a friendly rivalry between them and the American crew began with catcalls and the usual posturing. Both sides knew that the other consisted of professionals but it was a lot of fun casting doubts on that fact.

The club owned a very nice bell that hung from the ceiling. It was a much better bell than the one at Glenview that the squadron had stolen and which was now installed in the squadron's ready room despite the frantic efforts of the station to locate and recover it. Kruger eyed the bell and nudged another officer who looked at it and smiled in a knowing manner.

Earlier in the year Kruger's squadron had "kidnapped" the bell located in the Officer's Club at Naval Air Station Glenview in retaliation for the way the club manager had treated them during their previous two-week "cruise". The Station CO, Captain Merchant, wanted the bell returned and constantly harassed the Marine contingent on the station as everyone figured that only the Marines would be so brash as to steal a bell from an Officer's Club. The station's treatment of the Marines added flavor to the triumph of possessing the bell. The bell itself occupied a place of honor in the squadron's ready room. The squadron Commanding Officer delighted in ringing the bell to gain order in an otherwise very disorderly ready room. The Naval Air Station had so far not discovered the identity of the thieves. Thus encouraged the squadron CO had floated a trial balloon in one of the all officer meetings. He said, "Wouldn't it be nice if the bell in the officer's club at Bermuda could keep our bell company? Can any of you gentlemen think of a squadron that you served with that owned two bells? We would be famous."

That was all it took for a plot to be hatched with the result being the appropriation of the station bell that currently occupied a place of honor in the station's officer's club in Bermuda. Kruger was on the next crew to deploy to Bermuda. He was already planning.

Kruger's P3 arrived at the Naval Air Station Bermuda late in the day. His crew was "greened out" to operate a patrol the next day. There was just enough time to consume a few beers and joke about flying in the Bermuda Triangle, that subtended position on the earth that includes an area from Bermuda to Virginia to south Florida and is sometimes called the Devil's Triangle because of the odd things that seem to happen inside of it. Kruger was very familiar with all of the stories that attached to the Triangle but he had operated within it for years while he was on active duty without incident.

The next day he arose with the sun and, after his morning ablutions, he walked over to the local Navy "gedunk" or what passed for a fast food restaurant. There were three Navy wives ahead of him in line and he passed the time by going over the patrol mission for the day. When he was able he ordered eggs, hash browns and sausage figuring that nobody could really screw up an order like that. He wasn't disappointed and carried his breakfast to a vacant table that happened to be near that of the three wives who were engaged in some very important conversation. As Kruger sat down he saw a very large rat under the ladies' table that was busily engaged in harvesting any food droppings that happened to be present. The ladies were unaware that any of the local fauna was sharing their area. Tropical rats tended to be very large and this one was no exception to that rule.

Kruger cleared his throat and said, "Pardon me ladies, but is that a pet of yours?" He motioned toward the area under their table. All three wives looked to see what the weird pilot as talking about. You could never be sure about pilots. They tended to be sacrilegious and had a screwed up sense of humor. When they saw the large rat under their table pandemonium took over. They started to scream and hop onto the table or a chair in order to put as much space between themselves and the rat as possible. The rat was nonplussed and strolled over to a hole in the wall where he disappeared. Kruger ate his breakfast while watching all of the fun as food flew and women alternatively screamed and stamped their feet. When he was finished he bid the ladies a good day and walked to the flight line. So far the day was promising to be an interesting one.

During the preflight briefing the Air Intelligence Officer told the crew that a small power boat was missing and asked if the crew could keep a watch for it. The boat had been missing for 24 hours. Once the briefing was over and the preflight had been accomplished the P3 moved to the end of the runway. It was cleared for takeoff and soon was airborne. The crew was placed in battle station three and began to operate.

"Tacco, Radar, I have a small contact bearing 350 at 3 miles. That puts it in the general area of the missing boat."

"Flight, Tacco, recommend coming to 350 degrees and investigating."

"Roger, Tacco, I'm dropping down to 500 feet to investigate. All stations, heads up. Look for the contact."

"Pilot, I've got him at 11 o'clock at 3000 yards."

"Roger, good-oh, port side stand by for camera."

The crew took pictures of a cabin cruiser with a man atop the cabin waving his shirt, which had been removed from his torso, at the airplane. Obviously he was trying to communicate with the plane.

"That's got to be him, guys. Aft, toss out a long burner." The after station threw out a smoke light that would last for at least 30 minutes. The radio station transmitted both a latitude and longitude for the boat along with a Tacan range and bearing from the Naval Station. That was plenty of information for the search party. The crew now dismissed the boat and continued on the patrol.

When they got back to Bermuda the Naval Station was in a very upset, irritated and excited state. Kruger was met by the squadron's Air Intelligence Officer. He said that the station had been visited by a UFO. Four radar stations had held a very large airborne contact that was as large as a football field. It was traveling at an unbelievable speed and making right-angle turns, which are impossible according to our physical laws. It had been held by the Bermuda approach control radar, the New York Center radar, the Navy search radar and the Bermuda Center radar. In each case the radars in question had been examined by several technicians and they had stated that the contact was a "skin paint", which meant that there was something out there. No one could explain the radar contacts. The Intelligence Officer then said that the initial contact had "given birth" to several smaller contacts that had flitted about the area at unbelievable speeds and had then flown back to the "mother ship" where they were assimilated once again. The mother ship had then simply disappeared.

Shortly after the debrief an Air Force EC121 landed unscheduled at Bermuda. The Plane Commander stated that he had been chased or harassed by UFOs that could fly faster and were more maneuverable than he was in his plane. He was afraid and said that "he would not go flying until those UFOs were gone".

Kruger took all of this in stride. This was, after all, the Bermuda Triangle. What could you expect? This had been going on for decades. Kruger felt that he had been blessed with a sight into the unknown. It was exciting and wonderful; just what he signed up for when he became a pilot. Lots of other pilots had encountered what they would call a UFO but the reporting of them constituted more problems than they solved so most simply ignored the sightings and refused to "report or comment". Whatever this was it was light years beyond our technology and our ability to touch it or manipulate it was not possible. Kruger looked at UFOs like he looked at the brotherhood of flight. They were brothers in arms from wherever they came.

Kruger asked the intelligence officer what had happened when they picked up the guy in the disabled boat. The answer floored him. Search and rescue boats had gone to the area the P3 had identified and had found nothing. There was no boat, nor was there any wreckage. They searched for a couple of hours and came home. They intended to go back to the area the next day. Kruger left shaking his head. Just another manifestation of the Bermuda triangle.

The next day Kruger's crew flew another 10 hour patrol. When they returned to base and during the debrief Kruger again asked about the missing boat. He was informed that the search and rescue teams had returned to the same area and had immediately found the boat exactly where the P3 had radioed its position. It was as if the boat had disappeared and reappeared the next day. Once again, an unexplained occurrence in the Bermuda triangle. Things like this made being a pilot simply wonderful and exciting.

When he came back from the patrol Kruger showered and tried to relax at the officer's club. The O'Club at NAS Bermuda was staffed by a very proper British gentleman garbed in traditional Bermuda shorts. He even had a British accent. Kruger ordered a beer and looked around. The ship's bell was hung prominently from the overhead (ceiling). It was hard to ignore. He made small talk with the bar tender and found out that a contingent of Canadian pilots were in Bermuda also. After a few beers to relax Kruger left to his bed.

The next day Kruger's crew had a day off. There were a lot of things to do in Bermuda but a conference between Kruger, Jim Lipe and Jerry Pfennig took first place. It was imperative to formulate, plan and carry out a method of stealing the Bermuda bell. The planning session was scheduled for late in the day and numerous mugs of beer helped a lot in plotting the mission, which was set for that evening.

After the sun had set the three pilots donned dark sweaters, dark trousers and dark "tennis" shoes as they set out on their mission. The attack on the Officer's Club was set for the time when the club was closed. The three entered the basement of the club and attempted to gain entry that way. They found their way blocked by a hefty lock on the door allowing access to the main part of the club. A quick reconnoiter proved just as ineffective. All of the access points were soundly locked. The alcohol was wearing off and the night was late so two of the trio opted to retreat to their beds. Kruger was not to be put off, however, and a quick circuit of the club produced a good access. It was not the nicest but it would certainly do. It was a large garbage chute that ended in a dempster-dumpster at the rear of the club. The other pilots quailed at the thought of climbing up the slimy chute that just had to harbor all kinds of germs and obnoxious unmentionable things that surely could never be washed off of one's body. Kruger told them to wait at the nearest door and scurried up the slippery chute. He slipped a few times on unknown and unmentionable things but soon made his way underneath the rubber flaps that covered the exit of the kitchen area. He was filthy and slimey but successful, nontheless.

When he opened a door to the kitchen, which was actually a flap allowing the people who worked in the kitchen to toss garbage into the chute easily; he saw that several Philippine Stewards were cleaning the place up. Kruger waited until all of them were busy at a different place in the club and then scurried crablike into the kitchen hiding under a table. He held his breath as a few of the Stewards entered and left the kitchen. They were busy and wanted to finish and go home. The last thing they expected to see was an officer and a gentleman who was absolutely filthy hiding under a table in the scullery of the officer's club. In Kruger's experience no one ever looked above or below their normal line of sight. If you wanted to hide the best places were either above or below that line of sight. As long as you remained absolutely still and made no movement whatsoever no one would notice you. The Stewards soon finished and left for another part of the club.

Kruger took a deep breath and crawled from the scullery into the main part of the club heading for the bar. He was silent and every time a Steward entered the room where he was he remained as still as possible. His assessment of the situation was right on target. In a non-hostile arena people in that area tend to overlook anything that does not move. Not only that but they tended to ignore anything higher or lower than their normal line of sight. He made it into the bar undiscovered.

Kruger located the nearest exit door, paused at it as he assessed the situation and finally opened the door. His two cohorts quickly entered the bar trying to stifle giggles as they did so. A quick search provided a few bar towels which they used to wrap the bell clapper in order to remain as quiet as possible. Jim mounted the bar and quickly unscrewed the bell from the curved mount that held it to the ceiling. A few more bar towels were wrapped around the heavy bell and the trio opened the door once more carefully closing and locking it after they left.

They managed to transport the bell to a P3 on the flight line and stow it aboard unobserved. Jim was scheduled to fly back to Glenview the next day and the three pilots decided to call it a night and turn in.

The next day two sleepy pilots saw a third sleepy pilot off as he flew his P3 and his precious cargo back to the mainland and a rousing and cheerful arrival at the squadron ready room where the bell was introduced with honors next to the Glenview bell.

The mission was accomplished but Kruger wasn't finished. The next evening he entered the club and took up a position directly underneath the empty curved hanger that heretofore had held the bell. He ordered a beer and when the barman had drawn and served it Kruger thanked him and quaffed his drink deeply throwing his head back as he did so. Pretending puzzlement he called the barman over and said, "Pardon me bartender but wasn't there a bell attached to this bracket yesterday?"

The bartender, who was obviously irritated, said, "Thot's right, Sor. Some ruddy bostards stole it."

Kruger observed, "Are there no gentlemen anymore? Who would steal a bell from the Bermuda Naval Air Station?"

The bartender confessed, "Sor, we think it's your squadron what stole it. You Yanks seem to have a reputation for stealing things."

Kruger affected a hurt demeanor and said, "Aww, how can you think such things about us? We are gentlemen of honor. I can't help but notice that there is a contingent of Canadians aboard. I wouldn't trust them as far as I could throw them. I'll just bet you that they took the bell. Who else would do such a thing? Don't you know that all Naval Air Stations in the USA have their own bell? Why would we want another one?"

There were three Canadians in the bar while Kruger was talking to the bartender. They decided to leave and, as they did so, the bartender surprised them by yelling, "Bring back my bloody bell!"

The bell occupied a prominent spot in the squadron's ready room until one day a communication from the Admiral who exercised oversight on Bermuda sent the squadron a communication that directed the bell to be returned to the Naval Air Station. The CO of the squadron attempted to bluster over the stolen bell but, in the end analysis, a Navy

Commander cannot stand up very long to an Admiral. The Admiral, a fair man, said that the squadron could inscribe the feat on the bell if they wished but the bell would be returned as soon as possible, end of statement. Most of the officers watched the departure of their plunder with sadness.

Kruger had suddenly been given more responsibility. One of the smaller squadrons had an opening for a Commanding Officer. The previous one had been "fired" for non-performance and the squadron needed a new CO. Kruger was advised by a telephone call that he had been vetted for the new CO and that he would take over the next weekend. It was all too much too quick. Kruger had planned on being an Executive Officer for a couple of years before being thrust into the front seat. That was the normal progression but once again the Navy had "needs of the service" and Kruger was put on the tip of the spear, sink or swim.

His first course of action was to call his Executive Officer who lived in Denver, Colorado to find out what the old CO had done. Prior to this time Kruger wasn't even aware that his new squadron existed. Then he called his leading Chief Petty Officer to introduce himself and to lay out to the Chief what he wished on his first introduction to the squadron. Then he had to try to figure out for himself just what a Commanding Officer had to do. He was given no guide lines and really didn't even know what his chain of command was. Whoever his CO was Kruger thought that it was appropriate to call him and to ask him what was expected of him. Basically Kruger was on his own. He determined to run his new squadron in a fair and understanding manner. He remembered the cardinal rule he learned in Preflight, set the example. Kruger was determined to do just that. He had informed both the Leading Chief and the Executive Officer, the latter referred to as the XO, that he wished to have the entire squadron formed at 0730 on Saturday at which time he would introduce himself to the men, read his orders and tell his new squadron just how he intended to lead it and what he expected in return.

Just prior to the Saturday "drill" Kruger received a call from the TAR officer in charge who informed him that he was expected to attend a "CO's breakfast" on Saturday morning prior to checking in with his new squadron. The purpose of the breakfast, the TAR said, was to inform the CO of the Naval Air Station, Glenview, Illinois just what he intended to do with his squadron that weekend and how he intended to go about doing it. Kruger thought, "Just fucking great. I don't even know what the hell I'm going to do with my squadron. How the hell am I going to tell some senior officer what I'm going to do?"

Unfortunately for Kruger he had just been extracted from the operational portion of the Navy and thrust into the political portion. He was a babe-in-the-wood and was ill prepared for his new title. A stint as an XO would have cured that ill but he hadn't been given that little courtesy. He was the junior officer present at the CO's breakfast, which fell far short of a breakfast with only stale coffee being served. "I'm sure glad I skipped breakfast," he grumbled to himself.

Most of the officers present at the CO's breakfast were senior types and had been around long enough to have to justify their continual presence. The operating philosophy of the Reserve Navy was now categorized as "Youngest, Most Qualified". Most of the officers who attended the CO's breakfast were "has-beens" who had finished their service and were no longer really needed but who had not exactly assimilated that little fact yet. They were holding down billets as staff officers of one outfit or another that had been constructed to house older, more senior officers who had not yet realized that they desperately needed to go home and play golf or go fishing rather than to clog the works in the Navy by using up precious time justifying their existence. Kruger was reminded of the sign he had seen in a hanger that said, "If you have nothing to do, don't do it here!"

The various staff officers were oily and unctuous and had lots of posters and placards to show what they intended to do. The visual aids were accompanied by long and vociferous explanations that were obviously intended to impress the CO of Glenview as to the effectiveness of the has-beens on the staff. Kruger fidgeted and squirmed throughout the whole dog and pony show. When the CO's breakfast finally ended he hotfooted it over to his hangar only to find that his squadron had been standing in formation for an hour and a half awaiting his arrival while he sat through the absolute bullshit vomited by the fat staffers at the "breakfast". Kruger was, to say the least, pissed; Big Time.

As he walked onto the hangar deck the Leading Chief called, "Attention On Deck!" The entire squadron came to attention. As he passed the Chief, Kruger muttered, "Give 'em open ranks for inspection." The Leading Chief screamed, "Squadron, Open Ranks for Inspection . . . Harch!"

Kruger continued to stride toward the opened ranks. He was still mad enough to burn someone's ass. "Imagine," he thought, "My first introduction to my new squadron and I keep these poor long-suffering bastards standing at attention for over an hour while I play switchy-switch with a bunch of stupid staffers." The term "switchy-switch" came from an observation of a few junior officers who had determined that a few senior officers of the rank of LCDR engaged in the infantile occupation of stuffing one thumb in their ass and the other one in their mouth and then "switching" thumbs on command, hence "switchy-switch".

Kruger felt that he had to inspect the squadron because that's what all COs did on taking command. In the present case, though, the inspection seemed to only take up more precious time that was supposed to be allocated for training. Kruger was trying to make up for lost time. He was striding through the ranks as fast as he could, making the "inspection" more of a formality than a real inspection. His XO had to almost run to catch up with him. "Jesus, Ed," he whispered, "What are you trying to do? Look around you. You've got these guys scared stiff. First you keep them standing in ranks for over an hour and now you're striding through the ranks like you want to eat a bear. Look at them, for Christ sakes."

Kruger did as the XO said and was immediately ashamed of himself. That didn't do anything but make him angrier toward the goddamn staffers and the CO's breakfast. He cut the inspection short and took the podium the Leading Chief had furnished for him.

"Squadron, at ease!" he said. He looked at his new charges. They were something to be proud of; 100% volunteers and 100% patriots. He began by reading his orders giving him command of the squadron. Then he apologized to the squadron for keeping them in ranks until he showed up and explained why it happened. He told them what he expected of them and told them that he would back them to the hilt. He finally said that he expected to make his own Saturday morning musters and if the CO's breakfast kept him from that goal then he would time his musters so that he could make them. He said that the next Saturday the morning muster would be at 0830 instead of 0730 in order for him to make muster just like everyone else. The rank and file looked at each other and smiled. Now this was more like it. The CO didn't think of himself as a prima-donna. Things were looking up.

The next drill weekend the same thing happened. The staff pukes kept the entire assembly at the CO's breakfast until 0830 explaining what they intended to do in order to keep the Naval Air Station operating ad nauseum. Kruger was burned once again as he strode onto the hanger deck only to see his squadron standing in ranks once again. This time he apologized and told the squadron, "I fully intend to make my musters, once on Saturday morning in order to tell you what I expect from you and once on Sunday evening to tell you how much I appreciate your continued loyal service. If I can't make the musters then, as your CO, I will change the time until I CAN make them. Accordingly, the next Saturday we will muster at 0900. Banker's hours, people! Enjoy your morning sleep."

The TAR officer was alarmed at Kruger's pronouncement and said, "Ed, you can't do that. You have to give the government eight hours of service for your squadron." Kruger retorted, "I have to attend the fucking CO's breakfast according to you. I will attend my own musters. If the fucking staff pukes keep me at the so-called breakfast then I'll set my squadron's muster at a time when I can make it. If that becomes noon then so be it. As to the time served my squadron mustered early enough to satisfy any beaurocratic rule. They serve standing in ranks as well as working as a unit. And as to the fucking cry, "I can't" you can stuff that. I'm the fucking CO and I'll do whatever I think is appropriate for my squadron. If you don't like that then replace me. I won't become a dildo for some other officers who are staffers. I'm a line officer, remember? I command. I don't advise. And another thing; the people in my squadron ARE giving the government eight hours of service and then some. They can't help it if a few fucking officers are so inept that they are not given guidance to do anything but stand and wait for their CO to release them for real duty. The senior officers on this base need to pull their heads out of their collective asses and join the real, functioning world. Any questions?"

The next Saturday the station CO, Captain Merchant, said, "Gentlemen, it has come to my attention that some of our commanding officers cannot make their morning musters because of the length of this meeting. I think that their complaints have merit so from now on each person who briefs me in the morning will be limited to no more than five minutes of time. If you can't make your presentation in five minutes then perhaps you should find someone who can." Kruger thought,

"Hallelujah" and almost immediately thought, "Well, this won't endear me to the fat staffers on this station. On the other hand who needs them? All they're good for is three martini lunches in order to tell each other how effective they are. Nothing but alcohol and hot air."

Kruger was learning fast. He investigated a little and found that his Logs and Records officer was a Lt. Commander. Although Kruger had long ceased to be amazed about anything that happened in the Reserves he was still astounded to find a LCDR as a Logs and Records officer. Normally that lofty collateral duty was assigned to the most junior Ensign in any given squadron. It was a long way from an Ensign to a LCDR. Kruger put out a request for the Logs and Records officer to show up and soon a LCDR Pike asked for an attendance, which was granted. Kruger assessed his Logs and Records officer as a very weak individual. He was a navigator and not a pilot. Kruger asked him to come up with a report that would tell the new CO what the background was on every pilot and officer in the squadron. Specifically, Kruger asked for the total flight time and the time in each aircraft the pilot had flown. He said that he wanted the report by Sunday evening. Mr. Pike left after assuring the CO that he would comply.

By 1600 Sunday Kruger asked for LCDR Pike to show up once more. When this had been accomplished Kruger asked what the status was of the report he had requested be completed by Sunday evening. LCDR Pike whined that some pilots had three logbooks and that it took lots of time to "add up all that flight time that had been logged". Kruger took a deep breath and picked up one of the many logbooks that LCDR Pike had been working on all weekend. He turned to a page at random and held the book out for Mr. Pike to see. He pointed to one entry on the lower right-hand side of the logbook. "What does that say, Mr. Pike?" he asked.

LCDR Pike looked carefully at the open book. "It says 'total accumulated flight time,'" he said.

"What do you think "total accumulated flight time" means, Mr. Pike?"
LCDR Pike thought for a minute and finally said, "Oh!"
"Exactly," Kruger said. "How many logbooks have you processed?"
"About half of them," offered LCDR Pike.

"Mr. Pike, at the next drill weekend you will give all of those logbooks to your enlisted men with the orders to do with them what I asked you to do with them. You will inform them that the CO wishes the order carried out within the hour. Do you understand, Mr. Pike?"

"Yessir."

"You are dismissed, Mr. Pike."

When LCDR Pike left Kruger slowly shook his head.

One of the officers in Kruger's squadron also flew for Northwest Airlines. Lt Cecil Bell was a quiet, competant officer who asked nothing of anyone. One day he appeared in front of Kruger requesting the use of a plane so that he could fly to his family home in southern Alabama in order to check on a mistake in a surveyor's asessment of his family's farm. Kruger granted him the use of a plane for the weekend and directed the Operations Officer to pair the flight with a navigation exercise.

When Lt Bell got back to the squadron area he found Kruger in the officer's club and briefed him on how the task had gone.

Apparently he had "purchased" a black church complete, as Cecil said, "with a parson, three deacons and an organ player".

Kruger laughed and said, "Well, Cecil, every southern boy needs a black church so I guess you are fulfilled".

Cecil said, "I got the whole damned thing solved. I told the reverend that I didn't want his damned church and he paraded around with his hands in the air saying, 'Praise de lawd. Our white brother doesn't want to close down our church'".

Kruger was happy that he could solve such a weighty problem with the loan of only a P3.

One evening while Kruger was relaxing at the club with a beer three Marine officers approached him.

"Hi Ed."

"Hi guys. What's up? Are you slumming with the squids this evening?" Marines referred to Navy personnel as squids.

"Naw, we've got a problem though and we were hoping that you could help us out a little."

"Well, I'm always ready to help the handicapped so shoot. If I can't solve your problem I can always recommend a suitable handgun for you to use to do the right thing, so to speak." Kruger was referring to the ancient method of apology the Japanese used called seppuku.

"It's like this, Ed, the station CO thinks that we stole the ship's bell from the club. He's putting a lot of pressure on us to return it. We don't have it. We figure that you guys do. Be a buddy and tell us where it is so we can return it and get back in favor with the CO."

"Is that all you want? Hell, that's easy. Finish your beer and I'll even take you to see it." Kruger was no longer in the squadron that currently "owned" the stolen bell so he saw no disloyalty in letting the Marines know where it was.

The spokesman for the Marines, a young Captain named Nimitz, turned suddenly speaking to his group. "You," he said, pointing to one Marine, "Get a truck." "You," pointing to another Marine, "Round up a working party." He grinned at Kruger. "We're ready when you are, Commander."

Kruger led the little group to the hangar housing VP 90. As they approached the duty office the Petty Officer in charge looked alarmed as he said, "Good evening, Commander. What are you doing here this late? What are those Marines doing with you?"

Kruger chuckled. He recognized the young Petty Officer. "Good evening, Mickelson, do you smoke?"

"Yessir, I do."

"Well, now would be an excellent time to take a break and smoke."

The Petty Officer thought so too and hurriedly left the area.

Kruger along with his Marine friends mounted the stairs (referred to as a ladder by the Navy) to the squadron ready room. The bell occupied a position of honor on a table. It had been bolted to the table. The Marine working party immediately set to work to unbolt the bell and carry it to the waiting truck. It only took a few minutes. Kruger returned to the club while the Marines took the bell to the Marine barracks area and placed a guard on it to prevent any further moonlight requisitions.

The next day the bell was returned to its place in the Officer's Club to the delight of the Commanding Officer and the Club manager. The manager vowed to keep a better watch over the bell to prevent any further insult on it.

On the same day Kruger looked up from his desk and saw a delegation of enlisted men from VP 90 standing at attention in front of him. He smiled and said, "Good morning, guys, what's up?"

The spokesman for the group, a Petty Officer 2ond class with a large black beard said, "Commander, we think that you are a traitor."

Kruger grinned and said, "Why would you come to a conclusion like that?"

The Petty Officer said, "We know that you showed a bunch of Marines where our bell was and let them steal it."

Kruger smiled. He knew this Petty Officer and liked him. He had often thought that the man should have been an officer. He was bright and was more intelligent than a lot of officers that Kruger knew. He was a P3 Flight Engineer, no mean feat. The flight engineers were a "cut above" and were respected by all of the pilots. Kruger decided to have a little fun with him.

"Well, you're partially right. Yes, I did show the Marines where the bell was and allowed them to recover it for the station. But as far as being a traitor is concerned I'm not part of VP90 any more. I'm now the CO of RTU 60. As far as theft is concerned the way this game is played is for some group to steal the bell and for the original owner to recover it. VP90 had begun to think of the bell as theirs. It's not, of course. It properly belongs to the station that now has it once again. You guys should have kept a better watch over it if you wanted to keep it."

The Petty Officer thought that over for a few minutes and then said, "Well, sir, we are going to steal it again."

Kruger got serious. "Now hold on just a minute. This is a serious but comical game and is played by officers. You have to understand that technically what we are talking about here is outright theft of government property and it can be prosecuted to the letter of military law. You guys don't want to be swept up in something like that. Leave bell stealing to the officers and just stand on the sidelines and enjoy the discomfort of the guys who get caught."

"No sir, we are going to steal that bell."

"OK, but bear in mind what I just told you. If you get into trouble let me know and I'll do what I can for you." The little group left looking very much like a group with a mission in mind.

The bell had been back in the club no more than one day when a small group of Navy enlisted men in working clothes showed up in the club manager's office. They told the club manager that the CO wanted the bell removed from the club and placed in his office. The manager protested vociferously. He intuitively thought that something didn't feel quite right about all of this but the enlisted men seemed unconcerned and said, "It's OK by us. We don't really want to carry that heavy thing around anyway. We'll just go back to the CO and tell him that you wouldn't let us have the bell. I'm sure that he will figure out a way to have it delivered to his office. C'mon, guys. Let's blow this pop-joint."

The club manager didn't really want to have the station CO angry at him. It wasn't conducive to longevity in the workplace since the CO had hired him and could fire him at whim. As the working party started to leave the club the manager said, "Wait, wait, wait just a minute. You say that Captain Merchant wants the bell in his office?"

The leader of the working party, a Petty Officer with a large black beard said, "Yeah, that's what he said. Who else would want a fucking bell?"

The club manager nervously said, "Well, maybe I ought to call the Captain."

"Make up your fucking mind," said black beard. He knew that he was talking to a civilian and thus military courtesy was not required. "We ain't got all day."

The club manager caved in. He didn't want any more controversy. "OK, OK, don't get pissy with me. You can take the bell. I'll talk to the Captain later on."

Black beard shrugged, "Suit yourself. We don't care one way or the other. OK, guys, load 'er up and let's move. We got better things to do today."

The bell quickly disappeared.

Much later all hell descended on the patrol squadron hangars. The first inkling that Kruger had that the so-called shit had hit the fan was when a squad of civilian officers with automatic weapons burst into his office. They shouted, "Commander Kruger?" Kruger looked up and smiled. "That's me. What can I do for you gentlemen?"

"Sir, you are under arrest for misappropriation of government property. Please stand up and come with us."

Kruger remained seated and continued to smile. "Just what am I accused of doing?"

"Sir, you are under arrest for stealing the bell belonging to the Naval Air Station, Glenview."

Kruger said, "Interesting; I assume that you have a warrant. Does your warrant name me specifically in the charge?"

"No sir, it names the senior officer present attached to VP90."

VP 90 had deployed a week earlier leaving a skeleton crew to watch over the hangar.

Kruger said, "Well, gentlemen, you are in the wrong office. I'm not the senior officer present (known in the Navy as SeNav) of VP 90. I'm the CO of RTU 60."

The arresting officers were confused and muddled. They had been told to arrest Kruger on the assumption that he was the senior officer present of VP 90 and was known as a person who loved to instigate disorder in order to cultivate his sense of humor. His change of orders had been too recent for the rest of the Naval Air Station to assimilate the change. The leader of the flying squad who was, by now, completely confused by the rank structures of the squadrons said, "Who is the senior officer present of VP 90?"

Kruger laughed. He knew what was coming next and he delighted in telling the officers, "The senior officer present is Warrant Officer Bedlow. You will find him in the maintenance spaces in the hanger on the lower level. Please close the hatch as you leave and the next time you wish to have an audience with me please make an appointment."

The cowed arresting squad left quietly. They made their way to the hangar where Warrant Officer Bedlow was in charge. Warrant Officer Bedlow was a born-again Christian and testified to that fact often. He did not drink nor did he use foul language. He was an absolutely outstanding example of a fine officer and didn't understand at all when a bunch of ruffians descended on him, placed him in handcuffs and jack-marched him out of the hangar and into several marked police cars in the presence of all of the watch who stood around with their mouths open in absolute awe of what was happening to this most Christian of men. It didn't help, of course, that the officers were smarting over their recent attempt to arrest the most logical officer that everyone just knew was guilty as he had a long track record of bearding the goat at Glenview.

Within ten minutes Black Beard showed up at Kruger's office. "Commander Kruger, the station police just arrested Warrant Officer Bedlow!"

"Yeah, I heard. Remember that I warned you that this was an officer's game and could become serious."

"I'm going to confess to the cops." The Petty Officer was scared but still wanted to do the honorable thing.

"No, you're not. You are going to sit in that chair. I'm going to give you a cup of coffee and you are going to listen to me." Kruger poured him a cup of black but drinkable coffee, better known as Navy coffee. The nervous Petty Officer could hardly hold the cup without spilling it.

"This is still a game. I warned you about it. It can get rough. I predict that Warrant Officer Bedlow will be returned to the squadron in about a half an hour."

"Sir, I'm going to confess."

"Petty Officer Simpson, you will sit where I tell you to sit and you will not move your ass until I tell you that you can. Is that clearly understood?"

"Yessir."

Kruger thought once again that the man sitting in front of him should have been an officer. Damn, the man was intelligent and had high morals to boot. Kruger was not about to allow him to be sacrificed on the altar of fun just because he had more intelligence than the club manager or the security people.

Kruger took several telephone calls while "Black Beard" sat, sweated and fussed. One of them informed him that Warrant Officer Bedlow had been returned to the loving bosom of his squadron, sheepish but smiling, as he realized that he had been the butt of a monumental joke. Kruger informed black beard of that bit of intelligence, which seemed to relax him a tiny bit.

Finally Kruger took a routine telephone call and decided to have a little fun with the man sitting in front of him. As he hung the phone up he looked long and hard at the Petty Officer and said, "Well, I don't know what to say about that."

"About what, sir?"

"That phone call was from one of the sentries at the front gate. He said that they were looking for an enlisted man with a large black beard. He said that it was in respect to the theft of government property. They are searching all of the cars that are leaving the station. I'm sorry but you will probably have to shave off your beard and spend about a week on station. Do you want to call your wife?"

Black Beard hung his head and said, "That's it. I'm going to confess. There goes my whole career in the Navy."

Kruger laughed and said, "Relax, Simpson, I'm screwing around with you. None of that is happening. The whole thing is over. Nobody got hurt. No one is looking for you and they are not inspecting cars going off the station. I just want you to realize that what I told you early on is still true. The next time you want to steal something from the government make damned sure that some officer has authorized it. You don't have enough horsepower to weather an onslaught like this. Now go home and count your luck that you have a screwed up senior officer who likes you and looks out for you."

The very relieved Petty Officer with a large black beard grinned and said, "Thanks, Commander, you sure got me didn't you?"

"No, Simpson, you got yourself. Remember that the next time around, OK?"

"Yessir. Thanks, Sir."

"Go on, get out of here. Drink a beer and relax."

Kruger reflected that only in the Navy could you have so much fun and not get hurt.

Kruger flew the P3 for a year. It wasn't as much fun as the P2. It operated in a much different environment and had a much different mission. It sought the nuclear powered submarine, something the P2 could not do. It operated in the "middle of the air", at flight levels of 230 and 250 instead of the "lower air" like the P2 at 200 feet or lower on dark nights with the wind blowing at force three or higher. Kruger felt like a new kid in the plane. He had been in the P2 for far too long. He wasn't comfortable in this new plane with its new systems and operational imperatives. Face it, he was getting old. His priorities had changed. His family life was in shambles. It was time to go.

One evening while he was relaxing in the O'Club a fellow officer buttonholed him and asked, "Ed, how many years do you have now in the Navy?"

Kruger thought for a little while and said, "About 23 and a half years."

The other officer said, "Jesus, man, why don't you hang it up and give some of us other guys a chance to get enough years to retire?"

The officer was referring to the Navy policy of getting rid of officers who were too senior to hold down a "billet", or a position that warranted the senior officer's position. The Navy had a unique name for that. They called it being "riffed", short for Reduction in Force (RIF). The more Kruger thought about it the more sense it made. The application of large amounts of alcohol consumed as Kruger and his friend discussed the problem helped immensely. Kruger said, "Damn, I never really thought about it in terms like that. Are you in danger of being riffed?"

"Damn right I am and pretty shortly going to get the boot."

Kruger assessed his position in the Navy then and there. He wasn't happy with his new job. The squadron was a go-nowhere one. It really didn't matter at all. No one had even briefed him as to what the mission of the squadron was or what it was supposed to do other than stockpile officers for future use. Hell, no one had even briefed him on just who his Commanding Officer was or who he reported to. He had to find out everything for himself. No oversight, no counseling, no hints about anything whatsoever. That, in itself, told him everything about how important his squadron was in the whole picture. His flying days were now numbered and he was facing a life in the Navy like the fat, brain-dead staffers he had so much disgust for. He suddenly made up his mind.

"You are absolutely right. I'm just taking up space here. Tomorrow I'll put in my request to retire. Thanks for bringing that to my attention."

Kruger put in his request for retirement and soon was out of the active Navy, retired, a dinosaur, a has-been, an old man drooling on his shirt as he recited his accomplishments to an uncaring audience. He was a Commander, USNR-retired. Big goddamn deal! At least he didn't have to put up with kids who liked to fly into thunderstorms or Algee in the Glenview bar. He really missed some of the pilots and some of the Marines who brightened up the day even though they grated on the hard-asses who also frequented the bar. And he missed the bright enlisted kids who should have been officers.

He had survived a whole career in the Navy. It was one that could be equated to two and a half careers in civilian life. It had been an exciting one and one where life could be measured in seconds as any of several scenarios played out at hundreds of miles an hour. There weren't a lot of careers that could have offered that and Kruger had no regrets with his life in the Navy. None at all.

OK, it was time to go away. The old song says "Old Soldiers never die, they just fade away". There's not a song about old sailors. We just sail away, sort of, like the old Vikings did on their dragon ships. Put them into the ships, saturate them with booze (or mead or single malt Scotch whisky or whatever) set them on fire and set them adrift. They'll alight somewhere where the booze is cheap and the maidens are willing. Thor and Woden will watch over them. God knows that no one else will.

Part Two

Northwest Airlines

CHAPTER XII

Kruger thought that "flying the DC10" was a misnomer as far as he was concerned. He was a Second Officer on the plane and, as such, didn't do any of the flying at all. He was only a "flight engineer" and had to make sure that all of the systems on the plane were operated correctly. He balanced that with the wonderful time off he had as a crew member on the DC10 and the nice paycheck that he received twice a month. He didn't really consider himself to be an Airline Pilot as he figured that the title entailed actual flying and not simply "riding". Be that as it may, he did his job as he saw it and forgot about his goals. But it was boring, Big Time.

A major rub involved with his job was that he could not access any of the secure areas that the airports had laid out. He, as a crew member, could not get on the plane in order to preflight the beast but any biffy cleaner or sweeper could do so. Kruger had griped that situation for some time with no effect at all. When he had to leave the plane in order to preflight it he could not get back aboard because he did not have the appropriate "access code" for the lock on the jetway. At first he used to try to rundown a mechanic in order for that person to unlock the door. It was a real pain because the mechanic had his job to do and didn't have time to walk up the jetway and unlock the door for a crew member.

Finally Kruger adopted the method of carrying a book with him on his walk-arounds. When he had finished his preflight he would sit at the bottom of the ladder to the jetway reading his book. When the time came for the pushback someone would always find him and let him in the plane as the crew could not operate without the Second Officer. None of the so-called "managers, supervisors or vice presidents" could or would take note of the subtle protest so Kruger simply did what he wished and more than a few flights pushed back late because the Second Officer couldn't be located.

Northwest Airlines did not, irrespective of all of the rhetoric that passed for advertisement care about, or for, the paying passengers. The bottom line with the airline was, and still is, money, revenue or whatever you wish to call it. Top management said openly that the passengers didn't matter but, of course, that never got into the local papers except by innuendo. The only segments of the airline that cared one whit for any customer were the flight crews who took their jobs seriously and the front line Customer Service Agents who sold the tickets and boarded the planes.

The refusal of the airline to give any member of the flight crew access to a jetway grated on Kruger. The cleaning crew, some of which couldn't even speak English, had access to the plane but Kruger couldn't get on board in order to preflight even though the Navy had trusted him enough to grant him a top-secret clearance. Kruger had repeatedly spoken to a number of Chief Pilots and Station Managers but always got the same inane answer, "If we gave you access then we would have to give everyone access". Reason had nothing at all to do with this answer but then Northwest Managers were only "yes men" and were not hired to use their brains if, indeed, any had brains. Kruger acknowledged this as a fact and simply did his job while having fun with the "managers". He saw this as a game. He had always adopted the rule of an old Commander he respected in the Navy who said, "I can play any game you wish to play and win at that game. I only need to know the name of the game and the rules, if any".

One day Kruger reported to the airplane at a California station. He was on time and needed access to the plane in order to do a preflight and turn on the navigation devices in order to allow them to time out so the plane could get to its destination. There was no one at all on the concourse, no customer service agent, no passengers, no one at all. The jetway was pulled away from the plane and the number one hatch to the plane was open only about a foot. Kruger fidgeted for a few minutes and then found the key to the jetway was still in the key lock. He turned the jetway on and drove it up to the plane. He then scrambled under the hatch, gained access to the cockpit, turned on the battery, started the APU (the Auxiliary Power Unit), turned on the INS (Inertial Navigation Systems), programmed them, powered the entire airplane, turned on the air conditioning units and completed his preflight. The rest of the crew showed up much later and the passengers were boarded just in time to allow for an on-time departure.

When Kruger got back to Minneapolis he sought the office of the Chief Pilot, Donald Nelson. He told Nelson about the flight and how he had to do things that were not in his job description in order to allow an on time departure, something that was extremely important to the company. After his impassioned plea Nelson ponderously closed the door to his office and then said slowly, "You know, Ed, that you could get into trouble by doing things like driving the jetway." Kruger turned so that he was speaking to the wall. He said, loudly, "Why did I come in here? Jesus! I try to make a difference and get nothing but crap in return. I can fly airplanes but can't drive the fucking jetway. OK, I'm out of here."

He opened the door of the office and let himself out. He figured that every once in awhile he had to prove to himself that the office of the Chief Pilot was nothing more than the punitive arm of the company and nothing more. DF Nelson would never change. He was an elitist and a bully; two attributes that always grated on Kruger.

If the DC10 crews were a little more mature than the 727 crews they were much more entertaining. Kruger loved flying with some of them. One such crew was the team of Ev Tessmer and Jan Chrisman. Tessmer was the Captain and Chrisman was the copilot. Both pilots liked flying together and both were a hilarious comedy team. Kruger always came off these flights with a sore stomach from laughing so much.

One day Chrisman said, "Hey, I just found something up my nose!" Kruger looked up and saw that Chrisman had his finger stuck up his nose. Tessmer was trying not to gag and was looking out of the left cockpit window. Kruger discovered that Tessmer had a very weak stomach, in fact, he had the weakest stomach Kruger had ever witnessed. Chrisman knew this and capitalized on it. Chrisman grinned at Kruger and said, "Oh, this is a big one. If I dig around a little more I can get it."

Tessmer had stuck his fingers in his ears and was yammering a nonsensical litany of "Nah-nah, nah—nah" in order to drown out whatever Chrisman was saying. Kruger had doubled up with laughter by now and Chrisman grabbed the Captain's arm, pulling his hand away from his ear, and shouting, "Hey, you old woman, if you think that's bad look at what I can pull out of my ear." He immediately stuck his finger in his ear. By now Tessmer was gagging nonstop. Kruger was afraid that he was going to upchuck in the cockpit but obviously Chrisman knew his opponent and that had never happened. Kruger was hyperventilating due to laughing at the act. It went on nonstop until the trip ended.

On one of their layovers Chrisman told a tale of mounting a conquest of an old lady at a bar. Kruger recognized this as another attack on Tessmer but remained silent. Chrisman spun the tale of how he had met this lady at a bar and how she was "a little over the hill" and how she was "lonesome" and how Chrisman, "out of the goodness of his heart", had allowed the lady to take him to her home. Tessmer was gagging, by now, and was casting doubts on the honor of his copilot.

Chrisman said that the lady had a wooden leg and had apologized for that as he took her to bed. As Tessmer gagged and said, "Ah, you rotten SOB, you'd screw anything with a heartbeat", Kruger laughed until his sides hurt.

Tessmer not only had a very weak stomach, he was totally impressed with his position as a Captain. Kruger loved to poke fun at that image. On one flight Captain Tessmer left the flight deck fully dressed in the regalia of a Captain, blouse and cover. He roamed the first class cabin (the tourist class was not really for him) graciously accepting the adoration of the passengers as a Captain (or so he thought) and finally knocked on the cockpit door for entrance. Captain Tessmer would never stoop to carry a cockpit key like the other crew members. Kruger knew this and capitalized on it. He gathered up all of the coffee cups in the cockpit and opened the cockpit door just enough to enable him to hand out about six dirty cups to the Captain. He said, "Go throw these away and I'll let you in". The Captain tied to pull the door open growling, "Goddamn it, let me in". Kruger wouldn't budge and kept the cups in Tessmer's face. "Throw these away and I'll let you in", he continued to say. Finally Tessmer had to bite the bullet and take the dirty coffee cups to the galley like a normal crew member. Captain Tessmer obviously thought that carrying dirty cups was beneath the dignity of a Captain. It obviously grated on him and Kruger was laughing at him when he finally was granted access to the cockpit. Captain Tessmer had finally realized that he too was a JAP, just another pilot. Captain Tessmer got revenge on his Second Officer when he finally got back to the cockpit. He said, "Kruger, you could walk into an empty room and blend right in". Kruger laughed and acknowledged that the repartee was apt.

On another flight a different copilot made a pot of tea and dumped a piece of "hot ice" or solid carbon dioxide into the pot. It made a rather nice carbonated drink of tea and was refreshing although it was alarming to see as it "smoked" and bubbled. Captain Tessmer viewed it with suspicion. He wouldn't take a drink of it although the rest of his crew enjoyed it. Finally, after he had complained about the drink at length he got out of his seat to go back to the biffy. As he did so he stumbled over the pot of carbonated tea. He lost his temper, something that was normal with Captain Tessmer, and called the pot of tea an "ice tea carbonated cocksucker". The rest of his crew thought that the name was wonderful and referred to it for the rest of the flight. The offer of "pardon me but would you like a cup of ice tea carbonated cocksucker?" sent the rest of the crew into paroxysms while Captain Tessmer looked on with disdain.

Most of the cockpit crews passed the otherwise boring time in flight with levity of one type or another. Some pilots were openly and loudly comical. Others were deadpan and subtle in their humor. All had a well developed sense of humor. Often the humor revolved around jokes and tales, usually centered around the customs, imagined or real, of the sizeable portion of the populace of Minnesota, the Norwegians. These were identified as "Lena and Ollie" or "Sven and Ollie" jokes. The humor was harmless and paralleled the dry, matter-of-fact, earthy manner of those folk. Kruger thought that it was just about the funniest series of jokes and tales he had ever heard.

More than a few jokes revolved around the Scandinavian delicacy called lutefisk. Lutefisk is air-dried codfish, which is then processed by soaking in lye. The preparation for the table is fairly complicated but produces a smelly, semi-gelatinous mass called lutefisk. It is, one might say, an acquired taste savored mainly by Scandinavians.

A sample of one of the Norwegian jokes involves two Norwegians, Sven and Ollie, sitting in the living room of their house. A dog is present and is busy licking himself. Finally Ollie says, "Say, Sven, iss dat your dog?" Sven answers, "Yah, dat's my dog. Vy you ask?" Ollie says, "Iss he sick or sumting? He's been lickin' his ass for a half an hour now." Sven answers, "Nah, he's OK. Ve gave him lutefisk for supper and he's yust tryin' ta get da taste out of his mout'."

There are lots of other jokes but they are better told among friendly company rather than put into print.

Flying from home to work and back home was interesting. Kruger always tried to fly in civilian clothes so no one could identify him as being a Northwest employee. Sometimes he wasn't successful but he always tried to keep a low profile in regard to the paying passengers on his airline. He wasn't always successful and, at times like that, he tried to enjoy himself by trundling out his unique sense of humor.

One day Kruger was flying from Minneapolis to Miami. He had intended on driving from Miami to Naples. Before Northwest flew to Ft. Myers Kruger had to commute from Miami to Minneapolis. He had to drive the Tamiami Trail to Miami in order to get a Northwest plane to Minneapolis.

The day that Kruger chose to fly to Miami was very cold. That night the thermometer had bottomed out at 14 degrees below zero in Minneapolis. The flight was scheduled to be on a DC10. Kruger checked in and got a seat in first class. He always tried to fly first class on a pass whenever possible. The flight was scheduled to have a stop in Chicago before going on to Miami. The cold weather took a toll on the plane and it had a maintenance delay prior to pushback. The delay was announced over the PA. The anticipated delay was about one hour. The time was 0900.

Kruger settled down with a book. He was used to delays like this, especially when the temperature was so cold. At temperatures like this nothing really operated well or moved quickly.

In about 35 minutes the PA announced that the plane was OK and that general boarding was to commence right away. Kruger took his seat and the plane soon pushed back. It landed at Chicago with no problems.

After a 30 minute delay the plane was ready to proceed to Miami. The doors were closing but all of a sudden they opened again and a man ran onto the plane. He flopped down in a seat next to Kruger. He was unsettled at best. Kruger thought that he looked "frazzled". His hair was disheveled and his clothes were rumpled. The plane continued to push back. A Flight Attendant appeared and said, "Would either of you gentlemen like anything to drink?" Kruger declined but his new traveling partner said, "Yeah, I'd like a double martini."

As the Flight Attendant disappeared in order to get the drink Kruger's traveling partner said, "You probably don't know this but this damned plane came from Minneapolis. It had a maintenance delay there so I went to the nearest bar and started to drink." Kruger thought, "At nine o'clock in the morning?"

The companion continued, "The damned plane was supposed to be delayed for an hour but it pushed back after only 30 minutes. I missed it and had to run over to United and get another plane to O'Hare. Then I had to run from United to here in order to get on this fucking plane." During the whole monolog he was slurping his double martini.

He continued, "Do you know how fucking cold it was in Minneapolis last night? It was 14 degrees below fucking zero, that's how cold it was. My Dad wanted me to go into business with him in Miami but I had to go to fucking Minneapolis and start my own business. Well, fuck that. I'm done with fucking Minneapolis. I'm gonna go home and work with my Dad in Miami. Fuck Minneapolis."

Kruger was, by this time, having a hard time to keep from laughing. His partner was becoming louder and louder as he related his problem. About this time the flight attendant appeared again asking for more drink orders. Kruger's partner ordered another double martini. He continued to harangue Kruger with his tirade against Minneapolis. And he continued to drink.

When the Flight Attendants served breakfast Kruger's partner applied half of it to his inside and half to his outside by both drinking and spilling his martini. He was rapidly becoming "sloshed". He attempted to talk to Kruger. He said, "Wa's your name?" Kruger told him and asked him what his name was. He replied, "M . . . My name is F. F. Fred." He blinked as Kruger grinned. Then he said, "I don't s'pose you've ever been drunk in your whole fucking life?" Kruger laughed and said, "Oh yeah, I've been there a number of times." Fred stammered, "Well, you'd never guess it from the fucking shitty grin on your face." Kruger broke down and howled. This guy was better than a movie in flight.

Fred finally had to go to the head (biffy, toilet, whatever you wish to call it). When he returned he was wet all over the front of his trousers. He flopped into his seat and said, "If you go to the bathroom don't flush the fucking sink 'cause it will belch all over you." Kruger was having a hard time not laughing.

A number of Flight Attendants passed by and all of them greeted Kruger. "Hi Ed, going home?" Fred finally said, "Jesus Christ a lot of those stewardesses seem to know you. How come that is?" Kruger said, "Oh I travel this way a lot. I guess they recognize me."

Fred blinked and said, "Jesus Christ, want the hell do you do?"

Kruger grinned and said, "Can you keep a secret?"

Fred said, "Fuck yes I can. What the hell is it?"

Kruger said, "Don't tell anyone but I'm a pot dealer."

Fred blinked several times and blurted, "A po . . . pot dealer? Wha' the fuck? Whadda ya mean? Pot dealer".

Kruger whispered, "I sell marijuana. Don't tell anyone."

Fred blinked a lot. Then he said, "Jesus Christ. Imagine that."

Kruger had earlier found out that Fred was going to be met by a couple of aunts in Miami. He figured that Fred would need a gurney by the time he got into Miami so he resolved to meet the aunts and tell them that their nephew was soused and needed help. Fred shortly fell asleep and didn't bother anyone for the duration of the flight. In Miami Kruger found a couple of aged ladies, told them how to find their nephew and went home.

The next time he traveled back to Minneapolis from Miami he saw Fred waiting in line to fly the same flight. Luckily, Fred had no recollection of his old buddy from the previous flight, the pot dealer.

Kruger was on a trip that operated from Minneapolis to Newark. He was flying with a nervous Captain named Progger. Steve Progger introduced himself and seemed like a nice guy, only a little nervous. Kruger chalked it all up to flying with a new crew but Steve never seemed to calm down at all. By the time they got to Newark Steve looked like he was working on a heart attack. He smoked a foul smelling pipe all of the time. Like a lot of pipe smokers he was continually covered with dibbles of tobacco and smelled like an old ashtray. Kruger felt sorry for the guy and when they arrived at their hotel for the night he sidled up to Steve and said, "The copilot and I are going to go have a beer before turning in. Want to join us?"

Steve appeared startled and stammered, "Oh, I don't drink but you guys go ahead and I won't tell." Kruger couldn't believe that a grown man would say something like that so he said, "Won't tell? Steve, if I thought that you were going to "tell" I'd break both of your legs and stuff you upside down in a garbage can."

Steve's mouth dropped open and he almost lost his ever-present pipe. Kruger left him and walked away.

While Kruger and the copilot were drinking their beer Kruger related his conversation with Steve. The copilot shook his head and said, "I can't believe that you told him that. You probably gave him a sleepless night."

Kruger replied, "That wasn't my intention. I thought that he was extremely nervous and up-tight and only wanted to relax him a little. I guess I failed."

The copilot said, Steve's a closet drinker. He won't drink in public but, believe me, he does plenty of it in his room."

On a commute home Kruger had to take a cab from Ft. Lauderdale to Miami in order to get his car. The cab driver was talkative and curious. Kruger asked him a lot of questions and the cabbie asked if Kruger was a cop. Kruger laughed and showed the cabbie his ID as a pilot. The cabbie was impressed with Kruger being a pilot and asked him if he was interested in some "off the cuff" flights. Previously the cabbie had alluded to having a lot of contacts with drug dealers. Kruger said, "I don't do drugs or have anything to do with them. Do you have anyone who wants guns run?"

The cabbie said, "Oh, man, I'm a peaceful man. I don't like guns. I just want to spread love and peace around. I do drugs, not guns." Kruger grinned and thought that you could find just about anything in Miami.

Another time Kruger had just ended a flight from Europe and wanted to take a flight from Boston to Miami. He was still in uniform and had a seat in first class in a DC10. The pushback time came and went with no movement. After about 20 minutes Kruger buttonholed the First Class Flight Attendant and asked, "What's the problem?" The FA whispered, "It's a flap problem." Kruger knew that a problem with the flaps was serious and would probably result in a flight cancellation. He quietly began to gather his things and got up to leave the plane. The passenger next to him said, "Why are you leaving?" Kruger lied and said, "I've just realized that I have to be someplace else tonight."

As he left the plane he saw the passenger who had been sitting next to him gather his gear and get up. Another passenger across the aisle said, "Where are you going?" The first passenger said, "That pilot knows something. He's leaving and so am I." The whole airplane finally emptied due, primarily, to Kruger leaving the plane. He thought, "I hope that no one connects my name with the people leaving the ship like rats."

Commuting back and forth from Florida was tiring but it beat living in Minnesota with that state's high taxes and insular politics. On one commute Kruger had to fly to Memphis and Miami prior to getting to Ft. Myers. It seemed to take forever. During the stop in Memphis Kruger saw a retired pilot he knew waiting to try to get aboard the plane to Miami where he lived. The retired pilot told Kruger that he was worried that the plane would fill up and he would be left in Memphis. Kruger, who had a seat in first class, told him that if it came to that he, Kruger, would opt to fly in the cockpit thus freeing the seat for the other pilot. During the boarding process a seat became available so the retiree got to sit in first class. On the way to Miami he took ample opportunity to sample the free drinks that had always been served in first class. He had been, as the saying goes, "well oiled" before he even got on the plane and, as the flight progressed, he didn't get any more sober.

The cabin crew was staffed with a Flight Attendant who possessed a remarkable chest size. That lady was doing her duty in the tourist section. When the plane landed at Miami and before everyone had deplaned the retiree caught sight of the lady with the large chest. He stood in the middle of the aisle and shouted, "Hey, Kruger, did you see that Flight Attendant with the big bazzooms". He emphasized his shout by cupping his hands over his own chest and juggling them in an unmistaken parody of feeling large breasts. Kruger, who was in uniform sighed and thought, "Oh, man, how to dance on your crank. I had to be in uniform all through this." An elderly couple was seated in front of Kruger. The lady turned and looked at Kruger and said, "Young man, I hope that you take this incident in stride and never emulate your friend when you are retired." Kruger said, "Yes Ma'am. I've already figured that out. It gets embarrassing at times." The lady smiled and turned around to leave Kruger to his embarrassment in private.

Kruger had bid a trip that had a two day layover in Chicago. Chicago was one of his favorite layover places. It was a sleepy Saturday afternoon and he and the copilot, who was based in Seattle, decided to have a few beers in a local Red Lobster restaurant. They entered the near-empty restaurant and proceeded to the bar. The restaurant was empty and the bar had only three other people in it. They were watching a football game and having fun. Kruger and the copilot ordered a beer from the female bartender. She appeared to be having boyfriend trouble with some guy sitting at the end of the bar and spent most of her time cajoling him. All of a sudden he left the bar and she followed him. It was about this time that Kruger and the copilot needed a refill on their glasses. There was no one to refill the glasses so they sat for some time and finally, getting tired of no service, the copilot reached over the bar to the beer tap and filled his and Kruger's glasses. He said, "We can pay her when she comes back but I need a beer right now."

The three guys at the end of the bar watched this and yelled, "Hey, How about us?" the copilot said, "No sweat. Slide your glasses down here." They did so and the copilot then filled up their glasses.

It was about this time the restaurant manager appeared on the scene and roared, "You guys are thieves. I'm gonna call the cops." He immediately disappeared. Kruger was alerted to the impending danger. Northwest still mandated no drinking on layovers no matter how long the layover. A good friend of his, Thomand O'Brian, had been given a year off from flying status for just such a situation in Chicago. Kruger left the bar in a search for the manager. He found him trying to dial on a phone. Kruger placed his finger on the phone disconnecting it and said, "Let's talk about this. My buddy was out of line. We'll pay for the beer with no problem. You don't need to call anyone about this small incident."

The manager turned away from him and said, "No way. You guys are thieves and need to be arrested. I'm calling the cops."

Kruger hung the phone up again and said, "Now you don't seem to understand. If you continue to try to call on this phone I'm going to tear it out of the wall and thump you badly. That's going to hurt and cost you. On the other hand, as I said, I'll pay you and we will leave this place peacefully. I'm not arguing about the money. Tell me what you want and I'll pay it and you won't get hurt."

The manager blinked and said, "Will you pay cash?"

Kruger said, "Absolutely," thinking that he wasn't going to pay with a credit card or a check that could be traced back to him. The manager said "OK" and named a price. Kruger paid up and went back into the bar where his friend was still blissfully drinking. He said, "Come on asshole, we have to get out of here right now." Kruger didn't trust the vindictive manager and figured that he might call the police anyway.

The copilot said, "Yeah, just as soon as I finish my beer." Kruger said, "No, right now if you want to keep your job."

The copilot finally left with Kruger. As they walked out of the restaurant the manager followed them, shaking his fist at them and yelling, "And don't ever come back".

On the way back to the hotel Kruger began to laugh. The copilot wanted to know what was so funny. Kruger said, "I'll bet we are the only two Northwest pilots who have ever been kicked out of a Red Lobster."

The DC10 had long legs so it was the preferred plane to fly to Hawaii and Alaska, two places that Kruger loved. When he was senior enough he flew those lines of flying as often as he could.

Flying to Hawaii involved becoming INS (Inertial Reference System) qualified. The INS was an upscale navigation system. Each airplane had three systems installed, all checking each other constantly. The navigation was superb and only involved human intervention in order to check to make sure that no erroneous data had been entered by the human. Pilots were required to possess and carry an INS plotter and a compass in order to get a positive fix over land to check on the INS before striking out over water for hours.

One day Kruger was flying with a check pilot who got to fly the line that month. He was a no-nonsense, humorless pilot who carried his "check-training" attitude with him at all times. The copilot was a sharp guy who was both funny and relaxed. Once the flight was over water the Captain studied the navigation chart for a long time and finally said to the copilot, who was supposed to get the fix over land, "Let me see your plotter. This fix looks a little odd." The copilot shrugged and said, "I don't have one. I lost it a couple of months ago". The Captain stared at him and finally said, "You know the damned things are free. You could have stopped into any office and picked up one anytime you wished." The copilot shrugged again. His body posture said it all. He couldn't be bothered about an INS plotter. Finally the Captain said, "OK, give me your compass." Once more the copilot shrugged. "I don't have one of those either."

The Captain blew up. He ragged on the copilot for fifteen minutes while the copilot looked out of the right window generally ignoring him. Finally the Captain said, "Damn it, I've got to piss." He left the cockpit in a huff. The copilot turned to Kruger and said, "What got into him? He's acting like an old lady on the rag." Kruger was laughing so hard that tears were running down his face. He said, "You are the most relaxed copilot I've ever seen. If you were any more relaxed you'd shit your pants." The copilot just shrugged and grinned.

The company never trained the flight attendants in any aspect of flying other than to run them through a few evacuation emergencies. Most of their training was oriented around customer service, which is serving drinks and food. As a result the flight attendants were pretty ignorant about the geography they flew over or any aspect of flight at all. It wasn't their fault exactly. Most of them were right out of high school and had little exposure to the real world. The result was humorous from the aspect of the cockpit.

On one of the flights to Hawaii the plane had taken off from Los Angeles and had been airborne for two hours when a flight attendant came to the cockpit. She asked, "What lake are we flying over?" All three pilots stared at her for a few seconds and then burst out laughing. The Captain said, "Minnetonka." (A local lake near Minneapolis) The girl said, "OK" and started to leave. The crew all shouted, "Wait, wait,

wait." and explained a little about the earth's surface to her. It really wouldn't do to have her chatting to the passengers about flying over Lake Minnetonka. When she left the cockpit the Captain observed, "That girl's elevator doesn't go all the way to the top".

On another flight to Dublin, Ireland one of the Flight attendants wanted to know how long a ride it would be by train to go to London. After the laughter had subsided the pilots gave the FA a much needed geography lesson.

One month Kruger bid a trip that made a lot of stops around the Pacific Northwest. Part of the pattern was several short legs from Portland to Seattle. The crew had been back and forth a couple of times and had just left Portland. As they landed in Seattle the tower said, "Hey, Northwest, look back where you just came from. Mount St. Helens erupted just as you guys flew over it. You just missed it." As the crew turned the plane around to taxi to the terminal they saw a large cloud that looked exactly like a nuclear burst with the large mushroom shape. They marveled at the timing and wondered what it would have been like if they had been directly overhead instead of just past the mountain.

The trip sequence still had the crew going back to Portland. That entailed flying back over the mushroom cloud in order to get there. No one knew what that entailed. The Captain conferred with Northwest but got no help in that regard. Crew schedules were blind to everything but the printed schedule. Hurricanes, tornadoes, volcano eruptions or anything else didn't figure in their estimation. The word was "to go ahead and fly your schedule you cowards". The Captain buckled under and the crew set out for Portland with a number of unsuspecting and trusting passengers.

The crew skirted most of the large cloud that had to be made of pumice and particulate material. The flight was pretty uneventful and the approach was marginal with reduced visibility due to the dropout from the cloud. As the Captain taxied the plane to the terminal the windscreen was obliterated by the dust that, by this time, was blanketing the whole area. The Captain asked his crew if they thought that he should activate the anti-rain system. The plane had no windshield washers like cars have. The anti-rain system was a sticky substance that made water leave the windows. The substance needed copious amounts of water to work properly. With no water available if the anti-rain system was activated the windscreens would become absolutely unusable and no one would be able to see out of them. Kruger explained that to the Captain and said that he thought the best idea was to open the side windows and lean out in order to see. Both pilots did just that and they soon arrived at the terminal. The people were deplaned and Kruger did his walk around prior to flying back to Seattle.

When Kruger got back into the plane he looked like a man with terminal dandruff. The dust from the volcano was sticky and couldn't be brushed off easily. It was abrasive to the feel as pumice should be. The pilots talked about it at length. The initial problem was how to see out of the windows. Kruger said that you couldn't brush the stuff off. If you could it would become a problem about a few seconds later. The "dust" was accumulating like snow.

The Captain conferred with Northwest maintenance but no one had any suggestions and no one wanted to be the one who cancelled the flight back to Seattle. Flight time equated to money. Greed dictated that no one stuck his neck out enough to say, "Don't fly in that stuff."

Finally Kruger, who had been out in it all said, "Well, if you want my opinion I think that we could probably fly back to Seattle because it's a short hop but think what the pumice will do to all of the oil seals on the engines. I think that, if you fly in this stuff, you will have three engine changes. Pumice will ruin jet engines. My vote is to stay here until the pumice cloud goes away." The Captain called Northwest again with Kruger's assessment of the problem and Northwest finally concurred. The rest of the trip was scrubbed and the crew went to a hotel for the duration of the emergency.

When they got to the hotel Kruger looked at the "layover book" that contained all of the crew member's names who were currently at the hotel. He saw an old friend's name and called his room. There was no answer. He thought about where his friend would be at 10 O'clock in the morning and turned to go into the hotel bar. Just then the saloon bar doors banged open and his friend walked out wiping his mouth with an exaggerated swipe with his hand. Kruger thought, "Exactly! He was drinking the first beer of the day." The two buddies laughed and planned the rest of the day. The Captain fled to his room, not wanting to witness what was going to happen to his crew the rest of the day. He (the Captain) said, "Now guys, don't drink too much. The company might just want us to fly out of here any time." Kruger snorted when he heard that. Anyone with a brain could tell that the pumice cloud wasn't going anywhere anytime soon. Neither were any of the Northwest airplanes.

The crews stranded at Portland stayed there for three days until the pumice blew away. A rumor said that a United Airlines crew tried to fly in the pumice cloud and their 727 had to undergo three engine changes as a result. During their time there the Northwest crews partied a lot. One night Kruger was with a bunch of crew members who were going to a restaurant. One of the girls wanted some pumice for a souvenir. She started to scrape the layer of pumice off of a car's hood. Kruger stopped her saying, "Don't do that. The pumice will make hundreds of scratches on the hood. It will absolutely ruin the paint job." He scooped up a lot of pumice from the ground and filled a sack the girl had.

Three days later all of the crews headed back to Minneapolis not really realizing that they had been witness to a great event in history.

* * *

As was normal with Northwest Airlines the pilot's union, ALPA, called a withdrawal of services from the airline (better known as a strike) due to the failure of both parties to come to any sort of a contract renewal. Once more Kruger was on the street without a job until things sorted themselves out. It was getting to be a habit, an annoying one as far as Kruger was concerned. This time the strike was for a much longer time than usual. Tensions were high and soon the difficulty became one of "take no prisoners".

Several pilots tried to form a new pilot's union. They also "scabbed" or crossed the pilot picket lines to fly as the company wished. They were seen as traitors or turncoats by the largely military pilots who flew for Northwest. Most of the "scabs" were very senior Captains who figured that a strike during their last five years would impact their pensions, which were figured on the last five years pay they received.

They were correct and their worries were valid. Then there were two very junior pilots who were, by and large, weak pilots in both flying skills and moral turpitude. Some of the older scab pilots, who had been in the labor pool for much longer, attempted to dissuade the two young scabs as the older Captains knew what the younger ones would face for the balance of their careers. Most pilots, especially the ones who had military experience, valued their jobs highly. They also put a great premium on trust and loyalty and figured that anyone who would scab their own union, ALPA in this case, were only worthy of extreme contempt and derision.

The company tried, unsuccessfully in most cases, to protect the scabs. Tempers and tensions ran high on both sides, a dangerous mix. One of the scabs had his hunting cabin burn to the ground. Another had his yacht mysteriously sink. Several had their luggage disappear when it was left unattended for only a few seconds. One of the younger scabs, Gordon Schmidt by name, unwisely attempted to take the union head on. He would leave his car in the company parking lot with a large sign in it advertising, "Support the Independent Plots Union". This was the offshoot bastard union the scabs were trying to use as a replacement for ALPA.

The pilots union was not the only one that conducted guerilla warfare against Northwest Airlines. The mechanics union was a parallel union that had a beef against Northwest. It was the second strongest union on the property after ALPA. The mechanics had a grievance against NWA for some time.

Newark, NY had a mechanics lunch room that was shared by Northwest mechanics and Eastern Airlines mechanics. Actually, Eastern owned the lunchroom but allowed the NWA mechanics to use it. The lunchroom had a sandwich machine that all of the mechanics used but there was a problem with the machine. Since the lunchroom was small a time-sharing system had been set up with the NWA mechanics being allowed to use the lunchroom prior to the Eastern mechanics. When the Eastern mechanics wished to access the machine they found that the NWA mechanics had bought all of the sandwiches. This was a problem.

The station managers discussed the problem and came to a decision that would seem to solve it. Northwest Airlines bought another sandwich machine and installed it in the lunchroom. That would have seemed to have solved the problem but the NWA machine sandwiches were 20 cents more than the old sandwich machine owned by Eastern. Since the time share accommodation was not changed when the NWA mechanics entered the lunchroom they naturally bought the cheapest sandwiches available. The Eastern mechanics then had to buy the more expensive sandwiches and this caused a furor that amounted to a riot. There seemed to be no solution to the weighty problem.

One day the Northwest sandwich machine disappeared. A week later it appeared once more in Japan as a gift for the Japanese NWA station manager at Narita.

The Station Manager for Narita sent a message to the Station Manager of Newark-NWA to wit: "Thank you for the kind gift of a sandwich machine but why does it not take Yen and why were there old sandwiches still in the machine?"

Kruger, of course, was well aware of the ongoing struggles. Heretofore he had weathered the frequent strikes at Northwest without incident. He realized that strikes were a normal thing in the history of Northwest. The company was known industry wide as the only company that repeatedly was struck by any one of its unions. It was humorously referred to as "Cobra Airlines" for its tendency to strike. The humor was well deserved but for the more junior pilots like Kruger it was not exactly a humorous situation. As he returned from each strike Kruger had to start stockpiling cash immediately for the next one. Every prudent Northwest pilot did the same but the more senior ones made a lot more money than the junior ones did and it was much easier for them.

Kruger didn't like what the company did relative to its employees but was pretty well stuck with his choice. The Airline Pilot's job was not exactly mobile. If he chose to move to another airline, even if the airline would hire him, he would have to start all over again at the very bottom of the seniority list as if he had no experience at all. He tried to simply weather the storm and not fret about his lot in life. That attitude changed catastrophically one day.

Kruger's wife of twenty three years wanted a new life. She was tired of her old one, bought into the "woman's liberation" philosophy of the 1970s and considered that males of any stripe were duty bound to "keep women down and in servitude". She told Kruger that she no longer loved him and he cooperated by allowing her to choose a lawyer to aid her. Hand in hand the couple, in their ignorance of how the law worked, approached the lawyer and asked how to dissolve their marriage. The lawyer explained that he could only represent one party and Kruger said, "Well, she picked you so I guess that you ought to represent her". He still had no idea what he was getting into. The lawyer said, "OK, Mr. Kruger, if you will please step out of the office so that I may confer with my client . . ." Kruger began to suspect that he was in a war of a different kind.

Kruger weathered the strike in his home in Florida. He needed something to do that didn't take money away from the family. He was trying to conserve his cash reserve as he had no idea how long the strike would last so he put his time and efforts into teaching SCUBA classes with an old friend who was a professional SCUBA instructor in the Naples area. Kruger had earlier on qualified as a SCUBA diver in Minnesota as he intended to move to Florida and dive in the Keys looking for an obscure alga in the hope of forming a company that specialized in mariculture. His SCUBA checkout had been stringent as he intended to dive alone, a custom that was rigidly proscribed by sport diving groups.

When the strike was called Kruger was flying with an old friend, Captain Sam Martin. Sam asked what Kruger was going to do during the strike. Kruger said that he was going to sit on the bottom of the Gulf of Mexico with his air tank and sulk. Sam laughed and said that he was going to pan for gold around his home in Wyoming. Later on, comparing notes proved that both pilots did exactly as they said they would.

The strike lasted for six months. When it was over Kruger received a terse note from the Director of Flying, Bill Hochbrunn, which stated, "Work is available for you". It went on to say what Kruger had to do to reinstate his position with Northwest. He moved from the heretofore family home into his commuter apartment in Minneapolis in order to make himself available for flying. He left all of his possessions at the family home. He figured that he didn't have much left there in any case since his wife would have nothing to do with him any longer.

Going back to work for Northwest was not exactly fun. The returning pilots were made to feel like strangers by the company and everyone walked around like strange dogs did with each other, stiff-legged and sniffing cautiously. There were a few hoops to jump through. Every pilot had to undergo a two day "refresher" course in airline procedures and safety plus take a check ride in the simulator.

When Kruger had returned to the Minneapolis area he looked for his commuter car. He had parked it in the lot maintained by a local motel that he often used. He knew the people who ran the motel and had their permission to leave the old car there. It was not where he had left it so he contacted the motel people and asked about it. They said that they didn't know where his car was and that it had been in the lot all along. Kruger finally acknowledged that it must have been stolen, although he couldn't believe, for the life of him, why anyone would want to steal such a beat-up old car. In any case he reported the car as being stolen to the local police.

In his next class he found another pilot who wanted to sell his "beater" so Kruger bought another "airporter" or commuter car for four hundred dollars. The car was serviceable and Kruger soon was released to the line as a DC10 Second Officer.

One day as he was looking for a parking slot in the company parking lot he saw his old commuter car. He couldn't believe his own eyes. He parked his new car and reported for his flight. Inside the crew building he saw an old Captain that he had known for a long time. Things clicked.

About a year earlier Kruger was going on a month's long vacation leave. As he was driving past the crew building he saw an old friend, Tom Hennesey, waiting for a bus. He stopped his car, curious, and asked Tom what he was doing. Tom said that he was going to school to become a Captain on the 747, the largest and best paying plane that Northwest owned. He said that he took the bus to his motel each evening. Kruger told him that he could use his car while Kruger was on leave. He told Tom to leave the keys in Kruger's company mail box when he was done with it along with instructions on where the car was parked. Tom was overjoyed by the gift and complied with Kruger's instructions to the letter. He left a note thanking Kruger. The letter was so nice that Kruger looked Tom up. He said, "Tom, when I leave here to go home to Florida that car just sits in the lot. Why don't you keep the keys and use the car when I'm not using it. Leave a note in my box as to where you park it. I have first choice on it. When I'm not using it you can. Is that OK?" Hennesey was overjoyed at the arrangement. He was not asked for any money at all. He used the car for a year prior to the strike.

When the strike ended, 747 Captain Tom Hennesey was recalled right away because of his seniority. He saw the car that he had been driving in the parking lot of the motel and simply drove it without a thought of Kruger, who had not been recalled as yet. A month later Kruger reported the car as being stolen. Several months later he found Hennesey who told him about the car.

When Kruger heard the whole story he laughed. He told Tom that he was lucky that the cops hadn't seen the car as it had been reported stolen. Then he told Tom that he didn't need two commuter cars and that he would sell him the car that he was driving for $100. He said, "You have been driving the car for a year and a half now. You know what it's like. I don't need two commuter cars so give me a hundred dollars and it's yours."

Tom said, "Well, let's talk about that. When I saw the car it had set in the lot for six months. It had a flat tire and the battery had been stolen. I had to replace the battery and fix the tire before I could drive it."

The stories about the penurious ways of Airline Captains were rife. It was well known that the cheapest smack in the whole world was an Airline Captain. Kruger thought that the current situation was appropriate so he looked at the ceiling and heaved a great sigh.

He said, "OK, Tom, subtract the cost of the battery and the tire from the hundred dollars and give me what's left and the car is yours".

Tom thought about it for a few minutes and then said, "I guess I don't really need a car after all". He walked away leaving Kruger both amused and dumfounded at the epitome of the cheap Airline Captain.

Kruger subsequently sold his "airporter" to another pilot who was a wizard with cars and who owned a farm in Indiana. That pilot bought the car for $50 and cut it down to use it as a pickup truck. He drove it for years before it finally died an honorable death.

The strike was over but the animosity between the ALPA pilots and the scabs would never end. No scab could ever leave his luggage unattended. A few tried and their luggage disappeared. In a few more sordid cases their luggage was carried all the way to Tokyo and when opened due to the perennial request of "anything to declare?" by the Japanese customs people the customs police were horrified to find human feces deposited in the suitcase. It was said that you could always identify a scab by the way he had all of his clothes on (including his cover) and was standing with all of his luggage between his legs so it could not be stolen. It was not considered a good way to live.

The stories about the treatment of the scabs were horrifying to the uninitiated. One Flight Attendant told of having to serve a scab Captain his crew meal. She said that she had removed the little steak from the tray, wiped it in the biffy (toilet for non-airline types) a few times, replaced it on the tray and served it to the scab who ate it with relish. That added to Kruger's list of things not to allow. "Number 326; never allow your enemy to feed you."

On another occasion the scab Captain wanted to be served his crew breakfast. The copilot had not cleaned his electric razor in some time so he excused himself and did so in the biffy, saving all of the little whisker shavings. He then found the Captain's breakfast and emptied out the pepper shaker, which he filled with the whisker shavings. The Captain was then served breakfast. The whole crew knew what had happened and they watched with glee as the Captain salted and whiskered his eggs. The copilot reported that "You could smell the Aqua Velva on the eggs".

At every layover station at Hawaii or Narita a scab was "superglued" into his room. A favorite ploy was to empty a superglue tube into the scab's door lock so that he could not get his door opened. One copilot reported that he loved to come awake every morning to the sound of a high speed drill trying to get a scab out of his room.

One of the all time innovative acts against a scab involved an exotic dancer. On a layover in Honolulu a few pilots pooled their money and hired an exotic dancer from the "Forbidden City" night club that was operating at that time. She trailed one of the scab Captains to the nearest bar and "made herself available" to him. He, of course, thought that he was being hustled because he was "a good looking stud, a Captain and, what the hell, any woman would be happy to be noticed by him". The woman allowed herself to be talked into going to the Captain's room and once there went along with the usual foreplay that would end in coitus. She finally said (after having been prompted by the pilots who had hired her) "You know, what I think would be really sexy would be to make it on the balcony of your room under the full moon. Could you do that for me?" Of course the Captain would. By now he was panting so much that he could have blown up a whole blimp all by himself.

The exotic dancer talked the Captain into stripping buck naked and going to the balcony. She was naked also and, having been previously prompted by the pilots (along with a lot of money), said, "Oh, honey, I have to get my cigarettes. I'll only be a minute and then we can really have some fun, OK?" By now the Captain would have stood on his head for her. Of course he would let her get her cigarettes.

She reentered the room, closed and locked the door, dressed and left the room with the naked pilot on his balcony.

The pilot soon realized that he had been scammed. He tried to get back into his room but the door was locked. He finally, in desperation, leaped over to an adjoining balcony, a feat that would have received admiration in any other situation inasmuch as the balconies in question were on the twenty-third floor. Unfortunately he entered an occupied room and the pair of shrieking tourists soon got the attention of the hotel management and the police. The naked pilot had a lot of explaining to do before he was allowed to return to his room. Of course a complete report was made of the incident. After all, the hotel couldn't allow naked men to swing, Tarzan style, from balcony to balcony regardless of the reason. Rest assured that there were more than a few other pilots present who had been "aroused by the commotion and simply wished to see what was going on".

While all of this was happening Kruger was flying the line and spending all of his off time in the commuter apartment with five other pilots. Granted not all were in the apartment at the same time but enough were that Kruger was subjected to a constant barrage of anti-scab rhetoric. That, along with the stress of his ongoing divorce, was changing him for the worse. Heretofore Kruger had always felt that he was in control of his life. As a Naval Officer he was the epitome of confidence, command and control. He surrendered a lot of that in order to become an airline pilot and, as yet, that decision had not paid off. So far, if you averaged his annual pay, considering all of the off time for strikes and layoffs, he was behind what he would have made if he had stayed in the Navy. It was a sad commentary for a step-down in pride, satisfaction in a job and patriotism. And it was all due directly to his own decision. The "fault" was his and his alone. It made him angry. Anger and a lot of idle time is not a good combination. It forms a kind of synergy that bodes ill for anyone in the general area.

Kruger had learned "target identification" in the Navy. It was paramount if you wished to win any battle. The current battle was with Northwest Airlines but Kruger flunked target ID and targeted the scabs. He particularly targeted Gordon Schmidt, AKA Scab Schmidt, that sorry excuse for a human being, as the primary target with all other scabs and the company as targets of opportunity. It was probably a poor choice and allowed him to become "target fixated", a term that usually was applied to pilots who failed to pull out of a dive on a target and had "plumbered in" or crashed as a result.

One day, as Kruger had returned to Minneapolis from a trip, he saw Scab Schmidt's car parked in the company lot with a large sign in the front seat of the car that said, "Support the Independent Pilot's Association". It suddenly became too much for Kruger who hopped out of his car, grabbed a Gerber Mark I fighting knife that he kept in his flight bag, ran to the offending car and stabbed two of the valve stems in the rear tires. His intent was "to send a message" of disgust but he didn't wish to cause much damage monetarily. He figured that two valve stems would cause enough consternation given that most cars only have one spare tire in the trunk.

As Kruger left the car and hastened to his own car there was a sudden flash. He turned and saw two black-clad people with cameras taking his picture. In a flash he knew what had happened and how the car had been set-up by the company to catch someone just like him. For an instant he thought of attacking his new enemies. He had the Gerber in his hand and knew how to use it. Then rationality flooded his brain and he knew that was not the answer. He jumped back into his car and left the parking lot at what was commonly known in the military as "buster speed".

He had given a ride to an old friend who had been on the crew bus and couldn't remember where he had parked. Kruger had told him that they could drive around until he saw his car. When Kruger jumped back into his car and drove off the friend, George Handel, said, "Ed, what the hell is going on"? When Kruger told him George became quiet. He was an ALPA member and was active in the union. He asked Kruger what he was going to do and the answer was, "I'm going to call the union and ask for representation when the company calls me in to flay me". It seemed like the only choice other than to simply walk away from his job. He thought that he might have a 50-50 chance of keeping it. Better to fight than to run.

The company called him in about an hour or two and informed him that he would be in the Chief Pilot's Office tomorrow at 0900. He responded that he would be there pending the availability of ALPA representation. The Chief Pilot said, "You will be here or you will be fired". The next morning everyone showed up, Chief Pilots, lawyers, company officers, ALPA representatives and, of course, the culprit. A lot of rhetoric was bandied around, the lawyers postured and tried to look important and a court reporter was present to take notes. The only thing missing was the band and the farmers with pitchforks.

Kruger stepped right up and told the Chief Pilot, "I know what this is all about and I'll tell you what I did. I have nothing to hide". The company lawyer yelped, "We'll get to that soon. I have a lot of questions to ask you". Kruger ignored him and told the Chief Pilot what he had done and the reasons for it. While he did so the lawyer, a scrawny little guy with an ill-fitting suit, danced around and tried to get into the limelight. Everyone ignored him. He was obviously the lowest bidder for the job. His name was Horton and the pilots all called him "Harpoon Horton" because he had promised the company that he would "harpoon a few of the pilots who were making life hard for the 'non-striking' pilots; his name for the scabs. During the next few months he would prove to be the most ineffectual lawyer Kruger had ever encountered. He was also one of the most humorous, not that he tried to be. He was one of those individuals who could step on his toe and fall flat on his face with ease. In addition to all of that he had a face that made him look like a Norway rat. It wasn't a formula for success in any endeavor.

Finally the Chief Pilot fired Kruger with a lot of ponderous speech. As soon as he had done so one of the company officers, an ineffectual person named Benjamin Griggs, jumped up and said, "Hold on, now, I want to ask you a few questions". The ALPA lawyer, a very good one, said, "Ask him some questions? You just fired him. He doesn't have to talk to you at all. C'mon, Ed, let's leave this joint". They left with the company lawyer, the Chief Pilot and Bennie Griggs all sputtering.

Little Bennie Griggs came from a family with a lot of money. He was a "nothing" on his own and one day his mammy, who had the cash, approached Donald Nyrop, the president of Northwest, with an offer. She said that she knew that Nyrop needed some ready cash. She had some and was willing to part with it on the condition that little Bennie be given a nice job at Northwest, one that fitted with the family's prestige. Nyrop, no dummy, knighted little Bennie with a vice president's job, one that had lots of title but little actual power or responsibility. Benny was too dumb to know the difference. Some time much later when the flight attendants were striking the company a news reporter asked one of the representatives of the flight attendants about Griggs. She responded with the information that he was a vice president. When the reporter asked, "Vice president of what"? She responded, "Vice president of bullshit". She was more accurate than she ever knew.

Kruger had run into Griggs prior to this. Kruger had been a Second Officer on a DC10 when Griggs appeared in the cockpit while the plane was on the ground in Minneapolis. He had a very large stringed instrument of some kind, larger than a guitar, and wanted to put it in the cockpit. It seems that his kid was traveling on the plane and didn't wish his large instrument to be placed in the storage compartments like the rest of the peons flying. Giggs was trying to circumvent some federal air regulations by putting the cargo in the cockpit.

Now the DC10 cockpit is actually pretty small. It has adequate space for the three pilots but precious little for anything else, like the pilot's work bags containing the charts needed for their job and the luggage they needed for their layovers. There was no room for anything else, even the topcoats the pilots wore in the winter. Now here came Griggs trying to stuff his kid's bass viol in the cockpit. He began by saying, "I'm Ben Griggs and I'd like to put this in the cockpit".

Kruger was the only pilot in the cockpit at the time and he said, "Well, Griggs, that's up to the Captain. I can't allow you to leave that here without his OK. As you can see, there's not much room in the cockpit and we can't allow loose gear to be in here at any time during flight. It's an FAA rule." Kruger used Grigg's last name just as he would have used the last name of an enlisted man in the Navy. No titles for this idiot.

Griggs just stared at Kruger, who pretended that he didn't notice. Then Griggs said, "Do you know who I am?"

Kruger grinned to himself and thought, "Whoo, boy, another weirdo that doesn't know who he is. Am I supposed to call the authorities and see just what idiot has escaped from the looney bin? Do I have to tell him when I find out? Do you think he would think this is funny at all?"

He said, "Yeah, I know who you are. That doesn't change one little thing. The Captain still has to give his permission for you to leave that stuff up here. It's his ass if the FAA doesn't like it."

Griggs got red in the face and said, "Maybe I'll just leave it here. I'm positive that the Captain will allow it."

Kruger said, "That's OK with me but if he doesn't allow it I'm going to give it to the ramp guys who will toss it in the bulk cargo compartment. I'm sure that it will get to its destination. Your kid can claim it there."

Griggs was gritting his teeth by now. He glared at Kruger as if to say, "I'll get even with you someday". Kruger didn't even acknowledge him but went on with his preflight. So much for little Bennie Griggs, VP, Northwest Airlines.

Kruger left the company office and went immediately to the ALPA office where he filled out a grievance form, the precursor to the series of hearings that would be held to see if he could get his job back.

An old friend, Jim Watland, orchestrated a large turnout of pilots in all of the hearings. The intent was to show a solid wall of support for the pilot who was in trouble. The effect was not lost on the company, the lawyers and the neutral in the hearing. The company lawyers, Harpoon Horton leading the pack, vociferously protested the packed hearing to no avail. The decision to allow interested pilots in a hearing was decided long ago. The company lawyers were slow learners.

The hearings were supposed to be about Kruger being reinstated. In actuality they became all about Schmidt and his proven inability to either fly or make the decisions a Captain needed to be able to make. Schmidt was a "weak sister" and ALPA wanted to bring that fact into the public's eye. The company fervently wished to hide those attributes in their attempt to protect the pilot who had scabbed for them.

When the hearings were initiated Kruger was in the hearing room with the ALPA Master Executive Chairman, Tom Beedham. A crew trundled in a gantry containing the two tires that Kruger had flattened. Beedham shook his head and said, "I can't believe the dumb sons-of-bitches brought the damned tires in here. What do they hope to prove with them?" Kruger grinned and said, "Tom, want me to show you how I flattened those? It would only take a couple of seconds and I'd love to see Horton's face when he sees his number one exhibit flattened once more." Tom raised an eyebrow and said, "Ed, sit down in that chair and don't move until I tell you to." Kruger laughed but did as he was told.

The hearings were, as the saying goes, interesting. Side bets were tendered often with the odds in favor of ALPA only because of the ineptitude of the company's lawyers. Northwest had the reputation of being penurious to a fault. The amount the company paid their lawyers was a case in point. Northwest didn't have the top of the line lawyer staff and it showed.

Harpoon Horton stumbled and stammered through the whole hearing process. You might say that it wasn't his finest hour. Tom Beedham told Kruger early in the process, "This is going to be the death of either you or Horton. The company has put all of its big guns on this case. At the end of these hearings either you or Horton will be gone from the company." Horton quickly became the laughing stock of the entire assemblage. One morning when Schmidt stumbled into the hearing room late, Horton, without looking around to see just who had made the disturbance and thinking that it had to be one of the pilots, protested long and loudly to the neutral about how the pilots were disrupting the whole process. The ALPA lawyers looked on in amusement and, when Horton was finished with his diatribe, one of them casually remarked, "Counselor, I think that you ought to look at the disturbance. It's your witness."

During the whole grievance process the company had their lawyers file a civil charge against Kruger in order to cause him as much grief as possible. The charge was "tampering with a motor vehicle" and, if proven, could result in not only a fine but also some time in jail. Kruger called an old Navy friend who was a practicing lawyer in the area and that friend assigned a lawyer from his group to aid in Kruger's defence. The lawyer assigned to Kruger had been a prosecuting attorney for the city of St. Paul and knew all of the judges in the area.

When Kruger's lawyer visited City Hall in order to review Kruger's "file" he saw that the company lawyers had been there ahead of him and had tried to influence the prosecutor to "try this case only on the merits and evidence". Kruger's lawyer was apalled and said that this was not fair and not how cases like Kruger's was normally handled. Kruger told him how vindictive Northwest was and how the company pulled out all the stops in order to protect their scabs.

Kruger's lawyer talked at length to the prosecuting attorney and finally talked him into allowing a plea bargaining situation to unfold.

A few weeks later the PA called Kruger's lawyer and said that he could not allow any deals or plea bargaining as Northwest had gotten wind of the deal and had called him to threaten him with the loss of his job if he allowed any plea bargaining to go on. The PA said, "Now it's my job on the line and I can't allow your pilot to have any breaks here". Northwest was strong enough in the local area to back up their threat.

Kruger's lawyer was disgusted with the whole process and told him that they would adopt a new tactic of delaying any trial until Kruger had gotten back to work. At that time they would appeal to the judge showing how much Kruger had already been punished by the loss of wages and how that compared with the minor infraction of cutting off two valve stems.

Kruger's lawyer did just that, putting off two trial dates for later dates. On the third trial date Kruger met his lawyer at the court house and was told to wait while the lawyer conferred with a judge.

After an hour Kruger's lawyer showed up and said, "You're going to like this. I found a lady judge who thinks that pilots are neat. I told her all about this case and she is going to hear it in her chambers. You won't have to appear in court at all. When she asks you how you plead you tell her that you are guilty. You'll like the result."

Kruger and his lawyer appeared in front of a rather cute, very pretty little lady with granny glasses who was flanked by a court stenographer and her personal secretary. When they approached her desk she did not look up but read from some papers in front of her. She said, "Mr. Kruger, to the charges and specifications of tampering with a motor vehicle, how do you plead?"

Kruger said, "Guilty, your honor."

The judge said, "OK, Mr. Kruger, if you have no objections I'm going to place you on probation for six months and you will make restitution to Mr. Schmidt in the amount of six dollars and thirty-five cents for the valve stems you damaged . . . .". At this point she finally looked up and smiled at Kruger. She continued, "And, if you can leave the scabs alone for six months and not harass them your file will be expunged and you can honestly say that you do not have a police record. Is that satisfactory with you?"

Kruger could not say, "Yes, your honor. Thank you." fast enough.

And they were done. As they walked out of the court house Kruger's laywer said, "I would like to be a fly on the wall when the Northwest lawyers find out how we did an end run around them." Kruger's only thought was "I wonder if the little lady judge would accept a date with me"? Oh, well, there were always other little ladies who were cute and wore granny glasses and smiled a lot.

During the grievance process Kruger had to see the Vice President of Flying Operations, William F. Hochbrunn. Hochbrunn, better known as "Hockey Puck" by the pilots for his mental resemblance to that flat little piece of rubber, had fallen out of grace with the company higher ups. He currently had an office located on a remote area overlooking the freight area of the Minneapolis base. It was a greased slide on the way out of the company entirely.

There were numerous reasons for his fall from grace and you could take your pick from any number of them. For starters Hochbrunn tried to interview all of the pilots on an individual basis in order to see just why they seemed to dislike the company. Hochbrunn said that God had told him to do so. Now most pilots are very practical, down-to-earth people and they look with suspicion on anyone who is on a first name basis with God. Hochbrunn did not fit the working description of the pay-grade of prophet. When Hochbrunn's secretary called Kruger and tried to set him up with an interview Ed told her that he did not wish to talk to Hochbrunn. She said, "You don't wish to avail yourself of this opportunity to talk to Captain Hochbrunn?" Ed assured her that he didn't wish to talk to Captain Hochbrunn about any subject at all let alone to discuss Northwest Airlines. He did say that he would talk to Captain Hochbrunn at any time on any subject if he was paid by the contractual rate relative to the hourly pay scale.

Kruger promptly presented his body at the appropriate time for his interview with Hochbrunn relative to his firing. Although the topic of the interview was supposed to be about Kruger's conduct and the possibility of his return to flight status with Northwest Hochbrunn only wanted to talk about his own problems. He was approaching the magic age of sixty years when a federal law dictated that commercial pilots had to retire. He whined that he had taken the job of vice president in order to stave off the day when he had to retire but Northwest was going to make him retire anyway. He dwelt so much on the subject that Kruger decided to have a little fun at his expense.

Adopting a caring and concerned attitude Kruger said, "You know, Bill, that no matter what a guy has done, no matter how many honors he has won, when he retires society thinks of him as useless, of no value and he eventually thinks of himself in the same way. After a short time he simply gives up and dies."

Most people would have told Kruger that he was an idiot and laughed at the jibe but Hochbrunn looked sad and said, "I know, I know, that's what bothers me". Kruger actually began to feel sorry for the poor sap.

"Well, what are you going to do when you retire, Bill?" Kruger had given up on trying to talk the vice president into reinstating him.

Hochbrunn looked at the ceiling and said, "Well, I have my religious work to do and I just bought a recreational vehicle that I thought I would use to drive around and see the country. It's a nice RV. Maybe you saw it on your way in here. It's parked right out in front."

It was too good an opportunity to pass up. Now bear in mind just who Hochbrunn was talking to; a pilot who had flattened a scab's tires. And Hochbrunn had been a scab. Kruger bit his tongue to keep a sober face and said, "Why no, Bill, I didn't see it on my way in but you can bet I'll look for it on my way out." Hochbrunn had been one of the scabs who flew during the strike in spite of the fact that he was an ALPA member. The whole conversation went right over Hochbrunn's head. He had never been the brightest bulb in the package.

Kruger's visit to Hochbrunn turned out to be the non-event he had estimated it would be and he was not reinstated. He continued with the grievance process. During the whole process the room was populated by scores of pilots who showed up in support of Kruger. Occasionally a scab would show up but the whole tenor of the assembly was uncomfortable for a person like a scab. When Kruger had been asked why he was so fervent in his dislike for a scab he had a ready answer.

Someone told him that even old enemies like Americans and Japanese or Germans could lay their hate aside after a while and talk reasonably and without rancor about their old differences. If this was the case why couldn't someone like Kruger do the same with what he termed a scab, what the company called "the non-striking pilots?

Kruger's ready answer was that a scab was a traitor. Old World War II adversaries were mostly "honorable enemies" and each in their own case had fought for their side with honor and loyalty. A scab had no loyalty to anyone other than himself and could never be trusted. He used the example of Absalom who, according to the Bible, had turned on his own father during a war and was considered a traitor. From that biblical time to the present every man living in that part of the world, when passing Absalom's tomb, symbolically picks up a stone and throws it at the tomb. This was documented on the TV show 60 minutes one evening. The person reading the script made the statement, "The whole world hates a traitor".

One of the pilots named Jim Watland, when asked how the pilots could harbor a grudge for so long answered, "Refresh my memory please; who was Benedict Arnold?"

Nine months later Kruger was back on the payroll. The neutral had upheld his position. It seemed like more than nine months, more like nine years, but he was finally back to flying. Had he learned anything in that time? Sure he had. He had learned not to trust, that there was no such thing as a lot of good friends, that the number of real friends you have you can count on one hand and that the company demands loyalty up the chain of command but does not recognize it down the same chain.

When he reported for duty he had to see the Chief Pilot before he did anything else. He asked the ALPA attorney to accompany him. When he entered the Chief Pilots Office, Nelson chuckled and said, "Why, hello, Ed. You didn't have to bring your mouthpiece with you". Kruger smiled and said, "He isn't my mouthpiece. I speak for myself. He's a witness."

Nelson's smile disappeared and he became cagier. "Well," he said, "You don't have to be hostile. We're all on the same team. I just wanted to welcome you back and to tell you that there are no hard feelings. I'd like you to just do your job and not to talk up anything that happened to you. Don't upset the cockpit."

Kruger chuckled. He said, "OK, what am I suppose to say when someone asks me what the hell I've been doing for the last nine months? Should I say that I've been on a sabbatical? I'll tell them exactly what happened to me."

Nelson said, "Well, I don't want you to think that this office was after you . . ."

Kruger interrupted him by saying, "All right, then who sent me to the Mayo Clinic for a psychiatric evaluation?"

Kruger had to undergo a psychiatric evaluation before he came back to the company. It was not a fun test. The psychiatrist began things by saying, "So you have been a bad boy and they made you go see the headshrinker to punish you. Is that it?" The headshrinker asked him to count backwards from 300 by 13's among other things. Kruger did all of these things but afterwards wondered how he had done them. Northwest had only done that in order to see if they could get rid of him easily. The analysis from the headshrinker was that Kruger's thought processes and attitudes were not unlike those of the rest of the pilots at Northwest.

Later on Kruger bragged that not too many of the pilots at Northwest could be certain that the pilots they flew with were exactly sane but that he, Kruger, had a piece of paper to prove that he was sane.

Finally Kruger told Nelson, "I don't want you to think that I'm your friend. I'm not your friend. I was never your friend. I know that you are not my friend. Don't think that anything you say will convince me that we are friends. We are not. Don't think that you can smooze me. I know that you are not a friendly and that's that. Any questions about that at all?"

Nelson finally said that the session was at an end. Kruger and the ALPA lawyer left. Kruger had to see the assistant chief pilot next. The lawyer wanted to know if he needed him or not. Kruger said that he didn't and the lawyer left.

When Kruger entered the next office it was much friendlier. He talked with the assistant Chief Pilot for some time and all of a sudden Nelson entered the office. He glanced about, looking for the lawyer. When his eyes met Kruger's, Kruger grinned and said, "I didn't need him for this office". Nelson turned red and left the office.

In all future meetings Kruger realized that Nelson didn't wish to acknowledge him at all. Accordingly he used to position himself directly in the path of Chief Pilot Nelson and grin while saying, "Good morning, Captain Nelson". It always grated on Nelson to have to say "good morning" in return as he knew exactly what was happening. Nelson was never stupid, just repulsive.

It was an expensive lesson. Kruger had a plaque made with the Gerber Mark I knife. It was mounted on a barn wood base and had a brass nameplate that said "value, $50,000" along with the dates that Kruger had been off flight status. Kruger vowed never to repeat a stupid trick like that again. In the future his war with Northwest Airlines would be more on the order of a guerilla war. He had discovered that a war waged on those terms was hard to defeat.

During his stay in the commuter apartment in Minneapolis Kruger had the feeling that he was, once again, on a deployment. He had little in the way of possessions and knew that his new "digs" were temporary. Since he was going to be more or less a permanent member of the group he asked all of the other members if it was OK for him to live "more or less permanently" in the apartment. The vote was unanimous in that everyone voted for Kruger to stay as long as he wished. In response Kruger kept the place spotless. He did the cleaning and the washing of any dishes that needed washing. He cleaned the head and even did some of the laundry for any of the groaty guys who needed that sort of service.

Living in an apartment complex was taxing for an independent, freedom loving pilot. A lot of the tenants were simply "civilians", defined as people who had never had the training that was necessary in order to become one of the "elite". Kruger considered the majority of the people who lived in the complex as the great unwashed.

The apartment that the pilots had rented was sandwiched in between the top and the bottom floors. As such, it was privy to all of the sounds that emanated from all of the apartments adjacent to it. The apartment below Kruger's was owned by a single lady who had an alliance with a married guy who lived in a neighborhood apartment complex. You had to give the guy in question credit for guts since he would come to her apartment, have sex with her and then scream at her from her open window calling her a lot of really rotten names. (As if he had a lot of morals.) Kruger listened to the sex noises and the yelling for about two days. Then he decided to do something about the whole thing.

One day, when the guy below was yelling at the lady from her open window, Kruger decided to take action. There were several pilots in the apartment at the time and Kruger had apprised them of the situation below them. Kruger went to the window directly above the guy who was yelling at his paramour and said loudly, "OK, if you guys aren't going to free up the head I'm going to pee out of the window." Having thus made his announcement Kruger freed the screen and urinated out of the window onto the head of the asshole who was screaming at his paramour. The screaming of the asshole who had been heretofore calling his girlfriend a lot of names ended abruptly as the culprit exited the area in order to shower and clean himself up. Kruger had hoped that the guy would appear at his door in order to protest but that never happened. It did stop the yelling at the lady through her window though.

Soon he discovered that he was eligible to check out on the 747. He had applied for the position and was given it. It was a new era for him and opened a whole new vista of flying. Now he could fly to either Asia or Europe and he could do so by choosing either place on opposite months.

CHAPTER XIII

The 747 was the largest airplane Northwest had. It flew only long haul trips to Asia and Europe. Kruger was excited at the prospect of flying on it even as a Second Officer. It was the senior equipment on the airline. Kruger had visions of the South China Sea, Terry and the Pirates, the Dragon Lady and other childhood fantasies just like he had in the Navy when he flew the large Marlin P5M sea planes. This time he was assured of actually getting to the South China Sea.

But first he had to go through the checkout including another Boeing school. The instructor was an old Marine named Vic Britt who primarily lived in the training department. When the class was convened the instructor handed out the large aircraft manual to everyone. He then introduced himself and asked if there were any questions before he started to teach the systems. Kruger raised his hand and when he was recognized he asked, "Are we really supposed to read this thing or can we just fake it?"

The instructor grinned and said, "Hell, Ed, they really have got you scared and running haven't they? Imagine any pilot actually reading the manual." The class laughed. The instructor had adopted the habit of sucking and chewing on a cigar that he had not unwrapped. He would do that until about noon when he would actually light and smoke it. Kruger laughed and said, "OK, are you going to smoke that cigar or are you just going to suck on that thing?" The operative words were "suck on that thing". The class all knew what Kruger was referring to. The instructor laughed and said, "Well, if you're going to give some crap you have to be able to get some back." Thus relaxed, the class began.

The checkout took the better part of a month. The airplane systems were pretty familiar since Boeing made most of their planes pretty much the same. When Kruger stepped into the cockpit he immediately felt at home. His initial thought was, "God, this is a big plane." He familiarized himself with the whole plane. Not just the cockpit but the whole thing. He climbed into the bowels of the plane, opened the overhead panels to find the circuit breaker panels, inspected the Flight Attendants systems and generally looked over the whole system. He wanted no surprises over either the North Atlantic or the wide Pacific. On his first flight on an empty plane in order to check out he walked all the way aft and saw that the plane had a pronounced tendency to dutch roll in spite of the corrections Boeing had put into the systems to counter that tendency. A dutch roll was the tendency of an airplane to roll to one side and then recover by rolling to the other side while keeping the same altitude. The feel of the dutch roll was that the plane was corkscrewing through the air. He resolved to only fly in first class whenever he had to fly a long trip on the plane. You never felt the dutch roll in first class.

Kruger quickly fell into a habit of bidding flights into Europe one month and Asia the second month. The variety of flying was heady stuff. Kruger figured that he could do this until he retired.

On one of the first trips to Hamburg, Germany the copilot had just flown there and was loudly proclaiming the virtues of Hamburg as a layover spot. Northwest had just started flying to Hamburg and this was the third trip made there. All the way over the North Atlantic the copilot had praised the city and especially the restaurant that he had gone to the last time he was there. He kept repeating, "I don't know any German but I sure do know what to order there. I'll walk you guys through the whole thing, trust me." Kruger remained quiet throughout the whole trip.

When they finally reached the hotel where they were to stay they showered as agreed and met in the hotel lobby. The copilot continued his litany of praise for the "restaurant" where he was going to lead the other pilots. Kruger remained silent and let him lead.

When they had finally arrived at the "restaurant" Kruger saw that it was really a nice little bar, Hamburg style. They were seated and the copilot redoubled his efforts at convincing the other pilots that "he could get them something really nice even if he didn't know any German".

The German hostess soon came on scene and asked, in German of course, what they wished. Before the copilot could point to anything on the menu Kruger asked, "Haben sie dunkle bier am fass?" (Do you have dark beer on tap?) She answered, "Ja, wohl, mouchten sie drei?" (Yes, certainly, do you wish three?) Kruger answered, "Bitte" (Please) and she left. The copilot stared at Kruger and finally said, "Ah, you asshole", Kruger and the Captain broke out in laughter. The rest of the evening was just great.

Hamburg layovers were super but there were other places in Europe that were equally nice. Kruger loved Scotland (the home of his ancestors) and had a lot of fun in England. Northwest flew to Prestwick, a small airport about an hours train ride from Glasgow. Prestwick served a small town called Ayre. The English were fun to poke fun at. They were very stiff and formal and not prone to change. Kruger loved to ask some official why it was necessary to do some small formality. Usually the answer was made by the official looking over his glasses and down his nose at Kruger and saying, "We have been doing that for over a hundred years." Kruger would then look at the sky and say, "Oh, of course. Why didn't I know that? I must have been stupid. Of course you have been doing it that way for a hundred years. But did it ever occur to you that you have been doing it wrong for a hundred years?" Another response was, "It's policy". Kruger's response to that was always, "Oh, shit, why didn't I think of that? Of course it's policy. That certainly explains it all. Policy! What other explanation could you ever want? Policy! I should have known. Policy, the last bastion for the absolute bureaucrat. Policy!" Usually the bureaucrat would only blink rapidly, saying nothing.

One day on a flight to Prestwick, Scotland Kruger visited the local bank wishing to change some dollars for pounds. When the little lady at the bank asked him what he wished he said that he wanted to change some American dollars for pounds from the Bank of Scotland. Now in Great Britain pounds are pounds. It doesn't matter which bank issues the notes. The lady at the bank was curious and asked why Kruger wished pound notes from the Bank of Scotland. Kruger answered, "Tomorrow I'm going to fly to London and I want to make the Sassanach (A Scottish word for the English) take pounds issued from Scotland. The lady giggled and spent a lot of time counting out only Scottish pounds.

The layover hotel in England was fun. For a while the crews stayed at the airport hotel at the Gatwick airport. Then they moved to another hotel in Gatwick itself. Kruger soon learned that if he entered the bar in the basement of the hotel and greeted the barman, a very fat, ugly man with only a few teeth, with, "Hey, barman, how's it going?" the man would always shout, "Bloody fucking top-ho". Kruger thought it classic and always greeted the man in that manner. The bar was interesting. Kruger met all kinds of people from Irish Republic Army fighters to Ulster Light Constabulary (ULC) soldiers. It was about as interesting a layover as you could wish all coupled with copious amounts of good English beer.

One night when he was engrossed in a conversation with a member of the ULC the witching hour approached. In England, in bars supported by a hotel, all persons not registered at the hotel have to vacate the premises by 2100 unless "sponsored" by a person registered at the hotel. Kruger's friend was requested to leave. Kruger protested that he was "sponsoring" the ULC soldier and was told that he would have to pay for all of the beer the two consumed. Apparently the ULC man's money was no good after 2100. Kruger told the bar man that it was not a problem and he put the tab on his room check. The barman eyed him suspiciously for the rest of the evening.

Scotland was wonderful. The Scots did everything they could to make the crew's layover a memorable one. Kruger loved the place. He loved to roam the streets with their history. One day he wandered into a sporting goods store. The store had a lot of walking sticks, canes and authentic shepherd's crooks. Kruger had not, up until this time, ever given a shepherd's crook a passing thought. Here in Scotland they were not only real but were a necessary tool for the very real shepherds who operated in the hills. Kruger was told that old, retired shepherds made the crooks. They would select the wood, cut it and lay it in a stream to soak over the winter. In the spring they would retrieve the cut canes, strip them of bark and steam them into the familiar crook. The whole process took about a year. Kruger was fascinated. He asked if the store owner had any more canes and was told that he would have lots more in a week. Kruger said that he would be back in a week or two and would see what the owner had at that time.

When he returned to Prestwick (the town's name was Ayer) he went to the store. The owner had ordered a number of walking sticks and crooks. Kruger selected a number of sticks made of Irish Blackthorn, Cherry, French Chestnut and some other woods. They were all beautiful. He said, "I'll take these". The store owner's eyes bugged and he spouted, "All of them?" Kruger nodded, "All of them." He could tell from the look on the owner's face that he wished that he had ordered a lot more sticks.

When he flew back to the United States everyone had to declare customs in Boston. Kruger was carrying all of his canes and, as the shepherd's crook was long, he looped it around his neck. As he stood in the crew line waiting to be checked by customs he glanced over at the passenger line. A diminutive Scotsman was watching him with a grin and a glint in his eye. When Kruger looked at him the grin broadened and he said, "Are ya lookin' fer sheep, laddie?" Kruger grinned back and said, "Only pretty ones." The little Scotsman doubled up in laughter.

Scotsmen were friendly but hard to understand. One day a friend of Kruger's was in a local bar in Ayer when one of the locals wanted to talk to him. The local had a brogue that was hard to cut through. Jay didn't wish to be discourteous so he just nodded and said "OK" whenever the little Scotsman said anything. Finally Jay paid his bill and went to bed. The next time he arrived at Ayer he found the little Scotsman waiting for him as he exited the customs line. The local tipped his cap respectfully and said, "I've got yer veggies in the truck here, sor." Jay soon discovered that he had bought a truckload of vegetables while he was drinking at the local pub. He was gracious enough to pay the local man and tell him to deliver it all to his hotel. He figured that the hotel could figure out how to deal with the batch of "veggies".

On one trip Kruger was fortunate enough to fly with his old instructor, Ed Johnson. Ed had been recently divorced and was hurting as any guy would have been. Kruger decided to try to cheer him up.

During the trip as the two pilots flew from Gatwick, Scotland to London the controller, a female, called the plane and said, "Northwest, I have you descending. What is your altitude?" Kruger was flying and Ed Johnson said, "We are level at flight level 250". The controller said, "Your flight recorder has you descending." Ed looked at Kruger. What the hell? Ed Johnson disgustedly said, "I guess the recorder is fucked up". Kruger said, "When something like that happens here in England it's called a 'cock-up' not a 'fuck-up'". Ed picked up the mike and said, "I do believe there has been a cock-up in the box". The female controller almost choked with laughter. The flight continued with no other interruptions.

When they got to Scotland the two pilots found a small pub that had a lot of pictures of World War Two British pilots on the walls. Names like Tuck and Bader, World War II heroes, were all over the walls in pictures. The pilots couldn't resist eating in such a fine place and they did. When they had finished their dinner they repaired to the diminutive bar that could only accommodate four people. Ed Johnson and Ed Kruger each had a glass of single malt Scotch whisky. One led to two and soon both pilots were sound asleep sitting at the bar in the little restaurant. No one was discourteous enough to wake them but finally they awoke and were embarrassed enough to pay their bill and leave the establishment. It was a memorial time.

Kruger's crew had to get to London's Heathrow airport to deadhead on British Air. They complied with their schedule but BA had a few setbacks on theirs. First they were seated on an aircraft and nothing happened. Finally a PA said that the crew that was supposed to fly the plane had run out of time and a new crew was being shanghaied to fly the plane. Fifteen minutes later a very precise British voice came on over the PA to explain how that crew had been awakened and told to report to the plane for duty. The explanation went on to say that BA was very sorry for the delay and on and on. The pilot making the announcement did so in a very proper British voice that was pleasant to listen to. Suddenly the whole plane went dark as all power was lost on the plane. The cockpit emergency power came on and the very precise British voice said, "No doubt you have noticed that you have just been plunged into darkness . . ." It was so funny that Kruger's whole crew burst into laughter. The cockpit voice explained that the auxiliary power system had failed. It was not a good day for British Air but the humor of listening to the dry, proper Brit voice made up for the delay.

Flying to Asia was a lifelong dream come true. Kruger had finally arrived at the South China Sea. He never tired of flying to Japan, Hong Kong, Singapore, Thailand, the Philippines or Malaysia. He tolerated Korea and Taiwan but thought that they were still very interesting. The people in these exotic places were interesting and friendly also but the folks in Thailand made it a national attribute to be friendly. Kruger loved the place.

The Japanese were very formal, very polite and very regimented. Americans were viewed as raucous, informal, impolite and fun-loving, taking things the Japanese thought of as serious as comical. Flying into Narita put Americans in direct confrontation with the formal Japanese who worshiped rules. Americans thought that the rules were only guidelines while the Japanese saw them as gospel to be followed to the letter.

Pushing back from the terminal and simply taxiing to the runway necessitated following a large number of rules. You had to have permission to "push back", to ask for your clearance, to taxi (usually you had at least two or three controllers you had to ask permission from before you reached the end of the runway and to ask for permission to call the tower for permission to take off. If a casual American violated any of these rules he was required to write a letter of apology to the airport authority. The Japanese considered the writing of such a letter a "loss of face" or an embarrassment. The Americans thought that it was a minor inconvenience and meant nothing.

One bright day Kruger was flying with a crew that was a lot of fun. All three pilots had a good sense of humor. They were having so much fun that they forgot to ask for push back. The stolid controller cautioned them but they were having so much fun that next they found that they had pushed back without receiving a clearance for the entire flight. This was no big deal in the United States but was a cardinal sin in Japan. As they joked about the number of letters of apology they would have to write Kruger came up with a form letter of apology. The fill-in-the-blank letter began, "Prease excuse—for the very serious infraction of—. We promise faithfully that we will not break any rules until the next time . . . ." By the time the crew had perfected the letter they had arrived at the end of the runway and had broken another rule necessitating one more letter of apology.

Kruger soon learned and adopted much of the Japanese culture. The national yoke that all Japanese had to adhere to was the absolute adherence to obligation. Each Japanese was obligated to family, employer, the country, the government, friends, etc that amounted to a religion. Americans had one word for obligation but the Japanese had several such as "Giri" and "On". A similar situation existed among the Aleuts in Alaska who had about thirty different words for snow whereas to Americans snow was snow. Kruger's idea of obligation was, shall we say, enhanced by his association with the Japanese.

Kruger had made friends with several of the families that lived around the hotel the Northwest crews stayed in Narita. Northwest owned the hotel and keeping the crews there was a tax break for the company. The hotel management rented out the excess rooms to Japanese on vacations who wanted to visit the several shrines that abounded near the hotel. There were a number of families that owned property near the hotel. Those families ran restaurants the crews frequented. One day Kruger made a giant faux pas in regard to one of the families. He was going through a divorce at the time and took delight in the two little kids the family had. On a side trip to Hawaii he bought the kids several presents for Christmas. In doing so he put the father, Nobi Nokazawa, in his debt placing an obligation on him to repay that debt. In retrospect the obligation could never be settled because when Nobi gave Kruger a return gift it put additional obligation on him. Nokazawa-san and his wife gave Kruger two little dolls that Kruger was sure had cost way too much. Kruger finally gave up and remained in obligation to Nokazawa, which made that gentleman very happy.

Nobi's restaurant was an establishment that featured ton-katsu, which was a pork cutlet. He served go-hon or rice with each serving. Most of the crew members poured a sauce known as "bulldog sauce" over the rice. One day there was a tug-of-war between Nobi and one of the pilots over the sauce bottle. Nobi didn't want the pilot to adulterate his rice with bulldog sauce. Finally the pilots were treated to Nobi's lament. He said that he canvassed the whole area to buy only the finest rice for his customers and it broke his heart when they poured bulldog sauce over it. It was akin to pouring catsup over a fine filet mignon. It turned out that the Japanese had as many names for the different kinds of rice as the Aleuts had for the different kinds of snow. To the American rice was rice, end of statement.

All crew members had to pass through customs and agriculture inspections on entering Japan. Initially each crew member had to pick up a shore pass. This piece of paper allowed the person (gaijin or, more politely, gaikoku-no-America. Gaijin was a term that meant foreign devil, much like the Chinese Kwai-loh or Loh-fahn.) to travel in an area of 50 miles around the airport without having to show a passport. After picking up the shore pass the crew member went through Customs/Agriculture where the uniformed policeman asked, "Anything to declare?"

Chief among the proscribed things that you could not bring into Dai-Ichi Nihon was pornography. The Japanese idea of what constituted pornography was not the same as that in America. The Japanese allowed a lot of things the Americans thought of as smut but were horrified if any pubic hair was displayed. Playboy magazines were absolutely not allowed into the country. That was not to say that the Japanese men didn't like the magazine. It would have sold at a premium if any could be found. One Northwest pilot used to have a lot of fun with the customs police and, at the same time, made some of them very happy. When asked if he had anything to declare he would slowly pull the latest Playboy out of his flight bag and, with a grave face would mournfully say, "Hai, pornography". The customs man would silently confiscate the offending magazine. The pilot never got into any trouble over the "contraband" and, as he did the same thing month after month, an unbiased person could be excused if he thought that this was a normal thing and something that the customs people looked forward to.

The hotel the crews stayed at was a very nice one by Japanese standards. It was modern and had most of the amenities that Americans needed in order to feel comfortable. It boasted a nice restaurant that was top-of-the-line by Japanese standards but was found lacking by Americans. One complaint the "round eyes" had was that any breakfast order was delivered to the table in courses. If you ordered eggs, toast, potatoes and fruit you would probably be given the toast first. After, and only after, you had eaten the toast would you be served the eggs, then the rest in order but only after you had eaten the current course. This created a lot of huffing and abuse delivered by the round-eyes to the servers who were doing an excellent job by Japanese standards.

The hotel manager was a detestable man. He was draconian to his employees and cared not one whit for the people who were forced to occupy his hotel, that is to say, the Northwest flight crews. On the other hand he was obsequious to the occasional Japanese that stayed in the hotel. The manager tried to advertise the hotel to the locals by posting a very large sign in front of the property that said, in Japanese of course, "Come and see the beautiful American Flight Attendants in their swimming suits". An interpreter blew the whistle on him and he had to do away with the sign.

The manager that was on the property all of the time was a misunderstood soul who shouldered the entire rancor directed toward the head man as most of the crew members thought that the policies handed down were from him. Actually he was only the whipping boy for all of the grief meted out as the real manager would never step foot on the property. He was a serious man who possessed a keen sense of humor. One day he posted a notice on a bulletin board saying, "I am not the manager of this establishment. I only carry out the manager's orders. Please do not abuse me further for any policies set out by the management."

Northwest Airlines actually set the policies and the in-country manager implemented them. Most of the policies were intended to separate the crew members from their money as rapidly as possible. Those that had nothing to do with money made it hard if not impossible for a crew member to participate in any of the perks offered by the hotel to its guests. A hotel bus left the hotel each day for the town of Narita. The bus schedule was posted for all guests. When the bus seemed to fill with crew members a hotel employee would try to shoo them off in order to allow the Japanese guests to board first and take any seat they wished. This never worked because the Americans were not used to being pushed and shoved around as the Japanese were. Most of the time the hotel employee was lucky to escape with a full skin.

One day the day-to-day manager had to travel to Minneapolis for some reason. On the trip back to Japan the Captain realized that he was on board and made a special trip back to the passenger section to talk to him. This gave him a lot of "face" or recognition and he opened up to the Captain a little. When the Captain asked him why he had to go to Minneapolis he smiled. Bear in mind that, at the time period this occurred in, no Northwest crew member could drink any alcoholic beverage at any time on duty no matter how long the layover. When asked the question the hotel manager grinned and said, "Most important conference about camera monitoring the beer machine in the lobby of the hotel. Camera seems to be malfunctioning." Then he collapsed in a fit of laughter.

The hotel in Narita was a very nice one by Japanese standards but the Japanese were very rigid in determining what needed to be done relative to the infrastructure of their hotel. They ran the heat and the air conditioning according to the time of the year instead of the temperature existing at the time. Arguing with the staff was pointless. Kruger decided on a course of guerilla warfare. When the temperature was cold he would turn on the shower in his room full hot and let it run. Soon his room approximated an equatorial jungle. It was an option.

Insects and pests were a problem also. One night Kruger found a gigantic cockroach roaming his bathtub. He dispatched the animal as quickly and painlessly as possible by slamming it with the heel of a shoe. Then he placed the carcass on a piece of stationary provided to each room, put his room number on it, and carried it to the front desk of the hotel.

The desk was staffed by a young female. As he approached the desk Kruger bowed and said, "Komban wa." The young lady bowed and said, "Komban wa". Kruger laid the stationary with the insect on it on the desk and said, "Ah, so, cockroach desnae". The young lady gave an involuntary shrug and said something like "Ugh". Kruger bowed once more and left. In about 30 minutes there was a Japanese exterminator with a spray rig fogging Kruger's room. Mission accomplished.

When the crews arrived at Narita they were tired and needed to relax after a very long day. One of the best ways to do that was to imbibe one of the large bottles of Sapporo beer, a very excellent beer brewed by the

Japanese. The Japanese brewed some other beers but none of them was superior to Sapporo. One of them, Kirin (Japanese for Dragon) was a head splitter. Rumor had it that it contained a lot of impurities including methyl alcohol but whatever it contained it would give you a splitting headache. The Japanese seemed to love Kirin. Kruger figured that the Japanese equated pain with pleasure and they thought that they were having fun when their heads hurt.

The easiest way for flight crews to get cheap Sapporo was to go to a neighborhood store and buy it there. The hotel had a beer machine but, as was typical with a Northwest operation, it was a lot more expensive than buying it on the local market. The nearest local store was known by the flight crews as "Dirty Mary's". The name came from the proprietor whose name was Mary. The other name came from the fact that the place had never been cleaned. Mary was what you could call a loose woman. Never married, she lived in the back of her store with her mother and a bevy of little kids. She was always either pregnant or carrying a small child. Everything on the shelves of the place had a layer of dirt on it depending on just how long it had been on the shelf.

Dirty Mary's had received several awards for the most Sapporo sold in the Japanese Islands for several years. It was all because of the gigantic thirst the Northwest flight crews had generated. Of course that was all unsubstantiated rumor since the Northwest crews did not imbibe alcohol at all.

One of the pilots observed that the Flight Attendants always bought food from Dirty Mary's. He said that someone was going to be poisoned by eating the dirty stuff that Mary kept on her shelves. The pilots only bought beer and sake from Mary and always washed the bottles before opening them.

One day Kruger brought another pilot over to introduce him to Mary's. The pilot had never been to the store before this. Kruger briefed him about the cleanliness issue but it was apparent that the warning didn't register with the newcomer. The newcomer had bought a cup of yogurt or custard and was engaged in eating it when he entered Mary's. Mary appeared from the bowels of her home behind the store with a baby on her shoulder. As she entered the store the baby upchucked a load of white stuff all over Mary's shoulder. Mary didn't even flinch. She just went to the cash register in order to sell whatever the plots wished to buy, ignoring the episode happening on her shoulder.

The new pilot turned white, went to the front of the store and threw his custard as far as he could. He then told Kruger that he didn't think much of Dirty Mary's. Kruger briefed him on the pilot protocol of buying and imbibing beer from Dirty Mary's. They bought several bottles of Sapporo and left.

On one trip to Japan while airborne Kruger got an emergency message from the Flight Attendants. The message was sent via the crew communication system and the FA whispered the whole time. She said, "Please come down to the first class galley right now. I need you." Kruger tried to ask what the problem was but the FA would only say, "I need help right now".

Kruger alerted the rest of the crew of the problem, exited the cockpit and moved cautiously to the first class galley, which was screened by a drape that didn't allow anyone to see inside it. Kruger had no idea what he was going to encounter. This was the time period where Muslim extremists were blowing up airplanes or hijacking them according to the "Bojinka" project uncovered by the CIA. Kruger made sure that he had his large jack knife available. It was the only legal thing that he could carry in defense of any pirating attempt.

Kruger crouched and swept the curtain aside ready for whatever threat faced him. He only saw a female FA in the galley who motioned him inside. When he spoke to her he found that the problem was that she had an argument with a black male FA about where they were going to stow their luggage. Kruger was steamed as his adrenalin ratcheted down. He said, "Jesus Christ, here we are over the north Pacific and you guys can't solve a minor argument over fucking luggage. Where's the other person in this flap?"

The FA pointed to a large black male flight attendant who glared at Kruger like he was an old enemy. Kruger said, "OK come up to the cockpit with me and we'll talk about this thing". The FA loudly said, "You don't like me 'cause I'm black".

Kruger snarled, "I don't give a shit what color you are. You could be purple for all I care. You are acting like an asshole and the passengers can hear you. Lower your voice and follow me to the cockpit right now or I'll have you in a jail once we get to Narita." He turned and went to the cockpit followed by the surly FA. Once in the cockpit Kruger chewed the ass off of the FA and told him that he was out of line and if he persisted in his combative way he would be marooned in Narita and not allowed on another NWA plane until his immediate supervisor had made arrangements to get him back to Minneapolis. He said that the most probable outcome would be that he would be fired. That calmed the FA down and he was allowed to go back to the cabin. Kruger took a deep breath and reflected on all of the possible scenarios that could have happened. It was nice that this miniscule flap was just that.

Kruger had bid a trip that a friend had bid. Captain Bob Chance was a good pilot, a good friend and was an old Navy pilot; something that Kruger valued. The pilots had a nice time flying to London and when they got there they decided to have dinner at a local restaurant called the Thirteen Bells. The restaurant was named after an old church or abbey nearby that featured a belfry with a wide array of bells that could be used in melodies. The bells were operated by ropes that bell ringers used to play the tunes. The church was open to sightseers who would watch the bell ringers operate the bells. It was an additional perk for those who frequented the restaurant.

The restaurant itself was an old part of the abbey and featured several large fireplaces with roaring fires that were welcome in the frosty autumn temperatures. After their meal the pilots relaxed by the fires and drank dark beer. It was a wonderful evening.

They had walked from their hotel to the restaurant and expected to walk back. What they didn't anticipate was that the road they were walking on was a well traveled highway. Apparently there were rules that dictated when pedestrians could walk the highway. The pilots were walking along when a police car pulled up alongside them. A very pretty female police lady said, "Good evening, gentlemen. Where are you going?" Kruger, who had imbibed a little more than his share of beer and who had no idea about what the police were concerned with told the lady where they were headed. She said, "We would be most happy to give you a ride. Please enter the car". Kruger said that they really wanted to walk and a male police officer who was accompanying the lady said, "We really would prefer that you get in our vehicle". Kruger's obstinate gene along with his sense of humor kicked in and he said, "Oh, I don't think so. My Mom always said that I wasn't to get into a car with a strange man". The lady policeman laughed and said, "Well, I think that's a wise policy to follow. He certainly is a strange man but we really have to give you a ride since it's against the law to walk on this road". The pretty police lady convinced him and the pilots crowded into the diminutive car and allowed themselves to be taken back to their hotel. Kruger mourned that they had to find a beautiful lady who not only was a police person but was on duty and in England to boot. Asking her for a date was impossible.

On another trip to London Kruger was flying as a copilot. Another old friend, Dale Yeats, was flying as a training Captain and had to give "safety time" to another Captain who was just checking out. Dale met Kruger in the operations office and told him that he would not be needed on the trip to London and back so he could relax in his hotel until the flight returned. Dale mentioned that one of the Northwest scabs was the Captain that was being flight checked. Kruger said, "OK, if I stay here in New York who will you eat dinner with in London, the Scab?" Dale grinned and said, "No, I'll probably have to go by myself." Kruger continued, "And you'll have to drink beer by yourself, right?" Dale acknowledged that was true. Kruger said, "Well, I guess that I'd rather go on the flight in the jump seat so you won't have to drink all by yourself". Dale laughed and said, "God, I hoped you would do that. It would be a long flight with just that scab".

Kruger flew his trip in the first class section of the plane as there was plenty of space available. Most of the time he spent in the cockpit jump seat talking with his friend, Dale. During a lull in the conversation he said, "I watched 60 Minutes the other night on TV and saw a piece about Absolom's grave. I think that Dan Rather was narrating the piece. He said that Absolom was the son of David or Solomon and had carried out a war against his father. He was killed and his body was buried in the large tomb that was erected in his honor by his father. Every man who passes Absolom's tomb picks up a rock and throws it against the tomb. It is a custom that has been going on for centuries. Rather commented, "I guess that the whole world hates a traitor".

Later on Dale grinned as he said, "I knew that you were going to zing that scab. I didn't know when or where but I just knew". The two pilots spent a nice evening together and the next day they flew back to New York where Kruger picked up the rest of his trip minus the scab.

Earlier in the year Yeats and Kruger had flown together to Asia. On one of the legs they had a long layover in Honolulu. They rented a car and drove all over the island of Oahu seeing the sights and thoroughly enjoying themselves. Since Kruger was retired from the Navy they had access to Fort Derussey in downtown Honolulu where they consumed several Mai Tais. Then Kruger said, "We ought to go the PCT. I haven't been there for years". When Dale raised a questioning eyebrow Kruger said, "PCT, Pearl City Tavern. It's renowned for the monkey bar behind the long bar where you can drink and watch a gang of monkeys behind a glass window. All Navy people know about it. It was an old hangout when I was stationed here in 1962". Dale thought that was a good idea so they drove to Pearl City and entered the bar. It was just as Kruger remembered it.

They were drinking at the bar when Kruger whispered to Yeats, "Don't panic but that guy at the bar over there seems too interested in us". He indicated a young man who was sitting opposite them at the bar and smiling at them. Both pilots were aware that Northwest hired people to shadow pilots in an effort to find them drinking illegally. The rules had changed since Kruger had initially hired on with the company but no pilot liked the idea of someone spying on them for any reason. Yeats said, "What if he is?" Kruger said, "I'll thump him and leave him in an alley. I'm not going to allow some asshole to spy on me. I can take him and I will if he proves to be a company fink". After a few seconds of thought Yeats said, "I'm with you. I'll help out". The two pilots kept a wary eye on the guy at the bar.

Suddenly the person in question said, "I know you guys fly for Northwest Airlines. Can I buy you a drink?"

The Northwest pilots were startled and Kruger's adrenalin topped out as he contemplated battery on the upstart at the bar. Before they could reply he said, "My name's Terry. I'm a pilot for Molokai Air and I see Northwest pilots in here all the time because I drink here all the time. Relax. I'm not a spy. I know Northwest's policies and don't agree with them".

The ice was broken and the three pilots spent the rest of the evening swapping tales and telling lies like any other group of pilots the world over. Terry told them about his job which was flying trips to the leper colony, Kalapana, in Molokai. It was different, to say the least, but Terry was used to it and was happy to live in "Paradise" and fly planes there. He said that it was strange, the first time he shook hands with a guy with no fingers but that he soon got used to it. Leprosy wasn't catching and the disease was just about gone in the modern world so the leper colony was a dying tourist attraction. Meanwhile Terry flew tourists and supplies to the little colony and enjoyed life in Hawaii. Kruger and Yeats flew back to O'Hare the next day. Kruger reflected that only as a pilot could one meet people like Terry in places like Hawaii in a monkey bar and go back to Chicago the next day to resume life. Terry might have been happy but Kruger thought that he was probably happier.

One trip to Europe was memorable. Kruger was flying with a Captain named Tom Kelly and a Second Officer named Tom Malone. The trip patterns were from Ireland to Boston and back. Both the Captain and the Second Officer had roots in Ireland so they were happy to layover in places where they could check on their ancestors. On the leg from Dublin to Boston the plane was holding in a pattern over Boston in the "soup", IFR at 23,000 feet. The Captain was flying and Kruger was handling the communications. All of a sudden the pilots flying were rattled when the Second Officer screamed. He had seen a 727 pass close by the tail of the 747 they were in as the 727 descended in the clouds through the altitude Kruger's plane was holding in. This was definitely not supposed to happen.

As soon as Kruger had ascertained why Malone had screamed he immediately called the Center and asked what 727 had just missed them. The airwaves immediately became jammed by pilots all demanding answers and directions as there were many planes holding in the same stack as Kruger's 747 was in. The Center immediately called a Continental flight asking what altitude they were. The Continental flight said that they were at 21,000 feet. The Center said that they were supposed to hold at 25,000. Pandemonium ensued. The Continental plane was given a clearance to descend to 19,000. When the air cleared somewhat Kruger's flight was cleared to 21,000. As they began their descent the Center called Continental once more to inquire what altitude they were passing. Continental said they were still at 21,000, the same altitude that Kruger's plane had just been cleared to. When he heard that, Kruger hit the Captain on his shoulder and said, "Get the hell back up to 23,000". The Captain complied without comment. At this point in time Kruger had just assumed command of the plane.

He immediately called the center and said, "We are still at 23,000 and are going to stay here until you get Continental out of our way. Panic ensued once more. Continental and the Center flogged around a couple of more times with the Center almost putting Continental through another Northwest's altitude. Kruger's plane was finally vectored for an approach and landing and 400 passengers who never guessed how close they had come to being a statistic finally deplaned.

Kruger wasn't finished with the Center. On his layover he called the Center and demanded the tape of the incident. At first the Center refused until Kruger said, "If I have to get a lawyer none of you assholes will have a job with the government any longer and I'll be a lot richer". The Center finally said, "OK, you can have a copy of the tape but you have to come here to the Center and get it." Kruger's response was, "No, you'll mail the SOB to my home and you'll do it today". The Center finally caved in and did what Kruger demanded.

The next day the crew flew back to Dublin. They arrived on a Sunday and the Captain, who was visibly rattled, said that he was going to go to church. Kruger and the Second Officer said that they would accompany him. The rest of the crew, grateful to be still alive, went along. In the gothic church in Ireland a diminutive priest opened the service with, "May the Laird be witcha". Kruger thought that it was entirely appropriate considering the place and the time.

Kruger wrote a letter to ALPA documenting the near miss. He was called one day by an ALPA representative wanting to know if he would fly to Washington, DC and testify to a Congressional committee about air safety. Kruger said that he would do that and soon checked into a Congressman's office. He met the ALPA representative in charge of air safety there and they adjourned to the congressional hearing room.

Kruger was impressed by the room, the people in the room and the microphones arrayed around the room. Actually, "room" was a misnomer. It was an amphitheatre. A number of congressmen were seated in a high semi-circular area looking down on the people who were there to testify. Kruger was seated at a long table in front of the Congressman and invited to tell his story, which he did. He was then questioned by the Congressmen.

One of the questions asked of him was, "Do you think that the air over the USA is more or less safe since President Regan fired the controllers?"

Kruger responded, "How do you quantify safe or unsafe? Can you sell plane tickets based on the probability of getting from "A" to "B"? Our airspace is either safe or unsafe. In my estimation the air over my country is unsafe". The ALPA rep almost swallowed his tongue upon hearing this. It was not in ALPAs best interests to typify the air over the USA as unsafe. Kruger was the first pilot to tell the government this politically incorrect fact.

The Congressman continued, "Do all the pilots think like you do?"

Kruger responded, "I can't speak for all pilots but for the pilots I know and talk to most feel the same way".

The Congressman pressed on. "Do you know any pilots who have retired or quit because they feel that way?"

Kruger smiled and said, "No, and I can tell you why. Most of the pilots flying for the airlines today are ex-military pilots. They are used to flying in a lot more hostile skies for a lot less money than they are making right now. If you pay us enough we will fly anywhere in any conditions but can you sell tickets based on that? The probability of getting to your destination? I don't think so."

The congressional panel dismissed Kruger who walked out of the hearing room into a maelstrom of flashing lights and boom mikes. A large number of news media people wanted to interview him. One reporter asked, "Sir, you said that there were really two or more near misses. How can you say that since the same plane was involved?"

Kruger smiled and said, "Well, you seem to be a reasonable and intelligent man so I'm going to pose a question to you. If a plane headed toward another one and nearly missed that plane and then turned around and did the same thing once again would you consider that one near miss or two?"

The confused reporter stammered, "Well, I guess it would be two."

Kruger continued to smile and said, "There, I knew that you were smart. You just answered your own question."

Another reporter clamored, "You said that you were missed by Continental Airlines. What is the name of your airline?"

Kruger still continued with the smile but it was getting old. He said, "What purpose would it serve to identify my airline? The main news item here is that Continental Airlines almost cut off our tail. We had 400 passengers onboard and were operating legally. That's all you really need to know."

A little female reporter from US News and World Report stuck a mike in his face and said, "What is your name and address?"

Kruger said, "Why would you want to know that information?"

The little reporter said, "If I want to ask you anything else I would like to know how to contact you."

Kruger just smiled again and said, "Here's what I will do for you. Give me your card. If I can think of anything else you should know I will call you on my dime and tell you all about it." The reporter reluctantly and angrily handed over her card.

With all this public airing and with Kruger appearing in a Congressional hearing on behalf of, really, Northwest Airlines, the airline never responded about the incident to anyone or any office. Nada. Nothing. It was as if the whole incident had never happened. Kruger thought that this was par for the whole course. Northwest never acknowledged any efforts that had been made by its employees on its behalf. Kruger chalked it all up to his duty to the traveling public and had nothing at all to do with Northwest Airlines.

*   *   *

The layovers in Hong Kong were always wonderful. The people were friendly and exciting. One of the perks was the Hong Kong Aero club that was at the end of the airport at Kai Tak.

One day a friend of Kruger's was relaxing at the Aero Club with a Cathay Pacific Captain. Both Captains were drinking beer and having a nice time when a female flight controller who was British leaned over the Cathay Pacific pilot and said to the Northwest pilot, "I do so wish that you American pilots would use proper English instead of using slang like "By-By" and "So-Long" in your communications". Without even a glance the Cathay Pacific pilot said as he sipped his beer, "Well, if that disturbs you then the term, "Fuck Off" ought to really piss you off." The controller flounced off to the laughter of the American and the Brit.

Kruger continued to fly to both Europe one month and Asia the next. It was exciting, interesting and made for a wonderful career. On one of his layovers in the Scottish town of Ayer he decided to have breakfast in the hotel, which was an ancient one as far as he was concerned with lifts (elevators) that you operated yourself by closing two gates and operating a switch to go up or down. When he sat down in the little hotel restaurant he was given a menu that listed a wide variety of food. There were "kippers" (fish), "porridge" (oatmeal), scrambled eggs, a rasher of toast, orange juice, potatoes, bacon, steak, and several other items. Kruger was surprised by the variety of the menu. When the little waitress came to take his order he started to list what he wanted but she stopped him abruptly. Apparently the choices weren't ala-carte. The choice was "yes or no". The "menu" was breakfast. You either ordered it or you didn't. Kruger was amused but said "yes" and got more food than he could ever eat at one sitting. He thought that, if you had to work hard on a fishing boat or something like that then, you probably needed all that food. He ate what he could and left the rest, guilty because of his Mother's admonition to "always clean up your plate".

On one of his trips to Asia Kruger was flying as a copilot with an older Captain. The flight had been long and boring. As they approached Tokyo they made contact with a Japanese controller who took over the vectoring of the big 747. The Captain was fighting fatigue and it was apparent. Kruger kept an eye on him. The Japanese controller gave a direction; "Northo-Westo, turn right to a heading of 310 degrees". As Kruger watched the Captain, who was flying, began a slow left turn. Kruger, without comment, took the yoke and maneuvered the plane into a right turn. The Captain shook his head and continued to fly. No words were mentioned. The rest of the flight was uneventful but when the plane was on the ground and they were taxiing in the Captain said, "I want to thank you for correcting me in that turn and I especially want to thank you for not mentioning it at all". Kruger said, "We all get tired and we all make mistakes. We're human. Maybe that's why they put three guys in the cockpit instead of just one. No one's infallible. No one's perfect. I've made my share of mistakes and I expect that I'll make a lot more. What happened back there doesn't deserve any comments. It's over. We succeeded in getting the plane and the passengers to their destination. We should be congratulated, not that we will be. Most of us are simply average pilots; something that I call JAPs, short for just another pilot. No heroes, no supermen, just pilots. Don't let it bother you. It doesn't bother me, OK?" The Captain nodded and that was that.

The next day Kruger's crew flew to Hong Kong. Crews that "flew south" or in Asia west of Japan consisted of one "round eye" or American Flight Attendant and the rest of the F/As were Asiatic. When the crew got to the Meridian Hotel at the Kai Tak airport Kruger and the Chinese Flight Attendants took the elevator to their rooms. Just before the F/As exited the elevator the senior girl turned and faced Kruger. She smiled and said, "You have sexy ears" and fled. As the elevator doors closed the copilot said, "What's with sexy ears?" Kruger confessed that he had no idea what the F/A was talking about. He said, "I don't get off on ears.

It's got to be a cultural thing. Weird!" The copilot said, "Well, are you going to follow up on that come-on?" Kruger laughed and said, "Are you kidding me? Do you know how many pilots have been suckered in on an Oriental honey trap? One of the guys in my initial class did just that. He got a Chinese girl pregnant, married her, put her through law school and then she divorced him and took most of his paycheck and pension. Sexy ears my ass! None of those skinny girls turn me on in the least."

New Years was a monumental event in Hong Kong. Everyone wished each other "Happy New Years". Even pilots wished controllers, "Gung he fat choi". It was a happy time in Hong Kong. On New Year's Eve Kruger went to bed early as he had to fly the next morning. He was awakened, as expected, at midnight with a lot of explosions from high powered fireworks. He listened for a while and fell asleep again. Later he was awakened again by the sound of skirling bagpipes. Kruger prided himself as being of Scottish ancestry and the sound of bagpipes was overwhelming. He couldn't help himself. He arose, dressed and left the hotel following the sound of the pipes. He soon found the source; a bar that was populated with a lot of people and a fully dressed pipe band. He remained outside of the bar just listening and enjoying the music. Soon a pretty young lady appeared at his side and said, "I'm sorry, is the noise bothering you?"

Kruger smiled and said, "Oh yes, the pipes always bother me but not the way that you mean. I love them. I could stand here and listen to them all night". The young lady said, "My name is Anne Simpson and I own this bar. I would like to invite you into it. All drinks are on me. Aren't they beautiful?" (referring to the band).

Kruger said that he would love to do just that but he was a pilot and had to fly back to the USA the next morning. Anne told him that he was welcome to her bar anytime. Kruger went back to his hotel a little sad that he couldn't pursue his new acquaintance. He reflected that he had been without any real female company for a long time and this lady in Hong Kong was very desirable.

It was about this time that Kruger noticed a young Customer Service Agent at O'Hare. She worked for Northwest and was beautiful. Kruger had been divorced for some time and had batted around with a number of women during that time. He had been startled at the number of frantic women who were desperate to find a partner. They all seemed possessive to a fault and some were even scary in their possession. Some were like realtors in that, once they got your name, they seemed to think that they owned you. Dating had gotten very old but Kruger was still lonely. The Customer Service Agent looked enticing. And did I mention that she was beautiful?

Kruger maneuvered around and asked her name as he introduced himself to her. She seemed friendly but not exactly interested in an airline pilot. Ah, well, not everyone was taken by the epitome of mankind, a pilot. Kruger chalked it all up to fate and flew his trip to Japan.

Several months later he was in Chicago about to fly to Japan again when he noticed the same little Agent on one of the jetways leading to his airplane. She was too beautiful to be overlooked. Kruger tried to remember her name but was unsuccessful. He thought, "Jesus, how could I have forgotten this lady? I must be losing it."

He stopped the Agent in the jetway. She was busy with the flight and looked harassed. Kruger introduced himself again. He couldn't tell if she had remembered him from the time before. He thought, "Of course she remembers me. Who wouldn't remember a stalwart pilot? Every woman on earth dreams of a pilot like I am." Well, not really, but Kruger had the usual pilot's ego.

Barbara was busy trying to get the plane ready for its flight to Southeast Asia. She obviously didn't have any time to stop and chat with a pilot. Kruger tried to make small talk but he could see that she was tapping her foot. Finally Kruger said, "I'm flying this trip and I'll be gone for twelve days. When I get back would you like to have supper with me?"

Barbara snapped, "I suppose you're married." Kruger was surprised by the anger in her eyes. He said. "No, as a matter of fact I'm divorced." She snapped back, "Well, you'd be surprised at how many married pilots try to go out with me." Kruger grinned and said, "No, I wouldn't at all. I know all about that. Someone as nice as you are shouldn't be surprised either."

Barbara finally relaxed a little and said, "Sure, I'll have dinner with you. I'll check your inbound schedule and be waiting for you when you get back."

And so it started.

When Kruger got back to Chicago twelve days later he had to go to Minneapolis in order to retrieve some acceptable clothes for his date with Barbara. Then he had to fly back to Chicago. When he got into Chicago it was snowing and it was late. The longsuffering lady in question was waiting for him at the curb in her snappy little red car. Kruger took one look at her and thought, "Now there's a real keeper. Who else would have put up with all of this crap just to eat dinner with some pilot that she really doesn't trust? This lady bears a lot of thought."

At the end of the evening Kruger checked into a local hotel. He had successfully wrangled another date with Barbara and went to bed tired but happy. It had been some time since his divorce and he was really tired of the dating game. He had met a lot of nice ladies but a lot of them seemed frantic to "nail down" a partner, permanent or semi-permanent. Some were downright scary. Barbara wasn't in that category at all. She was beautiful, intelligent and very assured of herself. She was a bright spot in the clamor and cacophony of the dating game.

One statuesque blond Nordic type from Minneapolis took Kruger up on an offer for an evening out but wisely said that she would meet him at the restaurant instead of letting him pick her up thus putting herself at his mercy. Kruger gave her kudos for that decision but as the night wore on she drank a lot more than she could handle and when it came time to call it a night she was too blotted to drive. She was almost too blotted to walk. Kruger took her keys, bundled her into her car and was able to get her to give him directions to her house. When they arrived at her home Kruger saw that the lights were on and rang the doorbell. The lady's sister opened the door and Kruger half carried, half walked his date into the living room. The sister was spitting mad at Kruger, supposing that this was some nefarious plot of his in order to "have his way with her". Kruger tried vainly to tell the sister how the evening had progressed but she wasn't buying any of it. She was spiting mad at Kruger and blamed him for her sister's drunken status. Kruger finally quit trying to explain and asked the sister to call a taxi for him so he could go back to the restaurant and get his car. He waited on the front step in the cold for the taxi. It turned into a long night.

He never called the lady again. Sometime later on a friend who knew both of them said that she had asked, "What ever happened to that pilot I dated?" The friend, warned by Kruger, gave out no information concerning him. It wasn't altogether altruistic. The friend had designs on the lady and was happy to see Kruger disappear from her life.

Some of the ladies that Kruger dated smoked. Kruger had a short list of things that he wouldn't countenance and smoking was one of them. He also couldn't stand stupidity. He always said that, "Ignorance is curable but stupidity goes clear to the bone". You could have said that Kruger was an elitist and he would have half-heartedly argued with you but in the final analysis he wouldn't give or compromise on what he liked in a companion.

This "Barbara lady" seemed to typify most things that Kruger valued. He had long ago analyzed just what attracted him to the opposite sex and readily admitted that the first attribute was how the lady looked. After all, beauty was the only attribute that anyone could usually initially assign to anyone. Only when two people began to interact could you find out what was in the other person's head. In the final analysis the cement of any relationship, as far as Kruger was concerned, was how the lady thought, her attitudes, mores, morals and upbringing. Barbara seemed to have everything that Kruger valued and the more they dated the more Kruger thought that this was the lady for him.

* * *

Kruger loved flying to Southeast Asia. It was exciting, the people were wonderful and the layovers were long enough to allow travel and interaction with the folks of those countries. It was a very nice time to be employed by Northwest Airlines. Probably the biggest perk was that he was not under the constant scrutiny of the company. Asia was a long way away from Minnesota and the insular mindset of that sorry place.

Hong Kong was a favorite layover spot for Kruger. He loved the ethnic Chinese that populated the island. The whole place was a thriving morass of intelligent humanity that was fun to interact with. There were two streets in Kowloon that operated around the clock. One street featured hundreds of vendors that sold items for males and the other sold items for females. One night Kruger and another pilot decided to serf the street that featured male items. Kruger had decided that he needed a belt and he soon found a vendor that had hundreds of belts all rolled up with rubber bands on them. Kruger picked up one belt in order to examine it. The old Chinese man who owned the kiosk ran over and slapped Kruger's hand. Apparently he was not supposed to handle the merchandise. Kruger was insulted. In his world no one slapped anyone's hand for examining merchandise.

Kruger searched his memory banks and found a phrase that he had read from a novel written by James Clavel. The novel was "Taipan" and

Clavel had given the interpretation of all of the phrases that the people in his novel had uttered except one. It was "Dew Neh Mo Loh. Kruger had given the phrase to one of the Northwest Chinese interpreters and had come up with the following assessment.

"The interpretation will not be accurate since the inflection can't be accurate. You must understand that the interpretation is much more severe to the Chinese than to the Americans. The real interpretation means "Fuck you and your old wife". It is much more important and severe to the Chinese than to the Americans". Kruger had thanked the interpreter and moved on.

When Kruger had his hand slapped he faced the old man and said, "Dew Neh Mo Loh." The old man's eyes snapped open. He blew his cheeks out and stared at Kruger, who moved on. As Kruger and the other pilot walked along the street the old man stared at them. He actually dragged up a box to stand on in order to stare at Kruger. The other pilot said, "Damn, Kruger, I don't know what the hell you said to that guy but you sure got his attention. You're probably going to need to barricade your door this evening." Kruger just smiled and didn't respond.

A lot of the pilots in Japan had purchased mopeds to drive around. It gave them freedom, something an American cherishes above all. Kruger did a little research and found that a Japanese driver's license was not required for a moped. He looked around and found an acceptable machine in a local Japanese "used car lot". The moped didn't look like the top of the line machine but the price was acceptable. As he looked at the little moped the Japanese owner tried to sweeten the deal a little by energetically saying, "Ohhh, washee-washee. Changee oilee." That cemented it. Kruger was so enthralled by the Pidgin English that he couldn't resist the sales pitch. He was soon the proud owner of a moped.

Driving a moped around the tiny twisting roads that bordered the little rice paddies that populated Narita was challenging. The Japanese drove on the left side of the road so every turn onto a new road was an adventure. Couple that with the Japanese sense of humor that mandated they blow the horn when passing the moped as closely as possible and you can see the challenge that attended riding the little mopeds.

Ownership of a moped that primarily sat unattended most of the time created a new challenge. Initially the few mopeds that were owned by the pilot group weren't a problem but as more and more pilots and flight attendants bought them it became a problem. Japan has little unoccupied space and the growing moped population created big parking problems. The hotel, of course, was as uncooperative as always where flight crews were concerned. Initially a message was posted for the flight crews that said the mopeds were not to be parked temporarily in front of the hotel in the parking places provided for guests. Those spaces were for the use of "guests of the hotel". The implication was, of course, that flight crews were not guests but only tolerated second class citizens.

The problem was finally solved by a few of the pilots striking a deal with a service station located near the hotel. The deal was that every moped owner would only buy gas from that particular station and in return the station would allow parking behind the building in a vacant muddy lot.

Things were calm for awhile until it was pointed out to the hotel manager that the mopeds presented a good opportunity to make some extra money off of the backs of the crew members. The manager bought some prime real estate a half-mile from the hotel, fenced the property at a great cost, included a lockable gate and posted a message to the flight crews that said they could park the mopeds in the fenced property at an exorbitant rate per month. Not only that, but the gate would only be opened at certain times of the day and never at night. For flight crews that had a hard time sleeping it was a double insult. For the hotel manager it was a great loss of face as not one moped owner elected to rent the space and hike a longer distance to store their bikes. The attempt of the manager to entice the crews to the new "parking lot" was not lost on the populace that lived around the hotel and they delighted in the loss of face of the manager since he was not popular at all. Kruger had been accosted on the street by strangers who wanted him to know that the "manager not good".

Ownership of a moped gave one freedom to travel and see the Japanese countryside, which was beautiful. Kruger and his friend, Sam Martin, put miles on their bikes traveling around to visit parks, shrines, villages and tiny but excellent restaurants. Rubbing shoulders with the local populace was an excellent learning experience.

One day Kruger was riding around the Narita airport when he was stopped by one of the security people. The airport was a war zone. Long ago the farmers who used to own the property that was now Narita were promised by the Emperor that they would never be displaced. Then, inevitably, they were displaced as the new airport needed the space. The farmers were understandably upset. They banded together and protested as Japanese do, by applying for a permit to "demonstrate". They marched and demonstrated to no avail and finally bunkered in for the long haul. They flew large kites that they hoped would interfere with the airplanes that were landing and taking off. They flew large flags protesting the airport and did anything else they could think of that would irritate the authorities who had stolen their land.

The Japanese government retaliated by forming a pretty large army in order to "protect" the airport. The soldiers were dressed in combat gear and were called "R2D2" people after the Stephen Spielberg movie characters in Star Wars. They looked like robots in their black gear and long staves. They were all supposed to be experts in the several martial arts.

The soldier who stopped Kruger held up his hand. Kruger halted his moped and said, "Hai?" (Yes?).

The soldier slowly walked over to him and held out his hand. He said, "Driver's ricense".

Kruger knew that a driver's license was not required by the Japanese government in order to drive a moped. He asked, "Driver's license?"

"Hai", said R2D2.

Kruger rummaged in his wallet and produced his shore pass. He handed it to R2D2 saying, "Shore pass, des nei." (Here is a shore pass).

R2D2 looked confused. He questioned, "Shore pass?"

"Hai". Kruger was adamant and unmoveable.

R2D2 examined the shore pass with great scrutiny. Kruger waited patiently. Finally the soldier handed the pass to Kruger and came to attention. He saluted formally. Kruger accepted the pass with both hands, a custom that is very polite in Japan and bowed slightly. "Domo arrigato," (thank you very much) he said. R2D2 bowed in return and Kruger went on his way. He wondered what that had all been about. The inscrutable Japanese would give no clue.

*　　*　　*

Kruger finally, after much thought, decided to ask Barbara to marry him. He did just that on one of their dates. Barbara, typically, said that she would think about it and would let him know soon. Barbara was prone to deep thought before making any decisions while Kruger was a "hip shooter"; prone to action before much thought. In his defense it might have been a result of his being a pilot. Normally pilots don't have much time to make an important decision that usually makes the difference between living or dying. That's not to excuse how he operated but Barbara operated on a different plane. It worked for her and Kruger appreciated that. Perhaps the two differing attitudes would be synergistic and would be a roaring success. Who knew? Kruger would give it a chance if given a chance.

Kruger had an old friend at Northwest. His name was Sam Martin. Sam was a real "mountain man" like the old mountain men, like Jeremiah Johnson. Sam climbed mountains, flew hot air balloons and did a lot of other tough things in the name of fun. Sam was a senior pilot and finally got caught in the old honey trap in the guise of a Northwest Flight Attendant with a big chest and no morals or brains whatsoever. She was well known among most of the pilots who steered clear of her but occasionally she would find some lonely soul and would work her magic on him. Sam was, for some reason, tired of his wife and was a prime target for Nancy deLaPena. Many of his friends tried, unsuccessfully, to dissuade him of his new paramour but he would not listen to any of them.

Early on Kruger had been stopped before he went out on a trip by an old Navy friend who looked like he had been drawn though a key hole. Andy related how he had gone with Nancy for a couple of years, how he had figured that he would marry her and live happily ever after, how she was a thrill seeker and tried to seek out friends who peddled drugs and were the dregs of society, how she had finally figured out that he wasn't exiting enough and how she had emasculated him by telling him that he was no good in bed and that she had found several guys who were better, etc. Andy was a mess and in no shape to fly. Kruger had to go on his trip but told Andy that when he came back in four days they could get on Kruger's boat, sail to the Keys and have a good time while Andy got the woman out of his system and relaxed. Andy said that he would consider the offer but never followed up on it. Kruger saw him infrequently after that and he never seemed to be any better.

Sam married Nancy and they set up house on Sam's huge sail boat in Ft. Lauderdale. Everything was fine until Sam decided to spend the winter in the Caribbean. He told Nancy about the plan and she promptly said that she wouldn't go. When asked why she said that she had a lover that sold used cars and that she didn't wish to leave him. Sam experienced enlightenment over this announcement and booted Nancy off of the boat. The next time he flew a trip he went to the main base for Northwest and asked if his figures on what he would get if he retired that day were correct. When he was told that they were he put in his papers for retirement. Nancy had said that she was going to get a lawyer and sue Sam for divorce and get a lot of money from him. When Sam returned home he called Nancy and talked to her. He said that he wished to keep his Northwest pension intact. On the other hand he said that he realized that Nancy was young and wanted a lot of cash immediately. He offered to give her 50% of all of his earnings before taxes if she would sign a paper that gave him sole access to his pension. Sam made, at the time, around $200,000 a year. Nancy figured that $100,000 a year was pretty good so she signed the contract in the presence of an attorney. As soon as the ink was dry Sam retired from Northwest, his paycheck dried up, his retirement pension was intact and Nancy was marooned without a penny. Many glasses were lifted by the pilot group when they heard how Sam had one-upped a real gold-digging, rotten Flight Attendant.

There had been a long battle among the pilots of ALPA and the government about just when a pilot had to retire. The government had determined, a long time before Kruger had opted to become an airline pilot that a pilot had to retire at age 60. A large number of pilots had tried to lobby in an attempt to continuously work past that age. Finally the government allowed that a pilot could fly past age 60 only as a Flight Engineer, in other words, he could fly by attending to the Flight Engineers panel but could not occupy a seat as a pilot. A number of Captains who were approaching the age of 60 opted to do just that but it necessitated checking out as a Flight Engineer, the same checkout that a Second Officer had to undergo. A lot of pilots were against this move as they felt that the old Captains had had their "time in the sun" and needed to move on so junior pilots could move up to Captain status.

A number of Captains failed the checkout as they had rested on their laurels for a long time and really didn't know the aircraft systems. Some of the rest made the checkout but were not well received by the rank and file pilots. One of the most despised of the latter group was a diminutive pilot with a large head of hair named Warren Avinson. He had been a tyrant as a Captain but when he checked out as a Flight Engineer he assumed the stance of a lickspittle, asking for continual guidance and direction, more to ingratiate himself with the crews than to actually do his job. He was roundly looked down upon and most pilots would have nothing to do with him.

One day Kruger was scheduled to fly with an augmented crew from Narita to Los Angeles. As he stood in the lobby of the hotel among about 30 other pilots Avinson appeared and loudly said, "I'm scheduled to fly to Los Angeles this evening. I assume that you are the Flight Engineer on the crew." He had his hand out as he spoke. Kruger thought about how Avinson had treated his crews when he was a Captain and ignored the outstretched hand. He said, "No, your assumption is erroneous, YOU are the Flight Engineer. I am the Second Officer. His repartee was met with laughter from among the rest of the pilots in the lobby.

When the crew reported to the aircraft for the flight Avinson continued to ask for guidance and direction. Kruger tried to distance himself from the obnoxious pilot but was generally unsuccessful. Avinson kept getting underfoot regardless of the flags Kruger thought that he was flying. It seemed that Avinson couldn't take any hints.

Finally, just when the other pilots reported to the cockpit Avinson tugged at Kruger's arm and asked, "When you make up the crew bunk do you use one sheet or two?" Kruger exploded, much to the humor of the other crewmembers. "Jesus Christ! How long have you been making a bed? Have you ever made a bed? You are an old man. Has someone been wiping your ass all these years? Use one sheet or two or fifteen or sleep on the fucking floor if you can't figure it all out. Either way, I don't give a shit. Now stop sucking up and go to work or retire." That finally ended all future conversations with Avinson.

A friend of Kruger's, Jim Watland, had flown with Avinson when he was a Captain. Avinson was fond of complaining, "As airline pilots we make too much money". Watland was tired of hearing all of his pontificating so he finally said, "Well, Warren, if you make too much money how much have you handed back to Northwest Airlines or contributed to charity?" Captain Avinson only said, "Don't be ridiculous."

Kruger had an opportunity to fly with another Flight Engineer retread. This was a pilot who had originally been a Flight Engineer before Kruger had hired onboard with Northwest. He was a nice guy and kept a low profile as he knew that a lot of the pilots didn't like him. Kruger had flown with him when he was a Captain on the 727 and Kruger was only a copilot. He was decent and seemed to be a good pilot. Kruger had no quarrel with him. On that particular day Kruger was flying the 727. He had not paid particular attention to the trim of the plane as he flew it. Suddenly the Captain gave the rudder trim control a few turns to the right without any comment. It trimmed the plane up a lot and made it easier to fly. Nothing was said. Kruger tucked that little bit of information in his brain. This Captain was one of the good guys. He harbored none of the bad feelings of his group against the pilots who had tried to get rid of that group.

On the particular plane that they were on the throttles were controlled by a computer but the computer never took into consideration density altitude and kept a particular power setting regardless of the altitude. The Second Officer had to access a flight computer in order to set the power correctly so the plane could continue to climb and not stall on the way to the final altitude.

On this particular day Kruger was in the jump seat while the Flight Engineer was on duty. Kruger noticed that the power continued to degrade as they climbed. The pilots didn't notice it nor did the Flight Engineer. Finally Kruger pulled the computer, which was nothing more than a circular slide rule, out of its holder and held it up for the Engineer to see. "Has anyone ever shown you how to work this thing" he asked? The Engineer hurriedly shook his head "no". He obviously expected for someone to rag on him for his lack of knowledge. Most of the old Engineers were used to abuse from the pilot group. Kruger patiently explained the concept behind the computer and showed the Engineer that the power had to be added as they climbed. The Engineer added power and the plane took on new life as it took more interest in the climb. That took care of the problem and the Engineer thanked Kruger for the info. The pilots never knew that there was a problem and Kruger never enlightened them.

Kruger loved eating sushi. The Sushi restaurants in Japan were mostly top notch. One evening Kruger frequented a not so top notch restaurant and ordered sushi. It was a bad mistake. On his way home he had a bad headache. He couldn't seem to get rid of it. That was unusual as he never got headaches. When he arrived at Chicago his lady friend, Barbara, picked him up and they went to her home in Elgin. Kruger complained about being very tired and went to bed early. The next morning Barbara left for work and Kruger decided to mow her lawn. He accomplished that task but was so tired after the task that he took a nap. He was still "wiped out" that evening so he decided to go to his home in Florida the next morning to rest up.

When he arrived in Naples he was still fatigued and decided to go to bed early once again. He couldn't figure out just why he was so tired. The next morning he rose at 0300 in order to pee. When he urinated he was startled to see that his urine was the color of old mahogany. He looked in a mirror and was startled once again when he saw that the whites of his eyes were bright yellow. He thought, "Jesus, I don't know what's wrong but I sure hope that I can survive until tomorrow morning when I can see a doctor".

The next morning, early, found him in the office of his doctor and friend, Tom Field. Tom sent him to the local hospital for a series of tests that diagnosed him with Type A hepatitis. That type of hepatitis was spread by dirty hands and contaminated shellfish.

Tom told Kruger that he ought to enter the hospital. When Kruger asked what treatment was used for hepatitis he found that there was none. He told his doctor that if there was no treatment for the malady that he would just as soon go home and recuperate. Tom said, "I get the impression that you think that this isn't serious. You can die from this. If I send you home you have to promise that you will go to bed and rest. Pretty soon you won't want to eat but you have to do just that if you want to get well. Kruger promised that he would do just that and left.

Later on the Doctor said that when Kruger walked into his office and he saw how yellow Kruger was he really didn't want to touch him as he knew where Kruger flew and how he mingled with the locals. Dr. Field really didn't wish to contract some weird Asiatic disease.

Kruger went home and surrounded himself with a pile of books. He rested, contacted Barbara and anyone he remembered that he had contacted and told them that they needed to get a series of shots of gamma globulin as a preventative against type A hepatitis. He soon became bored and figured that, since his yard needed mowing, he could do that with no problem since he owned a riding lawn mower. After all, he only had to sit down and drive the mower. What could be easier?

He started the mower (it had an electrical starting system), jumped on and mowed one strip of his lawn. Then he shut the mower down and staggered into his house where he collapsed on his couch. God! He was exhausted! How long would it take to get over this? As it was it took the better part of a month before he really felt strong again and could go back to flying.

Kruger was accustomed to carrying enough books with him on his trips to tide him over on his long layovers. He usually bid twelve day trips. It seemed to be the most efficient way to fly as one twelve day trip was sufficient to fill up a schedule for the month. The rest of the month was his to do with as he pleased. It made for a perfect commute and, as Kruger lived in Florida, it was easy to plan.

Flying over the Pacific was not conducive to good sleeping habits. Kruger's day usually consisted of a twelve hour flight coupled with a long check-in period, a long preflight with a perusal of all of the weather that would be encountered enroute plus that of any alternate airfields that might have to be used, a long check-in period with whatever countries customs and immigration that would have to be navigated and then a long bus ride to the layover hotel. Then he had to check into the hotel and make sure that his crew was all taken care of. It made for a 24 hour day. Couple that with a destination that was on the opposite side of the world and the fact that the sun's travel was apparently fifteen degrees every hour and that made his jet-lag considerable. It wasn't something you could get used to. You simply had to accept it and make allowances for it. Kruger was used to waking up at 0300 Tokyo time, unable to sleep any more. Nothing was open in Japan at that time, even in the largest cities. Narita was a small, agricultural town. It was closed tighter than a Marine's ass in a conference consisting of homosexuals. Kruger's way of coping with that little problem was to immerse himself in a tub of very hot water and read one of the numerous books he had carried along for just this purpose. He lived in abject fear of running out of reading material on his layovers. Later on he would succumb to his jet-lag and take a nap around 1400, after lunch. He had tried, early on, to combat this syndrome but had been spectacularly unsuccessful.

An adjunct to the sleeplessness was that when he awoke he was usually hungry. Nothing in Japan was open at that time in the morning. The Japanese considered the early morning hours to be barbaric and perhaps they were correct. At any rate their customs didn't assuage Kruger's hunger one iota. He adopted the habit of carrying MREs (Meals, Ready to Eat, as packaged by the US military) in his luggage in order to have something to eat at those times in the early morning when it was impossible to find a restaurant open. It worked if you didn't mind MREs. Kruger had always excelled in his survival schools in the Navy. He could eat anything and enjoy it. Snakes were no problem. Kruger had eaten them with relish. He had enjoyed Possum, Raccoon, Bear, Deer and several other native animals that were usually not considered gentle fare. MREs were haute cuisine as far as he was concerned.

One day Kruger lined up for inspection at Japanese customs in Narita. The tiny official who was inspecting his luggage appeared to be about twelve years of age. He had coke-bottle glasses and, in spite of his thick lenses, he had to hold items up very close to his eyes in order to see what they were. He grabbed one of Kruger's MREs and asked, "What this?"

Kruger answered, "MREs".

That didn't really do it as far as the little Japanese Official was concerned. He continued to peruse the packet with his eye about one inch away from the cover. Suddenly he came alive. He excitedly screamed, "Beefu, beefu, beefu," holding the offending packet out as if it were contaminated. Obviously "beefu", or beef, was a proscribed item as far as Agriculture was concerned. The diminutive inspector excitedly gestured to his right, "Prease go to quarantine," he excitedly shouted.

Kruger was tired after his long flight. Other crew members in the line were looking at him as if he had the plague. He said, "OK, OK, keep your shirt on. I'll go to quarantine." He left the long line and headed to the office where several other, more mature officials were sitting. When he arrived at the quarantine office one of the officials asked, "What is probrem." Kruger explained about the MREs and the official said, "Ah, so, no probrem. Prease go back to inspection."

Kruger said, "Can you give me a pass for the MREs so the guy in inspection won't have a heart attack when I show up again?" The official thought that was funny and gave Kruger a piece of paper with Japanese Kanji written on it.

Kruger got back in the long line and when he arrived at the same customs official he was asked once more, "Anything to declare?" he said, "Yeah, I'm the asshole with the beefu, remember?" The unflappable Japanese took the paper and motioned for Kruger to leave the line. As he did so a United Flight Attendant behind him said, "You don't really eat that stuff do you?"

Kruger thought about that. He thought about how tired he was and how this civilian puke who didn't know anything about the military presumed to look down on the fare that the American fighting man was furnished with and said, "Yeah, lady, I eat that and a lot of other things. I eat snakes and babies too. I'd even eat you only you're too ugly. Any other questions you want to ask me before I turn in?" The Flight Attendant just stood there with an open mouth as Kruger walked to the crew bus that was waiting for him.

By the time Kruger got to the hotel and got a room he was beat. He thought about that a little. He was a lot older than he had been when he first hired on with Northwest. He had been up for over 24 hours. He was bone tired but not sleepy. He thought, "I guess that's what they mean by the term 'jet lag'." The usual thing for a pilot to do after he had thrown his bags into a corner of his room was to swiftly change clothes, brush his teeth and proceed to one of the nearest Japanese bar-restaurant combinations that were near the hotel. After a snack (the Japanese considered it a full meal) and two bottles of Sapporo beer the pilot was finally ready to collapse in his bed only to wake up at 0300 with nothing to do and nowhere to do it. It was at times like this that Kruger valued his books, MREs and the deep bathtubs in the rooms that could be filled with hot water. Usually the pilot could go back to sleep around 0700 and wake up once again at 0900 or 1000. A shower, shave and another tooth cleaning and he would repair to the in-house restaurant where he could chat with other pilots who were in the same situation that he was in. After breakfast the pilot would normally collapse in the lobby of the hotel where a few old copies of various newspapers from all over the globe were thrown, complements of the flight crews that had flown from those far off places. The Northwest pilots had christened those pilots as "lobby lizards". Flight attendants did not frequent the lobby as the lobby lizard group would normally revert to their military antecedents and the language that was bandied about was not for delicate ears.

One day Kruger was in the hotel lobby with a few other junior pilots. They were standing in a passageway and talking about their military exploits. A Northwest Flight Attendant pushed past them and, as she did, she sarcastically said, "Do you guys realize that this lobby is for everyone? So do you have to jam it up?" Kruger immediately said, "No, but you see lady, we are all Tailhook". The rest of the pilots hooted in accord with the thought. The Navy "Tailhook" debacle had just happened with the females in the Navy blowing the whistle on the attitudes of the pilots. There was no mystery involved. The male pilots had always entertained certain attitudes toward females in general and female pilots in particular and the current political attitudes couldn't change that. The Tailhook pilots had formed several lines that the female pilots had to traverse. I leave it to your imagination what occurred during the transits of those lines. For the male pilots it was all in good pilot fun but some of the female pilots didn't really see things in the same light. Complaints were filed and heads rolled as the result of several courts martial. The Tailhook debacle did nothing for comraderie between female and male pilots.

Japanese men loved pornography. Perhaps it was because the various laws mandated no pornography in the country or perhaps it was because of the formality the Japanese people lived with but regardless of the reason, it existed. Laws or not, pornography abounded in the Japanese society. Who said that you can legislate against thoughts or ideas?

One of the local restaurant owners loved to show pornographic movies to the pilots who ate and drank at his establishment. No one knew exactly why he did so. Maybe it was in order to gin up more customers or maybe he was just "weird". No one knew. The porn flics were free and so the pilots watched the free movies and cheered the main characters as they drank their Sapporo beer. About every half hour the patron would come into the room and drink a little sake as he watched his own movies. He would always leave after saying, "Americans have big cocks. I only have a little cock." No one knew what to make of the whole thing so they simply watched the movies and drank their Sapporo.

It was apparent that the Japanese people had the same concept regarding Americans that most American males had concerning black males. That idea was that the other male animal had a much larger phallus than did the indigenous animals. One evening the pilot group that was in one of the small restaurants that abounded around Narita was having a lot of fun. They decided that the "mama-san" who ran the restaurant was a nice, friendly lady and so they bought her several drinks in an effort to bring her into the friendly group. The lady unfortunately got the wrong idea about the friendly gestures because, as the group left to go back to the hotel and try to sleep, the lady approached one of the more straight-laced pilots, grabbed his crotch and giggled, "American big!" The unfortunate pilot was embarrassed beyond belief but received no help from his comrades who were cheering the giggling mama-san on to bigger and better things. Eventually the mamma-san had to be comforted with all of the yen that the pilots showered on her for a delightful evening.

One evening Kruger was drinking in one of the local establishments. The evening was wearing on and most of the patrons had left. Kruger and another pilot named Jim Jones were left and were having a deep conversation with the patron. Eventually the conversation got around to the subject of karate. The owner said that he practiced karate. Kruger, who had studied the art while he had been in the Navy asked what style the owner had studied. The owner thought about his English and finally said, "My style Kyokushinkai".

Kruger sat his beer down and said, "Ah, so, Mas Oyama." Mas Oyama was the originator of the style of karate called Kyokushinkai. He used to kill fighting bulls with his open-handed style of karate.

The Japanese blinked and said, "So des, you karate-ka?"

Kruger said, "Hai, watashi karate-ka. (Yes, I practice karate). Shotokan, Taikwondo, Shorin-Ryu."

The shop owner talked at length and finally got the idea across that the owner of a neighboring shop was a master in Kyokyshinkai and had studied under Mas Oyama. Did Kruger wish to meet him?

Kruger most certainly did. How often do you get to meet a celebrity that you've read about? Kruger, the Japanese and Jim took their beer and sake over to the next restaurant where Kruger was introduced to the owner of that establishment. He was an impressive man and immediately tried to teach Kruger how to "break" with his fingers.

"Breaking" techniques are called "Tomishiwara" by the Japanese and are simply methods of establishing confidence in the people who practice karate. The idea is that if you can "break" or shatter a board, a cement block or a brick with your bare hands then you won't quail about striking an opponent's head with your hands, the goal being to "break" the opponent's head or any other bone in his body.

The Kyokushinkai master tried to show Kruger how to break with his fingers by thrusting them into a bucket of rice in order to toughen them up. It was a fun evening. Everyone had consumed copious amount of sake. Beer had long ago been abandoned. Things got noisy. Customers left. No one seemed to care. The karate master finally figured that Kruger could break a board with his fingers held straight and by plunging his fingers into the board. Everyone celebrated the revelation by drinking a glass of sake straight with the toast of "Kampai!"

The Karate master produced a one-inch board and demanded that Kruger break it with his stiffened fingers. Kruger, cheered on by several onlookers, cleared his mind as the discipline dictated and shouted, "Hai!" as he shattered the board to the cheers of the onlookers. The Karate master pounded him on the back congratulating him. Everyone was happy. The happy group decided to go back to Aki's restaurant to celebrate.

Once more in Aki's restaurant the happy group decided to drink sake in order to celebrate. There is only one way to celebrate with sake. You hold up your tiny cup of warm sake, which is about 30% alcohol or 60 proof by round-eye standards, shout "Kampai!" and drink your sake quickly. After a few rounds of "Kampai" Kruger wiped out. Instead of recovering from throwing his head back after drinking his sake he simply kept on going; falling over backwards and taking out the coke machine as he fell. Everyone thought that was hilarious except Aki's wife who appeared on the scene and said that the party was over. She sent the karate master home and told Aki to take the drunken pilots back to the Narita hotel. This was accomplished slowly and carefully but successfully. The next morning none of the participants were anxious to arise with the sun. When they did manage to get out of bed they were all careful to wear their darkest sunglasses, even the karate master.

On a trip from Narita to Taipei as Kruger and the Captain entered crew schedules in order to make out the flight plane they were met with a towering FAA check pilot who said that he was going to give the crew a check ride to Taipei and return. Something about the man triggered a memory within Kruger's mind but he couldn't put a handle on it. The FAA checker got in the way a lot and Kruger finally told him that he had to stand to one side so he could make out the paperwork properly. The FAA man didn't argue but did as Kruger asked.

As they walked to the plane Kruger's memory banks were working overtime. There was something about this guy that he needed to remember. What the hell was it? All of a sudden he remembered. He turned abruptly and said to the FAA man who was walking behind him, "Now I remember you. You came through VP30 in 1968. I was your instructor and I gave you a down on one of your flights." VP30 was a squadron that Kruger served in as a flight instructor for anti-submarine warfare pilots. The FAA guy had been given not only a down, meaning a flunking grade, by Kruger but had a crew change since Kruger refused to fly with him further and he had his ass chewed by the squadron's Operations Officer.

The FAA check pilot laughed and said, "Yeah, I was trying to remember where I had seen you last too."

As soon as he could the Captain asked Kruger what that was all about and Kruger filled him in on the details. When the Captain heard about the episode he gritted, "Goddamn, you had to remind him of that before the flight check. This is his chance to get even." Kruger assured the Captain that a Navy Officer wouldn't do that, or at least most of them wouldn't. That didn't seem to relax the Captain at all. The flight went well and Kruger and the FAA pilot shared a lot of memories about naval service.

Kruger told the check pilot about his near miss over Boston. The FAA pilot said, "Kruger, if you are ever in trouble with the FAA don't talk to them. If they call you on the phone, hang the phone up. Don't say anything to them at all. Let an ALPA attorney talk for you. Most pilots who get into trouble with the FAA do so because they can't shut up. They pretty much convict themselves by talking too much. FAA attorneys are really bad. They are underpaid and do a bad job. If you just shut up they will probably lose their case." Kruger thought that this was good advice and thanked the pilot who said that he lived in Hawaii and that Kruger ought to look him up on one of his layovers in that city. Kruger appreciated the offer but figured that the last thing he wanted to do on a layover was to have a drink with an FAA guy.

Kruger was in the Narita airport one day to fly one of the legs on his trip. He looked out on the tarmac where the planes were parked and saw a Korean Airline 747 sitting at a jetway with 18 flat tires. There were numerous pilots and ground service people standing around and looking at the sad airplane. Kruger had never seen all of the tires on a 747 flat before. It was a startling sight.

On large planes like the 747 if the crew had to use the brakes a lot, as in an aborted takeoff, a huge amount of heat was generated in the wheel assemblies from the hard braking. A 747 that had a takeoff weight of around 800,000 pounds would have to sit on the ground after an abort for as much as 40 minutes in order to allow the heat to dissipate before another takeoff attempt. The heat would normally build up until fuse plugs in the wheels melted and allowed the air in the tires to escape before the tires exploded due to the heat. Exploding tires on a 747 had as much force as a stick of dynamite or more. Then too, tires that had deflated due to fuse plugs made landing a 747 a very hard thing to do.

The Korean crew had obviously braked very hard on landing and the fuse plugs on the plane had finally failed, melted due to the heat buildup and allowed all of the tires to flatten.

On one of the last flights Kruger flew to Europe he flew with an old nemesis, Ray Severson. When Kruger had last flown with him he had been on the 727. For some reason Ray had mellowed a lot after checking out on the 747. Kruger had been ready for battle when he found out that Captain Severson was on his flight but that soon dissipated once he found that Ray was quite amiable. This proved to be Captain Severson's last flight with Northwest as he was going to be 60 years old the day after his flight ended. Kruger and the copilot decided to make Ray's last flight a memorable one.

The flight basically flew between Scotland and Boston. On each layover the two junior pilots treated the Captain with dinner and a lot of drinks. On one leg from Prestwick to Boston Ray said, "It's a damned good thing I'm retiring after this leg. I don't think I could take many more like this." When they got to Boston the crew picked up a large cake they had ordered earlier that said, "Happy flight into retirement, Captain Severson". The Captain was touched. Kruger had carried a camera along on this trip and took some nice pictures of Ray standing near the nose wheel of his 747. He blew them up and sent them along to Ray later.

Kruger now flew mostly to Southeast Asia. Northwest had decided to fly the DC10s to Europe instead of 747s. That decision didn't make Kruger unhappy. He liked flying to Europe every once in awhile but his heart was in flying to Asia. Flying to Asia meant flying out of O'Hare and that meant that he could be with Barbara more so it was a win-win situation. On one trip that Kruger was on just before the plane pushed back Barbara, who was working the flight, came to the cockpit and put a paper sack on Kruger's panel saying, "I packed a little something for you for your trip." She left before he could thank her and as soon as the door was shut the plane pushed back. Kruger was busy and didn't have any time to even look into the sack until they were well into the flight.

They were well into the great circle route to Japan and at altitude at flight level 320 when he finally thought to open the sack. It didn't contain sandwiches or things like he thought were in it. He began to pull out items like a pocket watch, a coffee cup, some child's blocks and items like that. He was confused. He tried to make sense of the stuff and the off-duty Second Officer tried to help.

The blocks could only be joined in an order that said, "YES". The watch said, "It's time to say YES". Everything else in the sack said "YES". The off-duty pilot said, "I'm getting embarrassed watching this. I'm going to hit the sack". It slowly dawned on Kruger, the local idiot, that Barbara had given him her answer to his offer of marriage.

OOOF! How do you celebrate at 32000 feet over North Canada? Kruger had to keep his exuberance inside until he got to Narita and could call Barbara. Happiness was twice as many Sapporos as he normally drank. They were married some months later.

CHAPTER XIV

Kruger flew as a copilot on the 747 for years. He enjoyed his association with all of the various peoples in all of the countries that he stayed in. He thought that the people in Thailand, Malaysia, Hong Kong, Taiwan, Japan and the Philippine Islands were excellent. The people and the country of Korea were found to be lacking. Kruger thought they were cold and humorless. Nevertheless, the flying was excellent and the layovers were simply superior. Kruger had never been happier. He felt that he could do this job forever and be happy but he had to face reality. His job was rapidly coming to a close. The government had mandated, a long time ago, that all airline pilots had to retire at age 60. Kruger didn't have that many more years to go before that magic age rolled around. He had to face reality and maximize his retirement.

He opted to fly as a 727 Captain. That would put him into the training pipeline as a Captain. He was picked up immediately because of his seniority and had to check into a motel in Bloomington, Minnesota in order to have a place to stay while he was going through the checkout period. Barbara stayed in Florida as Kruger wouldn't have much time to do anything except to study.

Kruger jumped through all of the hoops that one had to jump through in order to become a Captain. In order to complete the training for a Captain everyone had to go through a simulator syllabus. The brief that had to do with the simulator had to do with the practicality of the machine. Kruger's instructor told him to treat the simulator like the machine it was. He said, "The "sim" doesn't fly like a plane so you will have to learn to fly it from scratch. It isn't fair and it isn't right but the company wants to use it in order to save money and the FAA goes along with it. Just learn it and after your check ride in it you can then forget all about it." Kruger thought back to the Aero Commander that he had to fly before he got off of probation. The 727 simulator was like that insult. It was simply another hoop that he had to jump through in order to become a Captain.

Staying in a hotel while he checked out was a boring existence. Kruger made friends with several pigeons by stringing a lot of bird seed on his window sill. The grateful little birds found the seed almost immediately and, via the jungle telegraph, soon told all of the pigeons in the local area about the nice man who was happy to feed them. He soon had a small flock of strutting pigeons on his window sill. He didn't imagine that the hotel owners appreciated his mini-zoo but they were comforting to watch and talk to.

Northwest had two 727 simulators. One was in Minneapolis and the other was an older type on loan to the local college in Grand Forks, North Dakota. The one in Grand Forks was the most miserable one to fly and, of course, Kruger drew that one for most of his training periods. He passed his Captain check ride with no problems and in normal time. A diminutive and self-important pilot, Will Tannahill, who had spent most of his time with Northwest in the training department gave Kruger the checkout and, when it was finished he leaned over the back of Kruger's seat, offered his hand and said, "May I be the first to congratulate you, Captain Kruger?" Kruger took the proffered hand and said, "Please, if we have to use titles simply refer to me as 'Commander'." Kruger had no use for self-important people. An old friend of his had once infuriated a Captain who thought that he was extremely knowledgeable and important by telling him, "The only difference between you and me is a few simulator rides and a check ride".

Kruger still had to take another check ride with the FAA, the ultimate cop. Most pilots hated to take a check ride with the FAA but Kruger wasn't fazed at all by the check. As it turned out the check pilot was based at O'Hare so Kruger flew there with his Northwest instructor on board. The Northwest instructor was as nervous as a cat and tried to brief Kruger as much as possible about the things that the FAA pilot thought were important. Kruger listened but was non-committal. His instructor said, "This FAA guy always likes to try to teach you something about the plane. He usually will want you to lower your left arm rest in order to rest your arm on it. He thinks that is important."

The flight was soon at O'Hare and Kruger met his check pilot who was a young, rather likeable sort. Kruger had to go to the operations office to file his flight plane and check the weather. As he left the cockpit he told the FAA pilot, "I know all of the people here. My wife used to work here. I'm going to tell them the FAA is in the area so they should watch their six". The FAA pilot laughed and said, "Do it! Do it!" They both laughed as the Northwest instructor held his breath at Kruger's familiarity with the "cop".

When Kruger taxied out to the runway the FAA checker said, "Let me show you how to taxi and fly easier. Let the left arm rest down and rest your elbow on it. It will make things a lot easier for you". Kruger had long ago tried that and had rejected it out of hand. He lowered the armrest out of respect for the check pilot who was just trying to make life easier for the "new Captain". After a few minutes Kruger said, "That's about the most miserable way of handling my arm that I've ever encountered but if you want me to fly that way I can do it, no sweat". The check pilot laughed and said, "Oh, hell, fly it any way you want to. I'm just trying to make life easier for you". They both laughed while the Northwest check pilot's eyes sought heaven in an attempt to beseech the Lord to rescue this dumb pilot who seemed to have no respect for the FAA. Kruger and the FAA pilot had earlier formed a very good relationship of mutual respect, unknown to the Northwest check airman. It had been subtle and was akin to the understanding that two Sumo wrestlers have just before they make contact while they are facing off. The understanding is non-verbal and in microseconds both wrestlers know, without a doubt, who is going to win and who is going to lose. The resulting match is only for the spectators as the results are already decided.

The rest of the flight was a non-event and soon Kruger had the blessing of the FAA to operate as a full-fledged Captain. He was released to the line.

Flying the line as a 727 Captain wasn't at all like flying as an international 747 pilot. Domestic flying consisted of making several takeoffs and landings, flying in and around weather fronts and storms and short layovers. Kruger began to feel his age. Flying internationally consisted of one takeoff and landing followed by long layovers, usually consisting of 24 hours or more. Kruger thought, "Face it; this is simply more like work". He was older than the rest of the crew and during the layovers he went to his room to sleep instead of running around with the rest of the crew like he used to do.

Kruger was used to command and had no problem with taking command of his aircraft. Several things had changed drastically since he had flown the 727. For one thing the airline had decided to put a lot of emphasis on something called CRM, short for Cockpit Resource Management. The concept of CRM was that the Captain would utilize any and all information available to him in his decision making processes.

This was not a new idea. Most Captains and, in fact, most pilots especially the military ones had used this concept for years. Specifically this entailed using all of the pilots in the cockpit and actively encouraging them to volunteer ideas and information in order to effectively optimize the conduct of the flight. There were, of course, some old pilots who would not brook any input from anyone regarding the conduct of the flight. This archaic attitude was, thankfully, limited to a few older pilots whose attitudes were entrenched in the early ages of flight. It was this type of an attitude on the part of the pilot in command that resulted in the deaths of hundreds of people when two 747s collided at Tenerife in the Azores. The CRM concept was simply something that some self-professed "expert" figured would make him a brilliant manager in the company shake-up and would embellish his bottom line.

Kruger had long ago used the concept of CRM even when he was in the Navy. The concept was used by any pilot who was even halfway competent. Northwest Airlines treated CRM as if it were a brand new concept and mandated that all pilots attend several classes to "teach" the "new" concept. A lot of the new pilots, especially the non-military ones, thought that it was a new innovative idea and the popular idea among these pilots was that CRM entailed a democratic process of "voting" on any procedure or decision that cropped up. Kruger had to quash that idea several times.

One day his copilot differed with him on some decision and told him that he was a "dinosaur" and had outdated ideas about how to conduct a flight. Kruger set that young gentleman, who was a competent pilot but who had limited experience, on the straight road by informing him that there was only one pilot in command and that he (Kruger) would always accept any and all ideas about how to conduct the flight but that, in the final analysis, the pilot in command was just that and would always make the final decision and would always accept the responsibility for those decisions. Command of an aircraft was not subject to the democratic process as the responsibility for the aircraft and the crew and passengers set directly on the shoulders of the Captain.

Something else that had changed was that Northwest had acquired another airline, Republic Airways, and had interleaved those pilots with the old NWA pilots. The Republic pilots were a mixture of the old North Central, Southern and Air West pilots and were considered by the Northwest pilots as being "cowboys" in that they flew their airplanes more like barnstormers instead of professional airline pilots. When the two groups were able to fly together there were the inevitable head-butting scenarios. In addition the Republic pilots disliked Northwest in general and the NWA pilots in particular. The NWA pilots reciprocated in spades.

When Northwest had acquired Republic initially the two groups were kept apart. Each flew their own airplanes and the two groups were not allowed to fly with each other. The Republic pilots had nothing but disdain for Northwest. They had lived for years next door to the Northwest group and had made fun of the NWA pilots whenever they had gone on strike. The idea that they were going to be integrated with their old enemy was distasteful in the extreme.

One day the inevitable happened. During a driving snowstorm a Republic crew was arguing about their merger with NWA and did not pay attention to the build up of ice on their wings or the flap settings prior to takeoff. The plane crashed at Detroit with no survivors. The Northwest pilots figured that it was the preview of things to come with the cowboys from Republic. Several months later the two groups were merged and they began to fly with each other.

The first time Kruger had to fly with a combined crew he drew a Republic copilot. His copilot was a well groomed young man who seemed competent but who seemed apprehensive about flying with an NWA captain. Kruger tried to put him at ease. On taxiing out of Detroit Kruger's 727 was behind a Republic DC10 that was taxiing very slowly. The NWA pilots always called the Republic pilots "ducks" based on the goose that decorated the tail of the Republic airplanes. Kruger smiled at his copilot and said sotto voice, "Will you get that fucking duck piece of shit out of my way"? His copilot was startled and looked at him but saw that Kruger was smiling. He said, "Go fuck yourself". Kruger laughed and, after a few seconds, the copilot laughed also. The tension was broken and the cockpit was relaxed afterward.

Kruger treated his copilot like he had all others and soon the crew was operating as well as any other. Kruger shared the legs like he always had with the copilot flying every other leg. On the leg from Manitoba to Minneapolis the copilot descended the way he had always done when he flew for Republic. The 727 had a maximum airspeed and, if you approached that speed, a "clacker" would sound in the cockpit to warn you. The copilot made the whole descent with the clacker sounding.

Kruger remained silent throughout the whole noisy descent. Once they were stabilized in level flight he turned to his copilot and said, "There are a lot of different ways to fly an airplane and most of them are safe and appropriate but you are now hired by Northwest Airlines and you ought to fly the plane the way the company wants you to. You can fly the way you wish but when it comes time for a check ride you will flunk hands down if you do what you always do. I used to teach in a military squadron and what I mostly taught was habit patterns. When the chips are down and you are in extremis you will revert to the habit pattern you always followed. If you follow the wrong pattern you set yourself up to crash and burn. I think that you know how NWA wants you to fly and it's not to descend on the airspeed clacker. If you really want to do that when you fly with me that's OK by me but some other pilot may kick you off of the airplane for that. OK?"

His copilot thought about that for about 10 seconds and then said, "OK, thanks for the heads up". They got along well after that.

On another trip Kruger had flown into Fargo, North Dakota. While he was looking over the new flight plan for the next leg into Minneapolis his Second Officer came into the operations office and told him that he had found that the plane was "hard downed" because of a bad hydraulic leak. A mechanic concurred with the Second Officer and Kruger called Northwest Operations to apprise them of the problem. Operations called crew schedules and they asked Kruger how long it would take to fix the problem as they needed his crew for an outbound trip from Minneapolis. Kruger reported that no parts were available and that it would take about 12 hours to truck them from Minneapolis. He also told Crew Scheds that a winter front was bearing down on Fargo and that it was a blizzard; that it was supposed to hit Fargo in the next 4 hours and that it was supposed to shut down the airport. He wanted to know what he was supposed to do with his crew.

Crew Schedules panicked. They told Kruger that a Republic 727 was leaving Fargo in 15 minutes and that he was supposed to get his crew on that plane. They said that the plane was full but that six paying passengers would have to be "bumped" in order for Kruger's crew to ride to Minneapolis.

Although Republic had been bought by Northwest neither side could fly each other's planes as yet although Northwest owned the other airline. Kruger felt sorry for the passengers who were going to be stranded in

Fargo. They were the real lifeblood of the airline but were usually treated like the janitors who cleaned the toilets. He asked the Controller who he was talking to if he could assign two pilots to the cockpit jump seats and two Flight Attendants to the F/A's jump seats thus saving 4 passengers the insult of being bumped. The Controller thought that was a wonderful idea and told him to go ahead with the plan.

Kruger briefed the crew and they hurried to the Republic plane. When Kruger entered the Republic cockpit he knew that he was in hostile territory. The Republic pilots generally thought that the merger with Northwest was a bad idea. They had long made fun of the Northwest pilots and their long struggle with their company. When Kruger entered the cockpit he saw that one of the jump seats was occupied by a Republic pilot who was flying the jump seat in order to get to Minneapolis. He told the crew what Northwest had decided to do with his crew and told the jump seat rider that he was sorry but that the welfare of the paying passengers was the important issue here and that, in a worst case scenario, the pilot could rent a car and drive to Minneapolis. Kruger himself had done just that several times in Florida, driving to a city where he could get on an airplane and fly to Minneapolis. The drive from Fargo to Minneapolis was a piece of cake compared to that.

When he had delivered his message the Republic Captain named Dale blew up. He screamed, "I hate this fucking airline. I hate you damned pilots. I don't like or agree with what is happening." He was so loud that the passengers could hear everything he said. As he ranted, spittle flew about the cockpit. Even his crew was intimidated. They adopted a heads down silence. As the Republic jump seat pilot silently left the cockpit Kruger smiled at the upset Captain and said, "You don't have to like it, Charlie. You just have to do it." He emphasized his command of the situation by patting the Captain on the head.

The Captain absolutely lost his head. He screamed and ranted. About that time Kruger's copilot entered the cockpit, smiled and said, "Hi guys. Mind if I ride here?" Kruger snapped, "Sit down, buckle in and shut up. This is a hostile cockpit." The startled copilot did as he was told and the trip commenced.

The Republic Captain hand flew the whole trip. He never calmed down and was as rough on the flight controls as an old cob of corn that has sat in the field all winter. Kruger watched him with utter disdain as he allowed his anger to dictate how he flew. He finally bullied the plane onto a final heading at Minneapolis and hit the runway with a landing that was about 3 Gs, just what a carrier landing would have been although the Republic pilot had proven that he had never received any Navy training.

After the hard landing and, as he rolled out, Kruger reached over and patted him on the shoulder saying, "Nice job, Charlie. I'm sure that your passengers appreciated your expertise and wonderful flight techniques. You'll make a wonderful addition to Northwest, at least until you bust your check ride due to your idiotic flying prowess." He laughed and left the cockpit as the Republic pilot ground his teeth in anger.

Kruger's copilot said, "Jesus, do you think that Dale (the Republic pilot's name) will make it?" Kruger said, "Naw, if he keeps this crap up he'll have a stroke before he's aboard 6 months. I wouldn't worry about him."

On one trip that Kruger had bid he was assigned a copilot that had flunked his Captain checkout. Northwest decided that the pilot needed to fly with a Captain who could possibly correct his deficiencies allowing him to undergo a recheck 6 months later. Kruger had been picked as he had been a check/training pilot in the Navy before he signed on with Northwest Orient Airlines. When they met before the first flight the copilot told Kruger about his new probation with the company. Kruger told him that his main problem was headwork. Kruger knew the pilot and knew that he could fly but his problem remained in not thinking ahead on any of his flights. He had relied on a Captain to prompt him and think for him for so long that it had become ingrained in him. Kruger had seen that syndrome operate a number of times on the airline. The job of copilot was so easy that it engendered laziness. The big difference between a copilot and a Captain was the ability to think ahead and situational awareness. Kruger's new copilot didn't excel in either attribute.

When Kruger had first met his copilot and heard his story he said, "OK, John, you lucked out and were given another chance at making Captain and keeping your job. A lot of other pilots haven't been as lucky as you so you are going to buckle down and work at becoming a Captain. Whenever it's your leg you are going to do everything a Captain does. You are going to check the flight plan, brief the crew, talk to the passengers and make all of the decisions with no prompting from me. Got that? No bullshitting or screwing around. Try to be professional for once in your life. Your copilot days are over one way or the other." John agreed and they walked out to the plane.

Kruger flew the first leg as was the usual thing for crews to do. On the next leg John did OK but when they got to altitude John was content to chatter on about anything at all. Finally Kruger said, "Well, fuck those passengers. They don't deserve any PAs about the weather or anything like that." John looked startled and said, "Oh, yeah, I forgot." He started to pick up the PA mike but Kruger said, "Planning, John. Remember that's what we talked about back there on the ramp. Don't open your mouth until you know exactly what you're going to say. Otherwise you'll sound like the asshole you are. Think and plan, dammit."

John stammered through a passenger PA and settled down to fly. Kruger handled the communications but refused to enter any dialog with John who sweated through the whole leg. He got through it by the skin of his nose.

On John's next leg as a "Captain" he chattered on and on. He did remember to brief the passengers but forgot everything else. Finally, as they approached their destination, Kruger said, "John, do you know where you are right now?" John looked startled and said, "Whadda ya mean?" Kruger said, "Well, we are supposed to land at Las Vegas. Do you know where Las Vegas is relative to our plane?"

John nervously glanced around and said, "Wha . . . Why no. I guess I don't." Kruger said, "I've got the plane." He rolled the plane up on one wing in about a 40 degree bank and said, "Look out your window. We are right on top of the damned place." John cursed and tried to grab the yoke. Kruger said, "I've got it, remember? You've got a memory about as short as your skinny dick, John. Now watch and learn. This is something that Northwest Flight Training won't teach you."

Kruger slowed the plane and brought up the speed brakes. Then he lowered the landing gear. You were not supposed to do both at the same time. The plane dropped out of the sky as the rate of climb instrument bottomed out. He looked back at the Second Officer and said, "If you can't keep up with the cabin descent rate let me know." The Second Officer, busy at his panel trying to stabilize the pressurization nodded. Kruger said, "We could also create a lot of drag by dropping the flaps but that would activate the spoilers in a one-to-one ratio and that might just put the plane into an unrecoverable attitude so we won't do that however, we could do one hell of a lot better if we could only plan the flight a little better and keep our heads out of out asses a little more." He glanced over at John who had his head dropped in an attitude of humility.

As they got down to a much better altitude and had contacted the tower after cleaning up the plane Kruger handed the plane over to John saying, "Well, I think that you might be able to land this thing as it appears that you have your head up and out of your ass for once so let's see what you can do from here on." John, without comment, took the controls and flew the approach and landing. On the landing he was rough and jerked the controls from side to side. Kruger placed his hands on the yoke and dampened out the wild side-to-side flops the copilot was making. John made no comment but continued the rollout.

After the flight Kruger invited his copilot to the nearest bar for some relaxing liquid refreshment. As they relaxed over a beer John said, "Something's been bothering me. I have to tell you that if you get on the controls the next time I'm making a landing I'm going to knock you on your ass." Kruger laughed and said, "Well, John, I have to tell you that if you think that I'm going to let you drag a wingtip because you can't fly the fucking plane then you are crazy as hell. I'll get on the controls anytime I think the plane is in extremis. That's part of my job and that's what you ought to be thinking about if you ever want to be a Captain. And another thing; anytime you want to take a swing at me you are welcome to do so. Just be aware that I'll swing back and I fight to win and not to be a gentleman. I'll wax your skinny ass, John. Now, if we have that all cleared up enjoy your beer and quit blustering." John, to his credit, grinned and did just that.

Kruger found out that John had finally seen the light and had grown up. He passed his Captain check ride and went on to a long career with Northwest.

Kruger always had a soft spot for commuters. He had been a commuter for some time, living in Florida and flying out of Minneapolis. Northwest, or at least some of the management people at Northwest, thought that commuters were akin to traitors. You see, commuters left the pristine areas of Minneapolis/ St. Paul for purely selfish reasons. They didn't like paying the exorbitant taxes the state imposed on its inhabitants. There had been a continual battle between Northwest and the commuters for years.

Donald Nyrop, the head of NWA, had participated in a luncheon with the governor of Minnesota, Rudy Perpech. During the lunch the governor asked why a lot of pilots were leaving the state of Minnesota. Nyrop said, "If you can't figure that out you shouldn't be the governor of the state of Minnesota."

One day Kruger was preparing to fly from Cleveland to Minneapolis. His plane was full. A Service Agent told him that there was a Northwest Flight Attendant who was trying to get to Minneapolis in order to fly her trip. Kruger's flight was the last flight of the day. The F/A was desperate.

Kruger was used to "letting it all hang out". He sympathized with the F/A and told the service agent that he would allow the F/A to fly in the cockpit in a jump seat but it had to be strictly on the QT. F/As were not allowed to fly in the cockpit under any circumstances. The F/A was overjoyed when told of the plan. She was cautioned to keep quiet about the plan as the Captain's head would be on the block if it got out. As the plane was boarded it became apparent that there would be one seat left vacant in the first class section that the F/A could occupy although she would have to pay for it with a pass.

The Service Agent came to the cockpit and told Kruger that there was a big problem. It seemed that the F/A, who was a young black girl, had been making a fuss about buying a pass in the cabin. She had been shouting that she had been offered a seat in the cockpit and she wanted that instead of one in the cabin. She had been abusive to Kruger's first class flight attendant and had made a real spectacle of herself in front of the passengers. Kruger's blood ran cold. He had put his job on the line by offering to put the girl in the cockpit. Now, with a seat in first class available, she wanted to opt for a free illegal seat in the cockpit instead of paying for a pass in the cabin. The monetary amount of the pass was negligible.

Kruger left the cockpit and braced the irate girl. He said, 'You are too stupid to deserve this job. I won't allow you to fly on my airplane under any conditions. You are disturbing our passengers. I don't care what happens to you from this point on." He left the stunned F/A and flew out of Cleveland without her. He never knew what had happened to her and didn't care. Some people were too stupid to live.

Kruger flew the 727 for about 8 months and enjoyed his status as Captain but always wished that he could be back on the 747 and the international schedules. One day the other shoe dropped.

Kruger had bid a schedule that had been bid by a Republic Second Officer and a Northwest copilot. He figured that it might be a long month. On the first leg of the first trip everyone trundled out their personal status items. The copilot had been in the Air Force as had the Second Officer. They were in the head-butting mode from the word go. Kruger was placed into the status of a referee in keeping the two from each other's throats. The Second Officer was particularly in the attack mode and was on the copilot's back a lot. Kruger was successful in making the cockpit environment mellow.

The Chief Pilot, Dick Edwards, had asked that a ramp manager be allowed to fly in the cockpit from Detroit to Tampa. Kruger met the man, who was an erstwhile Republic employee, and invited him to fly either in the cockpit or the first class section if there were space available. The manager opted to sit in the first class section but came to the cockpit for the final section of the flight.

As the flight approached Tampa Kruger invited the ramp manager to accompany the crew that evening. He said, "We have a long layover in Tampa and intend to go out this evening to have a few beers and eat some pizza. You are invited to go with us if you wish." Under the new rules on Northwest crews could drink alcoholic beverages if the drinking period was outside of a 12 hour period from drinking to the checking in period of the next flight. Since the layover was over 24 hours the crew was "legal" to imbibe.

The ramp manager declined the invitation and the crew gathered after the flight to have fun and relax. The Flight Attendants ate pizza with the cockpit crew and excused themselves. The three pilots continued to drink beer and finally returned to the hotel.

Upon arriving at the hotel the pilots decided to sit at the large bar in the center of the hotel and have a glass of wine before retiring to bed. Sometime that evening one of the pilots said, "We are about to go into the 12 hour period so we probably ought to stop drinking and go to bed". The others concurred and all three went to bed. The next day the flight continued to its completion.

A few months later Kruger answered a telephone call from his Chief Pilot. He said that Kruger had been accused of violating the 12 hour drinking rule and had been taken off of flight status pending an investigation. Kruger's wife, Barbara, was decimated. She was sure that the company was going to fire Kruger. Kruger assured her that the company might well wish to do so but that he had done nothing wrong and that ALPA would protect him. Barbara was not placated.

Kruger presented himself to the company people in due time with the representation of an ALPA attorney. The other pilots were in attendance. The ALPA attorney briefed them by saying, "You should know that this is not a friendly meeting. This is a hostile and adversarial confrontation and you should act accordingly. Kruger, you know this but the other pilots don't." Kruger was familiar with the process as he had weathered it before when he had been fired for cutting off the valve stems of a Northwest Scab during a strike. The ALPA attorney said that the Second Officer would probably lose his job since he was still on probation and the company could fire him for any infraction. The Second Officer was decimated and could hardly talk.

The meeting was complete with the Director of Flying, the Chief Pilot and a lot of ancillaries like court reporters and Vice Presidents. During the meeting the pilots were asked what had happened the evening of the occurrence. All of the pilots concurred about the happenings of the evening. Finally the Director of Flying said, "Well, we'll have to investigate this incident further." Kruger said, "How long will the investigation take?" The answer was a week or so. Kruger then said, "We are off flight status until the completion of the investigation aren't we?" The answer was "yes". Kruger then said, "Well, I can't give you a few weeks to investigate us. You asked me to come here from Florida and I did but I can't stay here for an extended time. Would it be OK if we came back here in a month to answer the charges? That would give you enough time to complete your investigation."

The company investigators thought that that was fine and complied with the terms. As the crew walked out of the hearing the ALPA attorney said, "Good call, Ed. In a month the Second Officer will be a member of ALPA and the company can't fire him unless it has cause". Prior to this the S/O was a probationary pilot and could be fired for any reason whatsoever. The crew members went home to await the next meeting.

The time seemed to drag slowly prior to the next meeting with the company. Kruger flew to Minneapolis a day early to confer with an ALPA attorney. He met the Second Officer and was startled to see how absolutely petrified with fear he was. Bob Holliker was carrying a Bible and repeatedly pointed out that he had been "studying it a lot". Other than that the only subject that he wanted to talk about was how he "would do just about anything in order to keep this million dollar job".

The ALPA attorney briefed the crew prior to the meeting. He said, "Ed, I know that I don't have to remind you about this but for the other two of you, you should know that this is not going to be a friendly meeting. It's adversarial. Watch what you say and think before you answer any questions. The company lawyers will try to prove that you are guilty. That's their job."

Kruger said, "Guys, I've been over this route a lot, both personally and vicariously with other pilots. Just remember that we did nothing wrong. I don't know who is trying to railroad us but we'll get through this because we are well within the rules".

Kruger was called first and grilled by the Northwest lawyers. He told them exactly what had transpired on the night in question and maintained that his crew was innocent of whatever charges someone had made against them. He repeatedly asked who or what had prompted the accusation but the company would not divulge that information. For some unknown reason Holliker, the Second Officer, was called next. Kruger later found out that he had told the company that the copilot had finished off a glass of wine 10 minutes into the 12 hour prohibited time period that proscribed drinking prior to flight. The copilot was called next and made aware of the charges the Second Officer had made against him. Bear in mind that the situation had now changed and that the Second Officer had made the charges against the copilot instead of the company as far as the company lawyers were concerned. The copilot became rattled and babbled that alcohol was a minor thing during his layovers and that he had not violated the 12 hour rule. In his excitement over being charged he said, "I'm pretty sure that I didn't violate the 12 hour rule. I might have but I don't think so". As soon as he said "I might have . . ." the Northwest lawyers adjudicated him guilty.

The crew, lawyers, Chief Pilots and a company vice president all convened and their verdicts were read. The copilot was fired, Kruger was given 30 days off duty without pay for allowing his copilot to fly "impaired" and the Second Officer was let off scot free. When the verdicts were read Kruger blew up, especially when he learned that the terrified Second Officer had sacrificed the copilot in order to keep himself out of the scrutiny of the company. Kruger shouted, "That's a damned lie. That did not happen. If you are going to fire someone for a 10 minute infraction you damned well better have the best clock in the whole world and a verifiable time hack. Who was keeping the damned time during all of this? Was it the crooked clock on the wall of the bar, the bar tender's Timex, the Second Officer's watch or what?" The company lawyers ignored him. As far as they were concerned they had just "won" the battle and they didn't give one damned shit about how it impacted any human. The Northwest management pukes went along with that attitude.

Kruger suspected that the Second Officer, Robert Holliker, had been petrified with fear that he might lose his job and that he had discounted the ploy that Kruger had played in order to save his job. Kruger had suspected that Holliker had called the company and had made a deal wherein he would sacrifice the copilot (who he disliked) in order to save his job as he had indicated he would much earlier.

Kruger and his copilot immediately went to the ALPA office to file grievances contesting the company's actions. Kruger refused to even talk to the Second Officer and vowed that every other pilot at Northwest Airlines would soon know of his traitorous actions. Kruger knew that the Second Officer had lied and sacrificed the copilot, who he disliked, in an attempt to keep the company from his "ass". Holliker, that damned Air Force officer, had absolutely sullied his office, his pride, his oath as an officer and his personal integrity as a pilot. In Kruger's opinion he was an anathema, someone you wouldn't stoop to speak to on the street. He was below contempt. Robert F. Holliker, a name that would live in infamy, to paraphrase a statement from Roosevelt.

When Kruger got home to Florida his wife was worried sick. She was sure that the company wanted to fire him. Kruger had been through things like this before he had married Barbara and assured her that they wouldn't be hurt. As Kruger said, "This is going to be a 30 day paid vacation in addition to my other vacation time. We are going to have fun. I'm going to win this grievance hands down. The company can't prove a damned thing that they allege and we did nothing wrong. We are going to fly to Seattle, rent a car, stay in nice hotels, see the sights, get on a ferry and sail to Victoria and stay in the largest, nicest hotel there that overlooks the harbor. Before we do that we have to make a short stop in Minneapolis so I can attend a hearing on the grievance. Northwest is going to pay for the whole damned thing."

And they did just that.

At the hearing in Minneapolis Kruger insisted on knowing just who had charged his crew with illegal drinking. The company wouldn't divulge that information in spite of the demands of the ALPA attorney.

The Northwest attorney tried to paint a picture of Kruger as a weak Captain who was deficient in judgment. He asked, "Captain Kruger, if you saw another pilot drinking illegally what would you do?" The company had long held that it was the duty of each pilot to snoop around other crew members and fink on them to the company. Kruger's old nemesis, Don Nelson, had tried to put Kruger in "his pocket" twice during Kruger's first year with Northwest. Kruger answered the lawyer; "I'm assuming that this is a rhetorical question so here's my answer. I could do a number of things. I could approach the pilot in question and ask him to cease his activity or to call in sick for the flight. I could approach his Captain and make him aware of the situation. I could call the ALPA professional committee and make them aware of the situation but there is one thing that I would not do."

"What is that?" The lawyer was smug in his attack.

Kruger grinned and said, "I absolutely would not call the company lawyers and say, 'Ya, ya, ya, I'm finking on a fellow pilot."

The lawyer was shocked at the flaunting of decorum on the part of Kruger during what he (Kruger) thought of as a kangaroo court.

During the hearing the neutral, a respected person who was an integral part of the grievance hearing, was increasingly bothered by Northwest's foot dragging against producing an interoffice memo that accused Kruger's crew of drinking illegally. Finally he said, "It seems to me that Northwest is hiding something that should be brought into the open. If Northwest persists in this avenue I will rule for ALPA and Captain Kruger right now." The company asked for a recess and the lawyers conferred in an anteroom. They were so engrossed in covering up evidence that they didn't even notice the little blond lady reading in a corner. Kruger's wife, Barbara, had seen them come into the room and immediately get into a huddle. As she listened to their conversation she heard them discussing how they could alter the incriminating sentences and perhaps run the altered document through a copy machine in order to hide the real evidence from the neutral. They finally decided that ruse wouldn't work and handed the document to the neutral.

Barbara was shocked at what she had witnessed. Ed Kruger just laughed and said, "Now you know what Northwest employees have to put up with all of the time. Northwest doesn't know what fair play is and lawyers are, and always will be, slimy things that will do just about anything to win."

The hearing was continued into the next month. When that date rolled around Kruger and a good friend, Jim Watland, showed up at the Northwest property for the hearing. The court reporter knew Kruger, the lawyers and everyone else but not Watland. She asked, "What are you?" thinking that he might be a lawyer. Jim smilingly answered. "Why, I guess that I'm a white, Anglo-Saxon, Protestant." She persisted until Jim gave his name and said that he was an "interested party". Northwest tried to exclude him from the proceedings but he had set a precedent a long time ago in packing hearings with "interested parties" that, in effect, told any neutral that the issue at hand was being followed closely by ALPA and a lot of pilots.

Robert Holliker was present at the hearing as the main accuser and kept his eyes on the ground the whole time. He refused to look at anyone in the room. The Northwest lawyers gave a weak presentation while the ALPA attorney gave an outstanding one that portrayed Northwest Airlines as a vindictive employer that thought pilots were uniformly against anything the company tried to do. It finally came out that the item that prompted the whole incident was a note from the Republic ramp person who had ridden to Orlando with Kruger. That person disliked the Northwest people and had sent the note in an attempt to get Kruger's crew into trouble. During the hearing, in which he was present, Kruger had whispered to the ALPA attorney, "Look at that guy! He's a recovering alcoholic and is off the wagon. Look at his complexion and his nervousness." The attorney agreed and during the questioning asked the man if he had been drinking during the time period that he said that he had observed Kruger's crew. The man was startled and quickly said, "I haven't had a drink since . . . (he gave a date and a time). It was apparent that he was a recovering alcoholic that had fallen off the wagon. That fact was noted by everyone in the hearing room, including the neutral. The hearing ended with the neutral saying that he would render a decision in a few months.

Kruger and his wife had their 30 day vacation on the company's dime. They flew to Seattle, stayed in the nicest hotels, rented a big car, put it on a ferry going to Victoria, British Columbia and stayed at the large, beautiful hotel overlooking the bay in Victoria. They enjoyed the beautiful gardens and the wonderful little restaurants. They really enjoyed the idea that Northwest Airlines was paying for the whole damned thing.

Kruger was back to flying after his 30 days suspension. Everything seemed normal except his legs seemed swollen and felt very heavy. He and

Barbara had to fly from Florida to Chicago to attend a wedding. Upon their arrival Barbara asked her brother-in-law, a Medical Doctor, to look at Kruger's ankles, which were very swollen. Dr. Pride took one look and sent Kruger to a local hospital against Kruger's loud protests. There was nothing wrong with him, he maintained. After a few tests the hospital found that Kruger's kidneys had shut down and he was hours away from becoming jaundiced.

He had to undergo a cystoscopy and the placement of a stent in his urethras in order to allow for the passage of urine. This was all new to Kruger who, prior to this time, had only been afflicted with measles his whole life. Several doctors took a look at him in an attempt to find out why his kidneys were afflicted. Finally after numerous tests an Oncologist informed him that he had cancer and that the cancer had squeezed the kidneys and urethras to the extent that they had been compromised.

When he heard that he turned cold. "Is that it for me?" he thought. "Is this the way I'm going to check out of this life?" The Oncologist, a very competent gentleman, told him that they would have to do several tests in an attempt to find out just what kind of cancer he had so that they could treat it. In the meantime Kruger had to remain in the hospital.

He would remain in the hospital for several months. It seemed like years. He had to undergo several operations in an attempt to find out just what kind of cancer he had and to keep his kidneys operating enough to sustain his health, as tenuous as it was.

Meanwhile, Northwest was notified of his condition and he was placed on long term medical leave. He had been leave for a month when his Chief Pilot, Dick Edwards, in Detroit called him to inquire about his condition. Dick had been a Republic pilot before the merger with Northwest and was well respected as a fine Chief Pilot who looked out after the welfare of his pilots; something most of the Northwest Chief Pilots were not known for. Dick had been party to Kruger's hearings and told him that he had gone to the company on Kruger's behalf and had gotten them to "throw in the towel" on his grievance. Kruger was stunned and humbled upon hearing this. Prior to this he had always figured that no quarter was asked or given anytime a pilot had run afoul of a Northwest Chief Pilot. Kruger thanked Dick profusely but told him that he would rather win the grievance than have the company "forgive" him for something that he was innocent of. Edwards chuckled at this and said, "I sort of figured that you would say that. I've learned a lot about you and know that you don't back down from a fight but I wanted to make the offer anyway." He wished Kruger good health and said that he expected to see him back on flying status soon.

Kruger had to undergo chemotherapy for 9 months and was finally pronounced "in remission". The Oncologist had explained that there was never a "cure" for cancer and that "remission" was as good as it ever got. The problem now was how to get back to flying status. Kruger sought the help of the ALPA Aero-medical team. Kruger's Oncologist had to write a letter to the FAA documenting his remission from cancer. He did so but couched the letter in language as if he was writing another doctor. It was too clinical. An ALPA member took the letter, with Kruger's name blanked out, and showed it to the FAA asking if they would put the pilot in question back on flight status. The FAA said, "No". The Aero-Medical group then called Kruger and said, "Your doctor had diarrhea of the mouth. All the FAA wants to know is (1) you are in remission and (2) you are free of drugs in your system. Get your doctor to put that down in a letter and resubmit your request for return to flying." Kruger's Oncologist was a little put out by that but complied and soon Kruger was back on flight duty.

During the time he was undergoing the chemotherapy he learned that another Northwest pilot had flown drunk from Fargo, North Dakota to Minneapolis. That pilot's name was Lyle Prouse. Lyle was an old friend of Kruger's. They didn't exactly run in the same crowd but Lyle had been a Marine pilot and was generally looked up to by most of the other pilots. The nitty gritty details were all on all of the news services and Kruger shuddered to hear and read about them. He pictured himself in the same situation. Most of his other friends on Northwest felt the same. Granted that Prouse had really screwed the pooch royally, most other pilots had been guilty of drinking "illegally" on layovers as seen in the light of Northwest's harsh rules. After some heartfelt thought Kruger got on the phone and called several other pilots about the situation. By this time Lyle had been convicted and had entered prison. Kruger was able to get a number of pilots to contribute $100 each for the time that Lyle was incarcerated in order to pay for his mortgage so that his family wouldn't have to be turned out in the cold. Kruger felt that, since he had to sit around and do nothing but endure chemotherapy he might as well do something meaningful. It seemed to work out OK. Lyle's family stayed in their home but on skinny rations during his stay hosted by the government. Kruger communicated with Lyle during that time and became closer to him during his sabbatical. They talked about their military times, their interest in karate and Lyle's Native Indian background. Kruger had long been interested in the North American Indian culture and had studied their ways and even the Plains Indian sign language. He had grown up playing with a friend who was a native American who lived in Michigan and he had several friends who were adult Chippewa's of the same tribal group. Kruger thought (hoped) that communicating with Lyle made his incarceration a little easier.

When he got back on flight duty he entered the training building for the first time in a long time. During the chemotherapy he had lost all of his hair and now looked like a Marine recruit with a shaved head only a lot older and more than a little rugged looking. As he entered the flight training building he ran into an old friend who had been in the Marines. Marine and Navy pilots have always engaged in good natured bantering and this time was no exception. Captain Dino Oliva took one look at Kruger and said, "Hey Kruger! Are you trying to look like a Marine with that haircut?" Kruger laughed and said, "Naw, it's from the chemotherapy." Oliva looked startled and said, "Damn it, I should have known that. I'm sorry as hell."

"Oh, stop blubbering," Kruger laughed. "That didn't bother me in the least. I'm just damned happy to be alive."

Kruger checked back out in the 727 but didn't fly it for very long before he got the chance to check out as a Captain on his old love, the 747.

CHAPTER XV

The timing for his checking on the 747 was fortuitous. Kruger was approaching 55 years of age and his pension, upon reaching 60 as mandated by the government, was based on his final average earnings over his last five years of flying. The checkout was fairly easy since he had flown previously as a copilot on the plane and knew the systems. The problem, as he saw it, was his strength. He would have to fly an approach with two engines out on one side of the huge plane to minimums and land. That would take a lot of strength on one of his legs. The 747 was a large airplane and the rudder forces needed to fly a two engine approach were huge. Normally a healthy pilot would finish that kind of approach with shaking legs. Kruger was very weak due to his cancer treatment that kept him in a bed for a long time plus all of the chemotherapy that he had undergone. He had to do something to boost his strength.

Since he was in a hotel he learned how to access the emergency stairway that every hotel possessed. Each morning and evening he would run up and down the stairs as fast as he could. He normally ended up sweating profusely. He thought of the Marine adage that "Pain is weakness leaving the body". When he first checked into the hotel for training he could not open his room door without using both hands. He simply couldn't turn the door handle with only one. He augmented the runs up and down the stairs with pull-ups on the door jambs and push-ups in the room. He kept to the adage that held that, "Eat protein for training and carbohydrates for fighting". When he had his check ride he did well.

During his prolonged stay in the hotel during his training period he was phenomenally bored. You could only study the airplane manual for just so long until you wanted to scream and throw the 5 pound manual across the room. Kruger solved that little problem by buying a sack of bird seed. He then opened the window of his room, no mean feat since the hotel didn't wish anyone to actually open a window anywhere on the property. That made no difference to Kruger who had taught himself how to open most doors with what is commonly called "burglar's tools". Kruger spread a long line of bird seed along the sill of the window. Then he closed the window and stood by, awaiting the results. As expected, soon a few pigeons landed on the sill and happily ate the seed. Kruger was careful to replenish the seed each night. It didn't take long for the "word" to spread and soon he had a whole flock of friendly pigeons strutting around and cooing. Kruger happily watched them as they did their own "thing" on his window sill. It was a welcome break from watching idiotic television and studying an aircraft manual. Of course he was sure that the management of the hotel would not appreciate all the pigeons that he had attracted to the area but Kruger figured that everyone had a cross to bear and the cross of having pigeons around was a small one.

He was soon released to the line. Line flying on the 747 was like putting on a comfortable old shoe. The only difference Kruger could find was that he was now in the left seat instead of the third or the right seat. He was now "The Man", the pilot in command. He no longer had to bow to some other pilot who Kruger thought was not quite capable of making the critical decisions that needed to be made while flying the large plane over thousands of miles of water. Kruger was comfortable. He had arrived.

It would have been easy for the position of a Captain on an International 747 to go to your head. In Japan or in most of the other countries in the Eastern Pacific countries the Captain was the principle person to attend to. The Flight Attendants were always miffed when the limo drivers would attempt to carry the Captain's luggage and would ignore the FA's luggage. Kruger always made the drivers take care of the FA's luggage. It was a cultural thing. The Captain was held in very high regard in those countries. It was heady and could go to your head easily. Kruger shook the feeling off and remembered where he had come from. He was, after all, just a JAP, just another nose-picking pilot.

Early on in his employment with Northwest Orient there had been a bid for several 727 crews to be deployed to Rangoon, Burma. The government in Rangoon felt that the Captain was sort of a "sacred person" and treated him as such. The Captain got a personal limo while the other pilots got to ride in another taxi. The Flight Attendants were hired from the local population and were treated like trash. There were only two or three crews in Rangoon and soon the Captains began to believe that they were, in fact, "blessed" and not really part of the regular Flight Crew. That was normally called "the Stockholm Syndrome". Kruger didn't wish to slip into that mind set.

A number of Northwest Captains had always banked on the computers and the copilots to come up with a flight plan with adequate fuel reserves for any flight. Kruger was not one of these. He insisted on his own analysis of the flight that was to be flown and refused to accept anybody else's analysis of what was going to happen in the future. Kruger had earlier seen a number of Captains who had been comfortable in their positions and had simply accepted the data that had been given to them in the flight plan that they had to sign and accept. Kruger insisted on checking the data on his own and refused to accept the conclusions of other pilots.

Kruger was a very junior Captain and NWA had earlier on come up with a new category of pilot; the International Relief Captain; the IRC (called the "IRK" by all of the pilots). As a very junior Captain Kruger was relegated to the position of an IRC. The IRC had to be qualified as, not only a Captain, but a Second Officer also. That way the IRC could stand watches as both a Captain and as a Second Officer on the long flights to South East Asia. Northwest Airlines had bargained that position in an attempt to, as always, save money regardless of any other considerations. The IRC could be used by Northwest as a Second Office or a Captain on either a single Captain flight or an augmented flight. On an augmented flight, that is, a flight with two Captains the IRC could also substitute for another Second Officer. The IRC position was a plum for Northwest as it saved the company a lot of money. Never mind that it put a whole lot of work on the IRC who was paid the same wage as a Captain while performing work that two pilots would normally do.

When Republic Airlines merged with NWA the pilot groups had to be merged also. When that happened some of the senior Republic pilots got to check out on the very senior airplanes that NWA possessed. The checkout procedure was brief and, as a result, the old Republic pilots had no real experience flying the long North Pacific routes as did the NWA pilots. It was very noticeable and the NWA pilots capitalized on that in terms of levity. One of the most laughable quotes was the one that was bandied about when a Republic pilot had been bumped back to fly the DC10 rather than the 747. He was quoted as saying, "Oh, well, the DC10 flies more like a fighter". Any military pilot who heard that doubled up in laughter at the idiotic quote.

Kruger didn't give that quote much credence until the pilot who said it told Kruger the same thing. Kruger could hardly believe his ears, but it happened.

Then there was the Captain (Republic) who told Kruger that he had navigated all the way to Japan by dead reckoning navigation. That got

Kruger's attention. He asked just how the other Captain did that and why. The old Republic Captain said that he had seen a "red light" on the Inertial Navigation System and had taken "appropriate steps". Kruger questioned him and found that the other Captain had turned off most of the Inertial systems (the INS systems) based on the little red light. He had not turned off all three systems or he wouldn't have had any airspeed, altitude or any other information. The INS systems were state of the art systems and were extremely expensive and accurate. There were three of them in the plane and they checked on each other all of the time. The "red light" that came on told the pilot that the INS units were "out of tolerance" with each other or, in other words, the system could only find the destination by a few hundred feet instead of a few feet. Kruger listened to the other Captain humorously and finally said, "You know, I've never experienced another pilot who had gone to Japan with only dead reckoning. I can't think of any other NWA pilot who has done so either. If I were you I would tell everyone about your wonderful feat. You ought to get some sort of medal for that." Upon further questioning it became clear that the "heroic" Republic duck had flown the airplane in VFR conditions the whole way and had actually followed the contrails of another plane that had been a few miles ahead of him and was headed to the same destination.

Kruger left the pilot thinking that the story would soon get around the airline to the dismay of the ignorant old Republic pilot.

The Republic pilots knew that they didn't have the experience that the NWA pilots had so they tended to bluster their way through the flight experience. One day Kruger had occasion to fly as an IRC with a more senior Republic pilot. The flight was from Seoul, Korea to Los Angeles. Kruger reported to the flight planning room and introduced himself to the other Captain. The Republic Captain was stuffy and, knowing that he was senior on the flight said, "I've already checked the flight plan so just gather all the stuff and meet me at the plane".

Kruger bridled at the attitude of the other Captain who assumed that Kruger was a "peon" and was on board only to "fetch and carry" the paperwork. He said, "I don't know if you are conversant with the rules but I'm supposed to sign the flight plan also as the other Captain. As such, I always check the plan. Only then will I sign it. You can wait or go on out to the plane. It makes no difference to me." The old Republic Captain (Actually, he was younger than Kruger) chose to wait and watch Kruger.

Kruger checked the flight plan like he always did. He saw immediately that the flight plan had his 747 go from Seoul, Korea to a position 100 miles east of Tokyo, Narita and from there back to Seoul and then to Los Angeles. The fuel load for that kind of flight was more than the plane was capable of carrying, never mind that the flight plan had nothing at all to do with what Northwest actually wished for the flight crew to do. Obviously the computer had belched.

Kruger wadded the flight plan up and threw it into the trash can to the dismay of the Korean flight planners. As he did so he said, "What a piece of shit" in a loud voice. That immediately got the attention of the other three crews in the flight planning section along with the Korean Flight Planners. When questioned, Kruger told everyone what his computer generated flight plan had come up with. Some of the other crews found that their plans had been the same way. Panic ensued. The Korean Flight Planners ran around in dismay muttering, "mistake, mistake", trying to make sense of the whole thing. The other flight crews were going over their flight plans in an attempt to correct the whole thing while the other Captain on Kruger's plane just stood and watched the whole episode with an open mouth.

Kruger took command of the flight without even talking to the other, more senior pilot, and the flight went well. Kruger was used to taking command of any flight in order to make sure that it operated safely and smoothly. It made no difference to him just who was "in charge". When it came to safety and the completion of the mission he brooked no idiots who said, "I'm in charge here" ala General Alexander Haig, and simply did what was necessary in order to accomplish the task.

On one of his trips Kruger had to fly to Bangkok, Thailand when there was a typhoon in the area. He had planned the flight way south of the weather in the South China Sea in an area that was usually not used since it was not the quickest way to get to his destination. During that flight communications became difficult and he soon lost the ability to talk to any land base. He was on an airway and was headed for a giant thunderstorm. He tried repeatedly to get a clearance around the storm but was unable to do so because of the lack of communications. Finally he made a broadcast "in the blind", that is to say he simply broadcasted his intent to fly off course 100 miles south of the track at an altitude that no other plane on a clearance would have flown at. He successfully circumvented the weather and finally arrived at Bangkok without incident.

Once he was at his home base he wrote a letter to the Chief Pilot describing what he had done. He did this just as he would have done when he was in the Navy, called an AAR or After Action Report.

One day while he was in the flight office at Los Angeles the Chief Pilot for that office, Sven Holm, buttonholed him.

"Say, aren't you Ed Kruger? I don't believe I've ever met you."

Kruger acknowledged that he was, in fact, the person that Swine Holm thought he was.

"I got a report from you about an off course deviation you made on your way to Bangkok. I really appreciate it. Most pilots would never send me a report like that."

Kruger said that he was used to giving his commanding officers an after action report when he was in the Navy and thought that it was still a good thing to do now that he was an airline pilot. He said that most COs thought that it was a nice gesture in that it kept them from being blind-sided when some higher authority asked them about the action.

Swine Holm was vociferous in his praise at the action and told Kruger that he had, in fact, done the same thing much earlier. He said that when he had to go off course he had turned off the collision avoidance system on the plane so that he "wouldn't be seen and given a flight violation".

Kruger was incredulous that Holm would confess to doing such a thing. For one thing Holm had discounted or maybe hadn't even known that all airplanes are tracked by satellite now and nothing the pilot could do could hide from that. Then, too, by turning off his collision avoidance system Holm had effectively made his plane invisible to other planes and had made a mid air collision all that much more possible. Holm was too stupid to fly planes in Kruger's estimation.

On another flight Kruger was paired with Don Debolt, a "simply wonderful" Northwest pilot (in his own assessment) who had his sights on glory. He bragged that he had flown on the SRT, the secret Air Force plane. Kruger knew that he had actually gotten a "ride" in one instead of actually flying one. Debolt was a braggart and was politically motivated. He saw himself as more of a management person than as a pilot. In short, he was insufferable. None of the regular pilots liked him. He was painted as "an 8 by 10 glossy" by one of the pilots.

Debolt was senior on the flight so he made the initial takeoff and landing at Narita. On the return flight Kruger was supposed to be in the left seat but Debolt said that he wanted to ride in the right one as copilot. Kruger was familiar with Debolt's attitudes of always wanting to ride in a pilot's seat. Debolt considered all pilots to be inferior to him and was paranoid enough to always want to be able to control the plane. Kruger told him that he could not ride in the copilot's seat. When Debolt wanted to know why he thought that way Kruger explained; "If we have an emergency I, as the left seat pilot, will be in charge and will call the shots. I have been trained to do just that and I have a lot of experience not only with Northwest but with the Navy in command authority. I don't need someone in the right seat who is going to question me and try to override anything I intend to do. I need a trained copilot who knows his duties and will accomplish them without question".

Debolt said, "I can do any copilot duties required". Kruger responded, "Maybe, but you think like a Captain and an overbearing one at that. I won't allow you to ride as my copilot". Debolt said, "Well, I have to ride in the right seat". Kruger saw that he couldn't win this fight since he was the junior Captain so he said, "OK, then you fly the fucking airplane. I get paid the same whether I fly or sit on my ass. I don't care about your particular paranoid attitudes and I sure as hell won't ever allow you to fly as my copilot."

And that's the way the flight progressed. Debolt hogged the seat time and Kruger relaxed but always kept an eye on Debolt, the world's most wonderful pilot. Kruger had seen his ilk before and did not trust him as far as he could throw the 747.

When the flight approached Los Angeles the weather was marginal all along the coast and there were riots in the streets due to the Rodney King incident. Gunfire was heard all over the area and all approaches to Los Angeles International were being conducted from the ocean side to preclude any gunfire being directed toward any plane on approach. The large, slow planes made ideal targets for any idiot who wanted to "protest" anything.

Kruger was sitting in the cockpit monitoring the flight. The Los Angeles flight controller was getting backed up by the volume of flights approaching the airport and asked Kruger's flight how long it could hold. The "hold" request was to ascertain how long the plane could remain in the air and still make a safe approach.

Without any thought or consultation with the rest of the crew Debolt answered, "We can hold for 30 minutes. Kruger glanced at the Second

Officer's fuel panel and said, "Call them back and tell them no more than 10 minutes. I'm not going to allow you to go into our fuel reserves. The weather is shitty all along the coast. If we miss and have to go to an alternate we will be in real trouble. I won't allow you to put the plane into extremis because of some hard-headed ego trip you are on. I'll take the fucking crash axe to you before I allow that".

Debolt looked startled but did what Kruger wished. Earlier he had been bragging that he was going to test-fly the newest Douglas plane during his layover. Kruger almost puked at Debolt's braggadocio. Northwest had definite proscribed caveats against doing just such a thing on layovers. Of course, with wonderful pilot Debolt, the rules didn't apply. When they got on the ground the real copilot asked Kruger if he had been serious about taking the crash axe to Debolt. Kruger assured him that, in the interests of safety and passenger safety he most certainly would have. Kruger had nothing but contempt and disdain for Debolt and didn't try at all to hide it at all.

During one of Kruger's flights he ran into an old friend that he had flown with as a second Officer. Ray had been a Captain as long as Kruger had been with Northwest. When Ray saw Kruger's Captain's hat he congratulated him but smilingly said, "We will always think of you as Second Officer Kruger". Kruger laughed and said, "Unknown to you and all the rest of the pilots at Northwest I have actually been in command of every plane I've ever flown in no matter what seat I have been sitting in". Ray thought about that and said, "Yeah, I guess I can believe that".

On one of his flights he was the IRC with three other old Republic pilots flying the plane. Kruger got along with all of them. They had a layover in Osaka. The next morning Kruger came down for breakfast and saw the other pilots seated in the lobby. He stopped by them and exchanged pleasantries. Finally he said, "I enjoyed flying with you guys. You know, if you'd stop talking about Republic Airlines no one would ever know you assholes were ducks." The other pilots were stunned for a few seconds and then started to laugh. Kruger was laughing also. It was, perhaps, the beginning of the healing process between the two groups.

Osaka was a nice layover but it was just a giant city like most others. The redeeming feature of Osaka was the elevator. Whenever you stepped into the elevator the first thing that you saw was the rug on the floor. It was changed every day. It always told you what day it was. That was very important to the flight crews who had traversed several time periods and the International Date Line several times and didn't really know exactly what day it was. The Osaka elevator solved that problem each morning.

On one of Kruger's layovers in Narita he came down to the lobby in order to join the rest of the "lobby lizards" who populated the hotel lobby drinking coffee, telling lies and generally bragging and doing what pilots have done for ages when in close proximity with each other. He soon saw that the group had devolved into two distinct groups; the old Northwest and the old Republic pilots. They were throwing figurative bricks at each other verbally. Finally a Northwest pilot, Jerry Leatherman, got between the two groups. Leatherman was acting as a peace maker.

Jerry Leatherman was a man's man. He was one of the few people that Kruger knew who had been both a Navy Seal and a Navy pilot. It was something that few people could brag about. Leatherman was a wild man. He was tall, lean and his hair looked like it had never been combed. He was one tough guy but he was never without a smile. Kruger had heard a worshipful Flight Attendant say, with dreamy eyes, that he looked like he had "just gotten out of bed". If you knew Leatherman you knew that anyone who had locked out of submarines at depth, had occasion to swim to a beach and blow up several things that needed blowing up and had then positioned himself, again at depth, in front of the sub in order to be gobbled up in a hole in the sub, was not someone you trifled with.

Leatherman, smiling like always, got between the two groups and said, "Now guys, we all are supposed to be professionals. We are all pilots and should be respectful of each other. Now you guys," here he pointed to the Northwest pilots, "If you would just back off a little, and you guys," here he pointed at the Republic pilots, "would just stop killing our customers," we could make a good company out of this shithole." The Northwest pilots erupted in laughter while the Republic pilots crept back to their rooms.

Leatherman was one of Kruger's favorite people. Kruger met him, one day, at the Northwest Credit Union. Jerry had a tiny dog, a Yorkshire Terrier, in his pocket. During their conversation Leatherman said, "I love this little dog. If anyone ever tried to hurt him I'd kill them." Kruger was absolutely positive that Leatherman meant every word.

Jerry Leatherman was one of a kind. He showed up one day for a check flight in the simulator with cut off jeans, a sweat shirt with no arms and shower clogs for shoes. When the Check Pilot observed that Leatherman was slightly "underdressed" for the check Jerry said, "What difference does it make how I dress? I thought that the purpose of this exercise was to see how I could fly." He passed his check ride with flying colors but the check pilot was somewhat miffed. Check pilots thought that everyone ought to show up in a three piece suit in accordance with the "lofty position" they held as airline pilots. Most pilots didn't share this pigheaded opinion of themselves. Those pilots who gravitated to "management positions" or lived in the training area thought of themselves as a position above that of the rank and file pilots. They desperately needed another opinion. The company had earlier floated a notice that said that a check ride was some sort of a lofty event and that pilots who were supposed to present their bodies for this inspection ought to dress for the occasion, like a coat and a tie. Most pilots treated this as the utter crap that it was. They, like Kruger, thought of themselves as a JAP, just another pilot.

Jerry had frequented a bar in Anchorage, Alaska that advertised "We have 13 beautiful girls and two ugly ones". He had become engaged in a dart game with several indigenous Aleuts (Eskimos) who were drunk. Jerry had imbibed a lot also. Jerry had just thrown two darts when one of the Aleuts approached the dart board in order to pull the darts. Jerry yelled, "Hey, you, I've got another dart to throw." The Aleut muttered something and started to pull the darts so Jerry threw the remaining one which buried itself in the Aleut's ass.

As you can imagine, that prompted a general melee and Leatherman saved his neck by virtue of throwing pool table balls at the guys who were trying to punish him. He told Kruger, "I really ought to cool down before I get killed on a layover."

The Flight Attendants had just signed a contract with NWA that stipulated that, in cases of deadheading, the Pilots and Flight Attendants would all be on the same seniority list when it came to choosing seats on the airplane. Prior to this the pilots had first choice on seats and would always choose the first class ones leaving the tourist seats for the flight attendants.

One day Kruger's plane had to land in Osaka with a deadhead to Narita. As the crew approached the check-in podium the lead F/A button-holed Kruger and said, "Our new contract says that we are all equal in terms of seniority so if there are any first class seats available I expect that we will be seated in them since a lot of us are senior to you pilots." Kruger just smiled and said, "Ah so, you know how things work in Dai

Ichi Nippon, desuka? Pay close attention to how I speak to the Japanese check in lady."

He then approached the Japanese Customer Service Agent who bowed respectfully in front of him. After bowing in return Kruger said, "Ohayo, kudesai. How are you this morning?" The diminutive agent bowed again and said, "I am well, Captain, and how are you and your crew?" Kruger complied with all of the niceties and then said, "I have three pilots and twelve flight attendants who need to deadhead to Narita. I would like the Flight attendants to be given any first class seats available and then assign the pilots and the rest of the Flight attendants seats as necessary in the tourist section. Please assign the seats in seniority order."

The little agent bowed again and assured Kruger that everything would go as he wished. Kruger then approached the Flight Attendants who had closely watched the whole thing. He said, "OK ladies, did you see that? I told the check-in lady to give all of the first class seats to the pilots and to seat the flight attendants as far back as possible in the tourist section. Did you see how she bowed? She's going to do exactly as I asked. Males rule here. Females are of no use."

The senior Flight Attendant blew up. She ragged on Kruger who just smiled. When it came time to board the Flight attendants were boarded first with the first class people. When the rest of the people were boarded the pilots were boarded last. As Kruger passed the senior Flight Attendant in the first class section she smiled at him and said, "I love you but you are still an asshole." Kruger just smiled and continued into the tourist section.

All layovers were interesting. On one layover in Hawaii Kruger was stopped by a young lady in a small red car honking at him. Thinking that she needed help or maybe directions he walked over to the car and the lady smiled at him and said, "Hi. Is that your wife?" She pointed to an older lady who was walking about a hundred feet ahead of Kruger. He laughed and said, "No". The lady then said, "Well, in that case would you like a little company this morning?"

Kruger laughed as he realized that he had just been propositioned and said, "Oh, that's probably the best offer I will receive this day or even this week but I have to refuse it. You are truly a beautiful lady and very desirable but regrettably I have to refuse because I have to go to work shortly." The lady said, "OK but if you change your mind I'll be around here all morning." Kruger waved goodbye and continued his walk.

Another time in Los Angeles He was on an elevator when a beautiful black lady jumped on at the last minute. As the elevator rose the lady smiled and said, "Nice evening isn't it?" Kruger admitted that was the case and the lady said, "How would you like a little company this evening?" Kruger gave his stock answer, "Oh, you are very beautiful and I'm sure that we could have a lot of fun but I'm really tired and I have to sleep as I have a busy day tomorrow." The lady said that she understood and got off the elevator at the next floor.

Kruger understood full well how a guy away from home with a few drinks under his belt could be snared in the old honey trap with all of these beautiful ladies making themselves available. This was, after all, the main way that foreign services snared people that were employed by the government into working for their governments as in spying or furnishing sensitive information to them.

Kruger loved flying to the exotic places around Southeast Asia. Saipan was a favorite. It was full of World War II memories. The normal trip pattern was to fly from Narita to Saipan and lay over for at least 24 hours before returning to Tokyo. On one such trip Kruger was privileged to have a crew that were all World War II history buffs. Their layover was for 48 hours. It was a wonderful holiday. The first thing they did on arrival was to rent a car. They drove all over the island visiting all of the historical sites including the suicide cliff where hundreds of Japanese families had jumped to their death rather than meet the US Marines who were assaulting the island.

Northwest had hired an old mechanic to service their planes on Saipan. He had been hired for years as their main service executive in Japan but when it came time for him to retire Northwest, in typical manner, fired him and hired him again as a contract employee for duty in Saipan thus negating his retirement pension. Smitty was loved by all the flight crews who hated the Northwest treatment of him. He was a bonified hero having served as a crewman with the AVG or American Voluntary Group aka the Flying Tigers during World War Two. During their layover Kruger and his crew invited Smitty out for supper and got him roaring drunk in the tradition of flying comrades the world over. The next morning Smitty showed up for the flight back to Narita and showed Kruger his scrapbook of pictures of him with the AVG in China. Kruger was awed and would have liked to have spent hours looking at that scrapbook but couldn't due to the launch time. Nevertheless, he always valued his time with a real hero; one that Northwest didn't value at all.

Kruger was always junior in his category and so he was always "on reserve". Being on reserve meant that one had to be at a dedicated base, and at the beck and call of crew schedules, anytime of the day or night. His time was not his own. One day he was called to fly a trip out of Seattle. Since he was based in Minneapolis he had to deadhead to Seattle to pick up the trip the next day.

When he reported for his trip he met a bunch of Seattle pilots that he had known when they were based at Minneapolis. There was a lot of jealous head butting between the two bases. Each base thought that the other was getting more in terms of perks than the other was. In actuality nothing could be farther from the truth but perceptions were controlling here. One of the pilots said, "Hey Kruger, what the hell are you doing flying out of here? Do you have super seniority or something?"

Kruger laughed, knowing that the other pilot was simply jealous over turf. He said, "Well, crew schedules knew that you assholes in Seattle couldn't handle this trip so they sent some poor puke from Minneapolis out here to handle things. Shape up and us Midwesterners will be able to stay home and tend to our farms."

When Kruger arrived at his plane he saw that he had a mixed crew. The other pilots were Seattle based and didn't seem to appreciate a Captain from Minneapolis flying what they thought of as their trip. Kruger didn't let it bother him but proceeded with his preflight. When his Second Officer came back onboard from his outside preflight Kruger asked him, "How did the plane look?"

The Second Officer was surly and said, "It looked OK except for the dent in the aft part of the plane."

Kruger said, "Tell me about that".

The S/O said, "Well, it looks like a payloader (a tractor that moves large airplanes) ran into the plane but the mechanic said that it flew into here that way so it's probably OK."

Kruger thought about that. He finally said, "Call a mechanic up here. I want that inspected."

The S/O said, "Why do you want that done? It was done on another flight and it's apparently OK. There's speed tape over the dent." Speed tape was known as 500 mph tape. It was adhesive enough to normally withstand a lot of wind over its surface before becoming unglued and blowing off allowing the wind to assault the underlying problem.

Kruger grated, "This flight isn't going anywhere until that so-called little dent is inspected. Go get the damned mechanic."

The S/O was peeved and showed it. He slammed out of the cockpit and soon showed up with an angry mechanic in tow. The mechanic seemed to think that he was in charge of the flight and demanded why the Captain wanted the "dent" inspected. Kruger calmly explained that he wanted assurance that the "dent" wouldn't fail at 32,000 feet at 550 knots. The mechanic said, "It flew in so it will fly out OK". Kruger said, "Well, I don't think exactly that way so go inspect the damned plane so we can fly, OK?"

The mechanic stamped out of the cockpit and Kruger made an announcement over the ships PA about the problem and what was being done to correct it. Much later Kruger found out that the mechanic had sought help from the foreman who had stripped the insulation off of the inside of the cargo hold in order to actually see what damage had been done. They had then called the main base at Minneapolis for help and the main base told them that the FAA had to inspect the damage since it included some of the structural parts of the plane. Several hours later the flight was cancelled as the FAA pronounced the plane as not safe to fly.

The Second Officer was noticeably silent as all of this was going on and Kruger thought it best not to rub his nose in his cavalier attitude toward flight safety. Kruger made an announcement to the passengers. He covered the damage to the airplane and assured the passengers that he would never accept or fly a plane that was not 100% safe to fly. He told the passengers that the flight had been cancelled and said that the agents were booking those who still wished to fly on another flight the next day. He also said that he would be standing at the door as everyone deplaned in order to answer any questions about his decision to "down' the plane. There were 400 people on the flight. Most deplaned without comment. There were several who said, "I'll never fly Northwest again". Comments like those were normal. Only one gentleman stopped and said, "I want to thank you. It makes me feel a lot safer whenever a pilot says that he will not accept any airplane unless it's absolutely safe to fly. Thanks for me and my family." Kruger nodded and the man left. It was worth all of the "aw shits" for one "attaboy".

Flying a large airplane over the Pacific with over 400 passengers in it while making sure that the flight was smooth, safe and comfortable for those passengers was trying at times but not quite as trying as the very few passengers who thought that the flight crew were somehow "domestics" who were there to cater to every whim of those passengers who had paid a fare to get from "A" to "B".

Kruger had a flight from Boston to Scotland one evening. The Boston people considered themselves to be a little above the average airline passenger and thus deserved a "little more" in consideration from the flight crew. Not all felt that way but a considerable portion of them did.

As Kruger waited in the passenger area for his plane to arrive a well dressed man approached him and told him that he had to call an important client in Scotland and that he wanted Northwest Airlines to pay for the long distance call as the flight was going to be late. Kruger told him that Northwest had no system in place for that kind on service. The man was nice but insistent. It soon became obvious that it was very important that he make the call and that he did not have any means to easily do so. After talking to him for some time Kruger said, "OK, I'll personally take care of it." He went to a bank of telephones and called the number that the man had given to him. Then he inserted his personal credit card for the call. He handed the phone to the man who completed the call, hung up the phone and walked away without so much as a "by your leave" or a "thank you". Kruger sighed and figured that it was just another charge that he had to take in order to make the passengers happy; not that Northwest gave a crap about that.

Kruger was in the Philippines in Manila when he was buttonholed by a man who said that he was a missionary who had been in the southern islands for some time. The missionary was sick and needed medical treatment. He said that he had a fever and needed to get back to the United States as soon as possible. He also said the he had no funds for treatment in the Philippines and that another airline had refused him passage since he had divulged that he had a fever. He wanted to know if Kruger could help him.

Kruger felt sorry for the guy. He was hurting however no airline would board him if he had a fever since the Japanese would slap him in quarantine and not allow him to travel any further.

Kruger said, "I would board you in an instant but you wouldn't make it past Japan. As much as it might gall you, you must lie and never tell anyone that you are sick. That's the only way you will be able to get out of the Philippines and through Japan on your way to the USA. If you don't wish to do that then you might go to any of the United States military installations here in the PI and throw yourself on their mercy. Ask for the Commanding Officer or the senior Medical Officer and do not talk to any minor functionaries about your situation. I sincerely wish I could put you on my plane and fly you out of here but it wouldn't do you any good once you hit Japan. I'm sorry."

The missionary said that he understood and would do as Kruger suggested.

Kruger continued to fly the 747 but things had changed a mite. Northwest had decided that the European routes would only be flown with the DC10 so Kruger was forced to fly only to Southeast Asia. That was OK with him. It was still a very nice job and the layovers were all great. And it was still flying around the South China Sea and Southeast Asia like his old childhood dream.

The company had purchased several 747-400s. It was a new airplane with new technology. It had what the pilot community called a "glass cockpit". Instead of dials and gages the plane had CRTs. All of the information needed to fly a modern jet was placed on the CRTs. It was a novel concept to the old time pilots who promptly called the -400 checkout the hardest checkout they had ever endured. One of the training pilots who had been one of the first to checkout on the new plane said, with a stare that approximated a 20 foot stare in a 15 foot room, "If I had known how hard the checkout was going to be I wouldn't have gone into it".

Kruger was selected to checkout on the 747-400 due to his preference card on file with the company. Other, more senior, pilots were afraid of the checkout and had not selected the plane due to their fear. They were content to wait and see just who had checked out on the new equipment and question them as to what they had undergone during the checkout. Kruger was very, very junior on the new equipment.

When he elected to initially check out on the -400 his wife, Barb, asked if he was certain if he was "up to it". The answer was, "most certainly". Once again, Kruger had to live in a motel in Bloomington while he went through training. Once again, he treated the local pigeons to a feast on his window sill.

When he finally completed his training and was released to the line an old training pilot, Bob Lee, buttonholed him and said, "I admire you. You got over a bout of cancer, got checked out as a Captain and then went on to a Captain as a 747 pilot. Then you checked out as a

747-400 Captain. That took a lot of balls and drive. Good on you". Kruger valued that assessment from a Marine pilot more than any other kudo. Marines knew what commitment was all about and they knew all about innovation, adaption and overcoming. Any complement from a Marine officer was wonderful, as far as Kruger was concerned. He thought back to his time in the Naval Preflight Program with Marine Gunnery Sergeants. Most of the things that he had learned during that time had emanated from the Marine Gunnery Sergeants teachings. Those ideas had not left him and he had operated with those ideas the rest of his life. He remembered the admonitions of "attention to detail" and "commitment". Northwest didn't care about any of this "drivel". All it cared about was the "bottom line".

Kruger entered the program for the 747-400 with enthusiasm. He had heard all of the caveats about the program but figured that he could make the grade without much grief. After all, hadn't he become a Naval Aviator after being a soft, flabby college grad? He could do this with no problem.

The real problem with the -400 (as the pilots called it) was that the senior pilots who were the ones that were chosen via the seniority system were not of the era that was conversant with computers. Oh yeah, there were several pilots who could keep up with the "kids" who had cut their teeth on computers but they were few and far between. The rest of the guys were like Kruger; just dumb pilots who were trying to do an average job. Just JAPs. Most of them were always behind the "power curve" meaning that if the airplane crashed the pilot wouldn't be hurt because "he was so far behind the plane that he wouldn't be present in the actual crash".

Kruger was fascinated by the cockpit display. Instead of dials and gauges there were 7 CRTs that, when powered up, would display any and all of the information anyone would ever want and usually much more than most of the older pilots could assimilate. It was awesome. The pilots were required to not only fly the plane manually like all of the other planes they had ever flown but had to fly the plane via the computers, which required knowledge of the internal computers and how to access them along with how to enter information on them. That was the real sticking point.

Then there was the lack of a third pilot. On most of the other planes that Northwest had owned there were three pilots. In the newer, "glass cockpits" there were only two. That meant that the work load was made heavier for the two pilots, no mean feat when you were traveling at over 500 knots. The problem was made greater when flying around Europe where the controllers had to issue clearances fast and the pilots had to react faster. Deleting or changing information on a computer and entering more information was much harder with only two pilots in the cockpit who had to not only enter the information, which entailed a "heads down" attitude, but who had to fly the plane and stay clear of other planes at the same time, a "heads up" situation. Throw in a few emergencies and you had a scenario for catastrophe.

Kruger finished the entire checkout with a "lot of sweat". A lot of his contemporaries either could not or did not do so. One of these, a pilot named Phil who was senior to Kruger, was one of these. Phil had been a Captain when Kruger was flying as a copilot on the 747. Phil was a good pilot but quailed at the -400 checkout. He sought counsel from Kruger and told him that he was fearful of the checkout. He said that he was going to drop out of the program. Kruger talked to him at length and finally went to the program manager, Murray Perine, saying that the company was about to lose a good pilot through his insecurity in the -400 program. Kruger had been an instructor with the Navy for two years and could analyze "students" pretty well. He could tell when a pilot was good, bad or indifferent and how to correct those problems. The program manager promised to oversee Phil's checkout with the goal of saving the pilot in the -400 program.

After Kruger had checked out completely on the -400 he was relegated to a "reserve status" due to his junior status on the plane. It was a lonely existence. He had to stay in a motel at the base where he was assigned subject to call. He had to be available in two hours for any trips the company wanted him to fly. The real fly in the ointment was that he didn't get called that often. The 747-400 was so new that no one wished to forgo their flight on the plane so the reserves didn't get that much time on the plane. Kruger was finally bumped off of the plane due to seniority after one year. He didn't have even a hundred hours on the plane and, as such, had to operate on "higher minimums, as a very junior pilot and one who had very few hours on the plane". The "higher minimums" rule meant that he had to add several hundred feet and some additional visibility minimums to the charted ones in order to give himself some additional time to assess the approach in low visibility conditions. It was like training wheels on a bicycle and in bad weather conditions he was of no use to the company due to his being unable to be dispatched because of the higher minimums rule . . . After a year on the -400 Kruger was bumped off the plane due to seniority as more and more senior pilots checked out on it. He was happy to go back to flying the 747 where he could actually fly a plane instead of simply setting in a hotel room.

Just before Kruger had been bumped off of the -400 he had to ferry a plane from Chicago to Minneapolis. He knew that he was shortly to leave that plane but it didn't bother him as he had always wanted to fly instead of simply sit in a hotel room and wait for a flight. He picked up his young copilot who was also soon to be bumped off of the equipment. Kruger felt sorry for the young pilot and told him that he could fly the plane to Minneapolis since that was to be his last flight for some time on the -400. When they taxied out to the runway Kruger said, "Well, we're empty. We don't even have any Flight Attendants aboard so let's have some fun with the plane, OK?" The copilot wanted to know what Kruger was up to so Kruger said, "Instead of using the low power settings the computer uses for an empty plane we will use the full power setting for a fully loaded plane. Let's see what this beast can do."

They made the takeoff and the flight guidance system pitched the plane up to a nose up attitude that neither pilot had ever experienced before. The rate of climb instrument topped out as the plane screamed for the heavens. The departure control called and wanted to know how the plane was doing what it was doing. Kruger told them that the plane was empty with only two pilots on board and that they were putting it through its paces. Departure Control admitted awe at the rate of climb while the copilot was ecstatic over the ability of the plane. When they deplaned at Minneapolis the copilot was vociferous in his thanks for Kruger allowing him to fly the plane and especially in that manner. Kruger's response was, "Well, we are pilots and we do what pilots do if we are given the chance. Enjoy the experience and one of these days when you are older do the same with one of your young pilots."

One year later Northwest called Kruger back up on the -400. He didn't really want to go back on that plane since he had never really flown it and probably wouldn't again. Kruger figured that he had hired on with the airlines in order to fly and not sit in a motel room. He was too junior to be on the -400. Nevertheless, the company wanted him to go back on the -400 and was willing to pay him a lot more for the privilege. Kruger bowed to the mindset of a whore where money is the prime consideration and said that he would checkout once more on the -400 but he had a problem with the whole concept. He said that it had been over a year since he had flown the -400 and that during his whole -400 experience he had accumulated less than 100 hours on the plane. He said that he would need an extensive checkout on the plane in order to feel comfortable flying it. The program manager, Perine, told him that he could have "as much time as he needed in order to checkout on the plane".

Kruger entered the simulator program for the -400 with Perine's words in mind. He was more concerned with the computerization aspects of the airplane than the actual flying of it. A 747 was a 747 and they all flew alike. The rub was the computer access on the 747-400. He asked if he could practice the computerization aspects on the simulators that Northwest had for that purpose but was denied that access. Kruger had said that he didn't wish to be paid for the computer practice and that he only wished to do it in order to be more familiar with the plane's systems. One would think that since it cost the company nothing and the only concern on Kruger's part was to be as familiar with the equipment as possible in the interest of safety his request would be readily complied with. In a less primitive company that would have been the case but then this was Northwest Airlines and any request by a pilot was viewed with suspicion and negativity. Once more he was denied access to the trainer.

The normal checkout for a pilot on one of Northwest's planes was three simulators and a check ride in the simulator. Kruger's first simulator ride was a series of emergencies like engine failures. Kruger was familiar with these emergencies and complained to the instructor that he needed practice on the computer aspects of the plane rather than the normal emergency items that he was familiar with. It apparently fell on deaf ears because the second simulator session was entirely taken up with the loss of all three INS computers. That left the plane with only the basic flight instruments and the practice entailed the copilot going through a long series of computer evolutions in order to regain the computers while the pilot (Kruger) flew the plane as if it were a basic trainer with only the basic flight instruments. The whole period had nothing to do with the computerization of the plane and was a complete waste from that viewpoint.

The third simulator period was more normal but at the end of the period the check pilot asked Kruger if he was ready for his check ride the next day. Kruger said, "Hell no. I was promised that I could have enough training periods so that I could fly a 747-400 plane with confidence. I don't have that confidence. I won't fly as a Captain if I have to rely on a copilot for more knowledge about the airplane than I have. I need practice on the computerization on the plane. I don't have that. I refuse to undergo a check ride under those circumstances."

The check pilot said, "Well, I'm supposed to certify you for either a check ride tomorrow or a board to censure you". Kruger blew up. He said, "I was promised, when I entered this fucking program, that I would be given the necessary training that I would need in order to safely fly this plane. I expect Northwest to keep that promise. If I am not given the time to accomplish that then you can expect a lawsuit about trying to force a pilot to fly a plane that he is sure that he cannot fly safely. I'm sure that the FAA would like to hear about this issue as would the Minneapolis Star and Tribune." The check pilot was helpless about the issue so Kruger buttonholed the program manager who said, "Well, Ed, you made a footprint when you entered the program and it can't be erased so you have to undergo a board if you want to opt out of the -400 program". It was obvious that the toady manager had been influenced by some higher up in the Northwest management that harbored a grudge against Kruger or was an accountant and was concerned with only money.

Once again, Ed blew up and said, "I have less than 100 hours on the plane. I haven't flown it in over a year. I don't feel comfortable flying it. I don't want to be a Captain on a plane where I know less about the plane than the copilot knows. I will not be a Captain on any airplane where I feel the same way. You originally promised me that I could have as much training as I thought that I needed in order to safely fly the plane. Once again, the operative word here is "safely". You are trying to force me to fly a plane that I'm not comfortable flying due solely to economics. Would you like for me to talk to the FAA and the local newspapers about Northwest's policies forcing Captains to fly planes that they are not comfortable flying due to safety problems?"

Perine opted to allow Kruger to go back to flying the 747 but he said that Kruger would have to undergo a "board" due to his "failure to complete the 400 checkout". Once more Kruger blew his stack. He said, "Screw your fucking boards. I haven't failed any check rides and I haven't done anything that would sanction any board. If you put me up for any board then you will see your name and Northwest's in the papers and an attorney will come knocking on your door."

Perine disgustedly finally said, "OK, just go back and fly your 747 until you retire". The fact that Perine had caved in on this issue was all the proof that Kruger needed to convince him that the situation that he was put in had nothing to do with any policy but everything to do with putting Kruger in a situation where he was sure to fail.

And that was just what Kruger did. Flying the 747 was actually flying and not sitting on your ass in a hotel room watching TV and hoping that the company would call you for a trip at 0300 when you had minimal sleep. Kruger was happy with the result.

Kruger flew the 747 into SE Asia until he was 59 years old. The FAA and the US government had long mandated that all pilots had to cease flying as a pilot after they had reached the age of 60 years. It had nothing at all to do with health, coordination, ability or anything else but had everything to do with politics. Kruger's career was nearing an end, big time.

The contract that Northwest Airlines had with the Airline Pilots Association mandated that a pilot's retirement was a lot better if he retired medically than if he retired normally. Kruger knew this and had been documenting pain in his hips and thighs as he sat in his seat for over twelve hours. Kruger's doctor had documented the debilitization and deteriorization of his hip bones called osteoarthritis. It was simply painful to fly to the Orient for over twelve hours. It was time to let go both from a physical and an economic reason. It also didn't hurt in that it would be a gigantic pain in the ass for Northwest Airlines.

Kruger was on a trip that flew from Los Angeles to Narita, Japan and back several times. It was a boring trip for the most part. Kruger's crew was superb, like always. On the leg from Narita to Los Angeles the copilot complained, "We are going to have to do this all over again tomorrow." Kruger said, "Well, you're going to have to check in a new Captain. I'm not going to be on the trip."

"What the hell are you talking about"? This from the copilot.

Kruger said, "I'm done flying. I called the company and told them that they needed to get a new Captain for the return trip to Narita. I'm done.

The copilot wanted to know why Kruger was doing this and Kruger explained his plan to them. His crew was incredulous. How could he just quit flying? Flying was what every pilot wanted to do. It was the epitome of all jobs anywhere. The idea of giving it all up was anathema.

Kruger said that he would have to stop flying as he knew it in only a year anyway. The government had mandated that all commercial pilots stop flying at age 60. Kruger was 59 and had a debilitating problem with his hips. He had a lot of so-called "sick time" accumulated on the books and could use that time until he was 60. ALPA had weathered strikes and a lot of collective bargaining in order to set up the "sick time" for just such incidences as this. Kruger intended to capitalize on this.

During all of the deliberations accompanying the talks among Northwest and the Airline Pilots Association about contracts ALPA had always told the rank and file pilots that "There is always just so much money on the table. We know it and NWA knows it. Most of the talks are oriented around what that money will be spent on. If, for example, you wish more sick time then you have to give up some vacation time. If you wish more money then you have to give up sick time and vacations. It's all a give and take. That's normally what takes so much time in the deliberations."

Contracts being what they were, as soon as the new contract was in place the company began to "parse and interpret" it. A good example was the so called "sick time". Sure, a pilot could call and cancel his trip due to being ill but the company then made him document the illness by a "note from a doctor". Sick time was treated as "malingering time" as far as the company was concerned. Never mind that the FAA and the Federal Air Regulations specified that a pilot MUST remove himself from flight duty anytime he FELT himself impaired by sickness or anything else that would derogate his performance as a airline pilot. Kruger knew this and had decided that he could "beard the goat" and make an end run around the company once again as far as his sick time was concerned. In the Northwest contract discussions the granting of "sick time" by the company took away the "money on the table" for anything else like pay, time off or vacation time. Once the contract was signed Northwest immediately began to "interpret" it and that included being draconian relative to the pilot's use of sick time. Kruger was going to subvert the company's strict regulation of the sick time that he was due per the contract.

This particular leg was being flown by the copilot. He was incredulous about Kruger's cavalier attitude regarding his "last flight". He asked if Kruger wanted to land the plane at Los Angeles and Kruger said that he didn't wish to. The copilot said, "I can't believe that you would not want to land the plane on your last flight". Kruger laughed and said, "I did land the plane on my last flight. It was my leg into Narita. This is your leg, not mine. Don't worry about it. I'm just fine with things as they are".

The copilot was really disturbed by Kruger's attitude. He thought that a pilot ought to be upset by flying his last leg or flight before his retirement but Kruger assured him that all pilots eventually had to face the same thing. Kruger said, "You will eventually have to face the same thing. At that time you will have to come to grips with the fact that your life has to change. Some people resist that and kick and scream about it. Some accept it and move on. This is your chance to observe what one pilot does at a time like this and learn. When your time comes to hang it all up don't be a baby and kick and scream about what is inevitable. I've had a whole lifetime flying both with the Navy and Northwest Airlines. You are just starting your life of flying. Enjoy it as much as you can and when it comes to an end brace it like a man, walk away from it and move on. There are lots of things other than flying, believe me."

The copilot and the second officer got the rest of the crew together and they made a small cake for Kruger. They presented it to him before they landed at Los Angeles. Kruger was touched by their concern and caring. It cemented his thoughts about how wonderful his contemporaries and all of the people he worked with at Northwest were. The people at Northwest were wonderful and that meant all of the people, the ones who flew and the ones who took care of the planes and the crews on the ground. He would miss all of them. He would not miss the company or the people at the top of NWA who thought of the rank and file as serfs and numbers to be used and discarded as necessary.

Kruger had mixed feelings about his decision to retire from flying. Flying had been his life for most of his life. The decision to stop flying was as traumatic as was his decision to separate from the active Navy and elect to fly with the airlines. It was tough but Kruger was used to tough decisions. He had always adopted the thinking that any decision was hard and maybe agonizing until you had made the decision. At that time it became reality and was, in all actuality, the "right" decision since you had to live with the results. Retrospection was useless. You had to look forward and not "cry over spilt milk".

Kruger had given crew schedules a "heads up" before leaving Narita and when he got to Los Angeles he cleaned out his crew box and headed for home. He met several other pilots who were nonplussed at his decision. Most pilots tend to ignore the age 60 phantom until it hits them in the face. It's a hard thing to contemplate or plan for. Nevertheless, Kruger kicked the dust of Los Angeles off of his shoes and headed for home.

He soon got a registered letter from the putative Chief Pilot for Los Angeles, Sven Holm. Sven was not held in high regard among the Northwest pilots. Most of the pilots referred to him as "Swine Holm". Holm was as untrustworthy and slimy as was his counterpart in Minneapolis, Donald Nelson. Holm's registered letter demanded a "diagnosis, prognosis and method of treatment" for Kruger's complaint of deteriorating hip joints and pain in sitting for long hours during his job as a 747 pilot on international flights. In addition he demanded monthly reports from Kruger's doctor concerning Kruger's status.

Kruger had anticipated such a letter and was, in fact, amazed that Swine Holm could put a letter like that together. He chalked it up to a superior secretary. He called his doctor and talked to the doctor's office supervisor. When he asked what the doctor got for writing a letter the supervisor was nonplussed. She didn't know what to say. Kruger said, "Do you think that $100 is an acceptable rate for a letter generated by your office?" She said that it seemed an acceptable amount. Accordingly Kruger answered the letter by sending a registered letter to "Swine" Holm that said, "I will accede to your request for an intrusive review of my personal data and the release of the sensitive information you requested but I have interviewed my doctor and he states that he gets $100 for each letter that he writes concerning his patients. I have also informed him that Northwest Airlines is normally late in paying any bills tendered to it so he says that he will only accept certified funds in advance before he generates any informative information concerning me. Once he receives the certified funds he will forward to you the information you have requested".

Kruger never received any answer to his last communication to Holm. He figured that Holm's reptilian brain had been overtaxed by reading Kruger's letter and simply didn't know how to respond or how to come up with the sum of $100 without begging from the bean counters at Northwest Airlines so he ignored the problem. That was fine with Kruger who simply chalked it all up to winning another battle with Northwest Airlines in the ongoing guerilla warfare the pilots and the company had always engaged in. Winning was sweet and the company would never stop fighting this war even though it persisted in hiring the ignorant, the incompetent and the cripples in fighting on its side. But, winning a battle with Northworst Arrogant was worth the time it took.

Kruger drew on his sick time, which was ample since he had used little of it over his career with Northwest Airlines. He had computed his time and figured that his sick time would take him through to age 60 at which time the government had mandated that he hang up his flying career no matter how healthy he was.

Since he had a lot of time on his hands Kruger thought that it was time that he introduced a dog into his life. Accordingly he read the classified ads and found a family that had just had a new baby and couldn't really keep up with a little Jack Russell Terrier. They wanted to find a good home for their dog. Kruger was just the ticket. He showed up at the home with a new box of dog cookies and saw a little, frisky white dog with black and brown spots checking him out as he got out of the car. The lady of the house was sorry to see her friend leave but she said that it was necessary since the little terrier needed a lot of attention that she was unable to give at the time. Kruger offered the little dog a dog cookie but his owner said, "He doesn't pay too much attention to food. He really likes to chase squirrels and Frisbees". Kruger saw a Frisbee lying on the ground so he picked it up and threw it. The little dog happily chased it, retrieved it and presented it to Kruger to throw once again. His owner said, "He will do that all day if you let him".

Kruger offered to pay for the dog but his owner wouldn't accept any money at all for him. She made Kruger take his bed and all of his toys as he was bundled into Kruger's suburban. It was a sad parting both for Kruger and the lady. The little dog, named Reggie for "Reginald of Crestview", watched his lady friend disappear into the distance as Kruger drove off. He was anxious about things but Kruger kept talking to him promising that he would have a good home with lots of attention.

Reggie took to his new home with gusto, as all Jack Russells do with life. He was a super little dog; as much as anyone would ever want. He soon won the hearts of everyone in the family and quickly established his dominance in the home. He was a delight and filled Kruger's life.

CHAPTER XVI

Kruger adapted to life without flying as well as any pilot could. He missed it a lot but "carried on" as any good military man would have done. No one lives forever. No one flies forever. Kruger considered himself a success in that he had never sustained a crash that was his fault and he had never been shot down, something that a lot of his contemporaries had undergone. He tried valiantly to enjoy life among civilians who didn't value military life or flying. It didn't really work.

One day he heard his wife calling his name. She had decided to walk Reggie for a while and suddenly a very large German Shepherd had materialized behind the little Jack Russell coursing along as a wolf would on a scent. Barb was terrified that the larger Shepherd was going to eat the Jack Russell for lunch. Reggie, on the other hand was anxious to do battle with the larger dog as Jack Russells have always considered themselves as much larger than they really are.

Kruger ran out and saw the problem. He immediately got a length of rope (line to a sailor) and collared the Shepherd, who was OK with that. The shepherd had no collar or tags. Kruger called several vet offices and other places that were concerned with dogs and got no information concerning the dog.

Kruger fed and watered the dog that seemed to appreciate the attention. What would they do with this monster? He was a very beautiful, healthy dog.

Finally they decided that they would put a long lead on him and let him lead them to his home. The dog was happy to lead the pair but didn't seem to have any interest in any particular home. Finally he seemed to like one house so Kruger rang the doorbell and asked the lady who responded if she knew who the dog belonged to. She did and disgustedly said that he belonged to a Mexican family on the next block who were not very caring for their animals as their dogs were loose and at large a lot.

Kruger approached the house and knocked on the door. A Hispanic person answered and said that they didn't speak English, a common ploy of the Hispanics in the area who didn't wish to interact with Anglos. Kruger asked if the dog belonged to them and that prompted a person who, remarkably, found that they could suddenly speak English. Yes, the dog belonged to them. It was housed in an outdoor kennel in a small, dirty, fenced-in area.

Kruger demanded to know if the dog was licensed. The owner assured him that the dog, whose name was Milo, was, in fact, licensed. The license was produced. Kruger then asked if the dog's shots were up to date. The owner said that they were not but that he would "get around to it shortly". Kruger said that he would check on the situation and that the owner had to get the dog's shots up to date.

Kruger followed up on the dog's welfare but the owner said that he had given the dog to another Hispanic who allowed Milo to run off. He said that he didn't want Milo and Kruger offered to buy the dog. He gave the owner five dollars and made him sign a bill of sale. Milo was now his.

He brought the dog home and gave him a bath in the yard. Milo was a beautiful dog with a heavy build like the European Alsatians. While Kruger was bathing him Kruger found a tattoo on his inner thigh.

Checking several sources for the tattoo number didn't produce any results. One source said that it was probably a Mexican tattoo and that Milo had probably been stolen as a puppy. Milo was taken to a vet who was awed at his size and demeanor. The vet said, "I'd be very careful around him. Look at how he stands. He obviously thinks that he is in charge here."

Kruger took Milo home and wrestled him to the ground in the front yard. He then pinned the large dog with his own body with his arm under the dog's chin so Milo couldn't bite. Milo tried to get up and when he couldn't he began to growl and bluster. Kruger just quietly held him on the ground. When Milo's repertoire of threatening was exhausted he began to whimper and cry. Kruger just held him until he was panting and rolling his eyes. Kruger then slowly sniffed him all over, like another dog would do. During this whole activity Milo rolled his eyes and was quiet. Dog etiquette dictated that he remained quiet and still when sniffed.

Finally Kruger allowed the dog to get up. Milo shook himself and wagged his tail at Kruger allowing himself to be roughly petted and stroked as Kruger talked to him. From that time on Kruger became the "dominate animal" in Milo's estimation. Milo would not leave his side and was the most faithful friend Kruger had ever experienced.

Some time ago a few of Kruger's friends had asked him what he was going to do when he retired. Retirement from flying was a real threat to most pilots. They seemed to be in terror as to what would replace their flying career. The thought of not doing anything except enjoying life and pursuing other interests didn't seem to be in the equation for most of them. When asked what he was going to do Kruger always gave the same answer, "I'm going to live and enjoy life". Kruger's outlook was always in respect to "BC and AC" (Before Cancer and After Cancer). Kruger always said, "Whenever I can see the sun come up it's a good day".

Looking back Kruger could say that he had experienced a very good, very exhilarating and exciting life; two of them in fact. He had survived numerous brushes with the Grim Reaper. Kruger had always said that the most exhilarating experience you could have was when you were right at the edge, when your life was in question, when you faced death and survived. He had done that a number of times. One of the old philosophers, Frederick Nietche, had said, "That which does not destroy me makes me stronger". Kruger believed that wholeheartedly.

His life was far from over. He had been named "Smooth" in his Navy life and was a "JAP" (Just Another Pilot) in his airline life. He had realized his boyhood dreams of flying large airplanes over the South China Sea and had combated pirates in the Gulf of Mexico. He figured that life in general could still hold a lot of exciting times yet before he "flew West" as all old pilots must do. In the meantime he would be ever watchful for that quest for adventure that always seemed right around the corner.

ABOUT THE AUTHOR

The author is an aviator with over 40 years of flying for both the airlines and the United States Navy. He has amassed thousands of hours of flying in a wide variety of aircraft all over the globe and in all types of weather. He has taught Navy pilots to fly and how to use their aircraft as a weapons platform by using a wide variety of weaponry. He has lectured in classrooms on various subjects such as conventional and nuclear weapons, undersea homing torpedoes, aerial mines, anti-submarine warfare and communications including classified codes with the Navy.

He is a retired Commander, United States Naval Reserve and a retired airline Captain who last flew the Boeing 747.

He now uses his time renovating a large 100 year old home in Elgin, Illinois and divides his time between there and his Florida home in Naples, Florida.

Notes